Moonlight Becomes Her

Moonlight Becomes Her

Meagan McKinney

KENSINGTON BOOKS

http://www.kensingtonbooks.com

KENSINGTON BOOKS are published by

Kensington Publishing Corp.
850 Third Avenue
New York, NY 10022

Library of Congress Card Catalogue Number: 2001090976
ISBN 1-57566-787-8

First Printing: November 2001
10 9 8 7 6 5 4 3 2 1

Printed in the United States of America

To Jude Nicholas Foret—
An Officer and a Gentleman

No other thought . . .

Prologue

September 1881

R afael Belloch pushed the leather curtain aside as his carriage rolled past City Hall. He thrust his head outside and called up to the driver, "Cut over to Baxter Street."

"But that's Five Points, sir. And dark's coming on."

"Correct on both counts. Now please cut over."

"It's full of rough customers, sir. The cradle of gangs and all that."

"I don't give a tinker's damn. Cut over."

"As you will, sir."

The driver sounded his yard-of-tin to warn other traffic. Then he slapped the reins across the team's glossy rumps, and the japanned coach veered around the next corner.

Rafe left the curtain pulled back and wearily relaxed into the quilted-satin seat, watching day bleed into night. A nascent moon had risen over the Upper Bay. From here he could glimpse the shadowy mass where the Manhattan tower of the still uncompleted bridge thrust itself boldly above the skyline over the East River. Its hanging maze of wire cables made a spidery outline against the darkling sky.

The editorials confidently predicted the unwieldy structure would collapse under its own weight any day now. But out west, he had watched his own engineers and workers blast train tunnels through "impenetrable" mountains of sheer granite. The bridge would stand. He would bet on it.

Anything men could dream seemed possible to achieve these days. Some believed the heady age had finally reached the useful limits of all knowledge. But Rafe scorned their smug blindness. Men could blast mountains, build towers to pierce the sky, but they couldn't keep a child from going begging in the dark alleys of Baxter Street. Progress was good for the bank account, but of no avail to the soul—or to the hardened heart of a man who lived mainly for vengeance.

The fast clip-clop of cabriolets and calashes faded behind him as his carriage left the well-maintained streets and bluestone sidewalks for the crumbling pavements of the slums. For a few moments, before the raucous bray of Five Points enveloped him, it was almost peaceful. So quiet and still he even heard the evening Angelus from St. Patrick's.

By day Baxter Street was no stranger to "respectable" men. Its Lower East Side location made it ideal for many City Hall officials. A man could visit his tobacconist and his whore in one convenient trip, for often they were in the same building.

Rafe knew the area had improved somewhat from the notorious era when rival gangs publicly broke each other's skulls. Charles Dickens himself had refused to enter its realm without an escort. But that was thirty years ago. A church mission now occupied the once dangerous Old Brewery. Nonetheless, most New Yorkers still avoided Five Points as though it were the mouth of hell, especially after dark. Which was precisely why he insisted on going there time and again— he, an exalted Patriarch of the Four Hundred, Mrs. Astor's elect. The Fifth Avenue Brahmins, as he scornfully called them.

Them? Us, he corrected himself. *Us.*

A drive through Five Points was just the antidote whenever he caught himself becoming complacent. The luxury and status of his newfound wealth was an easy bath in which to sink. He needed the vinegar of poverty to remind him: his role was revenge; revenge upon the very people who embraced him now. The same wretched rich who had caused his family ruin and shame. The same amoral persons who would have cast him to Five Points as a child and never looked back.

Outside, lurid shadows flickered in the gaslights; wooden houses rolled past, rotting and unpainted, interspersed with a few tall brick tenements. Sympathy warred with disgust within him as he glimpsed tramps and bummers, beggars and thieves, murderers, harlots, madmen, grifters. And everywhere the "street arabs," abandoned and orphaned children fending for themselves, competing with the stray dogs for a dry place to sleep.

Wall Street needs one more exchange, he thought. *A squalor exchange.* It was one of the city's most abundant commodities.

Abruptly, the carriage lurched to a stop. A moment later it was in motion again. Just off the Five Points, which was formed by three intersecting streets, was a confusing warren of dark, seedy alleys, home to the gin shops and demimonde rarely acknowledged except in the penny papers. Without warning, the carriage suddenly veered into one of these alleys and stopped again, so abruptly the tug chains rattled.

Rafe had been tossed off the seat in the violent turn. He thrust his head outside. "Wilson, damnit, what in blazes—?"

Before he could finish his question, a slim, well-formed feminine hand shot toward the window and pushed a damp pad under his nose. Rafe managed to avert his face, but not before he breathed in the stench of chloroform. It did not render him unconscious, but had the momentary effect of a stunning blow.

He sprawled back onto the seat, senses reeling. Everything seemed to be a ringing confusion of sounds he could not quite identify. Then someone jerked the door open.

"Climb out, Jack, and do it in one puffin' hurry or I'll shoot an air shaft through you."

Still unsteady, fighting down nausea, Rafe alighted on wobbly feet in the dusty, trash-littered alley. In the gathering twilight he could just make out a big man wearing a sturdy hopsack coat and dirty sailcloth trousers tucked into peg boots. An old dragoon pistol was clutched in his right hand.

Rafe glanced over his own left shoulder and saw a second man up on the box, holding a huge knife to Wilson's throat. Someone thrust a lantern up into Rafe's face, nearly blinding him.

"Look at these fine feathers," the man in the alley exclaimed, feeling the material of Rafe's greatcoat. "Our cornucopia runneth over, darling."

Darling, Rafe quickly realized, was the one holding the lantern— the same woman who had gassed him. A black domino mask obscured half her face, and a scarf of magenta silk sewn with beads restrained her thick dark hair. She wore a patched brown wool skirt and a dingy green velvet jacket that outlined the generous swell of her bosom.

She studied him right back with cool, glistening eyes that peered from behind the black domino like two chips of ice. He might have thought her heart was just as cold except for the unexpected emotion he saw in them. In the startling blue depths was a wounded, reproachful expression that seemed to have nothing to do with him, and everything to do with the world.

It told him she wasn't a completely hardened character. Not yet.

His stare brought a faint smile that lifted one corner of her mouth. The blue eyes flashed but looked away as if she were uncomfortable.

"Surely you recognize him?" she scoffed to her companion, her voice shocking in its refinement. "It's Rafael Belloch himself. The mountain mover, they call him. He builds tunnels and trestles for the Kansas-Pacific. Or used to, for I hear he's become an owner now."

"God's trousers! You're right, it's Belloch."

The robber up on the box snorted. "Sure, and this is Jay Gould up here."

"It's Belloch, damn you," insisted the large man who held Rafe with the dragoon pistol. "His picture was just in the *Herald*. There, look! Look at the harnesses—plated in gold."

"Of course it's Belloch," the woman's velvet voice affirmed. "His handsome face is not one a woman is likely to forget."

The very next moment, however, her words took on a mocking edge. "You're a long way from Fifth Avenue, Mr. Mountain Mover."

"Perhaps," Rafe replied. His head had cleared, and his fascination for her was quickly melting into outrage. "But I wager the three of you aren't very far from the Ludlow Street jail."

"If we need your opinion," snarled the man standing next to her, his face twisted with coarse insolence, "we'll beat it out of you. Hand over your wallet and watch. And *don't* try any of your fancy parlor tricks here."

Rafe withdrew the pigskin wallet from his inside coat pocket, then the gold watch and chain from his fob pocket and handed them over.

"Your coat, too, Baron," the woman added, her cold, bewitching eyes warming with merriment.

"Baron?" he repeated scornfully as he shrugged out of his greatcoat. "Have I acquired a title now?"

"Yes. You rank high among the peerage of the robber barons."

"If I'm the robber, then perhaps you three should raise your hands, not I."

"He's just whistling past the graveyard," scoffed the man on the box. "Just covering his milk-livered fear."

"Oh, he's not afraid," the woman answered, watching his face closely in the lantern light. "Mr. Belloch is neither timid nor fearful. That sneer on his face right now is not war paint. He's thinking how he'd love to thrash all three of us." She released a wicked, lilting laugh.

"Madam, you read thoughts—do you also interpret spirit knockings and tea leaves? Surely a woman of your obvious beauty and refinement can find a higher station in life than coarse thievery?"

The expression in her eyes darkened. The wounded child he had seen before in her eyes skittered away and hid, as if she was used to cloaking herself in shadows.

Right then Rafe knew one thing: this woman didn't like being reminded she had been born to better things. It was a sore point and most likely a great cause of the wounded expression she sometimes let slip into view.

"This, Mr. Belloch," she assured him coldly, draping his coat over her arm as though it were a blanket of roses, "is much more profitable than going blind doing piecework in a garment factory."

"You're a good one to talk, Belloch," sneered the man on the box, his voice caustic as acid as he tightened the knife on Wilson's throat. "You railroad toffs would steal the coppers from a dead man's eyes. At least we rob our victims honestlike, face-to-face. Your ilk hide on Wall Street and let the banks do your dirty work."

Rafe clamped his teeth rather than retort. He had no illusions about the two men's willingness to kill him. Instead he concentrated on studying the raffish beauty's face. He committed every pleasing feature—those he could see, at least—to memory. Her fine brow, the comely lines of her nose, and the sweet, luscious curve of her lips. He *would* find her again. The unmasking would be a pleasure.

But perhaps he stared too hard. For suddenly the ice appeared in her eyes once more. Wickedly, she said, "Don't stop with the coat, Mr. Belloch. Take the rest of your clothing off, too. It'll all bring a fine penny or two at the rag merchant."

"The rest . . . ? But surely to God you cannot be serious?"

Rafe winced when the muzzle of the dragoon pistol pressed hard into his sternum. "You heard the lady. Peel 'em."

"It's for my hope chest," she informed him, laughing seductively.

He bit back his rage. Tightly, he said, "Bethink yourself my puppet-master?"

"I *am* thinking, Mr. Belloch. You are clearly a proud and dangerous man. But no man is dangerous when he is naked."

"Is that theory or experience speaking?"

She looked away again. "I want to be sure the first place you go is home. Now disrobe."

"I'll need a bootjack," he insisted sullenly. "These boots are new and they're tight—"

"Plague take him!" the man up on the box burst out. "I'm shooting the bastard."

"No!" She spun around toward the speaker with the grace of a ballerina standing on her pointes. "No shooting!"

She turned toward Rafe again. Closer, he got a better look at her. For a few seconds her eyes were illuminated in the warm light—eyes that became the perfect blue of forget-me-nots.

So she was not all cold. Not all wicked.

"Strip quickly, sir, or I'll change my mind about the shooting." Her words were almost a plea.

Malice heated his blood, but Rafe complied. First he handed over his waistcoat, vest, and shirt of finespun linen. She was not at all bashful about keeping plenty of light on him.

"Who'd have known. The bloke's got muscles as hard as sacked salt," the man atop the carriage said.

Her gaze almost reluctantly wandered along Rafe's sloping pectorals. "I see why you're such a favorite with Mrs. Astor. Quickly, Mr. Belloch, boots and trousers."

The boots were a struggle, and he almost toppled over as he wrenched them off. The thief brandishing the pistol snatched them from his hands. "We ain't good enough to lace these boots, but by Saint Barbara we're good enough to steal 'em."

When the woman had his trousers, Rafe demanded boldly, "Underdrawers, too?"

Despite his angry contempt, her blunt answer caught him flat-footed.

"By all means," she told him. "The preamble has been pleasing, indeed. Don't disappoint me now."

Her faint smile goaded him again.

He hesitated.

"H'ar now!" protested her companion on the box, jumping down. "Never mind his damn skivvies, you little wanton. I'll not be sent to Blackwell's just so you can ogle this fancy man. Let's dust."

The two men pulled her along with them like the hooligan she was. Rafe watched as her sweetly shaped lips curved in another secret smile. She laughed full outright at her fun.

Even as the trio of robbers faded deeper into the murky alley, her taunting voice called out, "I'll always be wondering, Mr. Belloch."

His anger did not abate nor his humiliation. She had just thrown down the gauntlet, and suddenly his will clenched like a fist.

"Then, go ahead and wonder, you impertinent little wench," he muttered to himself.

Let imagination increase her appetite. It certainly would his.

For by all things holy, whatever she was secretly wondering about, Rafe swore she *would* one day find out.

Chapter 1

"Ladies and gentlemen," Paul Rillieux announced in a cultivated, resonant voice that showed no sign of his advanced age. "Among our number there exist some who possess the gift—as yet shrouded in mystery—of making contact with powers beyond our physical realm. They are sometimes known as 'sensitives.' I myself stake no claim to such a title. However, I do dabble somewhat in the mystic arts. Knowing of my interest, Mrs. Astor has asked me to provide a brief demonstration of telepathic mentalism, the well-documented ability to harvest the thoughts of others from the ether—that gaseous element which permeates our atmosphere."

An orchestra on a dais at one end of the gallery had been playing waltzes and operatic scores. But the musicians now surrendered their stage to the wealthy old inventor, explorer, and reputed clairvoyant.

"We all know," Rillieux added with a rueful grin, "that a request from Mrs. Astor carries the force of a government draft notice. So here I am, reporting for duty."

He bowed in the direction of a neatly coiffed matron with a waterfall of diamonds at her neck. She nodded graciously, and at this permission to reward his wit, delayed laughter bubbled through the decorated gallery and surrounding gardens.

Only a year earlier, District One in lower Manhattan was the first to be supplied with electricity from the new power plant on Pearl Street. Now, even in the Maitland mansion of lower Fifth Avenue, incandescent lamps glowed, steady and unwavering, from brass-and-crystal five-light sconces. These were cast in the shape of putti, grinning little cherubs, each sconce separated by large verdant tapestries.

"Mind is psyche," Rillieux yammered on, "but there is also pneuma, the soul or etheric double. Seldom are the two in harmony. The conscious mind may ponder what's for dinner while the soul secretly frets about some promise left broken or dream unfulfilled."

Poised and confident, courtly and gaunt, Rillieux surveyed the illustrious gathering before him, one hand resting on his slender rattan walking stick. Besides Caroline Schermerhorn Astor, his audience included Alice Vanderbilt; an émigré French nobleman, the Comte de Chartrain; debutante Antonia Butler, in line to inherit a fortune that rivaled that of the Vanderbilts'; and the evening's host, real estate mandarin Jared Maitland.

Mrs. Astor's presence proved that her rigid exclusivity had lately been attacked, then finally worn down, by the sheer numbers of new millionaires. Especially those from out west, who possessed fewer manners but much more money, than even her snobbery could continue to ignore. Indeed, thanks to all this new money, a radical new notion had recently emerged and begun to take root: if you know exactly how much money you're worth, then you can't be truly rich. Relentless, uncountable quantity was replacing inherited quality.

"Someone among us," Rillieux announced abruptly, "recently dreamt about a dearly beloved pet she lost some years ago. Now she secretly grieves anew. And someone else is trying gamely to be impressed by this evening's glitter, but in reality he's preoccupied by mundane thoughts of buying prime real estate on . . . why yes, on West Fifty-fourth Street."

An excited murmur broke out among a group of women standing near the dais.

"Why, Thelma says she dreamt of her Scottish terrier Jip only two nights ago," Lydia Hotchkiss, resplendent in chartreuse satin, called out. "And this is the first time she's mentioned it."

A male voice chimed in. "I wasn't aware I was actually thinking about it, but I admit I have lately been contemplating some land on West Fifty-fourth."

The speaker was attorney Albert Gage, whose Wall Street firm represented half of the city's nouveau riche as well as many in the old aristocracy.

"You were not *consciously* thinking about it, Mr. Gage," Rillieux corrected him.

For a moment Rillieux's gaze paused on a petite young woman who sat by herself on a laurel-pattern cast-iron bench, demurely watching. He made the slightest of nods, and a minute later she began slowly circulating among the distracted guests.

"Here's something else," Rillieux called out, his seamed face capturing the attention of everyone except the lady coursing through the crowds like a puma on the hunt. "Someone among us feels greatly irritated at . . ." He beamed a manufactured smile. "Why yes, at an upstart reporter for the *New York Herald*. . . ."

Perhaps twenty minutes after it began, Paul Rillieux's impressive demonstration concluded to an enthusiastic round of applause.

Even those who were not convinced, Mystere told herself, looked highly entertained. Popularity was assured when your champion was Mrs. Astor. Or destroyed if your name went into her bad book.

Mystere carried a misted glass of lemonade and a small fan of white lace as she slowly made her way back toward the cast-iron bench, weaving through a formidable maze of financiers and steel magnates, oil tycoons and railroad barons.

Only one of them, however, caused her any real concern. Although she kept her gaze shyly discreet, and like a proper young miss didn't once take a full look at the man, she was nonetheless aware of him watching her from his solitary vantage point. She could not make out his face but knew that he wore a dark suit of worsted wool, eschewing the elegant swallow tails of the Old Guard.

Brushing off her premonitions, she slipped, unnoticed, past Philip Armour, the millionaire meat packer from Chicago. He was holding forth for a group of his fellow merchants.

"The best property is taken now," he assured them, "and even if we do eventually force Brooklyn kicking and screaming into our civic ambit, the only way to grow is *up*. As Chicago is already doing. With ships passing through the Narrows at a record pace, we have no other choice."

Even Mystere, whose life was remote from the money fever gripping much of the city, knew it was Wall Street that had bankrolled the Union during the American Civil War. And now it was Wall Street reaping the astronomical capital gains of the long post war boom. By her headline-grabbing attendance at the Vanderbilt ball in March, Mrs. Astor had placed her rare imprimatur on these new "pick-and-shovel millionaires" she once condemned.

And the rest of the old aristocracy had dutifully followed her lead. Mystere noticed that Old New Yorkers, too, had turned out in force, radiating their sober, proper, Knickerbocker reassurance. However, old prejudices died slowly, and this group pointedly avoided Armour and anyone else who violated strict social punctillo by discussing commerce at evening gatherings. Mrs. Astor's core elite did not deny vulgarity, but they insisted on keeping it in its proper place. "Commerce is useful," as she once confided to Mystere, "but then so is a sewer."

Mystere had nearly reclaimed her bench when she felt a hand grip her right elbow.

"Miss Rillieux," a pallid and stout man of indeterminate middle age greeted her. "You look quite smashing this evening, young lady. I haven't seen you since the Vanderbilt ball."

"Thank you, Mr. Pollard. Yes, I'm afraid I've been quite the stay-at-home lately. Mrs. Astor coaxed me out this evening."

"Good for her. Although one can hardly blame a recluse these days," Abbot Pollard carped. "Why, we're being preempted on all sides. Have you *seen* the Upper East and Upper West sides lately? It's a regular blight of row houses and tenements. And the park? God help us, it's all hod carriers and shop girls crowding it now, coming in streetcars and that smelly, smoky, noisy El. One must go clear across the Harlem River for a peaceful carriage ride anymore. It's disgraceful, but there's Tammany politics for you."

Abbot was notorious for his snobbish tirades. Mystere gave him a tolerant smile. "The park was not built exclusively for the rich," she reminded him gently. "It was intended to be the city's drawing room, remember?"

"That's quite noble, my dear. You're still young and innocent, so I forgive you. But I, for one, do not allow any person into my drawing room who requires the services of a lice comb."

She was about to reply when a strong, masculine voice interceded from behind her.

"That's narrow-minded and cruel, Abbot. I have seen many a shop girl who is gracious, intelligent, and beautiful. Where is your spirit of noblesse oblige, sir?"

A slow, dreadful chill crept down her spine. Mystere turned around to meet the teal eyes of Rafael Belloch. The tight-lipped smile he gave her seemed to cost him an effort. His chestnut hair was cut unfashionably short and combed straight back from a strong brow and a fine Romanesque nose.

"Noblesse oblige," Pollard fired back, "has produced filthy wallows like the Fourth Ward and populist demagogues like Tom Foley, who bait the Irish and the Italians against us. The unwashed mobs nearly burned this city down in 'sixty-three. Next time perhaps they'll succeed thanks to all this new 'enlightenment' you champion."

Pollard stomped off, florid-faced with irritation. Mystere noticed, however, that Belloch hadn't really listened to the older man. He had only made his goading remarks to shoo Pollard off. Now his eyes took Mystere's measure with frank interest.

Her stomach knotted. She had managed to avoid the man since her introduction into society, but now here he was. Rafe Belloch. The notorious robber baron himself, with the gaze that probed too intently; with words that held all the softness of a razor.

"This crowd despises Tammany," he remarked. "But who else bothers to build hospitals and orphanages for the poor?"

"I shouldn't be too hasty, Mr. Belloch, in praising orphanages."

Mystere instantly regretted speaking up in a moment of unguarded feeling. But the words had spurted out before she could stop them. Feeling trapped by his stare, she added in a much lighter tone, "Mr. Pollard is just a harmless old sobersides. Did you enjoy my uncle's demonstration?"

The stare never wavered. "It was clever and entertaining, to be sure. And despite all the financial wizards in attendance, I don't think anyone has guessed his secret yet."

For a few seconds his unsettling words hung in the air between them, menacing and accusing. As his gaze seemed to probe her very soul, Mystere was gripped with panic. All the voices surrounding them, along with the soaring strains of a Strauss waltz, suddenly became grating noises screeching in her ears.

He knows, she thought in numb confusion. The awful moment of public exposure had come.

However, she had learned the art of dissembling from a true master. She gave him a demure little Mona Lisa smile. "Guessed my uncle's secret, Mr. Belloch? I'm afraid I fail to take your meaning."

"Why, it's quite simple. It is startling, Miss Rillieux, how much one can learn about any household by simply sending a servant to search through a parked carriage. Or even better, does your uncle find his information merely by passing some idle moments with a talkative upstairs maid, perhaps inducing her to read a private journal?"

Relief made her smile, and her confidence surged. Belloch only meant the little secret, not the Big One.

"I suppose that's possible," she allowed without much interest. "I don't profess any great belief in the occult. I look on my uncle's demonstrations as harmless entertainment. No doubt he has his little tricks."

"Of course. Encouraged by Mrs. Astor herself. Speaking of whom . . ."

He pointed with his chin—the great matron was even now aimed straight toward them. And of course her favorite minion, Ward McCallister, hovered at his carefully fixed distance like a moon orbiting its planet. Officially her social director, he was also less officially a matchmaker.

"Good evening, Mystere," Caroline greeted her with a genuine show of affection, bussing the younger woman's cheek. "You've been far too shy lately. You need not live in the shadow of your uncle's greatness. Don't forget that 'coming out' means precisely that. You're a debutante, not a cloistered nun."

Caroline turned to Belloch. "As for you, Rafe, *really*. You know perfectly well that one does not call a count 'monsieur.' One addresses him as *le comte*. I'm afraid poor Emile is terribly miffed."

Rafe bowed his head. "I'm truly mortified at the depth of my own ignorance, Caroline. Thank you for edifying me. I shall study to be deserving."

"You're scandalous," she assured him, raising a perfectly manicured hand to touch his cheek for a moment. "Mortified? You couldn't care less. And I am so smitten with you, you handsome brute, that I can't even be properly annoyed. Sensing my weakness, you abuse it."

Despite her bantering tone, Caroline sent him a low-lidded smile that went well beyond mere flirting, at least as Mystere understood the rules. Caroline turned to her again.

"Keep your guard up around this one, my dear," she confided. "New Orleans could not have prepared you for his species of male. Rafe is a jaded idealist, and your youth and naivete excite him. He's a man used to getting what he wants. And by the most direct path."

Caroline and Ward glided off, and Mystere hoped Belloch might follow them. However, he continued to stand close by, watching her from half-accusing, half-speculative eyes.

"Isn't this amusing?" he demanded, indicating the gathering with a wave of his hand. "The dryasdusts and the parvenus, all together under Caroline's newly expanded umbrella. And which are you, Miss Rillieux? Day coach or Pullman?"

"For one who scowls and makes acerbic remarks," she informed him, "you were certainly tame just now with Caroline."

"Of course. One does not visit Rome and insult the Pope."

She laughed even as she wondered: what did he want from her? Surely he did not recognize her. She looked very different from two years before. If anything, with her figure bound and strapped to appear younger, she had dropped an age instead of gaining one. Her education complete, her mentor Paul Rillieux had finally allowed her to earn her way out of her dirty, wretched rags. Her garb now was the most innocent blue satin gown Charles Frederick Worth could produce.

He couldn't recognize her, but oh, did she remember him, standing nearly naked in the alley in Five Points, rage and promise of vengeance hard on his face. He had been a spectacular sight, and she awoke from many a nightmare with his face etched in her mind like a photograph on albumen.

She glanced at him to reassure herself. It did no good. She swore he kept changing his position slightly, as if to study her from several angles.

She still knew little more about him than she had from the newspaper articles two years ago. He was a Patriarch of the Four Hundred. But whereas she and Paul Rillieux belonged only by special declaration of Mrs. Astor, Belloch could claim tradition of birth. There were vague rumors about some tragedy, although some preferred the word scandal. Perhaps so, for he was known to have many acquaintances but few friends. He had amassed a dizzying fortune in railroad ventures, lived part of each year at his magnificent estate in Virginia's hunt country, and owned a private steam yacht as luxurious as a small ocean liner. His yacht enabled him to take up local residence on Staten Island, deliberately snubbing Manhattan.

And, of course, he was an eminently eligible bachelor—which explained why, even now, Miss Antonia Butler was watching him like a cat on a rat.

"Miss Rillieux," he said, abruptly cutting into her thoughts, "what do you think about all this business with the Lady Moonlight?"

She did not miss a beat. "I confess I've given it scant attention. But it seems to have become a nine days' wonder in the press."

"Of course. After all, our thief is getting the best of the Four Hundred. Making all of us look like fools while robbing us in the very midst of our soirees. When she actually relieved Caroline of her best diamond bracelet, the Lady Moonlight's infamy was assured."

His probing eyes sent a message she couldn't decipher.

"It's a foolish name for her, if the thief is even really a woman," she opined. Her tone was polite but slightly bored.

"She's 'ethereal as a moonbeam, as elusive as a jungle cat,'" he quoted the papers, and they both laughed. Still, however, his greenish blue eyes seemed to be reading every detail of her face.

"She's also been described," Belloch added, "as a Valkyrie of a woman, huge and powerful. No match for a mere mortal man. But the only witnesses admit they glimpsed her only from behind in the shadows. And I suspect the press has seized on the Amazon angle to sensationalize the case. I'm of the opinion she is petite and extremely dexterous rather than big and strong."

"You seem quite immersed in the matter."

"I have a great interest, Miss Rillieux, in the methods and techniques of the society thief."

"Really? How amusing."

"Yes, isn't it?"

He moved even closer until she could feel his breath on her face, moist and warm and sweet from the brandy he had drunk earlier. The panic returned, and for a moment she feared a devastating exposure right here and now. Her legs felt watery and weak, and she wanted to sit down. But his intense gaze held her in place with the authority of a gun muzzle.

"You see, Miss Rillieux, the cleverest of thieves operate as teams or even vast syndicates." His eyes narrowed. "I shouldn't be at all surprised to learn that our infamous Lady Moonlight was once a common street thief, roaming with a band of coarse grifters. They stick together, these types, always prefering the safety of diversions to cover their activities. Perhaps she has even struck again this very night— while your uncle held us all in thrall."

She looked at him, ready to confront him with denial even though she longed to run away.

But she didn't expect to see the handsome grin on his face as he stared back.

"There it is again," he nearly whispered, his expression rapt. "That look—so full of reproach—so full of old wounds. What does a young debutante from New Orleans have to look wounded about?"

She turned away, choosing instead to focus on the ballgoers, but the parfait colors of satin ball gowns began to swirl in her vision as if washed in tears. Freezing up, she admonished herself not to be afraid. He had nothing on her. He was only speculating. As she had told herself a thousand times, she would do what she had to do to survive. For she had endured this long in order to keep alive the hope she would one day find her brother Bram. And when she did that, he would take her away from all the filth and lies. He would see that she was safe again, and all would be fine once more.

Then all the thievery, all the fear, would have been worth it.

The realization quelled her panic in a heartbeat.

"I can't imagine what you're talking about, Mr. Belloch. All this nonsense about syndicates and old wounds. I think you must have had too much brandy." She released a small laugh.

"How is it I've missed you during all these soirees? Tonight is the first night I've really looked at you, Miss Rillieux. I don't know how you've managed to stay out of my path at these functions, but now that I've seen you, I can't help but think you look familiar." The intent, mocking gaze raked down her figure. "Admittedly there are differences. The woman I recall was certainly more . . . robust, shall we say? She was not the pallid little mouse you appear to be, but that would be in keeping with my theory of diversions, would it not?"

"And no doubt," she taunted him with confident scorn, "my uncle is part of this wicked syndicate?"

"Perhaps," he answered with another wire-tight smile. "And perhaps you are the Lady Moonlight."

His tone left open the possibility that he was joking. But those dark eyes told another story altogether.

She felt a cold hand grip her heart, and her pulse leaped into her throat. Before she could reply, however, a startled cry rose above the music and the hum of conversation.

"Oh! My brooch! Someone has stolen my brooch!"

Chapter 2

Mrs. John Robert Pendergast of Grammercy Park clutched her neck as if garroted. At first, as news of the latest theft spread like grass fire through the assembly, everyone was at sixes and sevens. There seemed less concern for the missing brooch, Mystere noticed, than excitement about possibly spotting the exotic "Lady Moonlight."

"Well, Mr. Belloch," she forced out in a light tone, "it would appear that your clairvoyant powers rival my uncle's. You predicted this only moments ago."

Belloch folded his arms over his chest, watching her with all the alertness of a lion in the brush. "So I did. And to think I almost couldn't bring myself to attend tonight."

To avoid his probing gaze, she feigned an interest in monitoring the nearby commotion. Mrs. Pendergast, a stricken look on her face, continued clutching the high neck of her dress, open at the throat where the brooch was missing.

"Surely you must have dropped it?" Thelma Richards asked her. "*How* could anyone possibly have removed it without your knowing? Literally from under your nose!"

"How, indeed?" Belloch whispered, still watching Mystere. "Unless our Lady Moonlight is a true artist at her craft."

"Aren't you drawing some hasty conclusions, sir?" she challenged him without flinching. "A theft has not yet been established much less the gender of the thief."

She had begun to edge away from him with hopes of losing him in the commotion, but Belloch had other plans for her. Taking her by one arm, his grip firm and utterly merciless, he guided her closer to the hubbub around the victim.

It so happened that Chief of Detectives Thomas F. Byrnes was in attendance. He was a great favorite with the Four Hundred, for he had established the strictly enforced "dead line" north of Fulton Street that kept criminal predators out of the financial district. After a brief, confused search of the grounds and gallery floor by servants turned up nothing, he approached the distraught woman.

"What type of brooch, Mrs. Pendergast?"

"Why . . . a yellow-gold flower brooch, Inspector. There were five oval opals and twenty-two round rubies."

"Quite valuable, I take it?"

The matron paled. "Quite."

"Good luck to you, Inspector," Belloch called out through the crowd, though his gaze still lingered on Mystere. "You might have better results trying to hold back the ocean with a broom. It appears that our Lady Moonlight has struck again from within our very midst. Perhaps a thorough search of all our female guests would be in order?"

His tone was jesting, and a few men chuckled at his mild ribaldry while some of the ladies took obvious offense.

"That might prove most pleasant, Mr. Belloch," Byrnes admitted. "But also most unpolitic. I'd be demoted to a beat on South Street."

Antonia Butler caught Belloch's attention and smiled at him—showing too many teeth, Mystere criticized silently. She and Antonia had both come out this season, though, as Rillieux planned, Antonia was allowed to make the greater stir. Her father had originally made his fortune in Canton, Ohio, manufacturing carbon dioxide for the soda pop industry. But like Rockefeller, Carnegie, Armour, and so many others, he had moved to New York to put his fortune to work.

Mystere watched Antonia excuse herself from the group around her and cross toward her and Belloch. Thankfully, she felt Belloch's hand drop from her arm. In the crowd no one had noticed Belloch's manhandling of her.

Antonia looked quite fetching, Mystere had to admit, in a pinch-waisted sateen gown with black-velvet trim. Certainly it flattered her figure quite frankly, whereas Mystere's prim dress, while of high quality and an excellent complement to her opalescent complexion, had been selected to make her look more the girl than the woman.

The heiress was beautiful, Mystere allowed, but in the stiff way of a fine porcelain piece. In her ungracious mind, she thought Antonia radiated all the elan of a sleepwalker. And what little animation she possessed was mainly schoolgirl spite. She was purse proud and enjoyed parading her purchases in a way that suggested some early brushes with want. Worse than that, she had always treated mousey little Mystere as a sort of charity mascot for the rich and famous.

"Good evening, Mystere," Antonia greeted her with patronizing politeness. "Your uncle's little show just now was quite amusing. I didn't realize there was such theatrical talent in your family."

That was another Antonia trait—disparaging words delivered in a sweet tone. Everyone knew theater people were a socially degraded lot. Anger touched Mystere for a brief moment. But Antonia had already turned her toothy smile toward Rafe, and Mystere found herself grateful to the girl for her diversion.

"Mr. Belloch, you gentlemen have us ladies at a distinct disadvantage. *We* must languish at home while your sex is free to circulate at will. You might send up your card now and then, you know."

"Miss Butler, the prospect is daunting. The one time I did screw up my courage to visit, you were surrounded by a galaxy of hopeful admirers."

"Why, Mr. Belloch! So timid—and yet, you are the man who moves mountains."

Antonia's eyes flicked dismissively toward Mystere as she added, "I thought you were one to relish a challenge, Mr. Belloch, not the assured victory?"

"I do, Miss Butler, so long as some profit is likely on my investment."

His innuendo was a bit crude and direct, in Mystere's opinion, but Antonia did not appear offended. Still including Mystere in her gaze, she replied, "My father assures me that no one can hope to gain without taking great risks. I hope your success in commerce has not made you . . . too easily complacent in your personal affairs?"

Clearly pleased with herself, Antonia bid them both good evening and returned to her friends.

"There may, indeed, be a galaxy of men around her," Mystere commented in a neutral tone. "But it's quite clear *your* orbit has top priority."

"Oh, I may eventually play with her," he replied with scant interest.

"Are you playing with me, too? Is that what you've been doing? Amusing yourself?"

"Yes, but different women, different games, Miss Rillieux. Tell me something. I'm told that your uncle is a great favorite of Mrs. Astor's?"

His self-satisfied voice irked her, and she replied curtly. "She's been quite kind. We haven't been in New York long, as you know."

He greeted her answer with a rude bark of laughter. "At least two years, according to my count."

" 'Different women, different games,' " she coolly tossed back at him. "I do think you have me mistaken for someone else."

He ignored her words, his eyes narrowing again in speculation. "Caroline tells me your uncle went wide upon the world in his youth?"

"He has traveled extensively, yes. However, that was before I went to live with him in New Orleans."

"Ahh, that's right. After your parents were taken by . . . cholera, was it?"

"Yellow fever. It's a terrible problem in New Orleans. There was a particularly bad outbreak in 'seventy-one."

By now Mrs. Pendergast and Inspector Byrnes had withdrawn to the parlor to complete a more detailed report. Mystere gazed around until she caught old Rillieux's eye. He was seated at a marble pedestal table with Alice and Alva Vanderbilt. He nodded in her direction, and Mystere began to edge away from Belloch. But again the railroad plutocrat detained her with a grip like a steel trap.

"Yes, New Orleans is a charming city," he pushed on despite her evident desire to leave. "But the area is afflicted with a wretched climate. I was down there once on business. Do they still burn Beast Butler in effigy?"

"Who?"

"*Who?*" His face clouded. "Surely you're being ironic?"

Mystere fought off her distress, trying to place the familiar name. Then she remembered Rillieux's coaching. "Oh, of course. You mean

Ben Butler, the Union general who occupied New Orleans during the war."

"Yes. But I'm surprised a New Orleans native wouldn't know that right off. As I understand it, he's the most hated man in the city's history. He practically accused every lady in New Orleans of being a harlot."

"I have little memory of the war, sir. You forget my tender age. I just made my debut," she reminded him.

"Miss Rillieux, time does *not* heal all wounds. I was down there only five years ago. He was still reviled by one and all."

Mystere's uneasiness over all the questions gave way to sheer indignation at his bulldog tenacity. With a spirited wrench, she freed her arm from his grip.

"You've made your point that I must be a stupid creature, Mr. Belloch. Now, if the insults are through, I hope you'll excuse me."

Obviously he wasn't done with her, but she had had her fill of him. She turned quickly away before he could detain her again. If he even tried, she was prepared to cry for help. It would cause a scandal, but she could not let him get the upper hand. There was too much danger in him.

"Stupid is not the adjective I have in mind for you," his voice taunted behind her.

Without turning around, she stiffened her spine and left him to his mocking laughter.

As their carriage rolled past the great stone gateposts of the Maitland mansion, Paul Rillieux inserted a pinch of snuff behind his upper lip. Then he snapped his silver snuff box shut and said to Mystere, "Well now, my dear. Let me examine our latest sparkler."

She lifted her left forearm a few inches. The frilled cuff on the embroidered undersleeve of her dress was visible beneath the ermine lappet of the sleeve. A strategically located drawstring pocket had been sewn between them, obscured by the voluminous folds. After years of literal sleight of hand practice under Rillieux's exacting tutelage, she could remove and hide an item of jewelry so effortlessly even someone watching her closely saw nothing but a woman absentmindedly adjusting one sleeve.

She took out the brooch and handed it across to Rillieux.

He thumb scratched a lucifer, and the flaring glow of the match reflected brilliant points of color from the beautiful, richly jeweled piece.

"Superb craftsmanship," he pronounced in a reverent tone. "Mystere, I've had some brilliant protégés in my time. Your talent, however, is unsurpassed."

"Talent," she repeated, bitterness edging into her tone, "applies to painting or poetry or acting, not to stealing."

"Wrong. But at any rate, we do not 'steal.' I've told you that before. We arrogate. There's a vital difference. Stealing is low, vulgar, and common. You remember it well with your background, don't you, love? I plucked you from Five Points myself."

He gave a self-satisfied grin. "No, indeed. Stealing is a shameful, sneaky act by those who snivel when captured. Arrogation, in contrast, is refined, high-minded, and bold. It is seizure of property with no regard whatsoever for moral justifications. What the Romans called *pecca fortiter,* sinning boldly. How do you think the Four Hundred got so rich? By arrogating unto themselves that which they desired, that's how."

The match went out, and Rillieux dropped the "sparkler" into his coat pocket. "Speaking of the Four Hundred," he added, "what was Belloch saying to you? It certainly didn't look like polite small talk."

"He's suspicious of me. Even before the Lady Moonlight. It was the robbery at Five Points—he remembers me."

"Nonsense. That was two years ago. Has he accused you of anything?"

"Not in so many words, but—"

"Come now, my dear, you know how excitable you can be. You're building a pimple into a peak. You were masked at Five Points. Besides, you appear even younger now with, ahh, your womanly figure restrained."

"Yes, he perhaps thinks me seventeen and not the twenty I am. But that has him confused, not fooled. You should have heard him pressing me about New Orleans. And about you. He nearly tripped me up with a question about Beast Butler. Thank God I read the books you gave me and recalled him in the nick of time."

"Belloch had better keep his nose out of the pie. Simply avoid him."

"I'll try, but what if he won't avoid me?"

"He'll learn to, or he'll end up like the curious cat."

"What does that mean?" she demanded, a thread of alarm in her voice.

"Nothing that concerns you. Don't worry overly much about Belloch. He's an odd one. There's a rumor he's not quite right in his upper story. Some embarrassment involving his parents and their loss of fortune."

"He seemed quite lucid to me, odd or not."

The carriage crossed Broadway at Madison Square, the hotel district. The Ladies' Mile sprawled from Twenty-third Street south to Fourteenth Street, the world's unsurpassed shopping district. The Marble Palace, Lord & Taylor, and the other huge department stores were mostly dark and silent now. Only Delmonico's Restaurant and a few of the specialty shops were still open for business.

"Paul?" she said, her voice tentative now. "The brooch—will it bring a good price?"

"I expect so. That's up to Helzer, you know. Why do you mention it?" If a voice could frown, his did now. Mystere never asked such questions.

"I . . . that is, I only wonder if I might possibly have a larger share?"

"Whatever for? Do I stint you? Don't forget I must run a household for all of us. You have a fine home, good clothes, pocket money, liberal use of a carriage and driver." He wagged a warning finger at her. "My dear, you *must* stop playing ducks and drakes with your money."

For a moment his lecturing tone made her face heat with anger. Despite her fear of Belloch, right now she shared his apparent disdain for the Four Hundred. If they were so superior and discerning, why could a callow fraud like Rillieux so easily fool them with good tailoring and a Continental flair?

Perhaps her stony silence warned him. His voice lowered an octave, menace in his tone. "Mystere, there's one thing I will *not* tolerate and that is a Judas kiss. In our little group it is all for one and one for all. No one holds out on the others. Is that clearly understood?"

For a moment, with the darkness as her cloak, she felt tears sting her eyes and throat. "Yes," she managed.

But Rillieux, who knew her moods to a hair, shifted to a sympathetic tone. "Mystere, have you forgotten the orphanage I took you out of?"

Forgotten? Never would she be that fortunate. The freezing nights, the severe punishments, and there had been little to eat except panada twice a day—a sort of bread soup with some pieces of turnip floating in it. But thanks to Rillieux, she had left as an eight-year-old child and learned to thieve her way to the ripe old age of twenty. She had started as an alley thief and alongside Rillieux had worked her way into the highest ranks. She had shed the old suffering life as completely as a snake sloughs its old skin. But not, however, the memory of it or the fear of returning.

"No," she told him with feeling, "I haven't forgotten. And I'm grateful. You've been good to me."

She slid the curtain aside and glanced outside. Manhattan was still only partially electrified, and gas lamps lined the street. A rising moon lighted the spire of Trinity Church to a silver patina.

Rillieux's voice, still kind, sliced into her thoughts. "It's Bram, isn't it? You still miss him. You still think of your brother."

"He's twenty-six now," she mused, more to herself than Rillieux. "If he's still alive, he's the only family I have left."

"Wrong, dear. We are a family. All of us. I, you, Baylis, Evan, Rose, now even little Hush when he's ready. Concentrate on what you have, not what you've lost. Bram's been missing for twelve years. Frankly, those unfortunate enough to be shanghaied don't usually last too long. He'll not likely turn up."

Her eyes trembled, and again she felt the saline sting of tears. He was probably right, but she would not give up her secret, costly search to locate her brother. Hope was her waking dream, the only thing that kept her going.

Their carriage rolled under the El just as a late commuter train steamed overhead, and Mystere heard Baylis, up on the box driving the team, curse when soot rained down on him. Again, in flashes between the steel support beams, she caught sight of the pale moon. Despite her remark to Belloch about how silly the name Lady Moonlight was, she knew it was in fact eerily apt. And not because of that foolish "ethereal as a moonbeam" business, either.

The first time Lady Moonlight had gained press attention was after the grand, city-wide gala surrounding the opening of the Brooklyn Bridge last March. That evening, New York and Brooklyn had staged a spectacular fireworks show the likes of which the world had never seen before. For hours the night sky over the East River had blazed with brilliant colors. Everyone, rich and poor alike, had gathered outdoors to witness it.

Then, only moments after the last Roman candles blazed out, a stunning full moon had emerged from dark clouds and bathed the new bridge in an otherworldly luminous aura. The natural light show had entranced viewers even more than the fireworks—and it was then that Mystere, honed by twelve years in training under Rillieux, had removed Caroline Astor's bracelet.

Thus the Lady Moonlight instantly seized the public imagination and became a heroine to the less fortunate. Soon there was even a certain cachet to becoming one of her victims. After all, to be robbed by the Lady Moonlight was to be designated an elite—she never robbed the middle class, did she? Watching for her, speculating on her identity or next victim—all of it lent the rather dry lives of the upper crust a bit of titillation.

Again Rillieux's voice scattered her thoughts.

"Take this," he told her, pressing some folded bank notes into her hand. "Perhaps I can scrape up a bit more money for you now and then. But you must promise me you *won't* waste it searching for Bram."

Waste it . . . no, she thought, it would be wasted if it went for more gowns or perfumes. But the search for Bram was as vital to her as the breath in her nostrils. So her reply was at least a half truth.

"I won't waste it," she promised. "I really won't."

Chapter 3

Once Caroline Astor had fallen under the spell of Paul Rillieux's glib erudition and Old World charm, his acceptance was complete. No one even dreamed of investigating the claim that his wealth derived from French baronial land holdings. Thus, with no further references required, he had secured a roomy brownstone mansion near Great Jones Street and Lafayette Place, one of the most sought-after locations in Manhattan.

Mystere had been assigned an entire upstairs wing as her private quarters. She was awake early on the morning after the Astor soiree, for she had an appointment at mid-morning in Central Park.

She performed a hurried toilette and dusted her face lightly with powder. Then came a tedious daily ritual: wearing only pantalets, she stood before a sterling silver and green-velvet dressing mirror, carefully binding her chest with strips of linen. The procedure was cumbersome and uncomfortable, but Rillieux had insisted.

"We want a pretty debutante, not a beautiful woman," he had instructed her. "We want men to look at you and think 'Well, perhaps in a few years, but not now.' We want them to dismiss you and look somewhere else while you separate them from their possessions."

She finished wrapping the linen and donned a silk chemise. Then she crossed to a tall satinwood wardrobe and selected a black cambric dress. It was frumpy and stodgy, but that was precisely what she wanted for this meeting. After she dressed she drew her mahogany-colored hair back into a neat coil on her nape.

Quite drab and dreary, she approved, examining her appearance in the mirror. To check the final touch, she put on a widow's bonnet with a veil. Yes, that should do it—a poor widow could travel alone, unharassed. And covered by the veil, no one of the Four Hundred would likely recognize her at her assignation in the park.

A sudden knock at the door of her dressing room made her start. "Mystere? Are you awake?" called a woman's voice.

Hastily she took off the bonnet and stuffed it in her wicker tote— just in time—the door clicked open, and a woman of about thirty years of age, with her fiery red hair in curl papers under a mobcap, thrust her head into the room.

"Up and dressed already, la! I'm just up myself."

"Good morning, Rose."

Rose O'Reilly gave the black dress a skeptical glance. She had coarse-grained skin in a careworn face old before its time. "You've lost your pretty feathers in that raggedy dress."

Mystere ignored that. "Is Paul up yet?"

"Yes, he's with Hush in the downstairs parlor. Lesson time, you know."

"All right. I'll be down presently."

Rose started to shut the door, then hesitated. "By the way, it's all over the papers this morning."

"What—oh. You must mean Mrs. Pendergast's brooch."

"It's all the buzz. Evan says even the milkman went on and on about it. The police are vowing to catch the thief, Mystere. They're even forming a special team just to trap the Lady Moonlight. I told Paul he's paring the cheese mighty close to the rind, but he told me shush, he knows what he's up to. I sure to God hope so, or it'll go hard for all of us."

Having said her piece, Rose departed. But her warning words left Mystere feeling anxious and uneasy. Especially when she recalled Rafe Belloch and his dark, accusing eyes probing her last night. Paul dismissed him as "odd," but she sensed the dangerous, suppressed tension in him. The man was a caged tiger just waiting for some fool to open the door.

Nonetheless the risk was worth it. None of the others, not even the resourceful Hush, who was an astounding pickpocket despite his youth, were producing "sparklers" to match the hauls of the Lady Moonlight. They could not, for they were deprived of her easy access to the very wealthy. And the more she brought in, the more her share—or so Rillieux had promised. Money she desperately needed.

She unlocked the top drawer of a Louis XVI gilt bronze writing desk and took out a small birchwood box. The tattered and torn letter she carefully removed and unfolded had been written on foolscap, now dog-eared and faded from age, handling, and exposure. She chastised herself for handling it yet again, but there were times when she had to or else she might quit believing her struggle was worth it.

The most legible part was the printed letterhead, a split image of half an eagle joined to a man's arm holding up a dagger. The date below the letterhead was also clear, April 12, 1863. But the neat handwriting itself had nearly faded, and grew progressively dimmer as her gaze fell down the page.

Dear Brendan,

I pray God this letter and enclosed bank draft find you and your family well. I know how terrible things are in Dublin these days. Believe me, it was hard here in New York, too, when I first arrived.

However, I have prospered beyond my wildest expectations. I know your health is poor lately, but if at all possible, I urge you to bring your family here to New York City. Rest assured I have the means to make sure you will be well set up. Life here is turbulent and confusing, especially as we await the outcome of this terrible war. However, a man willing to roll up his sleeves will find ample chance to better himself and his children.

Speaking of that, also rest assured that whether or not you make it over here, you, Maureen, Bram, and Mystere have been provided for in my will. I could never have made it to America without your help. The money you gave me, at great hardship to you and your family, paid my way over. God bless you and answer my prayer that soon all of us may be united once again.

She could not read the final paragraph, however, which had faded too much. And try as she might she could not decipher the almost completely faded signature. At some point water had smeared the ink even before it faded. She had once taken it to a restorer of antique manuscripts, who tried without success to clarify the signature with tincture of mercury and zinc.

Nor did she even have a name to begin the search with, for she had never known—or had long forgotten—her last name. Brendan, her father, had died even before her mother received this letter, and Mystere had been only two when consumption took her mother, too. One of Maureen's final acts had been to place her and eight-year-old Bram on a ship bound for America.

Mystere carefully folded the letter and put it away. Memory amazed and frustrated her: It could run through a person's entire life in the time it took to tie a shoe. Yet it could also fail to answer the most fundamental questions about one's existence. She had no memory of her life in Ireland, only this letter and the things Bram had told her. And one thing he had insisted, over and over, was how their mother told him he and Mystere had rights to a great fortune.

Downstairs, the tall case clock in the hallway chimed the quarter hour and jolted her back to the present. She gave herself one final glance in the mirror and clutched the wicker tote that held her veil.

"Today," she said hopefully to her reflection. "Today Lorenzo will have something for me."

"Remember, lad," Rillieux's sonorous voice leaked through the hand-carved teakwood doors of the parlor, which stood ajar, "an excellent moment to exploit is during the first critical seconds when two acquaintances meet on the street. That moment when their eyes lock and they decide to acknowledge each other with the rituals of greeting."

Mystere peeked through the open doors into a sumptuously appointed room illuminated by gilt brass astral lamps, recently electrified. The even lighting accentuated a Persian Hamadan carpet of rose, blue, and green on a black background. Rillieux sat in a carved-walnut armchair, gesturing with his walking stick like a conductor with a baton. And young Hush, the only name they knew him by, had perched on a cushioned footrest, literally at the feet of the master.

"The greeting ritual," Rillieux lectured on, "is one that requires complete focus of attention for a few seconds. I once even relieved a gentleman of his portmanteau during just such an opportunity. But timing is everything, along with lightning speed and flawless movements. *The readiness is all,* Hush. That and absolute confidence, for you are an artist at your craft."

"An artist, sir?"

"Of course. Thievery—which I call arrogation—is a complex and beautiful art when done correctly. It should never involve threats, violence, or bloodshed. I absolutely abhor these Plug Uglies and Roach Guards who intimidate, injure, even kill their victims. Why would you kill a breeder of more rich men? Just as a good farmer treats his fertile dirt with respect, *we* must cherish those whom we separate from their costly baubles."

"Really, Paul," Mystere teased as she stepped into the parlor, "the boy is only twelve years old. You sound like Plato lecturing his disciples."

Hush scrambled politely to his feet when she entered, flashing the sadly disjointed smile that had instantly captured her heart when she first met him. The orphan worked as a rat catcher and lived in a basement hovel in Little Italy on the southern end of Mulberry Street. His trousers made of leftover Union blue shoddy were held up with a leather belt three sizes too big for him; his shirt was of wool, and it was clear by its dirty and patched appearance that the boy wore the shirt summer and winter.

Rillieux was in a good mood this morning and greeted Mystere with a smile. "Only twelve, yes, and just look at these. He is not just a disciple but a prodigy."

He pointed to the loot heaped up on a nearby marquetry tea table. Besides several billfolds, Hush's latest haul included a gold Italian rope bracelet and a pair of sapphire and diamond drop earrings.

"The lad has remarkable talent," Rillieux gloated. "I haven't seen his like since you, Mystere. What he's learned in the alley will graduate him to the Four Hundred, I tell you. Pickpocket hands that could easily master the piano or the surgical knife. The gold, by the way, is twenty-four karat."

She kept her face impassive, but his smug good mood about the child's deliberate corruption filled her with anger. Rillieux had a reputation as a world-traveled scholar. In truth, however, his "genius" was nothing but a near-photographic memory. This served two useful purposes: by dint of memorizing facts alone he could pose as broadly learned, and even more useful, he never forgot the location of any item of value.

"Did someone die?" he added, giving her somber black dress a puzzle-headed look.

"I think she looks beautiful, sir," Hush spoke up boldly. "Like a lady in some famous painting."

"We know you're smitten, lad. No one can blame you. She is a tonic to the eyes even in black. Will you be requiring the carriage today, Mystere?"

She had to be careful. It was part of the reason she wore the black dress. Widows out alone were usually left to their grief, while other young women out in the city alone, at best might be mistaken for prostitutes. And she was going into the city alone.

Certainly the carriage could take her, but she knew Rillieux had his private reasons for being so generous with the carriage. If Baylis drove her, he would dutifully report her actions to Rillieux. All of the servants, including Rose, were extremely loyal to him. After all, he had taken them away from places like Rag Picker's Row and Bandits' Roost, and given them a good place to live and some security in their heretofore desperate lives. Baylis genuinely liked her, and she him, but she had learned he would not keep any secret from Paul.

"I think the omnibus will do for me," she told him. "I plan to do some shopping on Broadway, and you know how congested it gets. Poor Baylis hates all that jockeying about for position."

"Well, at least call for a carriage. The Four Hundred do not ride on omnibuses."

"Good," she replied lightly. "Then none of them will be there to see me. I enjoy riding the omnibus."

Rillieux frowned, forming spiderwebs of squint lines at the corners of his eyes. "As you will, my dear. But make sure you're home by three P.M. We've been invited to a poetry reading at the Vernons'. Sylvia Rohr will be there—I've had my eye on a little trinket of hers."

"I'll be back in time," she promised, hiding her resentment.

On the face of it she had a highly desirable social calendar. Besides the numerous—endless, she corrected herself—balls, soirees, and high teas were the excursions to museums, operas, the theater, and lyceums. Yet despite it all she was in a state of unutterable loneliness. She was among people but not *of* them—she was there only to steal.

Hush followed her out of the parlor and through the main salon into the front vestibule. "Mystere?" he said behind her as she reached for the glass knob of the front door.

"Hmm?" She turned, her thoughts elsewhere, to look down into his dark, intelligent gaze.

"When will I be allowed to live here with you . . . uhh, I mean with the rest of you?"

She smiled, though his words gave her a stab. "Quite soon now, I think. However, that's up to Paul."

As was his habit, he shook his thick shock of dark hair out of his eyes. "Mr. Rillieux . . . he likes me, don't he? He thinks I do good work, right?"

Mystere believed that if she looked at faces very carefully, she could not only see what a person was, but what he would become. And she liked what she saw in Hush's face. Behind the grime and the scars and the tough veneer of a street arab, she saw an honest heart and a genuine depth of character.

"Hush," she replied, "he's quite satisfied, yes. Don't worry on that score. But you do understand, don't you, that no one is forced to . . . to become a thief?"

"Forced? I like it. It sure beats the hell out of crawling under houses to poison rats."

"I know. But remember, even while you do what Paul tells you, you can also pursue something you like even better. Something more honorable. Teach yourself a useful trade—can you read?"

He shook his head. "But I can cipher some."

"Well then, I'll teach you how to read. For a bright boy like you, it will be easy to learn. We'll start next time you come."

His face brightened at the prospect. She turned toward the door, but again his voice arrested her. "Mystere?"

"Yes?"

He sent a quick glance over his shoulder, making sure Rillieux hadn't left the parlor. "Are you . . . you know, forced?"

She searched his face. "You've guessed, haven't you? About the Lady Moonlight?"

He nodded.

"You *are* bright. Don't let on to Paul that you know."

"But are you? Forced to do it?"

Something about the curious glance he gave her reminded her of the way Rafael Belloch had looked at her last night, as if sounding the very depths of her soul.

She started to attempt a reply, then caught sight of the brass-and-glass mantel clock: already past ten A.M.

"We'll talk later," she told him, giving him a quick kiss on the cheek. "Just know this: Fancy words like 'arrogation' don't change a thing. Stealing may seem easy and profitable, but no matter how good one becomes at it, it is still a sin and a crime."

"Not when *you* do it," he insisted, his tone brooking no debate.

Paul isn't the only one corrupting him, she thought with a sinking feeling as she let herself out. Despite what he had just said, she was completely unable to meet his eye or utter a word of denial.

Chapter 4

No omnibus served Lafayette Place, but Mystere could walk a few blocks to catch an express car pulled by a huge dray horse. It took her directly to the park entrance at Fifth Avenue and Fifty-ninth Street.

Despite her nervous anticipation about what she might learn at her meeting with Lorenzo Perkins, she enjoyed the long, slow ride. It was a fine day, bright with unclouded sunshine while a steady breeze from the north kept the heat bearable. True, one could happen to glance south of Washington Square, where there was always that pall of dense, dark smoke floating above lower Manhattan—the factory district, choked with everything from chemical plants to tanneries—but Mystere simply accepted it as a fish accepts water, for she had grown up with the city, watching it push farther and farther north until the only rural part of Manhattan left was the upper end. There farm animals still grazed even as sidewalks were being laid out and gas lines installed around them. She had read recently that the last squatters and subsistence farmers were being chased out around Seventy-eighth and Seventy-ninth streets. Even the farm fields of Harlem were now being surveyed for housing lots.

The remarkable progress was evident all around her, especially overhead where a thick, tangled web of telephone and electrical wires blotted out the sky in some places.

She was about to enter the park when a handsome, loden green carriage rolled by on the opposite side of the avenue. The glittering gold harness rig caught her attention, and too late she realized who owned the coach. Before she could turn away, she found herself trapped under the almost physical force of Rafe Belloch's stare.

She dared not duck into the park as if hiding from him. So she simply let him scrutinize her at will, hoping her veil would protect her. From a sidewalk filled with prospects, he selected her to watch with minute attention. Despite her apprehension she couldn't help but notice how the window seemed to frame him like a painting, a portrait of a strong-browed, dark-eyed, dangerous young nobleman.

I have a great interest, Miss Rillieux, in the methods and techniques of the society thief.

Then, mercifully, he was past her, and she had safely entered the park.

She and Lorenzo Perkins had agreed to meet behind the *Angel of the Waters* at the Bethesda Terrace north of the lake. But, as usual, he was late. She found an empty stone bench that gave her a good view of the crowded plaza and sat down to wait. Water brawled from the bronze feet of the *Angel,* cascading down the tiers of the fountain.

Only sheer desperation to find out about her brother could have induced her to hire a former Pinkerton man. First she had exhausted every possible means. Interviews with Irish immigrants from her old neighborhood in Dublin, research at the university library—she even regularly lighted a candle to Saint Jude, the patron saint of all lost causes. Secretly, of course, for she was a devout Catholic awash in ruling-elite Protestants and attended Trinity Church with Paul.

But eventually she decided that God helped those who helped themselves. So she had also, at great expense and risk, engaged Perkins's services. So far, however, he had turned up little of any real use, only vague, unsubstantiated bits of information.

Thus ruminating, she didn't even notice Lorenzo until he sat down beside her. "What's with the widow's weeds?" he greeted her.

"Just a bit of prudence. Were you able to find out anything?"

Perkins looked at her with small, dull eyes like a turtle. He was somewhere in his thirties, she guessed, his teeth badly neglected. He was foolishly vain about his waxed mustache, which he carefully pointed every now and then with thumb and forefinger—perhaps to detract from his teeth, though it only pulled her eyes to his mouth even more often.

"I've been asking around on the quiet about that ship I mentioned to you, the *Sir Francis Drake.*"

"And . . . ?"

He shrugged, watching the motley flow of humanity all around them. Children in white linen were watched by nannies in blue serge. Mixed among them were the street arabs, the children like Hush who wore rags and lived virtually on the street. But even they were children and couldn't resist the sight of pennies in a fountain and the hurdy-gurdy man.

"Every lead just turns into a dead end," he told her. "This kind of search takes time. But I am closing in on your brother's whereabouts. I feel it in my bones."

"Yes, but that's precisely what you told me last time, Mr. Perkins. You've learned *nothing* since then?"

"What could you possibly know about the detective business? You must understand something—all's grist that comes to my mill. It must be sorted through at great pains. I'm getting there, I tell you, but you must be patient."

"But you've absolutely nothing to report in two weeks? What have you been doing?"

"I don't live in your pocket, you know. I have several other cases I'm working on."

"Yes, you told me. Debt skippers, I believe you said."

"Among other things," he assured her, his tone defensive.

A storm of anger began to rise inside her, but for Bram's sake she quelled it. Her attitude toward Perkins was forged of distaste and forbearance, for he was her only hope—yet, a forlorn hope. However, detectives were not so easily acquired, and she was not eager to search out another who might prove even worse.

"If he did sail aboard the *Drake,*" she pressed on, "wouldn't there be some record? Ship's log or something?"

"That's one nut I haven't cracked yet."

Among many others, she thought bitterly.

"I mean to look into it," he added, seeing the anger in her eyes and firmed lips.

In the distance factory steam whistles blew the lunch call. Mystere remained in a moody silence, watching a sudden, stiff breeze wrinkle the surface of the lake. The boaters were all forced to grab their hats.

But the water jogged her memory, and her inside eye saw Bram's abduction happening all over again.

It was only a few weeks after Rillieux had rescued her and Bram from the Jersey Street Orphanage. She had been eight at the time, Bram fourteen. One day, while they were wandering around Manhattan seeking victims to rob as Rillieux had instructed them, a dark carriage had suddenly pulled up beside them.

Four men dressed like ordinary seamen had grabbed Bram and thrust him into the carriage, evidently impressing him for duty on a ship. The carriage had then sped away, leaving her helpless, devastated, and bereft of family.

Bram had haunted her ever since. His disappearance was as if her very arm had been cut off. She was tormented by visions of what had happened to her only relative, the beautiful boy with the platinum blond hair so different from hers and eyes the exact green color of Ireland's dewy fields. Sometimes she wondered if the person who wrote the letter had found Bram. She tried to picture him living in a fine house, beloved and cherished—a man now of twenty-six, perhaps even with a family of his own. But if so, why would he have deserted her—or did he think she was dead?

"Once, when I was twelve," she told Perkins, breaking the long silence, "I thought I saw Bram. He was up in the rigging of a ship that was sailing from the docks on South Street. The same hair and eyes. But I was too late to board the ship."

"A packet ship?"

She nodded. "Square-rigged," she added, for she had done some reading about ships after that.

"Did you notice the name of the ship?"

"No, I . . . I was too upset to think of it at the time."

"Upset" was a vast understatement. She had called out Bram's name over and over, yet those magnificent emerald eyes had merely stared at her as she ran along the docks screaming, no recognition in his cold, blank stare.

Lorenzo watched her from a sullen deadpan. She had noticed that he rarely smiled, and when he did it was a scornful smirk that suggested a lack of ironic subtlety. He gave her one of those smirks now.

"It's not wise to stack your conclusions higher than your evidence.

He may indeed be alive. But it's also possible he's buried in a name-less grave in Potter's Field by now. Or locked up in the penitentiary on Blackwell's Island."

"If it's the latter," she pointed out, "couldn't you find out? The pris-oners' names must be recorded somewhere."

Shrewdness seeped into his eyes. "I can make some inquiries, yes. But as they say: An empty hand is no lure for a hawk."

Nor for a rook, she thought bitterly. Out loud she only said, "More money already?"

"It's not for me; it's to bribe the right officials."

Frustration sharpened her tone. "But, Mr. Perkins, I gave you one hundred dollars only two weeks ago."

He forced out a fluming sigh. "Yes, well, you needn't get your nose out of joint. I'm afraid I find myself temporarily in straitened circum-stances. My wife has been feeling poorly of late and requires much medical attention."

"Yes, you mentioned that last time we met." *When you reeked of liquor,* she thought. She suddenly remembered Hush, and it occurred to her: She could find out how Lorenzo was spending his time—and her money.

But for right now she only opened her purse and took out the money Paul had given her last night.

"This is all I have right now. Fifty dollars."

"It'll help," he assured her, tucking the folded bills into his fob pocket.

"When do you think you might know something?"

He shrugged one shoulder. "What's after what's next? Ask me something easy. I told you before I'm getting closer."

She had noticed he always got flip with her once he pocketed her money. By now her anger at him had driven her past the point of dis-cretion. Rather than risk a nasty, pointless fight, she abruptly stood up.

"Since it's needless to keep meeting regularly, will you please call me if anything turns up? Our number is in the telephone directory."

He stood up, too, his turtle eyes studying her clothing again. "Under Rillieux, right?"

"Yes."

"It's a small directory," he said, still watching her. "Few people can afford telephones. I see your name in the society columns, you and your uncle. So I'm naturally curious. Why do you keep it on the quiet that you've hired me? And if you know you're a Rillieux, why don't you also know your own brother's last name?"

The question had come up before. But she had not told him about the letter at home in its birchwood box. Bram had sworn her to secrecy about that, claiming only the right people should see the letter. However, he had been abducted before he could find those right people.

"I'm not aware," she replied archly, "that *I'm* the subject of your inquiries."

His little smirk-smile was back. "It might make my job easier if you were honest with me."

"I'm as honest as I need to be," she assured him. "I hope you are, too."

With that she turned and walked away, her hopes thoroughly dashed and a sharp pang of despair in her heart.

Chapter 5

Mystere had no appetite, but she felt slightly dizzy as she exited the park onto Fifth Avenue. Remembering that she had left home without eating breakfast, she stopped at a tea shop and ordered a light lunch.

She returned to the house shortly after two P.M. After a quick but relaxing hot bath in her quarters, she changed into a royal blue silk taffeta dress. Like most of her dresses, it had a high bodice and was cut to downplay her womanly figure.

She found Rillieux downstairs in the parlor with Rose, Evan, and Baylis gathered around him. Hush had gone.

"Baylis will take Mystere and me to the Vernons'," Rillieux was saying as she came into the room. "But he'll have ample time to drive back here and pick up Evan. I've culled the newspapers to determine who has gone abroad for the summer."

He handed Evan a sheet of paper and an odd-looking key Mystere recognized as a *passe-partout,* or master key. He made them himself in a lead ladle. Known simply as bar keys on the street, they included as many as four standard bits found in domestic locks of the day.

"Here are the addresses. Some will have left servants staying on the premise, some not. So use caution. Remember: only cash, good jewelry and time pieces, and good silver service. That's all Helzer wants at the present time."

"Not even good furs?" Baylis asked. Only in his twenties, he had a hard little face like a terrier and wore a derby hat with a grouse feather in the band. He had no beard except a line of hair between the chin and the neck—called a Newgate fringe because it covered the spot where a rope was placed in a hanging.

Rillieux shook his sleek white head. "Presently no. He has trouble disposing of them quickly."

"Helzer's getting mighty picky these days," Evan complained in his barrel-chested voice. At first glance the man who served as the Rillieux's "butler" appeared hulking and simian. But further study revealed a big, powerful man who was strikingly quick and coordinated for his size. A "cauliflower" left ear attested to many fights in his youth. Mystere knew that he and Baylis both still carried their knuckle dusters from the old days at Five Points—loops of heavy, shaped brass that fit over the knuckles in a fight.

"Yes, well, it can't be helped," Rillieux explained. "This new chief of detectives, Inspector Byrnes—he's brought in new methods that put pressure on our fences."

He turned his attention to Mystere, who had joined Rose on the carved rosewood sofa.

"You look quite charming, dear. An improvement over the rag you donned earlier. Did your shopping go well?" The old con's searching look told her he still suspected her story.

"Quite well," she lied, not backing down from his scrutiny. After all, she had learned the art of lying from him. "But mightn't I beg off from the poetry reading this afternoon?"

"Why? I thought you liked poetry. Don't you feel well?"

"I do enjoy it, and I'm not ill. Just a bit people weary, is all. It's been a hectic social calendar lately."

All that was true. She was tired. She hadn't slept well last night, and today's fruitless meeting with Lorenzo had drained her. She would love to spend a quiet afternoon in her quarters just reading and thinking.

"Buck up, Mystere. It wears on me, too. But remember, membership in the Four Hundred confers obligations as well as privileges. One of those obligations is to be a highly social creature."

There it was again, she fretted—the "kind choke hold" as she called Rillieux's grip on her. He had given her so much, but he required a great deal, too. Yet, he rarely made demands, for he could easily coerce her with kindness. And if kindness didn't work, then there was always the "other Rillieux" to go to work on her. That man was no gentleman of the Four Hundred. Paul Rillieux's dark side was in keeping with the liar and the fraud that he was. Deep inside him was a hard, cruel spirit that showed itself infrequently because he did believe one got more flies with honey. She had seen that man only once when she had refused to lift a brooch from a matron who was rumored to be on the verge of bankruptcy. Before the ball, Rillieux had entered her bedroom and beat her with his silver-and-ebony walking stick. And even when the stick broke under the strain of the lashing, he continued, his face frozen in hard, earnest contempt.

She had hardly been able to move at the ball, let alone dance with her beaux. He had been careful not to touch her face, so the bruises were well covered, and he gallantly attributed her new-found reluctance to dance as shyness. Despite her soreness and pain, she got him the brooch. But the memory of the episode was worked into her mind like a brand.

She and the others let Rillieux rule with his kind choke hold, for the other choke hold was much worse.

"I'll go to the poetry reading if you like," she said, quietly resigned to it. "But I can't guarantee I'll be able to take anything."

Rillieux nodded. "Mainly I just want both of us to get familiar with the place this visit. Trust me, we'll be invited back. If you see a target of opportunity, of course, then seize it. But you might be too busy keeping Carrie Astor entertained."

Mystere groaned. "You mean she's back from boarding school in England?"

"Yes, and she'll be with her mother this afternoon. Caroline wants you to be kind to her. The girl's very reserved, but evidently she's quite taken with you, Mystere."

"She does fancy Mystere," chimed in Rose, who had seen the two women together. "But she ain't 'reserved,' Paul—she's a reg'lar dimwit."

Old Rillieux snorted. "Of course she is, but she's also an Astor. Every blemish is a beauty mark when it's on the rich. But nothing has assured our own success with Caroline as much as her daughter's affection for Mystere."

He's right about that, Mystere thought. Proof that Mrs. Astor favored her could be found in the matron's sincere words, which never took on a cutting edge when directed at her or old Rillieux. Usually the only compliments Caroline gave were left-handed, always managing to insult even as she flattered. "Now *that's* a magnificent gown," she might bestow on some dowager, her tone implying that it was high time she finally dressed smartly.

"I'll be nice to Carrie," Mystere promised. "She's boring, but at least she isn't a horrid snob. But Rafael Belloch may show up, too. He's known for appreciating poetry. And if he's there, he'll keep a close eye on me. I still say he's trouble, Paul."

Rillieux's sharp, foxy face eased into a knowing grin. "Oh, he's watching you, all right. But has it ever occurred to you, dear heart, that it isn't *suspicion* that motivates his interest?"

Baylis, Evan, and Rose exchanged covert glances, all three of them joining Rillieux in a knowing grin.

"Mystere thinks them linen wraps make her a little Miss Pink Cheeks," Baylis said.

"They do," Rillieux insisted. "But that's my point. Some men don't *want* to wait for a girl to become a woman—they desire the girl and her innocence. It excites them, makes them want—"

"I take your meaning," she cut him off abruptly, flushing at his words. "But I assure you that none of his remarks suggest that sort of thing."

"What sort of thing?" Evan teased, and the rest all laughed.

"Words," Rillieux informed her, "were given to us to disguise our true thoughts. Belloch isn't trying to arrest you; he's interested in seducing you. Perhaps we could even coerce him into marrying you. It could prove a quite profitable union, Mystere."

"Especially," Evan chimed in, "when the groom dies tragically, leaving you everything he owns."

She felt her pulse speed up as heat flooded her cheeks. She directed her words at Rillieux. "Earlier today you told Hush thievery should never involve violence or bloodshed. Are you abandoning your credo?"

He frowned at Evan. "Of course not. That kind of talk is just more of Evan's air pudding. Now stir your stumps, Baylis, and hitch the team. We must get a move on."

* * *

Fifth Avenue's once middle-class brownstones had become Manhattan's Palatial Row, stretching north for miles. Nothing in the world rivaled it for sheer ostentation, especially the Vanderbilt chateau at the corner of Fifth Avenue and Fifty-second Street, built of imported marble at a staggering cost of three million dollars.

The Vernon mansion was located on the lower end of the avenue. While not so lavish as some, it was nonetheless a stately granite structure built in the style of a medieval cathedral—the ideal setting, Rafe Belloch told himself, to enjoy some good poetry, if, indeed, any were to be had today.

His sense of anticipation only sharpened when he was escorted into the huge second-floor library with its magnificent vaulted ceiling. Mahogany bookcases filled with leather-bound volumes were separated by paintings in gold scrollwork frames—privately owned masterpieces that occasionally graced the walls of the Louvre and Saint Sophia, for the Vernons were collectors of European paintings.

Tea was served in fine and rare Russian porcelain. For those desiring something stronger than tea, bottles of wine and liquor crowded a carved mahogany sideboard manned by a dapper bartender with neatly pomaded hair. Rafe had ordered a Scotch and soda almost the moment he arrived. Now, as usual at such gatherings, he stood off by himself, watching the crowd as he pretended to study an enormous floor globe on a walnut pedestal base.

As was the custom, Caroline Astor reigned over everything with matriarchal reserve. She shared a white brocade sofa at the front of the room with her daughter Carrie. But the sofa might as well have been a throne—every arrival, Rafe included, first paid obeisance to Mrs. Astor and Carrie before greeting the hosts.

He had met Carrie the last time she came home from school. The girl was maddening to talk to, for she floundered from notion to notion like a parrot among shiny objects. And while not precisely unattractive, she had a soft, lopsided mouth that irritated him.

Seeing the two women together made him grin inwardly at the ironies of life among the Brahmins. Everyone knew that Caroline had mentored him from the first moment he had returned to New York with his new fortune—despite his dark history, known to all in the Four Hundred, it was Caroline who made sure he was included in every social occasion.

She seemed quite fond of him—too fond, some whispered. The

matron of hyphenated New-York society would not lightly take on a lover, he knew. But if she ever did, he would bet his whole fortune she would make a play for him, Rafe Belloch. And he was eagerly waiting for the day Mrs. Astor let her heart get the better of her. Either for herself or for the vicarious thrill through her daughter, she would one day let down her guard with him. And it would cause her own social ruin. *Damn her,* he thought, *damn her and her kind to hell anyway.*

He felt the old anger rising inside him like a tight bubble. Those assembled here today had no idea what a ferocious grudge he harbored against them. His impeccable family lineage, and his massive railroad fortune, easily qualified him as a Patriarch. But their social aspirations were all a shallow, pathetic game to him. Twenty years earlier his own parents had been caught in the social noose that had only tightened under the reign of Caroline Astor and her court. The Belloch family background was unassailable, their fortune—when intact—had been old and immense.

But then his father, in one tragic moment of bad business judgment and unlucky timing, lost virtually everything in risky foreign bond investments. Two days later, on Rafe's fourteenth birthday, he locked himself in his study and shot himself. His mother died in a tenement bed right in front of him only a few years later, a lonely and broken woman, her "society friends" having turned their backs on her.

The pain and despair he saw during his drives through Five Points was not so far away from the life he once knew. And he would see the best of them—Mrs. Astor herself—take a taste of it if he could.

He consented to play Patriarch only as a form of dark ironic revenge. They were the architects of his family's demise, and he swore by all things holy that he would wreak havoc. He would crush their precious hierarchy; he would soil their debutantes and toss out their queen. The upper crust would crumble with a nasty public scandal—or even two. He despised the effete elite with their mordant wit and snobbish gossip. The women were bloodless harpies, the men softhanded barbers' clerks.

"Ease off, old son," he cautioned himself, for he felt anger and alcohol making him reckless.

Again he searched the room, cataloging the familiar faces of the enemy.

There was that pompous, arrogant ass Abbot Pollard, a fancy

foulard tucked into his shirt and making him look like an aging, bandy-legged dandy. And Antonia Butler's fetching amber brown eyes occasionally peeked at him over her palmetto fan, letting him know his advances were welcome. He smiled right back, anticipating the trouble in store for her.

Different women, different games.

And the one he gamed for now had blue eyes the frosty color of a moonbeam.

Lady Moonlight was feasting on the fools more quickly than even he could, and a begrudging admiration had formed inside of him for her. He had no real proof Mystere Rillieux was the notorious jewel thief, nor even the young bandit who had made him strip in the alley off Baxter Street.

But if eyes were the windows of the soul, then he had peered into that soul once before.

Mystere Rillieux's eyes were the same eyes that had haunted him for two years. No matter how many trips he and Wilson had taken to Five Points, the masked girl had never crossed their path again. But then, wholly unexpectedly, she had appeared to him, pale and girlishly straight, dressed in an innocent's gown. In his heart and soul he burned with the conviction that he had found her.

Different women, different games.

If he was truthful with himself, he knew he wanted her if only for the secret chase of unmasking her. He wanted her for the vengeful gratification of disarming her. And in the darkest part of his soul he knew he wanted her for the sweet sexual thrill of her surrender.

The reproach in her eyes, her wounded expression—those were things he would deal with afterward. He was a man first, and he hungered for conquest. Of the prey of his choosing.

But, as the poetry reading progressed, it appeared the Rillieuxs might not attend. Rafe couldn't escape a sting of disappointment. If there was one among them he ached to toy with, it was that beauty.

Then, only a few minutes into the reading, he saw Mystere enter the library on her uncle's arm.

Her glance touched him and quickly slid away.

His instincts raged, and his suspicions fired anew. He had noticed something else about the girl. She seldom smiled, but when she did it was a restive smile, the smile of a woman who knew too many secrets.

Staring at her, he watched her uncle seat her. Though it was not warm, she fanned herself with a small white lace fan. Her delicate shoulders were tense and knotted, and he wondered if it was their late arrival that had her on edge.

But then she made the fatal error of meeting his gaze.

Her hesitancy, her worry, sent an electricity through him that could have lit the whole of Manhattan for a week. And then he knew: she was the Lady Moonlight, and she was his back alley assailant. And she would be his whether she knew it or not.

It's about time, he decided, surveying the room full of rigid matrons and pompous buffoons, *that I make some inquiries about the supposed Creole miss from New Orleans.* He eyed Rillieux. *And that "uncle" of hers, they could both do with a little digging.*

A dark, derisive smile graced his lips. He ached for Mystere to turn and look at him again, but she sat as rigid as the matrons, seemingly transfixed by the reading, holding her secrets as close as stolen jewels.

Chapter 6

David Cyril Oakes, the much ballyhooed poet championed by Mrs. Astor, turned out to be a pop-eyed, wild-haired, white-bearded old man straight out of Genesis. A visiting professor at Columbia College, the Welshman's dark and gloomy meditations about death and dying, as well as his pompous worship of the pastoral life, struck Mystere as cloying and sickly sweet—just like the overpowering odor of the creamy gardenias Emma Vernon had chosen to decorate the library.

But predictably, those who were bored stiff feigned interest as good breeding required. The room erupted in loud applause when Oakes had finally dragged to a groaning, despondent conclusion with a verse called "Ode to a Mortuary."

"The man's dull as ditch water," Abbot Pollard muttered in Mystere's ear even as he clapped with enthusiastic vigor. "The ass waggeth his ears, and another society poet is born. 'Death, thou dusky demon.' What tripe! Pope and Dryden must be turning in their graves."

"He's certainly dour," she agreed. But even as she smiled at the perpetually displeased Pollard, she felt Rafe Belloch's glacial gaze like a cold hand on her neck.

An alarm went off inside her.

He's watching me, she decided. *Waiting for me to make the wrong move.*

Meantime, Pollard had got going on one of his favorite tirades: the decline and fall of New York's superior caste.

"It's a real disgrace how Caroline's head has been turned by all this new money. J. P. Morgan is the only one in that scrabbling, grasping crowd I truly respect. He, at least, appreciates rules and controls. These nouveaux riches are bent on seizing power and ousting the genteel aristocracy. But perhaps blood will win out—you may not know this, my dear, but the very first John Jacob Astor was an absolute savage of a man, ill-mannered and unclean in his habits."

"Mr. Pollard," she chided, still watching Rafe from the corner of her eye, "you sound as pessimistic as our gloomy old poet."

"Nonsense, *ma chere.* You are too young to remember Black Friday, caused by our greedy robber barons. But certainly Caroline remembers it. Or ought to, for pity's sake."

"I remember the Panic of 'seventy-three," she assured him.

"Yes, well, both resulted from railroad men and their criminal recklessness. Now suddenly all is forgiven them."

He aimed a spiteful glance at Belloch, and she wondered if there was something personal to Rafe's lone-wolf attitude toward the rest of the Four Hundred.

Pollard loved to grandstand, and his bold insults soon attracted a circle of listeners around them.

Mystere saw Belloch edge nearer. She hoped to latch on to Carrie, but the younger Astor was presently chatting with Paul and the poet. Oakes appeared to be showing them drawings or photographs, and Carrie had gone whey-faced.

"I've noticed something else," Pollard nattered on in his nasal baritone and affected pronunciation. "As Caroline's attitude toward the newly rich has altered, so has her view of the poor. She will soon jump on the bandwagon and blame the wealthy for their plight. Why, much of Oakes's sweet-lavender asininity just now was an elegy to the unwashed. What's next? Shall we invite Celts and Negroes to our next ice cream party?"

"Tell us, old roadster," Rafe's powerful voice spoke up behind Abbot. "Do you ever take time to smell what you shovel?"

Pollard didn't even bother to turn around. "I have never handled a shovel in my life, Mr. Belloch, and never will."

"Yes, believe me, it's shown in your physique."

Mystere was forced to cough to cover her sudden laughter. A few others smiled, while some frowned at Belloch's unseemly aggression.

"No doubt," Pollard responded with casual malice, "your own unfortunate childhood poverty has left you with a bias, Mr. Belloch. However, the Reverend Conwell is absolutely right. The poor have made their own beds; now they can damn well sleep in them. There are, indeed, 'acres of diamonds' for all with the will and courage to harvest them."

Belloch kept his hard gaze fixed on Mystere even as he directed his remarks at Pollard. "I might feel more impressed," he pointed out, "if I didn't know that your own fortune is inherited. What diamonds have you ever harvested?"

"Not one, I'm proud to report. Self-made men bore me. As usual you have the truth hind side foremost. Raw greed, sir, is no substitute for superior birth and breeding."

"Yes," Belloch said, his voice so quiet now Mystere had to strain to hear him. "I know all about your superior ways."

Mystere knew from Rillieux's schooling that Belloch was violating strict code by going on the offensive and "making speeches," although Pollard well deserved it. But again, she suspected Rafe spoke up more from some personal strategy than deep emotional conviction.

Just as his manner had done last night, his attack sent Pollard and the others packing. She looked up and realized Rafe had her all to himself. She wondered if it had not been his goal all along.

His intense dark eyes raked over her, frank and disdainful at once. But she refused to be intimidated. She had decided to take the offensive herself lest this dangerous man gain power over her.

"Well, you can certainly be belligerent, Mr. Belloch," she taunted him. "No one can accuse you of being a play-the-crowd man."

"Truckling to people of rank is fine, Miss Rillieux, if your only goal is to be a fawning lapdog like Ward McCallister."

"You have farther reaching goals, I take it?"

Those impertinent dark eyes seared into her. "Oh, indeed. There's no limit on my . . . desires."

Or my thirst for destruction, his tone seemed to add.

Despite her newfound resolve, his double entendre made her blush. "I'm curious, Mr. Belloch. Clearly you are a man of some passion. Also rich and, I might add, quite pleasing to the feminine eye."

He gave a gallant half bow to acknowledge the compliment.

"So why on earth is a good catch like yourself still off the hook? Is it us women you despise or just marriage?"

"Neither, Miss Rillieux, although I confess that marriage holds little appeal for me. While I do not find it totally inconceivable, in my case it must be, as they say, a *pisaller*, the last resort."

"The last resort for what?"

A smile tightened his lips. "Has this child a nurse? Does her mother know she's out?"

Again she felt his smug, goading, self-satisfied voice grate on her nerves. In his own way he was as egocentric as Pollard. But where Pollard was a harmless crank, this man was as dangerous as unstable nitro. She had no hard proof for her conviction, but she was convinced nonetheless.

"Perhaps," she suggested, pretending to study the gathering, "you had better inform Antonia Butler of your instinctive aversion to wedlock. She hasn't kept her eyes off you since I've been here."

"You noticed that, have you? Well, *I'll* not warn her. The eagle has no pity for the lambs."

She baited him with her smile. "Caroline Astor is no lamb. And her 'lapdog,' as you call Ward, has made some noise lately about a possible match between you and Carrie."

"So that's two women, so far, you've conferred on me. Are you assembling a harem for me?"

"Why not? *Eagles* take what they want anyway, right? Perhaps I'll make it three by adding Caroline herself. She so enjoys touching your cheek."

His eyebrows arched, and his mouth set itself in a hard smile. "This is interesting."

"What is?"

He gave a harsh bark of laughter. "You, that's what. It would seem that our helpless little kitten has discovered her claws since last night."

"Even kittens fight back when they are being bullied."

"Bullied? Come now, that's much too harsh."

Even as he spoke, however, his actions belied his words, for he had taken her arm in his iron grip. Full-length windows stood open to admit the breeze. He "escorted" her through the nearest one onto a scrolled-iron balcony. Then he stood between her and the window, blocking her escape.

"I don't wish to be out here," she informed him, biting off each word in anger.

"No? Then jump. It's only two floors. Perhaps your *innocence* will save you."

"Mr. Belloch, seriously, Caroline asked me to spend time with Carrie, and I—"

"Carrie's busy with your uncle. He charms all the ladies, I've noticed. Did you happen to see this morning's *New York World?*"

"No," she retorted coldly. "I barely manage to read the *Times.*"

His probing eyes forced her to break eye contact. "They have a very colorful story today about the theft of the Pendergast brooch. Indeed, the writer seems quite enamored of our Lady Moonlight. Sees her as a class warrior punishing the rich."

"As I said last night, Mr. Belloch, no one has even proved the thief is a woman. But frankly I don't care either way. I don't share your apparent obsession with common thieves. Now, if you will excuse me. . . ."

She tried to duck around him, but he was too quick. For a moment he detained her with both hands almost circling her waist. At the unexpected contact, she felt a current jolt through her, taking the strength from her legs. She strained to break free, but he held her back with effortless ease. His strength, she realized, was impressive— and daunting.

She met his gaze. A smoldering emotion touched the color of his eyes. He looked down at his hands, and a wry smile twisted the corner of his mouth. "If I weren't a gentleman," he whispered in her ear, "I might move my hands a few inches higher and test a theory of mine."

Alarm made her heart race. An uninvited, tingling warmth spread low through her stomach. She stared up at him. His gaze held hers. Her breathing grew faster and uneven.

"Please, Mr. Belloch, this is most improper," she whispered, almost pleading with him.

He leaned closer. So close she felt his breath caress her temple.

"You needn't fear me," he said, his voice a low rumble. "We're alike, you and I. We both prey upon the Four Hundred—"

"I don't know what you're talking about," she interrupted, struggling with his hold to be free.

"You don't, eh?" He chuckled, and his grip became a manacle. Slowly his hand rose up her corset. Slowly, as if he was relishing his greed and his suspicions. And his lust.

She grabbed his hand and gave him a poisonous stare. Paul had alluded to some trinket that belonged to Sylvia Rohr. But not only would there be no theft today; Mystere would be fortunate to get away with her disguise still a secret.

"If you don't remove your hands this instant," she threatened him, "I swear I'll scream for my uncle."

He released her, but he still blocked her passage.

Unable to face his mocking, accusing eyes, she turned and went to the balcony railing. The light of late afternoon had begun to take on the mellow richness just before sunset. A pair of silky English setters were playing in the garden below. She watched them while she got her breathing under control.

"It's not common thieves who interest me, Miss Rillieux," he said behind her. "As I told you last night, I'm fascinated by the society thief."

"Yes, and you also hinted that my uncle and I are part of some theft ring. If you have evidence, then why not go to the police with it and stop harassing me?"

"I don't have a shred of evidence. But almost two years ago I was robbed by a gang at Five Points. One of them was a woman. A beautiful woman who looked very much like you. Except that she was . . . hmm, shall we say fuller in her figure than you appear to be."

"Oh? Do you expect me to disrobe for you to prove my innocence?"

"Actually, yes. You see, the woman who robbed me also made *me* strip naked. Turnabout is fair play."

"Well, you'll have to go on being suspicious of me, for I assure you I shan't strip for you."

He laughed, though it was mirthless. His voice deepened, coarsened, and some animal part of her thrilled at the sexual urgency in his tone even as it frightened her.

"All I need to do," he reminded her, "is toss chivalry to the wind. I can reach out *right now* and see if those French wineglasses are really the full, succulent fruits I suspect they are."

"Do it," she flung at him, meeting his stare and matching wills with him. "Prove that Abbot Pollard is right about you and your kind."

"By God I will," he almost whispered, stepping closer.

"Mystere!" chimed a female voice from the open window behind him. "I wondered where you were hiding. Or have I interrupted plans for an elopement?"

For once in her life Mystere was overjoyed to see Carrie Astor. She rushed forward, sweeping quickly around Belloch. "Carrie, it's good to see you again. Oh, Mr. Belloch and I were merely discussing a point of anatomy in Greek statuary. How *are* you, Carrie?"

She took the new arrival by the arm and started back inside.

"You won't believe it," Carrie confided in a shocked tone, "but Mr. Oakes is showing photographs of cadavers. I was very nearly sick. The man is . . . rather queer."

"Miss Rillieux?"

Mystere looked back over her shoulder. "Yes, Mr. Belloch?"

"I'll always be wondering," Rafe said in a taunting voice, repeating her own words from that night at Five Points.

A sick dread engulfed her. He knew. He knew, and he was going to be ruthless until he could be certain.

She flushed, and he laughed outright. And despite her bravado, it was she who first lowered her eyes and turned away.

Chapter 7

Hush's first reading lesson took place in the same parlor where Rillieux and his unique retinue of thieves had met the day before. Mystere sat in the master's favorite carved walnut chair while her dirty-faced pupil straddled a three-legged stool close beside her.

The lad was smart, she already knew, but also undisciplined and unused to concentration—except for an amazing focus of attention when it came to learning thievery from old Rillieux, a master educator. So she contented herself, this first lesson, with making him memorize the letters A through L. This he mastered in mere minutes. Then she showed him how to sound out the letters while he copied them from a hornbook she had purchased for him.

"Now listen and follow my finger while I read aloud," she instructed him. "Notice how the letters sound. Especially those you've learned today."

She read slowly from *Leslie's Illustrated Weekly,* a breezy little piece about the recently opened Brooklyn Bridge. Hush followed along closely, as if the pleasure of being so near to Mystere was easily worth the pain of scholarship.

"There," she announced, closing the magazine and laying it aside on the coffee table. "That's enough for your first lesson. That wasn't so awful, now, was it?"

"Hunh-uh. You sure got a nice voice, Mystere. I really like hearing you read."

She smiled and tousled his wild dark hair. "Thank you, charmer. Would you like some more lemonade?"

"It's mighty nice of you and all, but see—lemonade is sorter for women and kids."

She bit her lower lip to keep from smiling at his serious manner. "Oh? I see . . . so what beverage do you think might be more appropriate for a young gentleman such as yourself?"

"I like a drink called Humpty Dumpty," he boasted like an old hand.

"I've not heard of it. Is it good?"

"*I'll* tell the world! It's ale boiled with brandy. Everyone in my tenement drinks it."

Mystere looked scandalized. "You are too young for spirits."

"Aww, Hookey Walker," Hush protested. He also scowled as if he hated nothing more than when she treated him like a child. "I'm too old for lemonade is what you mean."

"All right, that's fair enough. I'll serve you coffee or tea from now on."

"With a sup of whiskey in it?"

She wagged a finger at him. "Those who drink whiskey will think whiskey."

"Huh! And them as drink lemonade will think lemonade," he retorted.

That earned him an admiring laugh, and he smiled proudly, happy to have pleased her. She was about to remonstrate further when the heavy teakwood doors parted and Rose hurried inside. She wore her usual mobcap and crisp muslin apron, her red hair done in two thick plaits.

"Just a warning," she told them in a voice barely above a whisper. "Stand by for a blast. Paul's home from his club, and he's in an awful wax."

"Why?" Mystere demanded.

"You know how Evan and Baylis were sent foraging yesterday, among the homes of those vacationing this summer?"

Mystere nodded. "During the gathering at the Vernons', you mean?"

"Uh-hunh. Paul's alibi is fine, and yours, too, of course. But somebody botched it. They picked a house they thought was shut up tight for the season. Cleaned it out of clocks and silver and the Lord knows what all. But turned out a maid is staying there; she was only out shopping."

Mystere paled. "You don't mean they were caught?"

"No, they got out in time. But the robbery was discovered immediately and reported. Worse yet, the carriage was parked close by, and Paul's afraid that maid glommed it as she returned home. He's so angry he actually struck Baylis. I saw it myself. Oops, here they come now, saints preserve us."

Rose escaped even as Rillieux's anger-sharpened voice sounded out in the vestibule. "*Now* see what your carelessness has cost? Helzer will rook us now. A lot of money down the drainpipe, that's what it is."

"Why am *I* being pilloried?" the voice of Baylis howled indignantly. "It was this whoreson shirker who swore the place was empty."

"H'ar now!" Evan thundered. "Don't lay it at *my* door, chowderhead. I'm a mild man until I'm pushed; then I become a hellcat unleashed."

"Shut your infernal mouths, both of you!" Rillieux bellowed with amazing force for his age and physical frailty. "You're *both* a pair of bumbling idiots. My fault, though, for thinking you were exceptional men."

"We done what we was told," Baylis protested.

"Yes? Well then, it was done damned slapdash, was it not?"

All three men had paused in front of the partially open doors.

"Is the swag hidden in the coach house?" Rillieux asked a few moments later, his voice calmer.

"Sure," Evan affirmed. "That was the plan."

"Well, now the plan is changing. Take everything to Helzer immediately. We'll have to accept a lower price for rushing him. I have a paid informant among the police, a district roundsman. He tells me this investigation is being pursued vigorously. That maid may have seen our blasted carriage. Get rid of the swag. And just in case one of Byrnes's men comes nosing about, have some cock-and-bull story ready to explain why you were parked over on Riverside Drive without me or Mystere."

Mystere heard Evan and Baylis leaving. Moments later Rillieux stepped into the parlor. He showed no sign of his incensed mood from just moments ago.

"*Here's* my two prize pupils," he greeted them, crossing the parlor with the assistance of his cane. He bent to kiss Mystere's cheek. She smelled the cloying sweetness of his lilac cologne.

"Mystere's learning me to read," Hush bragged.

" 'Teaching' me," she corrected him.

Rillieux hardly seemed to digest any of it. "That's good, every man should be a reader," he said absently. The web of lines at the corners of his sloe eyes deepened as he studied Mystere closely, lost in some line of speculation.

"I noticed how Belloch herded you off to himself yesterday," he told her. "But judging from both your faces, he certainly wasn't making love to you. You were quite chilly toward him, evidently?"

"I was rather . . . crisp with him, yes."

Rillieux smiled at her word choice. "Fueling the flames, dear heart, fueling the flames. I still say this chap Belloch has a sweet tooth for nymphs."

Mystere sent him a warning glance, for Hush could hear every word and she didn't like such talk in front of him. Not that he didn't hear far worse in the streets, she reminded herself.

"It's not what you think, Paul, I'm sure of it. I think he's . . . guessed some things about us. Or perhaps 'intuited' is a better word."

"Nonsense. But even if you are right, that contingency can be dealt with."

"Whatever you mean by that, perhaps you are rating him too low? He strikes me as a dangerous and capable man."

Rillieux gave a snort of contempt. "Indeed? Dangerous and capable? And yet he strips bare naked *at Five Points* on the command of a mere chit of a girl? Oh, terror has me by the throat, Mystere! God save us from this nude *Ubermensch.* "

"Paul," she chastised him, glancing quickly at Hush.

"Oh, the boy's no baby; let him hear us. Actually, Mystere, you may have a point about Belloch, my teasing notwithstanding. I quizzed Caroline about him. She used the word 'harum-scarum' to describe him. She seemed to like that idea, too."

"What's that word mean?" Hush inquired.

"Reckless and unpredictable," Rillieux explained. He glanced at Mystere. "From now on I will take him a bit more seriously."

So will I, she vowed to herself. Several times, since yesterday afternoon, she had reflected on how close things had come out there all alone with him on the balcony. A mere move upward of his hands . . . Of course, she dared not stop stealing now that he was suspicious— that would only egg him on to persecute her even more.

The danger of discovery, however, was not her only fear involving him. How many times, since yesterday, had she indignantly denied the arousal his grip on her waist had fired within her? The strong, overpowering grip of those well-formed hands had stirred a pulsing loin warmth that left her weak and breathless, entertaining mental images that shamed her in their torrid frankness.

But she *had* to curb such thoughts. Not only because they were unseemly, but because they lured her into letting down her guard. And there was not a man yet born who could do that. She was a virgin still, and planned to stay one. Forever.

Indeed, sometimes a deep, dark loneliness engulfed her, but she knew her worth to Rillieux lay not only in her "art," but also in her untainted beauty. He often spoke of making brilliant matches for her. It couldn't be done for a girl who was not an innocent. If Rillieux ever found her with a man, if he ever found her taken, she didn't know what he would do. Kill her perhaps. The idea was not out of the question. She knew his brutality by her own first hand. While she had never known him to kill, she had never seen him that angry either. He might sacrifice her to get at Rafe Belloch's wealth, but she wasn't available for mere love and marriage. Until she broke from him, she was his property, and Rillieux would see her dead before his goods were spoiled. She would have to run from Rillieux, and from his care. Her only two sorry choices then would be to sell herself at South Street for a bottle of whiskey or endure the rest of her life sewing shirts in a sweatshop. Neither was endurable, so she would never take the risk. Never. She would remain hungry and lonely. And alive.

Her thoughts returned to Belloch. *You were in an emotionally charged mood,* she argued even now as if defending herself to Rillieux's tribunal. *You were keyed up and tense from his prying questions—certainly it* must *be that. No decent woman would desire such a conceited, devious man as he.*

While all of these thoughts whirled through her mind, Rillieux had turned to Hush again. "Well, b'hoy, we'll soon have you living here as our new footman. Did you bring anything for the family kitty today?"

"Not yet, sir, for I spent the morning trapping rats in a concert saloon on the Bowery. Also, as you taught me, I am avoiding the park for a few days so my face is not so familiar to the roundsmen. That purse I brought you on Sunday came from there."

"That's the lad—always be cautious and crafty."

"But now the bridge is open, I can easy cross over to Prospect Park. It's chock-full of rich toffs just like our park is."

"Good, good, have at it. Just remember, don't ever discuss what you do with anyone but us. Success in this game means keeping your mouth shut. And remember we're a family here, all for one and one for all. No one"—here his glance shifted to include Mystere—"may skim off anything. I will fairly distribute our collective wealth."

"Fairly," she realized, was his call. Just as "the family kitty" was merely Paul's term for "my own pocket." She had noticed something else about Rillieux: he assured the rest they were only pretending to be his servants, but in fact they were servants, servants trained to spy, steal, and gather information. She refused to treat them as menials except in public, but he had no problem with it.

Rillieux turned and started out of the parlor.

"Sir?" Hush called behind him. "You forgot something."

Rillieux turned back around. Mystere's jaw fell open in astonishment when she saw the pingrain leather billfold that Hush held out to him.

"Well, I'm a New Amsterdam Dutchman," Rillieux said, stunned by the youth's boldness. "You cheeky little rapscallion."

An eyeblink later, however, and the old man's eyes puckered in satisfaction, and he beamed with pride and greed. "Outfoxing the old fox, eh? *That's* the ticket, tadpole. Always keep an eye to the main chance. You're a credit to your dam—whoever she was," he added as he took his wallet back and discreetly counted the money.

Then he glanced at Mystere. "I've had only one other pupil show such immense promise, Hush. But she's left my wallet alone—so far."

It made Mystere nearly ill to see the gratitude evident in the boy's eyes. Poor Hush was fairly starved for some sense of pride in himself, and only look at the kind of praise Paul supplied for it.

After Rillieux had gone, she asked Hush, "Do you remember what I said last time you were here? About doing something *you* want to do, not just what others tell you?"

He nodded.

"Well, it doesn't really matter if someone older orders you to steal. There's an old saying: 'Those who hold a candle for the devil share his guilt.'"

"Is that what we do, Mystere? Me 'n' you—hold a candle for the devil?"

"Yes. And the crime of it isn't all. Sometimes, when you are good at what others tell you to do, you can give up your freedom just trying to please them. They become rich and powerful from your risks and skills. They are free to exercise choices while you are owned by them."

Hush, who could only see such abstractions in terms of his own life, said, "Do you mean . . . I should steal for myself?"

"I'm not sure what I mean," she confessed helplessly. She worried lest, in trying to lift the boy's morals too high, she might set him at odds with Paul's temper. For no matter how kind Rillieux might, at times, appear to be, she knew he could inflict some intense cruelties, especially on those who proved disloyal after he had placed trust in them.

But secretly she had another answer for Hush: *Yes. If you must steal, then do it for yourself, not for a master.* Tough talk. If she ever hoped to find Bram, she would have to stop talking tough and *be* tough.

Such thinking inevitably reminded her it wasn't just Paul about whom she had to worry. There was also Lorenzo Perkins. She felt a tumult of fresh misery sweep over her. How could she ever locate her brother so long as she could not trust the very man she had hired to find him? Yet, neither did she have the strength of will to dismiss him without proof. He had, after all, come up with some bits of information such as the name of the *Sir Francis Drake,* the ship aboard which Bram might once have sailed.

She made up her mind to do what, until now, she had only contemplated.

"Hush?"

"What?"

She took out her reticule and removed a five-dollar bill. "This is yours," she told him, "if you'll do a favor for me."

He took the bill and stared at it. "Jaysus! But you don't have to pay me, Mystere."

"Never mind, take it, but don't let Paul see it. Do you know Amos Street?"

"Sure. The dispens'ry is there. Where they give medicine free to the poor."

She nodded. "At the corner of Amos and Greenwich is a druggist's shop. You can tell it by the wooden mortar and pestle out on the curb. There's a man and his wife living in the flat above the shop. The man is tall and thin, always wears a rather shabby suit and vest, and has a silly waxed mustache that looks drawn on. I need to know something about how he spends his time. Are you willing to follow him, off and on, over a few days?"

Hush grinned. " 'At'll be fun."

"Good. But you *must* be careful. Don't let him know what's up. Promise?"

"Cross my heart," he promised.

A few minutes later she saw Hush off at the front door, then lingered a moment in the vestibule, as still as the marble letter stand near the door, her thoughts again returning to yesterday, the balcony, and Rafe Belloch.

What a crying shame, she told herself, that such a well-knit and handsome man could be so dangerous to her. Rafe Belloch struck her as a brutal enemy, and she vowed to avoid him by any and all means—never mind her electric response to his touch.

Perhaps, after all, she was wrong about his interest in her. Perhaps he was only sufficiently interested to be cruel, but no more. She hoped so. But some inner self doubted that he was merely toying with her. She feared he was like a young boy who had trapped a fly—her—and now he meant to pull its wings right off and watch it die.

Chapter 8

Unlike Manhattan, Staten Island had so far escaped the frenetic pace of urban progress. It still appeared cutoff and quiet, a rural respite of wooded lots and narrow lanes, wide verandas and rush-bottom chairs. Its population of fewer than fifty thousand was dwarfed by almost two million just across the Upper Bay. Here there were no tar-papered squatters' shacks such as those dotting upper Manhattan, and the only shapes thrusting up into the sky were a few modest steeples topped by weathercocks.

Rafe Belloch liked the sense of being isolated, yet conveniently adjacent to the vital nerve center of the Wall Street financial district. He maintained a suite at the Astor House, its location across from City Hall Park convenient for occasions when business or social obligations demanded he stay near his Manhattan offices. But whenever he could, he literally retreated to Garden Cove, his seventeenth-century country estate on Staten Island's Bay Street. When the ferry didn't suit his mood, there was always his private steam yacht in a nearby slip. The three-man crew lived aboardship, ready to sail at a moment's notice.

At the same time that Mystere was teaching Hush the front half of the English alphabet, Rafe was in his study at Garden Cove dictating letters to his correspondence secretary, Sam Farrell.

"In summation, gentlemen, I'm convinced the timing of events is propitious to our interest. The consolidation of our Midwest short-line railroads into one centrally managed corporation will greatly enhance service as well as profits. I direct that consolidation be put to a binding vote at the next regular meeting of the board of directors. Cordially yours, etcetera."

Rafe watched Sam's face closely, curious to gauge his response to this latest bombshell. Farrell often startled people at first meeting, for his snaggly-toothed grin was at odds with the deep-sunken eyes like a pair of wounds. Rafe had often thought that Sam's face blended the mask of tragedy and the mask of comedy into one disconcerting visage.

But right now that visage gave the boss no clues to his reaction.

"Can't you hear them howling already?" Rafe prompted. "And see my caricature in the editorial cartoons with octopus tentacles and a pirate's eyepatch?"

"Of course, it's predictable from that crowd of hyenas. Wear it as a badge of honor, sir. Joseph Pulitzer's ink-slinging, calamity-howling hacks can rip away at the railroad enterprise and robber barons all they like. The fact is there's been a booming bull market for twenty years now except for the scare in seventy-three. And it's chiefly thanks to the railroads. As for consolidation—the New York Short Line proves the wisdom of that, in spades. The Commodore did not abandon his beloved steamships for some pipe dream."

"Wear their scorn as a badge of honor, eh? That's good, Sam, I'll remember that."

Because much railroad work was dangerous, it had always been Rafe's company policy to hire and retrain injured blue-collar workers for clerical positions. But Sam Farrell—who had suffered a crushed right hip while dropping a coupling pin into place between two coal cars—had required little training. After reading glowing reports from his field manager in Ohio, Rafe had personally interviewed Sam and then immediately transferred him to New York with a hefty new salary.

In the years since, Sam had mastered law on his own time, passed the New York Bar, and now also served as chief legal advisor for

Belloch Enterprises. It had been his steady hand on the tiller when Rafe steered the rocky course from railroad builder to investor-owner. Through all the changes Sam remained a blunt, simple, fiercely loyal man with an amazingly resourceful mind.

"I'll post the letters this afternoon," Sam told him. "Yesterday you said there was something else you needed me to do? Some inquiry to New Orleans, I believe you said?"

"Ahh, that's right."

Rafe began pacing his study, Sam's question having jolted his thoughts back to Mystere Rillieux. His study doubled as a commercial office, an odd function for a wainscoted room enhanced with Georgian carvings. The Cornelius and Baker gas chandeliers were hung to the ceiling with ropes of dangling brass serpents. The light was further augmented by old seven-arm candelabrums. A Sultanabad carpet and Gothic armchairs struck some visitors as stately and imposing, others as simply cold and tasteless. For his part, Rafe liked it all just fine and agreed heartily with those who thought he lacked refinement.

Mystere Rillieux . . . He mused, again thinking of how his hands had felt with her tiny waist in his grip. And she had not needed the corset, for he had proved that to his own satisfaction. She was petite, beautiful, and harbored some major secret suggested by her very name. And by the Lord Harry, she possessed the most striking blue eyes he had ever looked into.

But damn her beguiling bones, for it was *she* who had humiliated him at Five Points, he was almost certain now. She was a fine actress, but he felt that something within her was at war with evil and almost *wanted* to be exposed. As if . . . as if she were some kind of noble-woman trying to masquerade in criminal costume.

"I'd like you to contact Stephen Breaux's law offices on Canal Street in New Orleans," he told his secretary. "You'll find the address in the files. I once worked with them on a contract to haul cotton. He's a good man and very discreet. Have his people make some inquiries concerning a Mr. Paul Rillieux and his grand-niece, Mystere, who claim to be from New Orleans."

Sam, taking notes in a flip-back pad, knew something about discretion himself. "Precisely what type of inquiries?" he pressed. "Financial information, legal records . . . personal matters?"

Rafe's expressive lips firmed in a cynical grin. "I see you're thinking like an attorney. Nothing for use as leverage. No. I think . . ."

His voice trailed off as he considered the matter. He crossed to his favorite thinking spot in the entire house, a casement window facing northeast across the Narrows.

His housekeeper always kept the blinds shut at this time of day so the sun couldn't fade the rugs. He tugged them open just in time to watch as a huge foreign steamship with three stacks cleared the Narrows and hove to for the docks at the Battery, passengers crowding the taffrail for their first good view of Manhattan. Those in first and second class would get a quick look-over and be on their way; those in steerage would be detained for processing and medical examinations at nearby Castle Garden.

But Rafe's inner eye saw only Mystere's flawless opalescent skin, smooth as some elegant lotion. He had thought more than once about sliding his hands and lips over that skin, feeling her pent-up need quiver to his touch. . . .

But no. He forced himself not to be distracted from the real issue of her true identity. There were light-skinned Creoles, all right. He knew that. However, how many of them from New Orleans didn't know who Beast Butler was the very moment his name was uttered? Damnit, first he must expose this woman to sate his own curiosity. Then he might see about seducing her.

"Chiefly," he finally answered Sam, "I'd like to verify their identities as well as their addresses over the past years, their general social standing. Get something about the old man's character. Frankly, Sam, I suspect they're both superbly clever grifters and thieves working as a team."

It was Sam's habit to scour every daily paper in the area. He was quick to see where this was headed. "Holy Hannah! The Lady Moonlight . . . you think she's Mystere Rillieux?"

"I suspect so, yes, but keep that to yourself. Do you know of her? Mystere, I mean?"

"Only through the columns. Her uncle receives plenty of ink since he's one of Caroline Astor's acolytes."

Rafe nodded, still gazing outside. From his spot in the window he had an excellent view of the terraced garden that surrounded the house on three sides. It was teeming with a bright confusion of colors, more of his undisciplined taste: China roses, narrow-leaved asphodels with yellow flowers, brilliant poinciana bushes and marigold beds. Rising up out of the center of this floral profusion was a patinaed bronze figure of Victory holding upraised laurel wreaths. In a paddock behind the garden, a pretty sorrel horse with four white socks was enjoying a lazy roll in the grass.

"Yes," Rafe resumed, "Paul Rillieux has made quite a splash in the 'best' circles."

Indeed, there was an irony in this situation that had begun to please Rafe immensely. For whoever the Lady Moonlight really was, she was in one bizarre sense his ally. Regarding the Four Hundred, she was a pox on *all* their houses. Cleverly sailing under false colors, she stole gems from the rich. He, in contrast, meant to steal their hearts and reputations. He would ruin Carrie Astor, and by ruining the queen's most valued possession, he would take Mrs. Astor and her ironclad position in society down with her.

Then there would be no more Four Hundred to follow her and mince about. The lot of them would suffer the humiliation of realizing they prayed to a tin idol. New York society would be finished. So let the Lady Moonlight relieve them of their trinkets. He, in fact, had plans to be the greater villain.

Such thinking, however, dredged up the anger seething just beneath his calm surface. Again he gazed at the bronze figure of Victory. Seeing it always steeled his resolve and gave him solace and strength. It made him understand something his father had somehow momentarily forgotten: a man must always see things through to the end; that was the real victory—to endure and prevail.

Never, if he lived a century, would Rafe ever forget the curt final message his father had left the world: *I am too ashamed to live a moment longer. Please forgive my weakness.*

Not one member of that group Abbot Pollard called "the elect" had turned out for John Belloch's funeral. The fact was quite conspicuous inasmuch as the successful investor had helped many of them prosper and even carried a few of them with quiet loans during the hard times.

It had killed Rafe's mother to be left a pariah, pitied and scorned by those who had once valued her company and sought her out. But her end had come more slowly, a lingering death by the self-inflicted torture of social shame. . . .

Rafe had watched it, seen what it was as it destroyed her, yet been unable to utter a word that might have prevented it.

But no more. No more.

For Sam, who glanced up from his blotter just then, the jut-jawed anger on his employer's face was all too familiar. Sam had guessed something few others even suspected: Rafael Belloch was that saddest of modern creatures, infinitely successful yet infinitely disappointed.

"Well then," Sam finally said, snapping Rafe back to the present. "Shall I send a telegraph or a letter?"

"It's not urgent, so use the mail. Tell you the truth, I'd like a little time to keep an eye on her—on them, I mean," he corrected himself quickly. "It's rather amusing, actually. What do I care if she picks clean the bones of Dame Astor's fawning lick-spittles?" He laughed. "Mainly, you understand, it's personal. You see, Sam, I'm very nearly convinced that Mystere is not *just* the Lady Moonlight. I think it was she and her gang of cutthroats who robbed me a couple years back."

Sam gaped. "You don't mean—the pert skirt who left you nearly naked at Five Points?"

"Yes, damn her. And don't worry about dragging the police into this, all right? I've some questions of my own before the police have at her."

Sam looked innocent as a parson. "The police? They're a heavy-handed lot of bunglers. I'd say you're far more likely than they to fit the punishment to the crime—pardon me the liberty of saying it, sir."

"No pardon needed, but I appreciate your good manners, Sam. Yes, you're right," he promised. "Our haughty little bandit will eat a good helping of what she dished out, count upon it."

"I believe you," Sam replied. "Then again, if she's who you think, I suspect you've got a bit of a road to travel just yet. She might prove your match."

Rafe snorted, and his dark eyes glittered with anticipation of the challenge.

Chapter 9

"My dear," Paul Rillieux said in the magisterial tone he had lately picked up from Mrs. Astor, "tonight you will see the sparkler of all sparklers, one that belongs under a bell jar, not on a finger. Caroline telephoned me today with the details. Antonia's newest play-pretty is a twenty-four-karat gold ring with a huge Indian emerald set in the center and eighteen radial-cut diamonds."

"She always prefers understatement," Mystere replied drily, although Rillieux hardly seemed to notice.

Through the uncovered carriage window she looked out on a pleasant stretch of Riverside Drive overlooking the Hudson. It was a cloudy night, and dark moon shadows prowled the river and the distant New Jersey shore. The restless, shape-changing shadows seemed to match her mood.

"Of course, you won't take the ring," Rillieux nattered on. "You will simply admire it along with everyone else—for the time being. The fate of that ring will be sealed at some later date, when less publicity surrounds it. Tonight, while everyone waits for Lady Moonlight to take the obvious bait, she will instead relieve Sylvia Rohr of a most charming sapphire-and-diamond brooch. Pin, my dear, not a clasp, so it's tuck and slide as we've practiced. I know her habits well by now, and I think she's due to wear it again."

Dr. Charles Sanford and his wife Catherine (nee Logan of the Boston real-estate clan) gave their Summer Solstice Ball every season, and it had quickly earned a reputation as bland and predictable, yet entirely unavoidable. Sanford had some remote connection to the British peerage, while his wife's fortune ensured their membership on Mrs. Astor's short list. Caroline herself would be there, and so it would follow that all the other Chosen would make an appearance.

"Do you really suppose," Mystere asked idly as she watched the well-illuminated Sanford mansion draw nearer, "that Antonia has actually planned it all out with the police?"

"Mystere, I do not depend on suppositions when it comes to such matters, you ought to know that by now. It's not just Antonia Butler—the entire scheme has Caroline's blessing, too. You must remember, the Lady Moonlight may be titillating the many, but most of the stately matrons are losing patience. This thief is flouting them, making a mockery of them. That's why Antonia plans to make it obvious when she removes the ring and places it in her handbag."

"I don't doubt your information, Paul. It's just hard to believe Caroline would actually permit that all the women present would be searched."

"Only in recognition of the ring's extraordinary value. The emerald is huge and can be cut up quickly into several fine stones. Don't forget the genius of the compromise Caroline worked out with Inspector Byrnes: each lady must volunteer to be searched, and needless to say, only police matrons will be allowed to verify compliance. Caroline knows that once she herself submits, the rest of the women will, too."

"Why are you so confident the same search will not take place when Sylvia's brooch is missed?"

He snorted. "I forget sometimes that you really *are* still young, Mystere. First of all Sylvia's family, while old money, has lost status over the years as railroads have cut into shipping. The Butlers, in contrast, are at their social zenith. Also, the brooch, while a lovely little prize, will fetch only one-quarter of that ring's value. Byrnes depends on the goodwill of the Four Hundred for his popularity—neither he nor Caroline will go forward with a search for anything less than that ring, count upon it."

Rillieux paused to take a pinch of snuff. "However, in the unlikely event that a search does go forward, you are an unequaled expert at sleight-of-hand, my dear. Merely deposit the brooch somewhere safe, preferably outside, where we can send one of our lads to retrieve it later. If we lose it? So, we lose it. Other baubles will await in the future, that ring among them."

A strong, sudden spurt of cool breeze blew in from the river and tickled Mystere's cheek. This section of the Upper West Side, Morningside Heights, was an acceptable if not exclusive area of Manhattan, still a bit barren and open but with the city's mass hunkering nearby and rapidly closing in around it. There was talk of soon building an academic grove out where the insane asylum was, for lately New Yorkers had begun to notice they lacked a high culture to match their high wealth.

They were only three long blocks from the Sanford residence now. The three-story mansion of gray masonry had an impersonal, functional design more appropriate to the financial district. Night's dark cloak masked the dull outside, but inside, Mystere knew from several visits, all was sumptuously appointed. Besides, the dance was actually being held in the adjoining gallery, which had been temporarily expanded with a sturdy dance pavilion that jutted right out over the Hudson. Because of the stiff winds, the ladies had been advised to wear gowns with weighted hems.

Rillieux's voice cut into her thoughts. "Mystere? You know that Belloch may attend? He's been quite the bon vivant lately. And everyone has noticed his disinclination to mingle—except when you're around."

The very mention of his name caused a curious, ambivalent kind of dread inside her. On the one hand, she feared Belloch's prying eyes and his prying questions. On the other, he stirred illicit feelings of pleasure and excitement she had never before felt—nor even suspected existed.

"What of it?" she replied carefully.

"If you must know, you and he have become a speculated about 'item' in the gossip columns. Or so Caroline reports. She doesn't read them, but Ward does. In fact, I suspect he even writes some of them since they're so preposterous."

Alarm quickened her pulse. "What kind of item would anyone write about Rafe and me?"

"That's still up in the air, of course. No one is publishing the banns, believe me. Caroline is offended by it. I thought perhaps she had her own Carrie in mind for Belloch—if not herself by the way she looks at him—but she punctured that balloon the moment I floated it. She doesn't want talk, and to quell it, she might be rather inclined to push Antonia Butler as her new choice for him."

"From what I've seen," Mystere said, "Mrs. Astor has very personal reasons for making sure Belloch does not pursue Carrie."

Rillieux sniffed, amused. "My, you *have* grown up lately. You've been quite observant, dear heart, and quite discerning. I share your suspicion—there is a naughty gleam in that woman's eye when she looks at Rafe. However, I doubt she would do anything so bohemian as take on a lover. At any rate it hardly matters. I think Belloch has made it clear lately he prefers his women almost scandalously young and innocent."

"You misunderstand his interest," she insisted again. "The man is not flirting—he's persecuting me."

"Perhaps he is digging at you a bit. But that's the way of some young men—he has the sardonic wit, as we say. For all your skills and talents, don't forget you've known little about men *as lovers.*"

The unmitigated gall of reminding me, she fumed silently. The smug tone was back in his voice, and again she had a glimmer of suspicion about Paul's ultimate motives for making her a rich widow. Nor had she forgotten Evan's remark about a tragic accident befalling Rafe after she married him.

She tried to convince herself she was being foolish. Evan said plenty of careless, sinister-sounding things that meant nothing. Rillieux was a thief and confidence man, yes, but no murderer. At least not yet. . . .

But there was the coldness in his eyes when displeased or disappointed. She knew by all her experience on the street that he had murder in him somewhere; the fear of what he could do was part of the choke hold. A man who methodically trained children to steal was not above furthering his career of crime. She could enumerate Rillieux's good points all she liked—the shackles he had placed on her, though kind, were nonetheless ironclad and binding. She was not free. And she might never be free.

The tug of a forbidden lure pulled on her. To be her own woman was to be awakened from a nightmare that had endured since she was a child and Rillieux had snatched her from the orphanage. Antonia's new ring beckoned her like bread to the starving.

The gem is huge and could be cut up quickly into several fine stones.

But no . . . first she must see what Hush had to tell her about Lorenzo Perkins. *It's one thing to want to be free,* she told herself; *it's another altogether to be foolish.* Life on the street was hard. She knew it too well. Rillieux was a devil, but he was the devil she knew. Besides, in her station, she had money to pursue Bram. She had to wait to see if the tree bore fruit before she cut it down. Lorenzo Perkins was worth the indenture if he was at least making some effort to find Bram where she could not. But it was another game entirely if she found out he was simply a thief.

Simply another *thief, you mean,* her conscience pricked her.

"Paul?" she burst out suddenly, motivated by guilt and some nameless but very real fear.

"Yes?" The new caution in his tone showed that he was instantly alerted by her voice.

"All this nonsense in the gossip columns—is it wise to call attention to myself while the press is also looking for the Lady Moonlight? I . . . all the attention, it frightens me. Can't we let it all die down, try something else? Perhaps not tonight. Not now."

Mystere rarely expressed such apprehensions, and Rillieux responded with alacrity. By now they were only a half block from the Sanfords', approaching at a trot. Rillieux slid back his window panel.

"Baylis!" he called out. "Walk the team in, we need a moment."

He reached across the space between their facing seats and took both of her hands in his. "Mystere, *look* at me."

She didn't want to; she just wanted to get out of the carriage and walk for hours, alone with her thoughts. But there was no resisting years of established habit between them. Although there was no electricity this far north yet, flickering gaslights gave off enough illumination to make out his sharp facial features and the mesmeric intensity of his eyes.

"Breathe deeply and slowly," he commanded her. "Not from the lungs but even deeper, lower. Slow and steady, that's our girl."

As his will mastered her own, she felt a calm confidence replace the giddy lightness of her limbs.

"I *trained* you to shine under the most brilliant lights, remember? Finishing school in London, a tour of the Continent, ballet lessons under the incomparable Mademoiselle Dupree. You are not some base thief pretending to culture, you are an *artiste*. Like any *artiste*, you fear the attention, the challenge. But you also thrive on the very things you fear. You turn your fear into your greatest triumph."

"Yes," she answered, rallying somewhat. "You're right. I'm . . . I'm sorry."

"Nonsense, you needn't apologize for being high-strung; it's in your fam—"

He caught himself. "It's your nature," he amended. "And remember something else, Mystere. For you and me, there is no middle way out. In one sense we are astride a tsunami, and we must ride it until it crashes. Or more precisely: until the moment *just before* it crashes, when we must escape."

"And if we miss our moment—what then?"

"Hah! What do you think, m'love? They'll give me the gibbet. As for you—even Caroline Astor couldn't get them to hang a woman. You will be 'reformed' in a women's penitentiary by wiry, horse-faced old virgins who stink of rejection and failure—and hate you for being everything they are not."

He patted her cheek fondly. "But we *won't* miss our moment, for timing is all, and timing is my great skill."

Mystere began to hope, early on, that Rafe Belloch might not show up. She saw no sign of him inside the house, where the Sanfords, and Mrs. Astor, and a few others had set up a reception line for the guests; nor anywhere outside among the invitees scattered between the gallery and the adjacent pavilion, at the near end of which an orchestra was tuning up.

Already the Vanderbilt sisters, Alva and Alice, formed the nucleus of a large gathering inside the porticoed gallery, socializing rather than pairing off for the dancing. Even three months after the widely reported Vanderbilt ball, the penny papers were still abuzz with articles about the costume Alice had worn. She had come as "Electric Light" in an astonishing gown of white satin aglitter with diamonds— real diamonds for a one-occasion gown.

As usual after the initial reception, the men joined the more seasoned old guard outside for cigars and politics. The matriarch herself, Mrs. Astor, regal in a flowing summer-weight cape with a sealskin collar, claimed Paul Rillieux's company.

"You," she told Mystere, taking her off alone for a moment, "are the picture of innocence, and I for one judge the picture genuine. Remember that when others throw a shadow over your name."

"Has someone done so?"

Caroline looked closely into the younger woman's face, then shook her head in wonder. "Most likely, or will soon. But never mind it, Mystere. The public has its insatiable thirst to know all the 'inside' details about the rich, you see. And publishing scoundrels like J. Gordon Bennett are eager to provide those details, even if it means informants who tell outright lies and slander us by name."

They moved a few steps, and Ward McCallister followed them like a ship's wake, always the same discreet distance—not close enough to eavesdrop, but ready to hand should his mistress need a date written down or some new occasion "gotten up" as Caroline called setting the social agenda. His sycophantic face and manners irritated some, but influenced others around her to a more ceremonial conduct. This visible loyalty made him more valuable than his menial services.

"You just enjoy yourself, dear," Caroline urged her. "Go mingle, let your youth take over and never mind those of us who have learned to sneer at everything. You have your life before you, and you are beautiful and men want you. I envy you, Mystere. But remember that scandals are easily kindled and nearly impossible to extinguish. You have no mother to advise you, poor thing, but I share Carrie's genuine affection for you. That is why I mention such things to you, dear girl."

With those startling words, she joined Paul again and left Mystere to her own devices. Nearby, a second large gathering had formed around Antonia Butler, mainly women paying homage to her new ring. Mystere did not hesitate, but moved forward to merge with the admirers, knowing she mustn't make herself conspicuous through aloofness.

"Mystere! How absolutely wonderful to see you again," Antonia gushed in the minor-key tone she reserved for those who did not quite rate her full enthusiasm. "You look quite lovely tonight. And well protected from any sudden chill."

This last remark was barbed and elicited a few hidden smiles, for it was an obvious slap at Mystere's wardrobe. Current evening fashions for ladies bared much of the back and shoulders, although decollete necklines were less daring than in the risque 'sixties and 'seventies. Mystere, however, as usual had worn a gown with a high bodice that hooked almost completely up the back, exposing only her delicate collarbones. Antonia, of course, assumed she dressed this way to cover her immature lack of feminine shape.

"Your new ring is gorgeous," Mystere forced herself to say in a sweet tone. She was genuinely impressed, however, by the size and purity of the emerald. For a moment, as the stone glimmered in the light from the Chinese lanterns, she was even caught in déjà vu. Again, as if the vision was embodied in the deep green center of the emerald, she saw a sailor's emerald eyes watching her, lifeless as the stone. They were Bram's eyes. And many a night she had awakened from a dream where she was again running down the docks after the departing ship, screaming Bram's name to the man who knew no recognition.

"Yes, it's quite nice, isn't it?" Antonia responded, already bored with Mrs. Astor's charity mutt. "It is frightfully heavy, though. Would you like to try it on?"

"Oh, might I?"

Antonia got it off with some slight difficulty. Both women were startled when the heavy, glittering ring proved to be a perfect fit on Mystere's finger.

"It might have been made for you," Antonia conceded, the sarcasm momentarily deserting her voice—the ring was not just a perfect fit; it was simply beautiful against Mystere's skin.

Suddenly aware how a dozen people were staring at her, Mystere slid the ring off and handed it back. "Nonsense, Antonia, it clashes with my eyes. It's perfect on you."

Mystere edged away and began chatting with Thelma Richards and Sylvia Rohr, who was, indeed, wearing the very brooch Paul lusted for. Thelma was still in a snit over the congestion, earlier that day, at the corner of Broadway and Fulton.

"Traffic was absolutely frozen for over an hour," she lamented. "A dray wagon had broken an axle, and barrels were tumbling everywhere. I do wish they would restrict commercial vehicles in the upper wards."

While Mystere nodded sympathetically, she searched everywhere for Rafe Belloch under the pretense of idly surveying the crowd.

Safe for now, she decided when she failed to spot him. However, Abbot Pollard was upon the little trio before she could think about Rafe any further.

"Ladies," he greeted them all, lifting each one's right hand with a gallant flourish and touching his dry lips to it. "What's this I see—no Lydia tonight?"

He pinched in his lips like some little schoolyard prissy who knew a secret. "And thereby hangs a tale, but *I* shan't tell it."

He didn't need to, Mystere knew, because everyone listed in the Manhattan Telephone Directory already knew about the latest scandal involving one of their own. It was a fait accompli that Mrs. Astor was the central figure in the best society of Old New York—the fixed pole around whom all the glittering stars rotated. But yesterday that comfortable universe had been shaken when one of the stars plunged from its orbit forever.

Lydia Hotchkiss, wife of a city magistrate, had been apprehended in an act of genteel kleptomania, as it was delicately called in some quarters. She was caught at Tiffany's trying to drop a locket case into her purse. Normally such crimes by the well-heeled were kept quietly hushed up.

Unfortunately for Lydia and the rest of the Four Hundred, class chivalry was dead at the *Sun*. An enterprising crime reporter bribed a store detective, and the matter quickly got noised about. Within hours Lydia's ruin was complete.

"Just think," cut in a strong, familiar voice behind Mystere. "If Lydia's genteel thievery has caused her such utter social ruin, how shall we treat our Lady Moonlight when *she's* finally . . . exposed?"

Chapter 10

Mystere spun graciously around, nodding a cool greeting to the late arriver. She felt heat leap into her cheeks as the rest, following Rafe Belloch's lead, all gazed at her, waiting for the reply.

"I'm sure I couldn't say, Mr. Belloch. Nor, unlike you, do I care overly much what happens to thieves," she replied coolly.

He threw back his head and laughed, strong white teeth flashing in the soft halo light of hundreds of translucent lanterns. Tonight, Rafe had shown up in swallowtails and a fancy frilled shirt. Women's gazes turned in his direction and lingered. The chestnut brown hair was combed straight back, revealing the strong angles of his brow. His teal gaze, more green than blue in the light, taunted her.

"Yes, I've noticed your apparent apathy about our infamous lady," he said, "but think of the excitement, the amusement—why it's better than Barnum's museum. One little slip, and our legendary thief winds up in a filthy holding cell at the Tombs."

"You have an odd idea of amusement," she demurred.

"Nonsense, you're turning into a humorless old stuffed shirt like Abbot here. I find the Lady Moonlight's activities quite diverting. Certainly more exciting than some pathetic larceny at Tiffany's."

Pollard, never one to suffer a slight in silence, pandered to the rest,

deliberately avoiding Rafe's intimidating eyes: "There's no account-
ing for taste, ladies. It's the same with these 'progressive' poets and
historians winning favor lately: the *bad smell* of an age is what they
choose to remember it by."

However, the clash of stags was cut short by the sudden arrival of
Mrs. Astor at the periphery of their group.

"Rafe, you've a stone for a heart," she accused, offering her hand to
be kissed. "You slipped past me deliberately and positively crushed
me."

Rafe assumed a contrite look, lifted her hand to his lips, then made
a point of holding it as he replied with sly gallantry: "Perhaps,
Caroline, I did so only to see if you'd even notice?"

"Oh? And are you experimenting on Antonia, too? She is quite
miffed at you, sir, though the dear holds it in well. You may toy
roughly with us old married women; we deserve what we get. But our
belles have certain rights."

She paused to look at Mystere. "This lass is quite lovely, and no one
can fault your interest in her company. But shall the rest merely
wither on the vine?"

Mystere watched her as she again touched Rafe's smooth-shaven
face with her fingertips, stroking it lightly.

"As to married women or virgin belles," Rafe assured Caroline,
"maiden or matron, *no* woman should ever feel neglected."

His obvious innuendo struck Mystere as scandalous and crude, but
Caroline only smiled mysteriously as she turned to speak with Thelma
and Sylvia.

Mystere turned to Rafe. "It's all a glass-bead game to you, Mr.
Belloch, isn't it? Utterly insignificant, like killing a fly?"

His eyebrows tented in surprise. "What is?"

"Women. Antonia, Caroline—I. Any of us."

"Perhaps, but after all, glass beads should not be disparaged. They
purchased Mana-hata from the savages."

She longed to put him in his place, but before she could respond,
she realized that Caroline had not joined their little group merely to
flirt with Rafe. Mystere watched her turn to Abbot Pollard and assume
a steely-eyed look that could have frightened a Hussar.

"You, sir," she bit off coldly, no trace of humor in her voice, "are in
my bad books."

This was not banter, but a literal statement of excommunication, and Pollard knew it. Pale by nature, he now went so alabaster he looked chemically preserved. "My dear woman, whatever for?"

"Crimes so vile, Abbot, that your usual blandishments and cunning wit will not save you. I shan't drag it all up now. It's sufficient to note that you've been making some rude remarks lately about me and some of those I happen to admire."

"Why, if it's that poet you mean, Oakes, we all deprecate at times; it's—"

"Do *not* interrupt me, sir," she nearly snarled, and Mystere saw a fierce, tyrannical power in Mrs Astor's eyes that chilled her blood. It cowed Pollard, too.

"Your rapier wit," she added, "is famous and often admirable. But when it skewers me continually, Abbot, it is misdirected."

Pollard opened his mouth to plead his case. But Caroline turned away and moved back to her group, leaving him to stare foolishly at the rest.

"Oh, well, *sic transit gloria mundi* and all that," he japed, putting a brave face on his ruin.

"If it's Latin you crave, old roadster," Rafe goaded him, "how about *persona non grata?*"

Refusing to buckle under the crushing rebuke, Abbot remained true to form. With an audience watching him expectantly, he piped up with spiteful gusto: "If it's rudeness you people abhor, why not pray someone of taste will finally hold sway in City Hall? Will someone here make a stand and prevent the vulgar monstrosity they want to erect on Bedloe's Island? I implore you. It's bad enough the rabble in France want to foist their populist dogma upon us. But why on earth would we help pay for it? Mark my words—that hideous statue will come to be a laughingstock among future generations. They'll show better taste and demand it come down."

"As usual, Abbot," Rafe dismissed him absently, eyes watching Mystere, "you're jabbering pompous nonsense. My God, gentlemen, has someone died?"

This last remark was directed loudly toward the orchestra. Earlier, shortly after Mystere arrived, they had got everyone's blood stirring with the rousing strains of the "Triumphal March" from Verdi's *Aida*. But at some point Abbot had collared the conductor, and now a gloomy, ponderous movement Mystere did not recognize, or like, filled the night with an incessant groan like dying elephants.

"It's not a railroad work song," Pollard jibed, "so you wouldn't recognize it, Rafe. It's from *Ring of the Nibelung* by Wagner. I thought it appropriate tonight as the master has only recently passed from us."

"He could have taken his infernal racket with him," Rafe muttered, strolling purposefully toward the conductor's dais. Mystere saw him slip some folded banknotes to the conductor, who seemed relieved by the request, judging from his new animation as the orchestra struck up three beats to the measure and broke into a lively waltz.

With no one yet dancing, she felt a jolt of alarm when Belloch returned and took her firmly by one arm. "May I have the honor?"

"I'd rather not, I . . . Mr. Belloch!"

But her protest meant nothing to him. His left hand fit itself to the small of her back, and he literally swept her out onto the empty outdoor pavilion.

She saw right away that he meant to intimidate her with his strength and skill, for it quickly became clear that Rafe Belloch was an excellent—if somewhat possessive—dancer. However, no matter how violently he flung her into a spin, she managed to turn it into a graceful pirouette, twirling back into his arms with perfect timing.

A raft of clouds floated away from the moon, and suddenly the surface of the Hudson behind the pavilion became a million glittering pinpoints of diamond light. For the first time that evening, the listless gossip writers spying from behind the iron palings out front began scratching furious notes.

"My compliments, Miss Rillieux," Rafe murmured against her hair, genuinely impressed. "I've been told that I lead too forcefully, yet you make me look meek."

She ignored him. Four gliding steps, his powerful thrust, and her perfect balance bringing her thrusting right back into him like a fencer.

"You always seem to be laughing up your sleeve," she accused.

"I'd rather take a look behind your chemise," he riposted, laughing when two splotches of color stained her cheeks.

Step, thrust, pirouette, and thrust again back at him. "You're also very quick with such improper evasions."

"Evade, parry, and *thrust,*" he replied, twirling her out at arm's length, and yet again some invisible counterweight within her brought Mystere spinning back into his arms with such graceful precision that spontaneous applause erupted around them.

Soon nearly everyone—including the journalists outside—had noticed how superbly Rafe Belloch and Mystere Rillieux were gliding and turning with such effortless artistry. Many even assumed it was planned deliberately to enliven another garden-variety ball.

By now their dancing had inspired a few other couples out onto the pavilion. The first to join them were the new-money crowd, New Yorkers now but few by birth. But then, just as she had publicly blessed the Vanderbilts last March, Mrs. Astor deigned to dance among them, Ward McAllister giving her ever-present escort.

"You're quite accomplished at everything you do, aren't you?" Belloch probed strangely, this time with no sarcastic intent.

Brought up short at the end of the dance, Mystere gave him a small, gracious curtsey. "I'd hardly say everything," she said in dismissal.

His gaze was merciless, giving her no place to run. "Well, of course I imagine there are many things you still haven't tried yet."

"Many, perhaps, but I mean to do some of them, sir."

He laughed, still holding her hands so she couldn't escape. "Oh, that's capital. You tossed the 'sir' in just perfect. Young and innocent, aren't you, the debutante come forth like a sweet new flower. Well, just remember—as to the things you haven't done yet, but mean to . . . thoughts need never submit to a master. No one can be arrested for one's own private mental images."

"I've figured all that out without your telling me."

His eyes lowered to her modest chest. "Of course you have, but it excites me to talk about such things with you."

She tried to pull free, but he restrained her, still studying her in the soft light.

"Yes," he said with newfound conviction, looking closely into her vivid blue eyes. He held a hand to the lower half of her face as if mimicking a domino. Then he stared, a triumphant smile growing on his hard mouth. "It was you. Indeed, the light was dim that night, but it was you. If I stripped you naked right now . . ."

The band struck up another waltz. He swept her around . . . three, four, pirouette and back. . . .

"What night?" she countered as if he had said nothing else.

But he only laughed again, a caustic bark, at her show of perplexion.

"You're a capable actress," he admitted, "but something deep within you cannot fully embrace deception as can your loving uncle."

Harder he led through the gliding steps, not guiding but forcing, and by now both of them were breathing like Thoroughbreds breaking out of the second turn. Soon his violence even commanded the musicians, who unconsciously picked up the tempo to match him.

Mystere gave thanks that other couples had joined them, for their presence seemed to rein him in somewhat. But she knew perfectly well what he meant by "that night," and he had unnerved her enough that she gave up any idea of stealing Sylvia Rohr's brooch. It would be too risky with his eagle eyes on her.

It wasn't just him, either. There lingered over everything and everyone a sense of dramatic expectation. It was cheap and sensational; few spoke of it directly. But in truth almost everyone present tonight had been poring through the smutty dailies produced by Printing House Row, hungry for more details about this celebrated thief who was all the rage even in the British and European papers.

But now, she thought, *right now* while they were dancing, Rafe did not expect her to make such a move. She must try something, just to prove her defiance, for obviously he now assumed he could strike terror into the Lady Moonlight by his mere presence.

For a moment, however, after her decision to steal, fear hammered at her temples. But Rillieux's lessons had taught her well. When she made her move, it was precisely executed and over in an eye blink.

Rafe had sent her twirling yet again at arm's length, a sweeping flourish that spun her right past Garrett Teasdale and his wife Eugenia. For a fractional second Mystere's trained eyes focused on the heavy gold pin in Rafe's black silk cravat; then she diverted him by looking at Garrett with smiling eyes. Garrett nodded in greeting, and Rafe's gaze followed.

With a swift whisper of a movement, her outflung hand brushed him, and the pin was gone. Tuck and slip, just like she was going to do to Silvia Rohr's brooch. In one continuous, fluid motion she stuck it safely inside her chignon, the entire gesture looking like nothing more than an absent pat to her hair.

Her empty hand came back to join Rafe's, and the theft was accomplished. She knew Rillieux would howl about the pin's scant value. But instinct told her the Lady Moonlight had to strike, had to shake Rafe's confidence that he was in control, or all was lost.

Sudden relief at her bold success altered her mood. For a few enchanted, heady moments, as the violins rose and he swept her along above the sparkling ribbon of water, she felt the power and masculine strength in him, the incredible agility that matched his pleasing face and form. In that timeless moment of enhancement, she felt, too, the thrill of life's promise, the sense that her own existence was a story still unfolding, felt her youth and her woman's hunger to be completed.

Then his breath was warm and moist on her cheek, intimate like a lover's, and he pressed closer until she swore she could sense the forbidden swell of his gender.

He had begun guiding her away from the other dancers with a purpose. In the shadows beyond the edge of the pavilion, he suddenly swept her into a nearly hidden gazebo.

"No," she protested when he crushed her to him, "what are you—?"

The protest was smothered on her lips by his almost bruising kiss. For a few moments her traitorous body responded instantly, her passion rising to equal his. Then, with a violent effort, she broke free of his embrace.

"*Stop* it," she flung at him. "Are you insane? People saw us come in here."

"This time I'll stop," he husked, his voice altered by his lust. "But as I just said, thoughts need not submit to a master. *I'll be wondering.*"

She pushed past him, face flaming when she saw all the heads turned in their direction.

Only moments before, she had felt transported to the very heavens. Now she came tumbling down to earth. Suddenly all of it, as she gazed round at the people and the pavilion, seemed falsely bright and artificial, like painted flats at the rear of a stage.

"That's twice you've said that to me," she managed to whisper, as if to herself.

"Yes, but only because you once said it to me," he taunted behind her in a voice for her ears only.

She turned to look at him one last time.

In his eyes was the promise of damnation. He gestured to his empty black cravat where his gold stickpin used to be. He had known all along that she took it. "And that will be your undoing, Lady Moonlight."

Chapter 11

Even before full sunrise the streets of lower Manhattan began to writhe with people and conveyances, all jockeying and jostling for position. Hush started watching the flat on Amos Street shortly after seven A.M. Just after eight A.M., by the bells of St. Paul's, a plump woman in a faded calico dress emerged from the private street entrance, on the ground floor right around the corner from the pharmacy. She walked across the brick street to a bakery, returning with a loaf of bread wrapped in wax paper.

The next two hours dragged by for Hush, as slowly as the preaching he had to endure before he could eat the free supper at the Methodist Mission. He occupied a good vantage point on the roof of a three-story warehouse across the street. By now he knew the Lower East Side so well that he could travel through much of it atop the buildings, avoiding the traffic, police, and gangs prowling below.

A steady stream of customers entered the pharmacy, emerging with mineral waters, salts, and patent medicines of every sort. The church bells gave ten peals, and still he saw no sign of the man Mystere had asked him to spy on. It wasn't Sunday, so why hadn't the man gone off to work? The area was no slum, but neither was it Rich Man's Row.

Bored and hungry, Hush climbed down the rickety back steps and hoofed it to Cherry Street. There he bought an apple and a wedge of suet pudding.

His appetite slaked for now, the twelve-year-old noticed a well-dressed elderly woman waiting at the corner for her hansom. A huge crushed-velvet bag dangled from her right arm. He noted the brass clasp with a studied eye, recognizing it as a type he could work with just one thumb.

He glanced around to make sure no roundsmen were nearby. Then he fished a jet earring out of his pocket—Rillieux had taught him to employ diversions when possible—and dropped it onto the sidewalk to the woman's left.

" 'Scuze me, ma'am," he piped up. "Did you drop your earring?"

He pointed at it, and her curious eyes followed his finger. The few seconds she spent studying the earring were more than ample for him to fish the Italian leather billfold from her purse and drop it behind the baggy front of his shirt.

"Why—no, it's not mine, young man, but thank you for mentioning it."

"Oh, well, finder's keepers," he said as he scooped up the earring and hurried off.

As taught, he would not steal in this neighborhood again for a few weeks. And he would not even look at the billfold's contents—it would go straight to Rillieux and the family kitty. The family . . . *his* family if he went by all the rules.

He returned to his post atop the warehouse. Again boredom quickly set in; but all he had to do was think about soon living in the same house with Mystere, and that funny knot was back in his stomach. She was right out of the top drawer, all right, even if she did practically admit she was the Lady Moonlight. He was determined to do good work for her. *Cripes,* he thought—after imagining her velvet voice and ivory skin—*I'd sneak into hell with a pocketful of firecrackers if* she *asked me to.*

Just past noon his patient loyalty was rewarded. A big, swarthy, mutton-chopped man with hairy hands and a splay-footed walk stopped at the door and banged the brass knocker. He was let inside, emerging a few minutes later with the man Mystere had described.

Hush scrambled down to the street and caught up with them as they aimed toward the unceasing racket and activity on Broadway. Dogging them from a few yards behind, he quickly recognized the big one from his odd walk—he was called Sparky, and he was one of the regular loafers who hung around the South Street docks, pitching pennies until laborers were called to unload a cargo ship. When he had worked long enough to finance his next drunken rout, he was a loafer again. The cycle went round and round.

Hush followed them across Broadway, no mean feat in the lethal traffic. Even a veteran like him had to leap at the last moment to avoid being run over by a buggy with its top up.

At first he thought the two men were headed for the Bowery, only three blocks east of Broadway, with its less-fashionable array of disportments. Instead, the pair aimed for the strip of concert saloons on lower Broadway.

Now and then Hush heard a glissando of piano notes growing louder as they approached. The two men ducked past the slatted batwings of a saloon, and Hush paused outside to study the sign with gilded wooden letters hanging over the entrance. For practice he sounded out the letters Mystere had taught him, and to his proud surprise he knew all of them except the last: "A . . . l . . . i . . . b . . . i . . . B . . . a . . . urr," he guessed for the last sound. The Alibi Bar. Cripes, thanks to Mystere he could already read a little.

The variety show did not start until later, so the toughs hired to sit inside the doors, brandishing billy clubs, were not yet on duty. Hush slipped inside the dim, smoky interior; it exhaled an odor of sweat, beer, and tobacco. He spotted the two men at an S-shaped mahogany bar, each with one foot up on the rail while Sparky talked and gestured. Hush knew he would be chased out, but he headed back toward them anyway.

Sawdust covered much of the floor, and unshaven men with cigarettes stuck to their lips played billiards and darts. Hush cast a longing glance at a huge joint of meat on the free-lunch counter. But it was only for those who purchased cocktails costing fifty cents and better.

"Two ales, Jimbo!" Sparky called to the bartender. "And draw 'em nappy."

So far no one seemed to notice the boy with shabby cloth trousers gone out at the knees. He edged in closer to the two men. Sparky's bray was easy to hear.

"I'm telling you, Lorenzo, we can make a fortune in Little Italy and never break a sweat. Just collect our fee on each rental. My hand to God, trained monkeys rent as high as thirty dollars a month. Add four dollars rent for the street organs, and Easy is the street we'll live on, b'hoy. All you need to get in the operation on equal shares is a thousand dollars. Can you raise the money?"

"Hold off a bit, Sparky—I'm damned if I'll train any filthy monkeys—"

"Shoo, *we* don't train 'em, slick; we pay some eye-tye brats a few bits a day to do it. We don't have to go near the damned monkeys; we'd just be the owners. Why, it's money for old rope. You're a fool if you don't buy in."

Both men had quickly finished their first huge schooners of beer. Sparky signaled for two more. Hush watched Lorenzo place his elbows carefully to avoid beer slops on the bar, evidently mulling Sparky's offer. He kept patting his mustache with three fingers as if afraid it might fall off.

"I may indeed be interested," he finally replied. "As to the money I must pay—that's no piddling amount."

"Nor no piddlin' profits, anh?"

"Perhaps, but at any rate I only have some of the money. I still need to raise about four hundred."

"Are you in the way of raising it quicklike? Nick has other takers lined up if we don't want it."

"I may be at that," Lorenzo replied, nodding. "I have a very wealthy client these days. You see, she—"

"All right, just so you get it. But remember, by the street of by and by you'll arrive at the house of never. We must move quickly, you and me."

Even as Lorenzo got drunker, Hush noticed, his voice held one flat pitch, rarely varying. He also liked to drink at Freeman's Quay—here came their third beer, and again Sparky paid for it. Odd, considering it was Lorenzo wearing the suit and vest. Unless Sparky was working a con on him. Sure, and Mystere was that "very wealthy client" Lorenzo had in mind.

By now the bartender had spotted Hush and thumbed him toward the door. But it wasn't long before the two men came outside, shook hands, and parted. Sparky headed back toward the waterfront while Lorenzo cut over only as far as lower Fifth Avenue.

Hush was surprised when he turned in under the Arch and entered Washington Square. He headed toward the northeast corner of the square, and at first Hush was sure he would enter the marble-fronted administration building of New York University.

Instead, Lorenzo aimed for a row of pleasant brick-and-masonry flats just behind the university. He tugged the bellpull at number 17 Washington Street and was admitted by a slim, smiling young woman who wore her dark hair loose and flowing.

Hush took a turn around the square, wary of a roundsman lingering under the Arch. One block west of the square, a group of young girls, having met their morning quota, emerged from a huge brick shirtwaist factory. While the cop was distracted calling out flirtatious exchanges with one of them, Hush ducked into the narrow strip of garden between number 17 and the next building.

He stopped at the first window he came to, where a gap in the curtains allowed him to see through the lace curtain. He glimpsed fleur-de-lis wallpaper, needlepoint tapestries, and tall glass-fronted cabinets filled with glazed porcelain figures. But the room appeared empty of people.

He slipped back to the next window. Here the curtains were tightly drawn. But he carefully pressed one ear flat against the glass. The noises he heard inside were familiar; he had learned them long ago from living in crowded tenements. Lorenzo's wife lived on Amos Street, all right, but obviously he kept a whore in Washington Square, too. And Hush had a pretty good idea, by now, just whose money was paying for her.

Much as he hated to, he decided it was time to go see Mystere.

"You ask me, all he's doing for your money is washing bricks," Hush informed Mystere almost the very moment his second reading lesson had concluded. She had insisted on the lesson first, suspecting the lad's report might upset her. "And he wants still more for some scheme to rent out monkeys and organs."

"I never said anything about paying him money," she pointed out, though neither did she bother denying it.

"Well, he's just sittin' on his pratt when he ain't drinking or visiting his wh—his sporting gal. And his pal Sparky, he ain't worth a rap. Ask anybody 'at knows him—all you'll get from the likes of him is short measure for a long price."

Hush held the McGuffey's primer Mystere had given him today. Both of them had taken their usual places in the downstairs parlor. Mystere was glad she had insisted on the lesson first—Hush's report, while in no way shocking, quickly scuttled her hopes for a good mood.

"You say he's quite the drinker?" she clarified.

"Huh! He don't just sip it down—he drinks it like he's a pipe through the floor."

Yes, she thought, *I know that pipe—the same one that's been draining off my money for months now.*

"Did you see the wife?"

He nodded. "She went to the bakery."

"Walked?"

"Sure, it was only across the street."

"She didn't look ill to you?"

"Naw. Fat and healthy."

Hush watched worry mold her face. He obviously wanted to say something to make her feel better. So he told her about sounding out the letters on the Alibi's sign and how he had guessed the *r* by himself. It did coax a brief smile from her.

"Good for you," she told him absently. "You must practice whenever you can."

Her thoughts, at the moment, had got into a confused moil. She was still trying to understand the events of last night at the Sanford ball. Then Hush had arrived with this latest confirmation of her fears. Clearly certain events were coming to a head, but she felt swept up by them, washed along, when she wanted desperately to somehow gain control.

There was some hopeful news, at least. As she had prayed for, Belloch had kept his mouth shut about the cravat pin she took last night, and there was no new spate of Lady Moonlight stories in today's papers—at least, not in the *Sun*, the *World*, the *Herald*, or the *Independent*, which Baylis had purchased as usual for old Rillieux's ritual morning perusal, along with the more respectable *Times*.

Unfortunately, some of the gap in Lady Moonlight fare was being filled with more speculative gossip about her and Rafe Belloch. The *Herald*'s wildly popular gossip maven, Lance Streeter, asked provocatively, "Exactly what transpired inside that gazebo? Will this *pas de deux* lead to wedding bells or ruinous scandal? A lady's innocence may well be intact, yet suddenly at issue."

If that was not painful enough for her, Streeter, so powerful he often sniped at Mrs. Astor by name, had even launched a new side bar column titled "Inside the Gazebo." He promised it "will take you, the curious reader, inside the private love nests of the wealthy and famous."

She had started to walk Hush toward the front vestibule when Rillieux suddenly pushed open the teakwood doors of the parlor, blocking their exit. His face was choleric with anger, and she instantly saw why: the monthly bills were clutched in his left hand. Paying accounts always left him in a pettish mood.

"Young woman," he greeted her without preamble, "I am fed up with your extravagances, do you mark me? All the cash I give you, yet *still* you charge on my name? From now on you must cut your coat according to your cloth."

He was not one to brook interruptions when he was in a rage, so Mystere only submitted meekly, letting him rant it out. He had maintained a stone-faced silence last night when she had given him the gold pin instead of Sylvia's brooch as he had expected. Now, however, he erupted, revealing the darker, more threatening side of his personality.

"Do you think the cream you poured on your strawberries this morning delivered itself free for your enjoyment? This lad"—he nodded toward Hush—"will need new footman's liveries when he joins us, complete with our family crest embossed on them. Do you have any idea what it costs to outfit Baylis as our coachman, to maintain the expense of a team and carriage? Or to keep a roughhouser like Evan in good suits and linen?"

You pay none of them any salary, you old piker, she wanted to fling at him.

"Your little gewgaw from last night," he raged on. "At face value, why yes, the pin's worth a few dollars. From Helzer, however, it will at best fetch perhaps forty."

Rillieux paused, leaning more heavily on his rattan cane, as if she were becoming, literally, an intolerable burden. Hush chose that moment to try and lift the master's mood. He presented the wallet he had stolen earlier while spying for Mystere. It had the unforeseen effect, however, of feeding into Rillieux's tirade.

"There, you see?" he demanded of Mystere, sliding an impressive sheaf of banknotes from the wallet. "Thank God the boy has taken up your slack, Mystere, or we'd've been dunned out of our home by now.

And do you understand what a dunning notice means for us? It means complete public exposure of our artfully constructed facade."

"You're right," she conceded. "But I promise to do better at the opera this Saturday."

"*That's* the gait," he approved.

He had forgotten all about Mrs. Astor's annual opera party, and Mystere's contrite tone seemed to temper his spleen somewhat. But it wasn't just a chance to throw a bone to Paul—once again it was an opportunity to ease the pressure on Lady Moonlight, for the suspect pool at the opera house would be much larger. And certainly all the ladies could not be searched.

Though somewhat appeased, Rillieux hadn't yet finished his admonitions. He slid the bills into his vest pocket and tucked the cane under one arm, all so that one fist could beat the palm of his other hand to underscore his points.

"Mystere, I mention the danger of public exposure because, ironically, *that* is the fear making you so timid of late. You've been educated too well, I'm afraid, in the ways of the upper crust. Now I think your fear is the shame it will bring you even more than the punishment."

"Perhaps," she admitted, but nothing more.

"Of course, but in our walk of life such conventional morality must be set aside now and then. Do not mistake my patience for indulgence. Nor is your gender fair excuse to go puny. Rose is not only a good maid, but she keeps a sharp ear and eye on the daily doings hereabouts, and still brings home some prizes now and then. You must earn your keep in this family as does everyone else."

She was forced to bite her lower lip until she tasted blood. His words angered her. *Earn her keep?* In the past three months alone she had brought in at least five thousand dollars for the household, no Vanderbilt allowance, perhaps, but a good sum at a time when workingmen kept families alive somehow on three hundred dollars a year.

Some of that loot, of course, never made it into the family kitty. Most of the stolen goods were kept hidden out in the coach house until they were taken to Helzer's front operation, a giant salvage yard down on Water Street. That way Evan or Baylis would be the scapegoats if it was discovered.

But Rillieux had quietly been skimming off cash and a few items of very special value, locking all of it in a safe in his bedroom. She had glimpsed the contents by accident only once. They included a beautiful diamond tiara she had stolen this spring, among the Lady Moonlight's first coups.

"You must stop fretting about the right and wrong of your actions," he concluded in a kinder tone. "Is it *right* for the fox to seize the chick? I assure you, where money is involved there can be no hypocrisy. You're succumbing to a humbug morality. *Sin bravely*, for then you will get away with it."

A canny gleam seeped into his eyes. "Apropos brave sins—what *did* happen inside that gazebo, dear heart?"

She flushed to the roots of her hair. It pleased a chuckle out of Rillieux.

"There, there, never mind," he soothed as if she were a child. "Your color speaks volumes. At any rate, those few moments, and your dancing, have insured a memorable Sanford ball this year."

His eyes narrowed as they focused on her, accusing. His voice hardened. "But don't think I don't consider what's going on. I see how Rafe Belloch may be the perfect way out for you."

"Way out?" she repeated, his meaning escaping her.

"Of course. You act like you've grown sick of thieving. You admit you're worried about a devastating exposure. Marry Rafe and you'll never have another money worry except how to spend it all before you die."

"Never minding, of course," she interjected hotly, "the fact that he is too conceited to ever submit to the sacrament of marriage. Or that I find him an arrogant beast."

Rillieux's lips formed a crude wolf grin, revealing his gold crowns. "Can you look at me and say he doesn't make your blood hot?"

This time she had to turn away, he shamed her so.

"Oh, don't overdo the ingenue," he snapped impatiently. "You'll not be trapped in any marriage. When you tire of his ... conjugal attentions, Rafe will have an accident. You'd have nothing to do with it."

She stifled her first impulse to argue this point, trying another tack. "You fail to understand him, Paul. Even if I agreed to such a plan, even if by some incredible series of events, he proposed to me and I accepted—he is no old man careless of his wallet. He would be a fearsome adversary if violence confronted him, I'm sure of it. The man is dangerous."

"Humph. Trust me, *any* man becomes a pussycat once his blood is hot for a particular woman. I have seen how he looks at you, practically licking his lips at the flat-chested little nymph—"

"Paul, that's enough." She frowned at such improper talk in front of the boy. But Rillieux only chuckled again, tousled Hush's wild mop of dark hair, and went upstairs to his quarters.

"What does 'dunning' mean?" was Hush's only question before Mystere let him out of the house.

He knew he was woefully ignorant, but even a blockhead understood that men who courted real ladies like Mystere must know their letters. And even write poetry and such gimcracks to impress the fair sex, he thought, for they were a deep-feeling lot; he could see it in Mystere's expressive face as Mr. Rillieux raked her over the coals. *I must never,* he vowed solemnly to himself, *let a lady see my rat pail when it is filled brimming.*

"I'll tell you what it means at our next lesson," she promised. "I'll show you how to use the dictionary."

One important task remained. After Hush left she went into the little telephone niche midway down the hall and lifted the handset from its wall-mounted cradle. She turned the magneto crank, ringing up a hello girl, and nearly yelling into the receiver, asked for a connection with a bicycle-messenger service located near Fourteenth Street and Sixth Avenue.

A tinny, faraway voice that could have been either gender answered, and she dictated a brief message for Lorenzo, telling him she would be waiting at the usual place tomorrow at one P.M. She hung up, heart racing, for she sensed she had reached a critical juncture in her life.

She wasn't sure what she was going to tell Perkins—or what he might do. But if she ever hoped to find Bram, she had to become her own woman in a hurry; she was sure of that much, at least. As Paul's chilling remarks about Belloch had revealed, she must also put out the flames, his *and* hers. Not only was Rafe a threat, but he was *threatened.* No matter how much he infuriated and frightened her, she would not even entertain the idea of violence against his person.

If only she could be strong enough, tomorrow she would begin to take control of her own destiny.

Chapter 12

"**A**wake already?" Rose called from the bedroom doorway, breakfast bell in hand. Mystere, eyes open wide but her attention obviously inward, was clearly visible through the hyacinth blue French silk hangings of her four-post canopy bed.

"Since well before sunrise," she confessed, "but still lying here like a slug-a-bed."

"Well, perhaps you should humor His Nibs and join him for breakfast this morning," Rose suggested tactfully, adding, "I heard him hollering at you yesterday in the parlor. Mother Mary, he rattled the shutters!"

"Perhaps I should join him," Mystere agreed, throwing back the counterpane.

She had not been loafing, however, so much as paralyzed by worry. Her newfound resolve of yesterday had somehow weakened during the near sleepless night. The thought of what lay ahead—today with Lorenzo, and beyond with Paul, with Rafe Belloch—made her want to burrow under the bed linens and never come back out.

"Rose?"

"Hmm?"

Mystere's gaze went to the writing desk beside the east window. But she fought down the urge to handle the letter yet again—she had nearly worn it out. *Reading it again,* she lectured herself, *will reveal no secrets.* Yet, there was a secret—she knew that as surely as she was alive. And no matter what, she would, she *must* learn that secret. Because somehow it was linked to Bram's disappearance.

"Yes?" Rose reminded her gently, used to Mystere's dark moods. "Do you think of Ireland much?"

The question did not seem to surprise Rose. Even though she was not from Dublin, as Mystere was, but from the farm country bordering the Irish Sea, she seemed to understand Mystere's curiosity. Because Rose was older and had remained in Ireland longer, Mystere often plied her with questions. Indeed, the young woman's thirst to know about her homeland, and her family roots, was insatiable. All her reading, the endless questioning of Irish expatriates . . . Mystere had even gone to the American Museum every single day while Barnum's elaborate scale model of Dublin had been on display.

"I do think of my family some, but I still say I don't miss the place much. I was born in 'fifty-three during the midst of the crop failures, although the very worst of it was over."

Mystere had a shadowed, faraway look in her eyes. "So many died in the famine that killer hunger seems to be our only national identity." She retreated farther into her black thoughts. She herself was Irish. Enduring the open contempt the predominately Protestant Four Hundred heaped on the Irish, and of course Catholics, was one of the most difficult aspects of her deception.

She rose, shrugged into a dressing gown, and crossed to the satinwood wardrobe. Whatever she chose to wear, first would come the tiresome, undignified ordeal with the linen wraps.

"At least you have *some* memories, good or bad," she pointed out. "I think that's better than none at all."

"No doubt. I remember that things were still bleak in the countryside by the time I came over in 'sixty-three—no prospects for the young, which is why my parents sent me. I went straight to the Five Points, where I had an uncle. But he had died of cholera. That's another reason they hate us so much here, you know—there's no denying the cholera some of us brought over."

"If so, it was mostly Irish who died of it."

"Yes, may Uncle Liam rest in peace. Mystere, the Five Points is still a rough place now, but in 'sixty-three? It was corruption and death for children, especially them as had no family. If Paul hadn't taken me in, I'd've copped it sure as the Lord made Moses."

Rose did not say this with intention to make her feel guilty, Mystere realized. But her remark was a goading reminder of Mystere's rebellious plans. Rillieux had rescued her and Bram, too, and now only look how ungrateful she was.

But within, her bold new self spoke up in vigorous defense of individual liberty, and Bram was the very reason she needed her freedom, needed also to get rid of that blood-sucking leech Lorenzo Perkins. She was "arrogating" thousands each year for Rillieux—why, she could live decently and still finance a thorough search for Bram, for their roots, too, if she could only keep some of that money herself.

Money . . . without willing it, she suddenly thought of Antonia's pure emerald, of that soft, dewy green shade exactly like Bram's eyes. She wasn't overly superstitious, but couldn't help wondering if that ring was meant to spur her will. It was a mere show trinket to Antonia, but for Mystere could mean the independence to continue her all-important search.

"Try to hurry," Rose reminded her softly just before she backed out and shut the door. "It always cheers him when you have breakfast together. He is so fond of you."

"He's fond of all of us," Mystere conceded. "Perhaps that's our problem."

Rose started to respond, then abandoned the effort and hid behind her careful housemaid's face.

"Rose?" Mystere managed just before the door closed.

The mobcapped head and twin red plaits came back around the door. "Yes?"

"I . . . I mean, it's not *my* idea that Paul and I should live so finely and be waited upon." Mystere knew all about the cramped cubbyholes in the attic that were provided for servants, stifling in summer, unheated in winter. And they took every meal in the servants' dining room in the basement. Rillieux insisted on it, claiming the ruse was vital to their deception.

"Push all that right out of your head," Rose deprecated. "My room is dry and clean and has a lock on the door. We all eat well, and Paul does not begrudge us time off. Though he occasionally thumps the boys, they're used to it and would not respect him if he didn't." Her eyes clouded, as if she was thinking of the incident when Mystere had gotten her beating. "He's never hit me," she offered, as if it was some kind of excuse. "Besides all that—you have no special privileges that you have not earned dearly. The risks you take . . . la! Worry about your own lot, poor thing, for he's become quite dependent upon . . . well, never mind, I'm running on. I pray for you, Mystere, and feel no envy or resentment, none at all."

Mystere joined Rillieux for a pleasant breakfast in the solarium, and he was on his best behavior after the abusive remarks he had made yesterday. He did, however, make a pointed remark about having his kid gloves and silk topper cleaned for Mrs. Astor's upcoming opera party—and thus, holding her to her promise that she would make up for the paltry take at the Sanford ball.

He did not question her story, however, that she would be spending much of the day at the park and then Macy's reading room, for she often wiled away an hour or two there after a trip to the park. Nor did he offer the carriage since he required it himself.

Despite her new resolve to economize, however, Mystere flagged down a hansom cab the moment she was out of sight of their brownstone.

"How much for a trip to Brooklyn, then back across to Central Park—say a couple hours or a bit more?"

"Set rate, ma'am," he lied without a blink. "One dollar an hour."

The price was dear, based on his quick assessment of her fine cotton linen skirt and side-lacing silk boots. But today she could spend recklessly.

"All right," she agreed without haggling, and he handed her in without relinquishing his seat at the rear.

Long before the bridge had opened, Mystere had begun taking trips on her own to Brooklyn when she had something important weighing on her mind. The quiet residential city was a relaxing, calm, reflective place compared to the teeming behemoth just across the river. There were five ferry lines back then, though she had almost always taken the Wall Street ferry.

Now, of course, the bridge made the trip faster and offered a spectacular view, especially for the pedestrians dawdling up on the elevated promenade: a busy confusion of steamships and barges and the sturdy cargo packets of the Black Ball line far below them, with smaller skiffs and sailing boats flitting among them like water bugs.

But though Mystere's eyes registered all of it, all she could really dwell on were Rafe Belloch's cruel, fascinating eyes, all she could think of, his violent, passionate mouth igniting her body like a flambeau.

"Where to now, lady?" The driver's voice slapped her rudely back to awareness, and she saw with a little start that the gothic arch of the Brooklyn tower of the bridge was passing.

"Take a turn through Prospect Park," she directed him.

Ashamed by the . . . warmth of her prurient thoughts, Mystere resolved all over again *not* to let a few wanton moments of unseemly sexual ardor be her undoing, socially or emotionally. Not for a king's ransom would she surrender physically to such a conceited, arrogant man. His behavior toward Caroline and Antonia proved the wisdom of avoiding him as did the way he had practically . . . why, practically shanghaied her into that gazebo to force himself on her with the manners of a common gardener's boy. . . .

Abruptly she became aware that the cabman was peering at her through the small opening between the covered vehicle and his seat, peering at her with his face squinched up anxiously.

"Pardon me?" she managed, suddenly disoriented for she had lost all track of time.

"I said are you all right, lady? That's twice now I've asked where you wish to go next. We've been around the park twice."

"Oh, I'm sorry. I'm fine, I just—"

"Look, are you *sure* you can cover the fare?" he challenged, his tone skeptical. "For aught I know, you escaped from Bellevue and stole them fancy clothes."

"Here's three dollars now to calm you." She handed the bills through the opening. "What time is it, please?"

"Nearly eleven."

Her heartrate slowed, for it was not so late as she had feared. But she *must* stop thinking of Rafe Belloch and concentrate on the immediate problem of Lorenzo Perkins.

"Take High Street for a bit," she decided.

They left the park and headed north, following the pleasant, tree-lined parkway through blocks of comfortable rowhouses. Land was cheaper here, and the less-affluent could afford decent homes, yet be proximate to their work in Manhattan.

But Perkins, *Perkins,* she forced herself to stay focused. She had an unsettling feeling that canceling his services would be neither quick nor cheap. All his prying questions about her and Rillieux . . . all this time she had pinned her hopes on him, and for what? Less than mince pie. Perhaps it would even turn out worse than a waste of time and money.

Again Mystere thought of her letter at home, its strange, intriguing letterhead—her forlorn hope of locating Bram, perhaps even of inheriting a great fortune. But she could not stake her rightful claim unless she at least found out her family name. Bram had told her so much, but not that—*why* not that?

Now, blood prickling her nape, she recalled what Rillieux had almost said that night in the carriage, on the way to the Sanford ball: *It's in your family.* She had thought it was just a mistake, a simple slip of the tongue. She had no idea why he almost said it. But suddenly she wondered if he knew something he wasn't telling her. And if that was the case, the sheer irony of it would almost drive her mad. Here she had been secretly searching the world for information on Bram, and the information may have been at home all along. Withheld for reasons she knew would not prove good.

Again the driver's voice startled her like a cold touch. "Quite a view, eh, lady? I've a cousin means to build near here before long. A ward boss," he added proudly. "You'll find no hominy on *his* plate, I'll warrant."

He had reined in his horse atop the airy bluff, overlooking the East River, that gave High Street its name. The view was a breathtaking panorama in the late-morning spun-gold sunshine.

She gazed across the crowded river and saw boys playing under the Manhattan tower of the bridge, insect-size from where she stood as were the day laborers rolling heavy barrels of fish across the docks.

She could see the proud spire of Trinity Church, the eight-story Equitable Building on lower Broadway, the massive spans of the bridge . . . all of it heaven-grasping grandeur and wealth. But she could also see the crazily leaning tenement buildings crowding the waterfront of the East River, each one so poorly built that it leaned against its neighbors for its main support. No longer just the Lower East Side, either—the slum blight now covered much of the east and west shores of Manhattan, human beings "packed in like maggots in cheese" as one shocked reformer had described the population density of Manhattan's tenements.

However, it wasn't reform on her mind now; she didn't have the capacity for good works beneath Rillieux's heavy thumb. But seeing all of that darker side of the metropolis, she was suddenly numbed by the old insecurities and fears. For in reality, much less than a half mile separated her from horrid squalor.

A horrid squalor she knew like the back of her hand.

Unless she somehow became dependent on no one but herself, the threat of poverty would continue to hang over her. She was only one man's whim away from disaster at any moment, one glaring headline from becoming one of those desperate women she saw everywhere: shabby-genteel creatures fallen on hard times, proud but destitute, scrabbling to attach themselves to the wealthy in some menial capacity.

But *no,* she mustn't let the destructive fear engulf her; she must be strong for herself and Bram. Even today she could visualize the big brass plaque that she, Bram, and the other children had been required to read every night before prayers at the orphanage, the pithy wisdom of Cornelius Vanderbilt: *Let others do what I have done and they need not be around here begging.*

All right then, she decided, *from here on out I'll be tough and iron-willed like the Commodore.*

"Driver," she called up, "please take me to the Bethesda Fountain now."

"It's the devil's own work," Lorenzo began his report—perhaps the only part of it, she thought, that would be true. "These last few days I've been going at it hammer and tongs from sunrise to dark."

That was a bald-faced lie and she knew it. His dull little turtle eyes peered out at the boaters on the lake, avoiding her scrutiny. His usual sullen, apathetic mood was replaced by an urgency she hadn't figured out yet—though she remembered Hush's report that Lorenzo and Sparky were cooking up some scheme that required money.

However, before she could even accuse him of lying, he pressed on with precipitate haste, as if sensing why she had asked to meet him. "But I think all my efforts might have paid off," he vouchsafed. Despite her determination to end this, Mystere had to let herself take this much bait, just in case.

"And . . . ?" she encouraged him.

"It's this fellow out on Blackwell's, you see, a guard at the penitentiary. He *may* have had your brother locked up in his cell bay some time back."

"He 'may' have? Doesn't he know?"

Perkins expelled the long, fluming sigh of a patient, put-upon man. "Of course he knows. But you've no idea," he assured her, "how greedy and rough and cunning these prison screws are. Oh, they're a sweet bunch, all right."

"I see. You require more money, is that it?"

He spread both hands in a gesture of helplessness. "It's not for me but to oil their tongues."

For a few moments, literally sickened by his lying face, she turned her eyes to the magnificent bronze figure of the angel rising triumphantly from the water. Right now the statue gave her great solace, for she believed that despite Lorenzo Perkins and all she had suffered, this was the same angel who had guided her here to New York to fulfill her destiny. And she *would* fulfill it.

"Mr. Perkins," she told him in a voice of unwavering resolve, tinged by anger, "you have *not* been working on my case at all these past few days and you know it."

The little eyes blinked rapidly from a face gone blank with surprise. Caught flat-footed, he fell back on his favorite tiresome maxim. "Never stack your conclusions higher than your evidence."

"Well, how's this for evidence? You spent the better part of yesterday at home, as well as drinking beer with a pal on Broadway and then visiting a . . . female friend at Washington Square."

His jaw went slack.

For such a dishonest man, she thought, he was a poor liar.

"That's barmy," he protested. "I took some time off yesterday, sure. She who pays the piper calls the tune, I agree. But the piper decides what key to play it in."

That was actually quite clever, for him, she thought. "It's not just yesterday," she insisted. "You've been nowhere near Blackwell's Island recently."

Actually she couldn't prove that, but it must have been true because he offered no denial. He simply glowered at her as if his foul mood meant more than her grievance. When she refused to be cowed, he demanded as if he had a right to know, "Who says so?"

"It really doesn't matter, Mr. Perkins. The report is reliable, and I'm terminating your services, for I mean to find my brother on my own."

"Balls. You'll make cheese out of chalk first."

"Perhaps, but that's my plan."

She gathered her skirt and made as if to rise from the bench. But his sullen, menacing tone stopped her.

"It's Belloch, ain't it?"

"I beg your pardon?"

"Beg a cat's tail," he snarled, his coarseness surfacing under this pressure. "I've had my stomach full of you acting so fine haired and la-de-da. My wife reads them tattletale columns; she's told me all about you and your fancy man."

"Would that be your ill wife, Mr. Perkins, or your secret one?"

He ignored that, or pretended to. She watched him rapidly turning this new problem back and forth in his mind, studying its facets, looking for the angle he needed.

"It's Belloch," he repeated with bulldog tenacity, having seized something he refused to let go. *"That's* why you're giving me the boot. You've got your claw into him, and you don't want him finding out all the skeletons in your closet. Now you've cooked up these false accusations to fire me."

"That's utter nonsense, I—"

"You must understand, *Miss Rillieux,"* he cut her off, dark innuendo seeping into his tone, "that I've come to depend on your reg'lar payments. We have what the law calls a spoken contract."

"Mr. Perkins, that's preposterous. You are not on permanent remittance; I hired you for a specific service that you have not even remotely performed. Furthermore, I paid you generously and certainly owe you no more money."

With that she again started to rise, her nexus to the boorish lout permanently severed in her mind.

Obviously, however, he had a different view of it.

"You'll pay me," he snarled, "or I'm going to Belloch."

Alarm tightened her throat, but the warmth of anger made her cheeks feel as if they were swelling. "And telling him what?" she challenged.

Here his certainty crumbled somewhat, but it did not crack completely. Nor did his spiteful belligerence. "It's my profession to find out that sort of thing," he assured her. "Call yourself Rillieux, do you, but don't even know your own brother's hind name? P'r'aps I'll just see about this fancy-dan uncle of yours, too."

His threat shot chills into her extremities, and she only hoped he was as inept in other matters as he had been with her case. For a long moment she felt the despair of those who wonder if the game is even worth the candle. So many impediments, so many traps and obstacles such as this dull, grasping man who threatened her now.

Just then, however, her eye latched on one man among the flow of humanity crossing the terrace. He strolled slowly among the throng, leafing through a copy of *Leslie's Illustrated Weekly*. She focused on the bold type of a full-page advertisement on the last page: WHAT ABOUT BUB 'N' SIS?

Seeing the familiar words at that very moment, hot tears instantly filmed her eyes. The popular phrase "bub 'n' sis," was used by everyone from politicians to advertisers. "What about bub 'n' sis?" had come to mean "Say! Let's not forget the children." Bub 'n' sis were synonymous with hearth and home. And even though it was just silly commercialism, seeing the phrase now pinched her throat shut and trapped the sob trying to get out of her.

"Here now," Perkins ventured awkwardly, misreading her reaction and feeling guilty at having frightened her too severely. "No one wants to harm you, Miss Rillieux, I—"

"Never mind, Mr. Perkins," she cut him off in a peremptory tone, rising from the cast-iron bench. "I consider my arrangement with you terminated. Should you choose to carry out your absurd threat of blackmail, only remember that adultery is a felony and carries with it a prison sentence."

"You've not heard the last of me!" he shouted behind her. "Damn your threats, we have a contract, and by God you'll pay one way or the other!"

Chapter 13

Even the weather seemed to come under Mrs. Astor's wide circle of influence. The Saturday evening designated for her annual opera party turned out storybook perfect, with a sky full of dazzling stars and a gentle, warm, caressing breeze. But Mystere wondered when her enchantment would be shocked out of her by Rafe Belloch's prediction that she and Paul would soon be officially exposed as frauds and criminals.

"Man alive!" Baylis exclaimed when he caught sight of her emerging, on Rillieux's arm, from the brownstone. The carriage waited in the crushed-marble cul-de-sac. "You'd make a gelding feel like a stud, girl."

"Baylis," Rillieux snapped in an undertone, "stop that tomcat talk in front of the boy; you'll ruin him for his job."

"What, mooncalf there?" Baylis jeered. He meant Hush, who stood near the open door of the carriage, uncomfortable but proud in his stiff new scarlet-and-gold livery and visored cap. The sight of Mystere in her silver satin gown with hand-sewn crystals swagged over her hips, emerging from the house like a sudden vision, had arrested him in the act of holding the door open wider.

"Hush!" Irritation raised Rillieux's voice to a shrill. "You're a footman now, not a love-struck puppy. Keep your eyes in your head and stand at the ready beside the door. As we approach, you look to be sure the step is down and secure. Then you simply hand us in. That's all. Do not gawk like a bumpkin nor speak unless spoken to by one of us."

"Yessir!"

The lad hastened to open the door and swing down the step for them, somehow disciplining himself not to gaze at Mystere in the flickering glow of the gas yard lights.

Baylis stood nearby with his hands in his pockets, watching all of them and shaking his head in amusement. Rillieux frowned at the coachman's slovenly appearance.

"If you must wear that ridiculous neck beard," he snapped, "can't you at least trim it?"

Baylis proudly combed his Newgate fringe with his fingers. "Nix on that, boss. I endure enough of this high-handed carrying on. It's the royalty in Europe, the Astors in America, and the same damned story—all the land for a few great lords. A poor man might at least have dominion over his own damned beard."

"I don't give a hang about your politics," Rillieux grumped as he settled into the carriage, careful of his creases. "We're *robbing* the great lords, you blockhead. Isn't that enough revenge for you?"

"Yes," Baylis ventured just before Hush shut the door and climbed onto the high seat. "Others rob them, however, while you prate about among them and damn well seem to like it."

"Insolent dog," Rillieux muttered as Baylis took his whip from the socket and lashed the team into motion.

"I don't blame Baylis. You *do* enjoy passing yourself off as one of the Four Hundred. It's gone to your head that Mrs. Astor's latched on to you, and you talk to Baylis and the others as if they were actually your servants."

She rarely challenged him like this. He frowned so deeply his silver-white eyebrows touched. In the shadowy illumination of the street-lights his face looked thin and sharp-nosed, younger and vaguely menacing. But he surprised her by only saying mildly, "If youth but knew and age could do."

He studied her in silence for perhaps thirty seconds. "Mystere, Baylis clings to his pathetic politics because it offers castles in the sky to poor, ignorant men who are less than drops of piss in a cesspool, to put it bluntly. But one cannot inhabit castles in the sky, do you at least see that much?"

She still said nothing to all this. As if sensing her turmoiled mood, Rillieux became even more patient.

"As to your constant harping lately about treating the rest as servants—only think a moment. I *must* run a tight ship. What happens the moment one of them slips up in front of the wrong person and somebody twigs our game? A consummate actor takes on a role and *lives* it to be convincing."

"There you go again, comparing sneak thievery to an art."

"Young woman, what I've taught you is, indeed, art, and you are an artiste, deny it or no. Has it occurred to you how *minimal* I have kept our apparent household staff? Mystere, even merely middle-class households these days generally keep four to six servants. Households among the Four Hundred employ twice or three times that number. Mrs. Astor has tactfully overlooked our lack of a resident gardener and a parlormaid, but acquiring a footman was de rigueur."

"I suppose you're right," she surrendered a little, though grudgingly. "But you mentioned castles in the sky—our own house is built from cards and must eventually collapse."

"Dear heart, should a man stop eating forever because someday he might choke on a bone? Ours is no profession for those who worry about the disasters that *might* happen. You can wail that your best friend is dead, or you can declare with joy that *once he lived*. Both are equally true, yet how one chooses to see it divides life's happy from the wretched. Do you take my meaning?"

Strangely enough, she did. Sometimes he made great sense—she did see the truth of his observation. And thanks to his training she could discipline everything except her emotions, which refused to be curbed. Especially the emotion of fear, for she sincerely doubted that a positive attitude would ever turn Rafe Belloch into anything but what he was—a serious threat to anyone who crossed him.

"Let not your heart be troubled," Rillieux continued in his soothing, authoritative voice. His sloe eyes burned into her, powerful and compelling, and years of submission quickly brought her under his mesmeric spell. "Tonight you will take Sylvia Rohr's brooch. You will do it quickly and be out of her proximity before she even misses it. Right?"

She nodded. "Right."

"That's the girl. Just remember: Be sure that your eyes do not tele-graph your movement or intention. Use some natural diversion as your cover. Be confident, fast and fluid, one single movement to take and conceal."

Again she nodded, obedient as ever, appearing to be the weak reed bent to his will.

But tonight she was stealing only to mollify Paul. Next time it would be Antonia Butler's fine emerald ring, and Mystere meant to keep the money, after selling it, for herself—for Bram.

Any gathering of Mrs. Astor's drew press attention. But tonight, Mystere quickly realized, the press scoundrels had turned out in throngs. To ogle the high-and-mighty in their finery, of course. What truly had them slavering, though, was the hope of more Lady Moonlight non-sense.

Even she, jaded by the false glitter of high society, was impressed by the roll call at tonight's event. Before their conveyance even reached the Astor Place Opera House, just off Broadway, they were engulfed in a crush of expensive carriages, surreys, calashes, and other vehicles forming a congested knot, all heading for the opera.

"H'ar now! Are you bolted to the damn pavement, Jack?" Baylis screamed at a driver just ahead of them. He added a string of curses, and Rillieux angrily thumped the carriage ceiling with his walking stick.

"Keep a civil tongue in your head, Baylis!" he called out.

Mystere, in contrast to Paul's irritability, had begun to feel a stir-ring of anticipation despite her dread of seeing Rafe Belloch again. A renowned company from Madrid was performing Bizet's *Carmen*, one of her favorite operas.

As they inched nearer to the opera house, Rillieux pulled a curtain aside.

"There's Inspector Byrnes," he said grimly. "He's entering by him-self, but rest assured he will be prominent in the Astors' box."

"Watching for the Lady Moonlight," she remarked, feeling the irony of it. "And never once suspecting he's sharing a box with her."

She had naturally assumed she would be among the Astors' immedi-ate party since Paul was. But now he cleared his throat, his gaze evasive.

"You'll not be with us, my dear, during the performance. I forgot to mention that."

"Why won't I be?"

"Well, I'm sure you've heard the Duke and Duchess of Granville are visiting the city with a large retinue. Many from Caroline's inner circle will be seated in adjacent boxes."

Excluding myself, of course, his smug tone added.

"And with whom will I be seated?" she demanded, suddenly suspicious.

"Oh, someone will claim you." He shrugged off the question. "Of that I have no doubt."

"Hmm," was all she said, although she suspected treachery was afoot.

However, they had finally gotten their turn at the curb, and too many sights and sounds, as well as a flurry of greetings, distracted her. Hush had leaped down to let them out, but he was edged aside by a dignified porter wearing gold-braided livery with the Astor crest.

The cream of the upper wards had turned out. In one sweeping glance, she spotted steel magnate Andrew Carnegie, several of the Vanderbilt clan, and Wall Street fixture George Templeton Strong. Speaking quietly and earnestly to Strong was Trevor Sheridan, whose sister Mara was now the Duchess of Granville. Sheridan was tall, broad-shouldered, and uncommonly handsome. He was an Irishman through and through, but the story was that he had succeeded in spite of his shunning. And then a great Knickerbocker beauty had fallen in love with him. He and Alana Van Alen Sheridan were considered one of the great love matches of the century. Whenever his wife was not at his side, there was an intense grimness to him. It was said of him that he hoarded his smiles like he hoarded his gold, but when Mrs. Sheridan appeared, the harshness rolled away. Anyone could see that he still had eyes only—and always—for her.

And there, about to enter the opera house, were Caroline and Carrie, Mrs. Astor looking every bit the regal matron in a foxskin cape. Antonia Butler milled nearby on the arm of some insipid little English count Mystere had once danced with and forgotten. He looked as though his chin had melted half away and seemed fearful of the beauty on his arm.

And there—there was Sylvia Rohr, and just as Paul predicted, she wore the beautiful shoulder brooch Mystere had promised to "arrogate" this very evening.

She glanced to her left, immediately challenged by the commanding teal gaze of Rafe Belloch. Many of the older men, Paul included, wore shiny silk top hats and wide trousers. Rafe, however, was hatless and wore the patent leather shoes and thin trouser legs currently in fashion with young captains of commerce.

"I knew you'd be here tonight," he said, masterfully walking to her and bowing to kiss her hand.

Her heart hammered in her chest. Fear was a metallic taste in her mouth. He was dangerous. He suspected too much about her. Now he toyed with her like a cat with a mouse. It was a good thing she was soon getting out of the game.

"How did you know I'd be here, Mr. Belloch? Have you learned the telepathic arts from my uncle?" Her voice was cool and assured, not revealing any of her fear.

"Nothing so occult, Miss Rillieux. It's quite predictable that a lady with your . . . interesting secret life would adore the character of Carmen."

"Oh, yes, excuse me. I'd forgotten that I am the Lady Moonlight," she said in a mocking little tone.

"Indeed. And after all, Carmen is a wily seductress who dupes all the men around her."

She boldly matched his stare. "I rather prefer the bullfighter who stabs her."

He took her arm in his before she could pull away. "He's my favorite also. I compliment your taste, madam, even as I ponder: Should I search this dangerous beauty for weapons before I share my box with her?"

"*Your* box?" She halted.

"Yes, it's all been arranged," he divulged, the issue apparently settled. Then his voice and his eyes softened. "By the way, you look quite beautiful this evening. As you always do."

Numbly she allowed him to escort her again, knowing they were being watched by all and sundry. Forcing a confident smile when she was anything but that, she said, "How kind of you, but I fear I'm just a brown house wren next to Antonia. I certainly can understand if you would prefer to accompany some other—"

"I would not prefer," he interrupted, brooking no discussion.

Her smile turned brittle. Coyly, she warned under her breath, "You're in danger of appearing gallant, Mr. Belloch."

His hand turned to steel on her arm. "I fear that impression may soon diminish."

The buzzing throng slowly made its way into the lobby with its Bergama runners and huge portrait of John Jacob Astor in a giltwood frame centered on one wall. Electric lamps with milky glass shades emitted a soft, pleasing light.

"I don't believe my eyes," Mystere remarked, determined to show that Rafe wasn't rattling her. "Look. It's Abbot, and he's escorting Caroline and Carrie. After just being excommunicated by her only three days ago."

"Oh, Abbot has tremendous influence with Mrs. Astor," Rafe assured her. "Don't forget, she heartily agrees with his vitriolic snobbery when it's not directed at her or her Chosen. What you see tonight is his public penance. He must meekly escort her and Carrie because opera bores the Astor males. They seem to want no part of it."

Mystere had to smile at the truism, for she had once known Astor to exclaim that all operas were female nonsense "except that one with that sly old rascal Figaro in it; now *that's* a capital show."

Rafe met her gaze again. "Caroline will put him through his facings. But remember, a family tree as old as Abbot's cannot easily be uprooted, even by Caroline. Never mind that he has squandered much of his fortune, that he's refused to wed and leave an heir."

Then, a rarity in Mystere's experience with him, Rafe lost his ironic mask, and pure malice glittered in his eyes. "The *only* mortal sin, to Caroline and her ilk, is poverty. Against that they will close ranks. As for Abbot, he will submit, for after all he is a Patriarch of the Four Hundred."

"As are you, Mr. Belloch."

"As is your uncle, Miss Rillieux."

His gaze was minatory and mocking all at once. But she refused to be cowed, holding his stare with bold defiance.

The faint shadow of a smile touched his lips. "Good, that's good. I see you've decided to fight. I like it when we fight."

"The way you made me fight at the Sanford ball, you mean? Forcing yourself on me like a drunken boor?"

"Ahh, that's been on your mind, has it, Lady Moonlight?"

"Here comes a woman who might not fight you off at all," she observed drily, neatly sidestepping his question. Antonia had left her insipid count to greet Rafe. She wore her beautiful emerald ring, and

Mystere had to force herself not to stare at it covetously. *Soon,* she promised herself.

"Rafe Belloch, you heartless rogue," Antonia greeted the railroad plutocrat, flashing her excess enamel and virtually ignoring Mystere. "You do force us women to be shamefully forward, don't you?"

"You'll *have* to be forward with that British biscuit of yours," he replied with scarcely disguised cynicism. "But don't hurt him. He looks fragile."

"This was Caroline's iron hand—she keeps all of us away from you, especially Carrie. Does that hint at her thoughts? The shameless woman is saving you, Rafe, and who could blame her?"

What's truly shameless, Mystere thought, *is this brazen, unseemly talk.* But only look how Rafe was grinning, cunning as a wolf, and how Antonia made a wanton of herself in public.

However, Mystere missed the rest of the unseemly exchange, for Abbot had eased away from the Astor ladies to mutter in her ear.

"I've disliked that man"—his hostile eyes settled on Rafe—"from the day I met him. We shook hands, and God strike me down now if *his* wasn't callused. The man's as common as a ditchdigger. You deserve better, my dear. Watch him, for he's a scoundrel."

Alarm constricted her throat—so she and Rafe Belloch were, indeed, an item now. In one sense or another.

"Take care yourself," she replied lightly. "Caroline is looking daggers at you for leaving her side."

"The woman's like Satan with a sunburn," he agreed, already turning to head back. "But she's predictable, and I can play her like a piano." He gave a last glance at Rafe, who stared back, a ferociousness in his eyes.

"You, however," Abbot sniveled before fleeing, "are handling a mountain mover—quite volatile. Be very careful, or he'll have you blown to bits, too."

Chapter 14

"**G**lasses, miss?" inquired a polite usher, offering Mystere a dainty pair of pearl-and-gold-inlaid opera glasses as he led them to Rafe's private box.

"Oh, this young woman has excellent eyes," Rafe interceded, tucking a banknote into the man's hand and waving him off. "Especially for anything that sparkles."

Dread stabbed at her heart. Had she stupidly let him see her staring at Antonia's ring? Was she walking into the lion's den? Certainly it looked that way. She would have to have her whip and chair ready at all times.

"What can I do to convince you I'm not the dark and mysterious Lady Moonlight? After all, I thought we were to see the opera tonight, so must we ride this hobbyhorse all evening?" she asked wearily, gazing round the plush interior of the Astor Place. Romanesque arches and swagged boxes lured the eyes above, and from thence to steep tiers of velvet plush seating, all narrowing as they approached the proscenium-arch stage and the orchestra pit.

He smiled wolfishly. "But that's your lure, my love. I want to be seduced by such a siren. Yes, all evening and beyond. In the meantime, I would like my stickpin back whenever you should find it convenient."

She ignored him, glancing around the roomy opera box. "This could easily seat four more persons. Who will be joining us?"

"Not your make-believe uncle, certainly."

She ignored him again, and unfortunately found his hand on her back as he chivalrously seated her.

He taunted, "No, you're completely in my clutches this evening. But never mind that, artful dodger. I'm waiting to hear your protest, for I just called your uncle make-believe."

"I heard you, Mr. Belloch; it's just that I feel foolish encouraging your obsession. Do you have proof he's make-believe, or is proof un-neccesary when you exalted Patriarchs make accusations?"

You. The word seemed to sting him like buckshot. His mouth firmed in anger. "Proof is on it's way," he told her bluntly. "A very capable employee of mine has begun some inquiries. Mail now moves fairly quickly up and down the Mississippi. I expect news from New Orleans any day now."

Despite her resolve to resist his bullying, the announcement made her face suddenly tingle. No doubt she paled, too, for he laughed. "I believe the ladies' press calls that a 'blanche.' "

"So what if I did blanche? How *should* I react when I learn that an obviously obsessed man is investigating my life?"

"What matters that to an innocent and untried flat-bosomed girl like yourself?"

She gave a look that knifed him. "Can't we at least leave my bosom out of this?"

He chuckled. "You've been trying to, haven't you? You've done some handy disguising, too, for as I recall you at Five Points, you had plenty to 'leave out.' "

"You are absolutely disgusting," she announced with cold, angry precision, pointedly ignoring him while she surveyed the assembled crowd below. Those not privileged enough to sit in the boxes included Thelma Richards, Dr. and Mrs. Charles Sanford, Jared Maitland and his wife Constance, Garret and Eugenia Teasdale. . . .

She lost her concentration, aware that he continued to study her from a smug, knowing face that angered her.

"Tell me something," he requested. "Sam, that resourceful em-

ployee I mentioned to you, has already told me some things about
you. Is it true you can handle a Thoroughbred as well as any man? I
heard tell you learned to foxhunt at that fancy school Rillieux sent
you to in Britain."

"Yes, I can ride very well, thank you, and that's no secret, Mr.
Belloch."

"No wonder you handled me with such graceful contempt during
our waltzes. You're obviously used to handling power."

He leaned across the narrow space between their gold-embroidered
armchairs.

"But I'm no animal used to a bit and harness." He shocked her by
stroking the fine hairs at her nape, his hand behind them where no
one could view the impropriety. "The strumpet who robbed me at
Five Points," he confided in a low tone, "was also quite graceful."

"Strumpet? So she was a prostitute also?" she asked stiffly, praying
his hand would leave her nape, praying the ceaseless tingling that
electrified from his fingers would refrain from running down her
spine and heating her entire body.

"You tell me."

Mystere didn't move. Her thoughts stumbled over one another.
He's more suspicious than ever, she realized. *Why?* For a fleeting moment, she thought of Lorenzo Perkins and his veiled threats of blackmail when she had sacked him.

"It's a shame you never got to know her better," she rebuffed, running her own hand down the back of her neck, chasing him away.
"Obviously you're quite smitten with her."

His eyes bored into her. "She was indeed comely. I liked her audacity, but she's sorely in need of a keeper."

"Because she bested you?" Her gaze met with his. She was a fool to
show the audacity he had just lauded, but it was freeing and exhila-
rating at the same time. She was no mincing debutante to run at his
every scowl. Her only true fears were of the law and Rillieux, both of
whom were seated in the box with Mrs. Astor.

He tipped his head back and laughed. The strong—and, indeed,
Pollard was right—callused hand again went to her nape. This time
with a hangman's grip. "She bested me not once, but twice. I relish
the moment when I get to show her who her master is."

His tone, suddenly harsh, made her resolve to speak with Paul as
soon as possible. She *had* to make him understand the danger they

faced, especially once Rafe heard from New Orleans. But would Paul listen? Even now she could glance to her right and see his sleek white head amidst those in the Astor box.

Then another possibility besides Lorenzo occurred to her. Paul had already made ominous remarks about "an accident" befalling Rafe Belloch. Would news of Rafe's inquiry to New Orleans cause Paul to exercise more caution, or would he instead have Evan and Baylis rough him up? No matter how reprehensible she found Rafe's talk and behavior, she refused to be a party to violence against him or anyone else.

"Your fascination in this matter is ill-advised, Mr. Belloch. I'm not the adventuress you imagine. I'm just having my first debut, hardly the kind of woman for a scandal, or a romance. So I must point out that your efforts are failing miserably."

The house lights winked out, and the opera began. But in the darkness Rafe was even more of a threat and a presence. He leaned close. So close she could feel his breath against her temple, his heavy, strong thigh against hers. Wretchedly, he stroked her cheek with all the intimacy of a lover.

"You're no schoolgirl. Look at me."

She complied to his demand, her eyes wary even in the dimness.

He took her face in both his hands. If the lights had been up, she would have struggled, but no one could see them in the darkness, half-hidden behind thick velvet curtains.

"Please, Mr. Belloch—"

"Rafe. My name is Rafe."

A surge of unwanted emotion caught in her throat. In truth she shouldn't have desired his hands on her face, or the intimacy of using his first name, but the notion of both moved her. And she didn't know why. She didn't even want to know why because it might prove her more vulnerable than she ever thought possible.

"Please, Rafe," she nearly begged. "I'm not the one for you to pursue. Your fascination may even prove dangerous to us both. Believe me, I can't bring anything good to you—"

"You bring to me a kind of truth I've rarely seen in this crowd. I can't help it if I'm drawn to it."

"There is no truth. None," she whispered, her voice harsh with strange, unshed tears.

"You're wrong," he whispered back harshly before his lips crushed hers.

The kiss was long and hard and wet. She wanted to scurry away, but the iron hold on her face was unrelenting. Slowly he coerced her rebellious mouth into surrender. The molten pink flesh of her lips parted; he gained free entry.

His tongue penetrated her with the thoroughness of a wine taster. Again and again he entered her, until her loins ached with emptiness. Shuddering, she fell against him, her breathing irregular and hard. Her heart pounding and yearning all at the same time.

"You played a ruffian's game at Five Points, Lady Moonlight," he said against her hair when they parted. "But that means you must honor ruffians' rules. You see, it's far better to kill a man and be done with it than to shame him and force him to revenge."

"You're either a madman or having me on," she whispered back. "I'm not sure which, but I warn you, this is dangerous. I'm not available for these games. They're dangerous, I tell you. Dangerous."

"It's you who are in danger, Mystere." His voice turned dark and rich. "I find myself wanting you. And I always get what I want."

She wanted to lower her head to her hands and weep. Moaning, she turned away from him. "You're a fool, then," she told him, thinking all the while of Rillieux and his murderous notions.

"I can assure you I've never been a fool for any woman, but never have I met a woman like you, Lady Moonlight. You steal men's jewels and their good sense."

A sob caught in her throat. Unable to speak, she placed her fingers to her mouth that still burned with his kiss. His ominous presence prevented her from enjoying the opera. Though the production was spectacular, the arias elaborate, the costumes, sets, and lighting lavish, she was too overwhelmed. Inside her, it was as if several productions were competing at once, none of them ever touching her distracted heart except the dark torment of his thigh against hers, his wicked torturous hand at her nape.

During the intermission Rafe made a point of dogging her like a shadow, as if daring her to steal something under his very nose. She was thinking about doing just that when Carrie Astor somehow made her way across the crowded lobby to briefly join them.

"Enjoying the show?" she greeted them.

Mystere, busy searching for Sylvia Rohr and her brooch, replied absently, "Yes, it's wonderful. I especially like the lead tenor."

"Is that right?" Rafe mocked her. "Well, I saw Colonel Cody's new Wild West show last summer, and this production tonight is quite similar. It's all noise and spectacle. All they need are a few whooping savages."

His eyes narrowed suggestively. "Although that's not so bad—a few Indians would certainly prove *diverting*," he finished on an emphatic note that subtly accused Mystere.

She couldn't prevent a sudden flush, for he was letting her know that he understood what she was up to. He laughed at her, and poor Carrie seemed confused.

"My mother asked me to remind you," she told them just before she left, "that she'll be hosting a late supper and cocktails at our house."

"Oh, the two of us will be there," Rafe assured her. He deliberately raised his voice, Mystere thought, so that a nearby gossip writer would overhear him.

With Rafe watching her like a prison guard, she had no opportunity to approach Sylvia. And by now his constant vigilance had stretched her nerves to the breaking point. Just before the lights dimmed to signal the end of intermission, Inspector Byrnes's gaze met hers.

His eyes only brushed lightly over her, moving on. But icy fingers touched her heart. Suddenly everyone seemed to be watching her from sly, caged eyes. And Rafe's words echoed menacingly in her thoughts: *Mail now moves fairly quickly up and down the Mississippi.*

Despite all that weighed on her mind, Mystere eventually found herself being momentarily transported by the drama unfolding below her on the stage—and especially by the music of the rousing "Toreador Song."

A powerful thumping of timpani, a plaintive crying of violins, and suddenly she saw herself again dancing out over the moonlit Hudson with Rafe. His forceful kiss burned anew on her lips. Again that strange sensation that all time had been suspended, and there was only this quivering effulgence of joy within her, her heart wildly pulsing *I want, I want.* This sense that her own life, too, was a dance unfolding moment by moment.

But then she glanced over at Rafe, and his alert, taunting eyes made her taste fear like a mouthful of corroded pennies. The orchestra slowed to a sleepy interlude, and he bent close to whisper in her ear.

"You've already stolen something, haven't you?"

"Of course," she lied in a whisper. "I'm the Lady Moonlight, remember? 'Elusive as a jungle cat.' "

"It's hidden on your person, but where?"

"Quiet, you two," came Caroline's hissing whisper from the adjacent box.

But Rafe only drew his lips even closer, until his hot breath tickled her ear. "Hidden where?" he repeated.

She shook her head and touched her lips, warning him to be quiet. Rafe only smiled at her and scooted his chair closer. She realized why when, gasping at the shock of touch, his right arm encircled her just above the waist.

"I asked politely," he muttered. "Now I'm searching."

"You wouldn't!" she protested, whispering harshly, grasping his right hand in her left and trying to break his grip on her right hip.

"Shh," he responded, touching his own lips in a mockery of her gesture only moments before.

In her effort to pry his hand loose she noticed the calluses again. Rafe Belloch had calluses to go with his muscles. His hand began to move around to her thigh, and despite her outrage she also felt that electric, erotic response to his intimate touch.

Her breathing quickened, deepened, and though she still placed heavy resistance against his hand, secretly she was almost willing to tolerate this new sensation, this fiery stirring of desire in a place now shamelessly close to his intrusive fingers.

But suddenly he surprised her by sliding his hand quickly up across her stomach, stopping only a fractional inch from discovering her tightly bound chest.

In a panic, she began exerting more pressure to force his hand down.

Rafe was so amused he emitted a coughing chuckle. Caroline's face turned in their direction, and even the dim box lights showed the angry set of her features.

Again he pressed his lips against Mystere's ear, the touch thrilling and galling all at one time.

"Show me all your treasures, Lady Moonlight," his whisper goaded, his lips a silky caress to her ear that both thrilled and reviled. "Let's make a wager, little beauty. Allow me to move my hand just one inch higher. If my suspicion about you is wrong, I shall have purchased a virgin bride. If right, I'll have exposed a treacherous siren. What say you?"

The mail from New Orleans, she realized in a moment of breathless fear, was a remote threat, indeed, compared to the danger now. Her only chance was to resort to the deceptive skill Rillieux had instilled within her.

"As you will, sir," she whispered back, eyes boldly meeting his. "But a gentleman's word is his bond, and I take your wager at face value. If you are wrong, then I must insist you marry me for the sake of my honor. I believe the threat of marriage will stay your hand, Rafe Belloch."

Brave words.

However, her heart sat out the next few beats as her fate remained in doubt.

Their eyes held a mutual, unblinking stare. As if to verify her confidence, she removed her hand from his. Now nothing restrained him—one little flex, and he would settle the issue once and for all.

But for reasons she could not fathom—unless he was simply less cynical and debauched than he behaved—he suddenly removed the offending hand.

"Ahh, but it's the *suspense* that keeps life interesting," he surrendered. "As to that body of yours—the time is coming when I shall learn much more about it than I can in this opera box."

"You'll have better prospects with Antonia Butler. Much better prospects," she answered emphatically.

"Perhaps. But something tells me your body has a different opinion than your sanctimonious speech."

By now neither one of them was even pretending to watch the drama unfolding onstage, where Carmen had just escaped from jail by manipulating yet another man. They had begun by whispering, but Mystere's voice had risen with her anger. Mrs. Astor was again sending her a reproving glance. But Mystere couldn't resist one last thrust.

"Are you truly human, Mr. Belloch, or just a beast? Have you ever *loved* anyone?"

For a moment his face became clearly angry. And as she was finding out, with anger came danger. "That's good, coming from you. Shall I have the usher fetch us some water so you can baptize me?"

Before she could reply, however, Mrs. Astor suddenly entered their box.

"You two are spoiling the opera," she announced in her formidable tone. "Rafe, push your chair back where it belongs. I'll be sitting between the two of you for the rest of the performance. Now your names, too, are in my bad book."

Chapter 15

R afe Belloch inhaled deeply, relaxed his body, and sighted carefully along the barrel of his .22 target pistol. Slowly he took up
the trigger slack until the gun bucked in his fist.

He fired six times, emptying the weapon.

Sam Farrell peered through binoculars to study the target fifty
yards downrange.

"Boss, you shoot that gun like you run your business," he reported.
"Solidly in the black. Six bull's-eyes."

Rafe snapped open the loading gate of his custom-made Belgian
pistol and thumbed brass-shell cartridges into the empty chambers.
"My father taught me to shoot, Sam. He was a line officer during the
War Between the States, you know."

"Yes, I do know," Sam replied as if reading information from a file
card. "The 15th New York Rifles Regiment. He was wounded three
times and won the Distinguished Service Medal for valor at Cold
Harbor."

Rafe smiled. "You amaze me. Does anything slip past you?"

But a moment later the smile faded as he added, "A man stands tall
in the teeth of enemy fire, then kills himself to avoid the shame of
poverty. Makes you wonder, doesn't it, just what courage really is?"

"Killing an armed enemy is one thing; killing a chimera in the mind is another."

"Yes," Rafe agreed softly. "Good point. 'Kill me the chimera.' "

He thumbed the safety on and slid his weapon into a flap holster slung over one shoulder. His private shooting range was located on the northeast shore of Staten Island, shoe-horned between the main grounds of Garden Cove and the Upper Bay.

"Had any breakfast yet?" Rafe asked his correspondence secretary.

Sam shook his head. "I spent most of the morning perusing the papers in my quarters."

"Ahh, good man. One of us has to read the damned things. Well, let's wrap our teeth around some food. Anything interesting in the news? Did our Lady Moonlight strike again?"

Both men had begun walking back to the house, following a graveled path through a magnificent flower garden. Long, narrow fingers of sunlight poked through the leaves of oak trees surrounding the garden. Rafe set a slow pace to accommodate Sam's ruined left hip, which caused him a pronounced limp.

"If she did, it wasn't mentioned," Sam replied from his usual deadpan. "But Lance Streeter's column in the *Herald* was . . . notable."

"Streeter? The wag who writes that Gazebo thing?"

" 'Inside the Gazebo,' yes. Only, this morning's installment is more like 'Inside the Opera Box.' "

Rafe chuckled. "I knew the gossip merchants were watching. Did Streeter lay it on thick?"

"Your name was repeated a dozen times, as was that of Mystere Rillieux."

Rafe smirked, bending down to pluck a white carnation. He poked its stem into a buttonhole of his jacket.

"Good," he replied with enthusiasm. "Was the word 'scandal' also used?"

"Implied only."

"Even better. The substance of real scandal, Sam, lies in what's left unsaid."

Despite Sam's careful control and blank expression, Rafe knew him well and sensed his silent disapproval.

"Well, old son, if you've something to say, I want to hear it. You're my trusted advisor—so advise me. You don't approve of this shameless public scandal business, do you?"

"My approval isn't the issue. Most prudent men avoid scandal; they don't deliberately court it."

"I see. After all, I have my lofty position to consider, right?"

Sam nodded. They had cleared the garden by now and were crossing a wide, immaculate lawn toward a white-painted house sprawled atop a low rise. Built in the 1790s by a Dutch merchant, its batten shutters and numerous French doors were flung open wide to admit the warm sunshine and gentle breeze.

"My business accomplishments are important to me," Rafe conceded. "And I fully understand, Sam, that the wrong publicity can damage a company's stock value. But in that event the mantle of leadership can be passed on. If I become too great a liability to Belloch Enterprises, I'm stepping down and you're taking over."

"I appreciate your trust, but I like my present job just fine."

Rafe smiled sympathetically but stuck to his guns. He had decided it was high time to rock Mrs. Astor's staid, comfortable world with a scandal the Fifth Avenue Brahmins would never forget. Exposing Paul and Mystere Rillieux was not his main priority—his investigation of them was for purely personal reasons, not public exposure. He meant to verify his belief that Mystere was both Lady Moonlight and the forward, acid-tongued wench who had robbed him at Five Points.

He would then get his revenge, but not by exposing her and her uncle. No, his greatest prize would be the public ruin of Caroline or Carrie Astor, and Carrie seemed an unlikely prospect for scandal. She was an inspid, shallow bore, though harmless and sweet in her own way, and he had little heart to hurt her. But Caroline was another matter. . . .

A floored breezeway led off the west wing to a comfortable breakfast nook. Just before the two men entered it, Rafe paused. He turned around and from this high-ground vantage point gazed across the bay past Governor's Island to crowded Manhattan.

"Baron Rothschild was right, Sam. The whole world *has* become a city. That thirteen-mile-long island will soon lose its last cows and chickens."

"But never its rats," Sam added, and both men laughed.

Rafe liked to converse freely at mealtimes, free of servants' prying ears, so breakfast waited, as usual, in covered chafing dishes on a sideboard. Each man helped himself, then sat at a wrought-iron table commanding a good view of ship traffic in the Narrows.

"Any word yet from New Orleans?" Rafe inquired.

Sam, busy spreading marmalade on a scone, shook his head. "It's only been five days since I posted the letter to Stephen Breaux's law offices. I predict we may hear something in about a week."

Rafe said nothing to that, for in his mind's eye he was back in his opera box with Mystere. *Why* hadn't he simply moved his hand one inch higher and proven to himself that she was hiding her full breasts under wraps of some kind? After all, his guess had by now become almost a certainty.

Perhaps, despite his deep cynicism, the Code Duello of the gentleman still governed his actions. Or perhaps he was foolishly falling in love with the little imposter, and he feared being right about her. He was willing to wound, and yet afraid to kill.

"Tell me, Sam—how could the devil's daughter be such an innocent-looking beauty?"

"I take it you mean Mystere Rillieux?"

Rafe nodded.

"What other form," Sam reasoned, *"should* the devil's daughter take? For she must, above all, beguile—the very essence of the infernal."

Again Rafe nodded, seeing the wisdom of that. But he warned himself: He must vigilantly battle his emotions. For he was a man on a mission, and Mystere was a threat to its success.

"Hush, clean your ears or cut your hair," Paul Rillieux snapped at the youth. "I've told you before *not* to hover near Mystere. When the footman is not attending to his carriage duties or running an errand, he waits in the main hall to answer the door or telephone. Now scoot."

"But, sir, I'm not hovering. Mystere said I could have a reading lesson this morn—"

"Glad you reminded me," Rillieux cut him off, aiming a disapproving glance across the parlor toward Mystere. "I want this reading-lesson foolishness to stop."

She stopped her coffee cup halfway to her lips and set it back in its scallop-rimmed saucer. "Why, Paul, that's unfair. You yourself said the boy should know how to read."

"Well, I was wrong. He'll simply get foolish ideas. Look what rubbish these radical pamphlets have stuffed into Baylis's and Evan's ignorant heads. *Scoot,* I said," he repeated, and Hush did.

"Really, Paul, he's not a dog," Mystere rebuked him.

"Oh, *bother* your do-good claptrap. He was a filthy street urchin before I gave him a home. I'm tired of your damned complaints."

"I don't understand why you're in such a foul mood. I got Sylvia's brooch for you, didn't I?"

The same brooch, she hadn't the courage to add, *which went into your private safe, not the family kitty.* She had managed to snatch it at the Astor residence, after the opera, waiting until Rafe had gone and striking during the hectic flurry of good-byes. The theft hadn't even made the morning papers, so most likely Sylvia hadn't noticed until she had arrived home, if then.

"My mood has nothing to do with that," he replied. "Don't you realize that you and Belloch nearly spoiled the opera for us. After all my hard work to penetrate Mrs. Astor's inner circle. You two were worse than schoolchildren, and Caroline was quite miffed at me on account of you."

"Paul, you're missing the important point. Caroline's anger isn't the real issue. I told you last night, Rafe Belloch is about to expose us. He told me he's written to New Orleans about us."

"I say that's all bluff. Why would he *tell* you anything about it before he'd received some kind of reply?"

"That's the kind of man he is—arrogant and cocksure."

Paul snorted. "Yes, I forgot you've had so much experience with men. But let's assume, for sake of argument, that he has, indeed, made some inquiry. You're telling me that your response is to avoid him from now on?"

"Yes, of course, he—"

"They always talk who never think. Use your head, you naive little fool. If you have a sliver in your finger, do you cut your arm off at the elbow?"

"That's a clever question, but I don't see how it's relevant."

He sighed impatiently. "Look, clearly the man is infatuated with you, burning to debauch you. If he *is* snooping into our past, then you had better be prepared to . . . appease him if trouble comes. You have the one thing that Rafe Belloch, with all his money, doesn't own and dearly desires."

Paul's bluntness was coarse, but she had to admit his logic made some sense. But could she "appease" Rafe in the sense Paul meant? She wasn't convinced that Belloch could be so easily controlled. Nor convinced she could be that debased.

He seemed to pluck that last thought from her mind. "Needs must when the devil drives," he assured her. "I'm only warning you what might be required assuming your fears are justified. Even if Belloch isn't bluffing, don't forget that I was careful to establish the legitimate existence of Paul Rillieux in New Orleans."

"Yes, but there's no record you had a niece there, no record of Mystere Rillieux."

"That's problematic," he conceded, his tone conveying the bored arrogance he had picked up from Mrs. Astor. "But only if a more in-depth investigation is pursued."

His voice seemed to hammer at her brain. Earlier Hush had gone out for the morning papers. Now Paul crossed the parlor toward her, holding out the *Herald*. She smelled the cloying stench of his lilac cologne.

"Read Lance Streeter's column," he told her, his tone less harsh.

"I did." A warm flush crept into her face as she remembered the opening sentence: *Every private box in the Astor House was crowded last night except that of a certain wealthy mover of mountains.*

"Well then," he admonished her, "use your head. Rafe Belloch is a powerful, important man. Yet look how willingly he lets himself be-come embroiled in juicy gossip so long as you're involved. That's not the behavior of a man engaged in a woman's destruction."

"You mustn't be so sure. He's not like other men."

"Of course not, he's wealthier than most."

"No," she protested, "I mean . . ."

But perforce she fell silent, at a loss for the right words to convince him a trap was closing around them. She would never make Paul un-derstand because *she* didn't understand. Never in her life had any other man evoked this strange response of fear and desire all at once.

Out in the hallway the telephone shrilled. She heard Hush answer it. A moment later he thrust his head into the parlor. "Telephone for you, Mystere."

"Thank you. Who is it?"

"I dunno. I asked but he wouldn't say."

Mystere recognized Lorenzo Perkins's voice the moment he said hello.

"What is it, Mr. Perkins?" she asked with cold precision. "Our business arrangement has been terminated."

"Not yet. I'm calling to let you know that five hundred dollars will buy my permanent silence."

"Silence about what, Mr. Perkins?"

"I'm thinking Rafe Belloch might be quite interested to learn that his fancy lady has been searching for a brother whose name she don't even know. A brother that was once shanghaied like a common mutt."

"Just as I'm sure your wife, Mr. Perkins, will be quite interested to learn about your visits to 17 Washington Street."

With that she hung the earpiece back in its cradle, heart hammering from this latest threat.

The noose was tightening, and no matter which way she turned disaster loomed just over the horizon. Worse, Paul was so taken with his newfound popularity that he felt falsely secure—dangerously underestimating Rafe and his intentions.

Five hundred dollars . . . a staggering sum even if she agreed to pay it. But she wouldn't.

What about bub 'n' sis?

Tears stung her eyes, and she tried desperately to renew the resolve, the confidence she had felt during that cab ride to Brooklyn a few days ago. She *would* become her own woman and use her new freedom to find Bram. Without him she was truly alone in the world, bereft of any real family.

But time was a bird, and the bird was on the wing. With a new sense of urgency she again resolved to steal Antonia Butler's emerald ring and, eventually, flee to another city, assume yet another identity. The main difficulty would be holding the ring back from Paul. She would have to fabricate a very clever plan.

Hush, watching her from the opposite end of the long central hallway, called out, "You okay, Mystere?"

Somehow she mustered a smile. "I'm fine," she lied.

She beckoned the lad closer with her finger. Lowering her voice so Paul wouldn't hear from the parlor, she added, "Later, bring your primer up to my quarters and we'll have that reading lesson."

Chapter 16

Mystere remained upstairs in her quarters on Tuesday morning, preparing for the impending disaster that Paul stubbornly denied was about to engulf them. With both Rafe Belloch and Lorenzo Perkins each mounting threats, she wanted to be prepared with an emergency escape plan in case of sudden crisis.

She readied a trunk, filling it with clothing and essential personal belongings such as the mysterious letter written long ago to her dying father. Leaving the city was not in her immediate plans because the search for Bram was still centered there. But there were some respectable ladies' boardinghouses on Centre Street. She could don widow's weeds again, and take a room under an alias. It wouldn't protect her indefinitely, but she might buy some time that way.

Her fall-back plan was far from perfect, but she tried to school herself in the belief that it would protect her. It wasn't just shame, social ruin, and prison she faced—exposure and capture meant the end of all, even the end of her dream to locate her brother.

She was just closing the leather trunk when Rose poked her head into the room.

"Telephone, Mystere. It's Mrs. Astor."

"Thank you. Oh, Rose?" she called just before the redhead shut the door.

Her mobcap-framed visage came poking back around the jamb. "Yes?"

Mystere hesitated, unsure what to say. She wanted to warn Rose and the other "servants" that trouble might be looming—serious trouble. But it would get back to Paul, and he would be livid.

"It'll keep," Mystere told her reluctantly.

On her way downstairs to the telephone she felt a little stirring of apprehension. While phone calls from the great lady were not exactly rare, she was still in Caroline's bad book over the disturbance at the opera on Saturday.

"Hello," she said in a loud voice.

"Good morning, dear," Mrs. Astor's distorted voice greeted her, rendered metallic and high-pitched by the phone mechanism. "Have you plans for later this morning?"

"I have none, but I believe Uncle Paul has an appointment with his dentist."

"Never mind Paul, it's you we wish to see."

Again Mystere felt an inner stirring of unease. "We? You and Carrie?"

"No, Carrie's taken the steamer up to West Point to visit her cousin Andrew. I mean Abbot and I, sweet love. We'd like you to accompany us to a lecture on Fourth Avenue. Afterward we'll all lunch at Delmonico's."

"I'm flattered you thought of me," Mystere assured her.

"Yes," Mrs. Astor replied, accepting that as her due. "But you might not like what we have to say."

It was Caroline's way to be brusque and cryptic. Nonetheless, her remark sent fear pulsing through Mystere's limbs. Had the trouble begun already?

"We'll go in my landau," Caroline added. "It's a gorgeous day to ride with the top down. We'll be by at half past ten."

Paul had come downstairs during the call. He watched Mystere suspiciously as she hung up the earpiece. "Who was that?"

"Mrs. Astor."

"And she didn't ask for me?"

"She wanted me. She and Abbot are taking me to a lecture and then lunch."

"You alone? She doesn't want me along?"

Mystere shook her head, wondering if Paul was going to act like a jealous child. Instead, he unexpectedly smiled at the news. "Well, well. This is quite interesting. You are a charming young woman, Mystere, but Caroline isn't seeking out your youth or your charm. She has an ulterior motive for everything she does."

"Such as . . . ?"

"Rafe Belloch."

"Do you mean—she's still angry about last Satur—"

He silenced her with an impatient wave of his hand. "No, you goose. She's not your governess. I suspect she has matchmaking on her mind."

"That's preposterous," she told him sincerely. "And even if Caroline did have such intentions, it wouldn't matter. Rafe Belloch does not have matrimony in his plans. Caroline ought to know that better than anyone."

"Rafe clearly has *you* in his plans, my dear."

"Yes, but not for the reasons everyone thinks."

"Please don't start with all your alarmist theories again. Belloch may or may not be in love with you. But he *is* burning with lust for you, your modesty notwithstanding. Considering his fortune, lust is enough to build your hopes on. Caroline knows this and is doing you a great favor."

"Favor? Caroline? But you just said she always has an ulterior motive."

"Of course," Paul agreed. "And that motive is to protect Carrie from Rafe. I think she sees now that Belloch is the kind of man who's a fine catch—for someone *else's* daughter. Caroline finds Rafe intriguing and attractive, but the mother in her also recognizes the man is dangerous."

She shook her head. "If matchmaking were on her mind, why would she warn me I might not like what she has to say?"

Paul started to reply. Just then, however, the front door opened, and Baylis and Evan entered the house, embroiled in an altercation.

"Teach your grandmother to suck eggs!" Baylis fumed. "I don't need you to tell me how to hitch a team!"

"Ease off, dunghill, or I swear I'll—"

"*Both* of you shut up," Paul snapped. "I won't have you carrying on inside the house like this! Mrs. Astor will be here shortly, mind your-selves. Evan, brush your jacket off; it's filthy with lint. You, Hush!"

The lad sat dutifully in a ladder-back chair near the front door. Now he leaped to his feet. "Yessir!"

"Get rid of that confounded pipe. Smoke in your room, not in front of guests. Look sharp when Mrs. Astor arrives."

"Yessir!"

"I'll go change," Mystere said, turning toward the spiral staircase.

Paul detained her with a hand on her arm. "You saw the invitation that arrived yesterday?"

She nodded. James and Lizet Addison were hosting a ball this coming weekend, and the guests of honor included the Duke and Duchess of Granville.

"Pretty sparklers galore," he gloated. "The ladies will wear their best jewels. You may even have a chance at Antonia's prize emerald. She often takes it off, I noticed, and carries it in a little beaded retic-ule."

"Yes," she agreed, taking care to meet his gaze frankly. She had Antonia's ring on her mind, all right, but that was one sparkler she had no plans to turn over to Paul.

But his perception, at times, was daunting. She wondered if a sub-tle clue in her face made him remind her, "I'm a mild man until pushed. No one in this family holds out on the others, understood?"

Then what about the private safe in your room? she wanted to shout at him. Instead, she only nodded obediently.

"Of course," she assured him. "Have I ever held out before?"

"Probably not," he conceded. "You're a good girl. But you're also highly notional, and I fear your impulses. Especially concerning your brother Bram."

"You've nothing to worry about."

"I hope not, sweet love, for your sake." His steady, menacing gaze sent a cool feather tickling down her spine. "Disloyalty to the family is one sin I cannot forgive."

"Careful of the dashboard, miss," Mrs. Astor's driver warned Mystere as he handed her up into the four-passenger landau. "I forgot to men-tion earlier that it's freshly blacked and may rub off."

"Why in God's name," Abbot carped, taking his spot in the seat facing Caroline and Mystere, "should any man bake his own bread and then write a poem about his pure digestion? That's just twaddle."

"I rather enjoyed Mrs. Hanchon's perspective," Caroline disputed. "She's been a Methodist missionary to the poor for nearly thirty years; she understands their mindset."

Mystere, too, had enjoyed the lecture on "Creating Self-reliance Among the Working Classes." However, Mrs. Hanchon had spoken about a worker's commune in New Hampshire. And it didn't take much to spring Abbot's hair-trigger contempt for "that sweet-lavender crowd who flock to utopias like flies to a molasses barrel."

"Abbot, you're incorrigible," Caroline admonished absently, her attention fixed on Mystere. "As Mrs. Hanchon advised—despise poverty, not the poor."

Was that a subtle innuendo? Mystere fretted. *Is she on to me?*

"My dear," Abbot told Caroline, "the rabble need to be kept down, not stirred up." This pronouncement was delivered while they passed Vanderbilt's Grand Central Depot at Forty-second Street and Fourth Avenue. Across the depot clock tower ran gigantic letters spelling out NEW YORK & HARLEM R.R. As the landau eased away from the curb, Abbot cast a sneering glance at the four-block-long depot building. His ire at the Four Hundred's acceptance of the *nouveau riche* Vanderbilt clan was legendary.

"What do *you* think, my dear?" Caroline turned to Mystere. "Can the poor be morally uplifted? Or are they simply depraved as Abbot insists?"

Again, in her apprehensive mood, Mystere feared that Caroline was somehow toying with her.

"I know of no evidence," she replied, "that moral depravity is the exclusive domain of the poor."

Mrs. Astor nodded. "Well put. Look at our own Lady Moonlight. All evidence suggests she is one of our own."

Mystere's heart suddenly began racing; her throat felt constricted. *They* are *on to me*, she despaired, trying to keep her fear out of her expression. It took great effort for her to meet Mrs. Astor's gaze. Yesterday's papers had created a great stirring and to-do over Sylvia Rohr's stolen brooch.

"Yes," she agreed. "Lady Moonlight is a good example that hits close to home."

"You're both pouring kerosene on a burning building," Abbot insisted. "Give the hoi polloi an inch and they'll seize an ell. Look what these filthy malcontents in the Fourth Ward are howling for now—a land tax on the rich to subsidize public transportation for the masses. It's gotten so that we can't even escape them anymore."

Even as Abbot launched his tirade, however, Mystere could see scores of slat-ribbed children on the sidewalks gaping at their landau. They stared with the vacant, glazed stare of hunger and chronic illness. She herself had once been one of them, and her heart ached to help them. But she would never be able to do them any good if she found herself returned to that abject hopelessness or in prison.

As they passed the massive arch at Washington Square she again thought of Rafe Belloch. All that power at his disposal, massed against only her ingenuity and quick wits. The prospects for her survival seemed daunting, indeed. Especially right now, with Mrs. Astor keeping her in suspense—she couldn't think what the powerful matron was going to tell her.

Delmonico's was located in the Ladies' Mile, towering department stores surrounding it like steep canyon walls. The maitre d' made a noisy fuss over Mrs. Astor and her party, escorting them to a roomy table covered with an ivory-lace cloth, aglitter with long-stemmed glasses and brilliant silver.

Mystere, her stomach nervously churning, ordered only artichoke salad and a bisque. After their waiter had departed with their order, bowing obsequiously to Mrs. Astor, the grand dame fixed her steely eyes on Mystere.

Here it comes, she thought, her heart in her throat.

"My dear," Mrs. Astor began with regal formality, "you are young and lack the advice of a knowledgeable female who has your best interests at heart. Your Uncle Paul is a dear, dear man who obviously loves you as a daughter. But he is *only* a man"—here her eyes cut to Abbot, a disparaging glance—"and he is incapable of understanding the finer points of, ahh, feminine decorum."

A great weight suddenly lifted from Mystere. She wasn't sure yet where this lecture was going. Clearly, however, it wasn't the crisis she had feared was coming.

"You must never forget," Caroline resumed, "how easily the word 'scandal' can attach itself to a woman. The very same actions which only increase a *man's* social standing can plunge a woman into ruin. Do you take my meaning?"

Mystere said, "I think so. You mean Rafe Belloch."

Caroline nodded. "The days of public respect for the wealthy are behind us, dear. There was a time when our private lives were never discussed. But John Gordon Bennett and his damnable *Herald* have changed all that. He has placed paid informants among our servants, even put his reporters in disguises to infiltrate our private gatherings."

"Thanks to that scoundrel," Abbot chimed in, "hounding the rich has become a veritable sport."

"And now that Lance Streeter has got hold of this . . . evident intrigue between you and Rafe," Caroline pressed on, "you *must* be cautious, dear. I admire Rafe greatly and recognize his appeal to our sex. But I fear he is a reckless bounder who flouts convention."

"You're gilding the lily," Abbot scoffed. "The man is base and utterly without honor."

"That's too harsh," Caroline objected. "He is an honorable man, but follows his own code of honor, not ours."

Abbot snorted. "By that reasoning, every convict on Blackwell's Island is honorable."

They fell silent as the waiter arrived and served their lunch on French Limoges porcelain, each piece with pale blue and floral borders. Every time the swinging doors of the kitchen burst open, Mystere glimpsed the restaurant's famous roasting range of brick and mortar with its beautiful copper canopy to channel smoke and smells into a flue in the chimney.

"At any rate," Mrs. Astor continued when they were alone again, "you must be more assertive with Rafe, my dear. Make it clear that *you* value your virtue even if he does not."

Before she could think of a reply, Abbot suddenly muttered, "Oh, *this* is delicious."

His ironic tone made it clear he wasn't praising his lunch. Mystere and Mrs. Astor followed his gaze, and suddenly Mystere felt herself flushing: Rafe Belloch had just been escorted into the dining room, Antonia Butler on his arm.

It took Mystere by surprise when she realized her first reaction was not fear, but jealousy. Nor did Caroline seem very pleased at the sight of Antonia gazing up at Rafe in clear admiration, laughing at something he had just said, flashing her excess of enamel in an otherwise beautiful face.

However, Mystere had no time to wonder at Caroline's puzzling response. Rafe had spotted them, and he and Antonia were aiming straight for their table.

"Sorry, old sock," Abbot greeted him, contempt clear in his tone. "Our table's too small to accommodate two more."

Caroline scowled at Abbot's boorish rudeness.

Abbot flushed, swallowing so hard his Adam's apple jumped visibly.

"Really, Abbot," Caroline objected, "you do exaggerate."

"Nonetheless, we can't join you. I've a room upstairs," Rafe bit out methodically.

Caroline Astor stared at Antonia. Everyone knew what the private rooms upstairs at Delmonico's were for. Very little of the culinary delights were appreciated once the doors closed.

Antonia, to cover her nervous fluster, began making small talk with Caroline while Abbot scowled at his plate. Mystere found Rafe's intense teal gaze upon her.

He stepped behind Mystere's chair and brought his lips close to her left ear.

"Lady Moonlight," he whispered.

Before he straightened up again, the hot, moist tip of his tongue briefly tickled her ear. The touch should have disgusted and enraged her; instead, a hot wave of response passed through her.

He bade Caroline good day, then took Antonia's arm again and steered her off to the staircase.

"Antonia and Rafe," Abbot said speculatively. "Well, perhaps the gossip columnists will leave you alone now, Mystere."

"I shouldn't read too much into what you're seeing," Caroline cautioned him. "Rafe Belloch is a complex man with a purpose, and the surface events do not reflect what he is really after."

The matron's eyes rested on Mystere as she added, "And one thing he's after, I'm beginning to suspect, is deliberate public scandal."

By now Mystere could trust her voice again. "But, Mrs. Astor, why would he do something so reckless and pointless?"

"Reckless, yes, for that's in his nature. His father had it, too, and it ruined him. But pointless? Perhaps not, to him."

Mystere wanted to ask what she meant about his father's ruining himself. But Abbot spoke up first.

"Belloch wants everyone to see him as the tortured idealist," he said in a voice sharp with scorn. "An idealist with a grudge to avenge."

Mystere turned immediately to Abbot. "What grudge?"

"Never mind, it's ancient history now," Caroline said dismissively. "Young lady, I need a promise from you."

"Yes?"

"This weekend, at the Addison ball—will you promise to be more circumspect with Rafe?"

Mystere felt heat flooding into her face. "*I?* It's not I who force myself on him."

"Dear, men are aggressive by nature, particularly American men. It is the woman's job to curb that aggression. You are young and still learning—"

"Unlike Antonia," Abbot cut in, "who is young and well-versed, evidently. *Look* at her, the little wanton—assenting to go upstairs with the man. In public."

"Cut me off again, Abbot," Mrs. Astor rebuked him with cold authority, "and your credit will be worthless in this city."

Abbot turned fish-belly white.

Again Mystere felt an unwelcome sting of jealousy—and anger over the intimate liberties Rafe had taken. Now he was with a woman she absolutely detested.

Caroline turned to Mystere once more. "Promise me you'll nip this scandal in the bud, dear. I admire much about Rafe Belloch, but I will *not* stand idly by and let him ruin you, Mystere. Promise me you'll not let the Addison ball or yourself be ruined by scandal."

Even now, torn in several directions by conflicting emotions, Mystere felt the irony of Mrs. Astor's request. Caroline had evidently dismissed the threat of scandal from Lady Moonlight ruining the ball. Why was she so confident?

"Of course," she replied, meaning it sincerely. "I promise. I *will* avoid Rafe Belloch. And if he won't let me avoid him, I promise to discourage his advances in the strongest possible manner."

Chapter 17

On Friday morning Mystere finished packing her "escape trunk" as she had begun calling it. She was tucking fragrant sachets among the clothing when a knock sounded at the door of her dressing room.

"Just a moment," she called out, recognizing Paul's knock. "I'm still dressing."

Hurriedly she closed the leather trunk. With some effort she pushed it behind her dressing screen. She hurried to the connecting bedroom and shut the door behind her.

"Good morning," she greeted Paul, letting him in. "You're up early."

His dry lips brushed her cheek in a kiss. "So are you. What's this? Wearing that stodgy black dress again? Dear, we want you to look younger, not frumpy and bereaved."

"I like black," she lied. In fact she decided to wear widow's weeds again so she wouldn't be recognized when she went out to rent a room. The bonnet with its black lace veil was tucked into her wicker tote once more.

"To each her own," he said gallantly. But something in his tone and manner alerted her to trouble.

"What's the matter, Paul?"

"Now, now, calm yourself, my dear, it may be nothing at all. Here, let's sit down, shall we? My bones are older than yours."

They settled into a pair of upholstered mahogany chairs.

"You know," he began, "that I have a paid informant among the city roundsmen?"

She nodded, her stomach suddenly in a nervous flutter.

"Well, evidently," Paul resumed, "that special police team—the one set up to apprehend Lady Moonlight—is planning a trap to catch her."

"A trap? How? I mean, what kind of trap?"

He shook his head. "Evidently they're holding their cards close to their vest. But something is definitely afoot. This past week Inspector Byrnes has been paying visits to Mrs. Astor and others in her circle. I fear they mean to spring their trap tomorrow night at the Addison ball."

Although this was bad news, it wasn't the killing blow she had feared—such as a full report from New Orleans, exposing her and Paul for the imposters they were.

"Unfortunately," he resumed, "our informant is not high enough in the constabulary to be privy to much useful information. Clearly, however, something is in the wind. Regretfully, I think it's best if Lady Moonlight goes into retirement—at least temporarily."

Mystere had no response, at first, as the irony of this latest development struck home. Such a suggestion would have been welcome had she not decided to keep the next sparkler for her own needs. And she had planned to retire Lady Moonlight tomorrow night assuming she managed to steal Antonia's emerald ring or something else of high value.

"What . . . what about the lost income?" she asked him. "Can we afford to retire her?"

"Afford it? Of course not! You've seen our monthly accounts. Rent alone costs a small fortune. And now that Hush lives here with us, his duties have cost us the sparklers and extra cash he used to bring in."

"So . . . what will we do?"

Paul's sharp fox face revealed nothing of his inner thinking. "Do? Well, in the short run, I suppose we can send Evan and Baylis out more often. It's vacation time, and many wealthy homes are only lightly guarded."

"You saw what happened last time," she reminded him. "A maid nearly caught them red-handed."

"Yes, well, I suppose Rose and Hush, too, can return to pickpocketing on the streets. I hesitate to take that risk, since they might be recognized as our servants. But the alternative is even worse."

"That's only for the short run," she reminded, watching him closely. "What about the long run? Will we have to resume highway robberies?"

He shook his silver head. "Of course not. At least—you won't need to *if* you pursue other, far safer and more lucrative avenues, armed only with your considerable charms."

Suspicion formed in her stomach like a cold ball of ice. "Other avenues such as . . . ?"

"Such as marrying Rafe Belloch," he replied with blunt candor.

She wanted to laugh outright, this was so preposterous and thickheaded. Instead, she only shook her head in negation, urgent to convince him how wrong he was to think this way.

"Paul, I've told you all along that Rafe Belloch is *not* marriage-minded."

"But he—"

"Yes, yes, I know, he's shown great . . . interest in me. You call it lust, and perhaps that's in the mix. But lust alone will not compel a man like him to the altar."

"All right then, but scandal might compel him where lust leaves off."

Heat crept up her neck and into her face. "I would rather rob a man at gunpoint."

"Mystere, where money is involved there can be no hypocrisy, don't you see that? Do you think John Jacob Astor or Cornelius Vanderbilt acquired their fortunes through chivalry? Do you have any idea how many are killed in dangerous mines so that New York's upper-class women may sport gold and diamonds? And personally, I don't give a damn."

"Even if I could ensnare Rafe in scandal, even if I *wanted* to marry him, it wouldn't matter."

"And just why not?"

"For one thing, he is out to destroy me, not seduce me. Destroy us, Paul, you and me."

"If that's the case, why does he seek every opportunity to get his name paired with yours in the gossip rags? This isn't some foppish dandy in the theater world, where scandal only enhances one's reputation. Rafe is a solid man of empire! Why should he risk so much for mere ink in the penny papers?"

"I can't answer that, for I have no window into his soul—assuming he has one. But he is the very last man you should be trying to manipulate," she implored.

"He'll have to be the solution, Mystere."

Rillieux's ominous tone sent a prickle of alarm down her spine. She knew it well, always a prelude to trouble.

Early on Friday afternoon Mystere rented a small but reasonably clean room at 720 Centre Street, a neighborhood of shabby-genteel homes, most subdivided into apartments and rooms.

She used the name Lydia Powell, explaining that her husband had recently been killed in a steamboat explosion on the Hudson and she had sold their home in Brooklyn. The landlady seemed inclined, at first, to require letters of reference; however, a month's rent in advance, plus the young widow's wealthy appearance and manners, swayed her. She became even more genial when she learned that Mystere would not be taking meals with the other boarders, yet requested no discount.

With the key safely in her purse, and the boardinghouse a block behind her, she quickly removed the uncomfortable bonnet and veil and tucked them away. The day was warm and humid, and besides, she had no great fear of being recognized now.

But one unpleasant task remained. Paul had not been generous lately with her allowance, and she had just spent most of her ready cash to rent the room. So she had brought a few pieces of her own jewelry to be appraised. There was a reputable pawn broker in the heart of the commercial district; she knew of him through Paul. A legitimate jeweler, he discreetly bought some nice pieces from time to time.

It was the final irony. The Lady Moonlight pawning her very own jewels.

Trouble struck again on the morning of the Addison ball; only later, when it was too late to save herself, would Mystere realize the day's bad beginning was an omen she should have heeded. By now, however, sheer desperation and chronic worrying had skewed her judgment.

She had come downstairs early, for she meant to visit the Columbia College library in midtown Manhattan and spend a few hours doing some research on heraldry. She had recently read that they had a new collection of armorial insignias, and she hoped to track down the coat of arms, if that was what it was, that served as letterhead on that frustratingly incomplete letter to her father.

She could hear Hush's voice while she was still descending the staircase, rising in volume as if he were arguing with someone.

Another set-to with Evan or Baylis, she assumed at first, for neither of them liked the lad very much, considering him Paul's spoiled brat. She hurried her step, meaning to quiet them before they woke Paul. But as she reached the central hallway, she heard a loud, boisterous voice she did not recognize.

"You'll shut your gob, you insolent pup, or I'll give you more than the rough side of my tongue! I said go get Miss Rillieux, and, mister, I mean *now!*"

"I will not," Hush insisted, standing his ground. "Not till you state your business."

"Why, you little cur, I'll—"

"Stop that, sir!" Mystere exclaimed, hurrying toward the two of them. "Leave the boy alone."

Hush had leaned one shoulder against the front door, doing his best to prevent the forced entry of a rough, unsavory-looking man she had never seen before. He was almost as burly as Evan, swarthy, with shaggy muttonchop whiskers the color of wet sand.

"Well now," the roughian greeted her belligerently, "here's the great lady her ownself, I'd wager. Be you Mystere Rillieux?"

"I am. Do I know you, sir?" she demanded.

Hush spoke up first. "This is Sparky, Mys—I mean, ma'am. You know—that one fellow I already told you about?"

For a moment she drew a complete blank. Then she remembered. "Oh, yes. Lorenzo Perkins's friend."

"More in the way of a business partner, miss, than a friend," Sparky corrected her.

"What do you mean by forcing your way into our home?" she asked, although she knew he must be here with blackmail on his mind.

"Now, lookahere, let's come down off our high horse, missy." Sparky, half-in, half-out of the house now, took her in with a leering glance. Despite his size and evident strength, he had unhealthy skin like yellowed ivory.

The elegant luxury of the interior seemed to intimidate him somewhat, for he suddenly lost interest in hurling insults.

"Please state your business, sir," she told him, her voice firm but her knees feeling watery and weak with dread.

He slid a folded sheet of paper from the pocket of his frayed and stained work shirt, a cheap "reach-me-down" as the new ready-to-wear garments were often called.

"The thing of it is," he began, his voice brimming with swagger again, "I'm actually on my way to deliver this to a certain railroad toff known to both of us. Seems you two been mentioned in the rags quite a bit lately."

Without a word she moved up beside Hush to take the paper from Sparky. Then she moved off a few paces and unfolded the sheet. The note was printed in black ink, carelessly blotted, and although the spelling and grammar were almost sound, the tone was both childish and pompous at once.

> *Dear Mr. Belloch,*
>
> *I am a detective who happens to be in the way of knowing some inturesting facts about a certain young woman. Facts you might want to know. For instance, why is this woman searching for a brother whose name is different than her own? Why does she wear a disgise when she meets me in the park to pay me? And if she is so high-society, why would her brother be forced to sea as a commun sailor? If you desire more information, send a message to me at 21 Amos Street.*
>
> *Yrs. truly,*
> *L. Perkins*

While she read it, Hush moved back closer to her.

"Sparky and that other man," he reminded her in a low voice, "are looking to get rich in Little Italy—remember, the monkeys and street organs?"

She nodded, folding the sheet back up. She could tell, from the vague phrasing of the letter, that the two inept blackmailers actually knew very little about her—in fact, ironically, nothing she hadn't already disclosed voluntarily to Lorenzo. Unfortunately, given Rafe Belloch's obvious vendetta, the wealthy industrialist would pursue even a dubious lead to learn more about her.

"The five hunnert is to be paid in cash," Sparky stipulated. "You can pay me now or take it to Lorenzo at the Bethesda Fountain by five P.M. today. Elsewise this note gets delivered."

Obviously, Mystere lamented, her thoughts a confused riot, the threat to expose Lorenzo's adultery hadn't scared him. Although probably lying about ever being a detective, he was evidently smart enough to realize she would have to expose her own secrets to expose his crime—and that she had far more to lose than he did.

"This is just absurd," she told Sparky.

He snatched the note out of her hand. "A good joke, is it? Then, we'll share it with Belloch."

"I—that's a huge sum," she protested. "I don't have that kind of money."

"So you say." Sparky's fleshy face twisted into a smug smirk. "I know *b* from a bull's foot, missy."

He kept his head past the door far enough to take in the hallway's long Persian runner and the fancy marble letterstand behind the door. "Aww, come now, muffin. Why *look* how you live! This here's a reg'lar palace. We ask very little of you. The dog must be bad, indeed, that is not worth a bone."

"Five hundred dollars is hardly a bone," she retorted, panicked.

Hush didn't like any of this one bit, and he started to speak up. But Mystere silenced him with a hand on his shoulder. She had decided on a stalling tactic. If only she could hold them until she had Antonia's ring, then she could escape all these threats that were about to overwhelm her.

"I cannot possibly pay the total amount at once," she reiterated. "I'll send Hush to the fountain today with a payment."

"How much?" Sparky demanded.

"Fifty dollars."

"T'ain't near enough."

"You roll fish barrels all day long for *one* dollar," Hush jumped in, anger spiking his voice.

"Roll a cat's tail, you insolent pup," Sparky snapped.

"Fifty dollars," Mystere repeated. "With more to come."

"When?"

"Soon. As soon as I can raise more."

Sparky pretended to consider her offer. But she knew the prospect of fifty dollars had enticed him.

"Well—by five o'clock, then," he told her. "Cash money. And *no* parlor tricks, muffin, or we spill it all to Belloch."

"Spill *what?*" she challenged, staring straight into his bloodshot eyes.

"Hunh!" Her blunt demand called his bluff, and he promptly left. Even if the note was really all they had, however, she knew it could be plenty in the hands of Rafe Belloch, who could afford a bevy of detectives far more competent than Lorenzo.

She had managed to keep up a strong front until then. The moment Hush shut the door, however, she felt the full weight of her growing despair. Her legs suddenly began trembling.

"Mystere!" Hush exclaimed when she stumbled and almost fell, near the point of fainting. He took her arm and led her to an old-fashioned Sheraton chair near the telephone. "Can I get you something?"

The boy's face was pale with concern. She patted his cheek. "There's a decanter of brandy and some glasses in that corner cabinet in the parlor. Would you be a dear and pour me some? Just a little."

He nodded before hurrying into the parlor. How, she wondered glumly, had her life come to this sorry state of affairs? All she desired of this world seemed so straightforward: to find her brother, and to find out who they were. Without Bram she was all alone in the wretched world, and without a surname she was deprived of any family history, left without any blood connection to the world around her.

But the forces arrayed to prevent her quest were more complex—brutally so, as this ruffian's visit just now had proved.

"Here you go, Mystere."

A solicitous Hush returned with brandy in a balloon glass. The stricken look on his face touched her heart. She set the glass on a stand beside her and gave him a big hug.

"I want you to remember what we've talked about," she told him. "A lad with a sound education can land an honest trade. One that makes him proud. You're a bright boy with a wonderful heart."

"What was in that letter he showed you?"

"Never mind that. Do you promise to keep up your education no matter what?"

He nodded.

"And promise me this. If . . . trouble comes to all of us, trouble with the police—I want you to tell the proper authorities the truth about how Paul gave you lessons in stealing."

"Trouble?" he repeated. "Is something gonna happen to us, Mystere?"

"Maybe, but whatever happens you just be truthful and respectful with the authorities, and you'll be all right. Promise me?"

Reluctantly he nodded. "What about you? Will *you* be all right?"

"I hope so," she replied honestly. "Do you know where the big fountain is in the park?"

"The angel?"

"Yes."

He nodded.

"Later today I'll give you some money to take to Mr. Perkins, the man with the waxed mustache. The man you followed."

There went her research time, she thought despondently. Instead, she would now have to visit that pawn shop on Broadway and sell her favorite gold drop earrings set with large black pearls. They had already been appraised at fifty dollars.

"Them two got no right to treat you like this," Hush declared angrily.

"Never mind," she told him gently. "We'll be all right, both of us."

But her mind's eye saw Rafe Belloch's cruel, handsome face accusing her, and even the warming glow of the brandy could not quell the cold fear within her.

Chapter 18

Retired State Supreme Court Justice James Addison and his wife, Lizet, spent each winter at their villa in Mexico City, returning to Manhattan and their upper Sixth Avenue estate by late April. Their annual summer ball had evolved into a great favorite among Mrs. Astor's elect, in part because it had become de rigeur that visiting foreign dignitaries attend. New Yorkers, labeled money-grubbing boors in the haute circles of Paris and London, were anxious to show their cosmopolitan side.

Mystere welcomed all the stirring and to-do, for it drew press and public attention to something besides Lady Moonlight or Lance Streeter's gossip. Especially tonight, for the Duke and Duchess of Granville were in attendance—which added old money and ancient title to the mix.

Soon after Paul and Mystere arrived, they were briefly presented to the duke and duchess. The duke brimmed with irrepressible youth and energy while his attractive young wife's charm was more sedate but no less genuine. Mara Sheridan was a black-haired Irish-American beauty who may have shared her older brother Trevor's good looks, but she showed no sign of his notorious quick temper or his condemning glances.

Both seemed quite taken with Mystere, the duchess twice complimenting her sleeveless dress of creme de menthe silk. But Paul surprised Mystere by suddenly acting almost shy, taking her hand and pulling her away before she had finished speaking to the duchess.

"Mustn't dawdle, dear, there's a line behind us yet," he muttered.

"But, Paul! She asked me a question, and you jerked me away in midsentence. You were rude, and I saw it in her face."

"Oh, never mind her, I've something more important to show you."

As Paul and Mystere left the reception line, a footman escorting them into the gallery ballroom, Paul leaned closer to speak in her ear.

"Don't stare, but there's Inspector Byrnes over by the orchestra. There's a rumor that several of the 'servants' here tonight are actually his men. And notice all the pretty sparklers on display this evening. Some kind of trap has been laid, all right. Desperate though we are, better resist temptation this evening, my dear."

"Believe me, I will," she promised, and at that moment she almost meant it. But a quick glance around verified two reassuring facts: Rafe was not present and Antonia was—her emerald ring conspicuous.

Soon, however, Mystere's anxiety and wrought-up emotions gave a sinister meaning to every circumstance, even those that seemed favorable. Rafe's absence, for example. Had he finally heard something from New Orleans? If so, his absence might well be part of the trap Paul mentioned. Intentionally designed to make her bold. And that could mean the police already had her in mind as a suspect.

However, she had to balance the very real danger against her increasingly desperate plight. Paul's notion that Rafe could somehow be their financial salvation was absurd. Her only real alternatives were stark: either take Antonia's ring, or passively await exposure, capture, humiliation, and imprisonment.

She circulated among the glittering throng, trying to remain part of the background. Twice she danced, a waltz with lawyer George Templeton Strong, a longer quadrille with a stiff young naval cadet who flushed beet red when she coolly rejected his attempts at flirting. The last thing she wanted was a man on her elbow all evening.

Alone again, Mystere visited the cocktail bar and requested a glass of lemonade. Abbot Pollard, working on his third or fourth gin-rickey judging from his unsteady gait, suddenly appeared at her side.

"I spotted Lance Streeter among the throng of newspapermen outside," he greeted her. "Looks like you mean to disappoint him tonight, eh? Congratulations."

"Whatever for?"

"Why, on your ability to avoid that vulgar lout Rafe Belloch. Just as Caroline and I advised you. Good girl."

"Avoid him? That's not very difficult since he didn't come this evening."

Abbot gave a little snort. "No? Then that must be his twin brother dancing with Carrie right now."

Utterly confused, she followed the direction of Abbot's gaze. Suddenly, among the swirl of dancers, she spotted Rafe and Carrie.

Immediately alarm bells went off within her. It wasn't like her to not notice something like an arrival. Particularly when it involved a man who was fast becoming her nemesis. She was slipping. It wouldn't do for her to fall apart on this, her last night. Again she worried that it was all part of some clever trap.

"Did he just this moment arrive?" she asked Abbot.

"I couldn't tell you, love, nor could I care less. Just keep up the good work. Belloch's money be damned, the man should be selling mulberries on Apple Street. Oops, mixed my fruits."

However, as the night progressed, Mystere realized her promise to Mrs. Astor was moot, for it was Rafe who was doing the avoiding. All except for his probing eyes, which seemed to follow her relentlessly.

He had evidently attached himself to Carrie, dancing with her repeatedly despite the angry, accusing stares of Antonia Butler. Whatever mischief he was up to, Mrs. Astor clearly meant to disrupt it. After Rafe and Carrie had danced yet again, Caroline interceded. She paired Rafe with the duchess, Carrie with the duke, and both visitors seemed well pleased with their escorts.

Paul managed to detach himself from Caroline's group long enough to get Mystere alone for a moment.

"You just *have* to upset the cart, is that it?" he accused her in a low, urgent tone.

"What are you talking about?"

"Belloch, you little fool. Can't you see he's flirting with Carrie to make you jealous? Go talk to him."

"I will *not* approach him. Besides—your overseer, Mrs. Astor, has ordered me to avoid him."

"Fine," he muttered with quiet anger. "Send us to the almshouse—or worse."

"It's not I who squanders our household money on spurious investments to impress the wealthy."

"It's necessary to our deception," he riposted venemously, adding, "You young fool."

"You *old* one."

Paul composed his face for the crowd, then abruptly left. Mystere found a dimly lighted corner where she could monitor everyone under the innocent guise of watching the dancers. She expected Rafe to escape the Duchess of Granville at any moment so he could torment Lady Moonlight anew.

But again he surprised her. Perhaps an hour and a half into the ball, she realized he had simply disappeared. In Rafe's case that was not really unusual, for he rarely stood on formalities when it came to departing a social function. However, Mrs. Astor, too, had clearly missed him, judging from the way she was scanning the entire gathering, her face puzzled.

Mystere didn't believe he had simply decided to quit tormenting her. Yet, if it was all part of a trap, she couldn't puzzle it out. With Rafe gone, no one seemed at all aware of her presence. It was reassuring to feel so anonymous.

Yet . . . wasn't it perhaps a bit *too* reassuring? she wondered. She could almost believe that the guests were watching her with caged eyes and slanted glances.

Nonsense, her mind commented. *Do you honestly think everyone present is conspiring to trap you? Perhaps even the duke and duchess are in on this grand scheme. Paul's right, you* are *a fool.*

In the midst of these conflicting thoughts, a neatly mustachioed face suddenly seemed to detach itself from the crowd and approach her.

"Are you all right, Miss Rillieux?" Inspector Byrnes inquired solicitously. "You look a bit pale."

For a moment her throat closed in fear. Then she realized: if she was the object of a police net, the lead detective would hardly approach her and comment like that, bringing attention to himself.

"I'm fine, Inspector. Thank you for asking, it's very kind of you. It's just a slight headache. I'll take a powder for it when I return home."

"Shall I bring you a spot of champagne? My wife often takes a glass against headaches; it seems to work well."

"Why yes, thank you, that might be just the tonic I need."

He went to fetch it, and she felt some of her old confidence returning like strength to a muscle. Again she told herself he would not approach her like this if she was under suspicion. He returned with her libation, and they made pleasant small talk for a few more minutes. Then, with the propriety required of a married gentleman talking to a single woman, he excused himself and left her alone again.

Thus bolstered, she turned her attention to Antonia and her dazzling ring. Mystere had found an excellent vantage point along the back wall of the gallery, obscured somewhat by an uncovered harp with gilt strings. Anyone watching her saw only the prosaic sight of a young woman idly plucking at the harp strings as she enjoyed the dancers.

In reality she was carefully studying the entire gathering while also following Antonia, who no longer served as the duke's escort.

Finally, the opportune moment seemed to arrive.

Antonia, perhaps miffed that Rafe had ignored her for Carrie, had been freely indulging in wine. Never one to play the wallflower, she was now flirting animatedly with the same young cadet Mystere had discouraged. His uniform, she surmised, might be lulling any policemen present into a false sense that Antonia's ring was safe for now—for certainly very few people even seemed to be eyeing her.

But opportunity alone was useless if Antonia decided to wear the ring all night long. Mystere was immensely talented, thanks to Rillieux's drilling, but even she could not remove a ring from a finger undetected—though she could sometimes remove a bracelet from a wrist. The ring, however, was heavy and uncomfortable, and in the past Antonia had always removed it at some point, sometimes several times in the course of an evening.

A few moments later she did just that, unconsciously slipping it off her finger and placing it in her small beaded handbag.

Mystere felt her heart pounding like fists on a drum. She had prepared for just this contingency, tucking a small pair of sewing scissors into her chatelaine before she left home.

As inconspicuously as possible, she began moving toward the engrossed couple even as her eyes ran quickly over the entire gallery, "judging the moment" as Paul called the final decision before a theft.

No one seemed aware of her. Apparently Caroline had convinced Paul to put on a little demonstration of "mentalism." Many who weren't dancing had congregated around him in a far corner, including a totally absorbed Inspector Byrnes.

Seize the moment, an inner voice urged her—the experienced voice of a master thief. Yet, even as she drew nearer to Antonia and the cadet, fears and doubts threatened to paralyze her will. Under the best of circumstances this would be a difficult theft. She would have to brush fairly close to Antonia and move with lightning speed, with absolutely no margin for clumsiness.

She was on the verge of changing her mind. But suddenly Bram's image filled her head, that golden-haired sailor she had cried out to years ago. Abruptly filled with new determination, she bore down on her target.

Now Rillieux's long years of excellent training took over. *Graceful and smooth, Mystere, like a ballerina executing a plié; swift and decisive like an eagle killing a hawk.*

She snapped open the clasp on her chatelaine so it would be ready. Timing her approach with great concentration, she waited until a moment when Antonia was absorbed in something she was telling the cadet. The beaded handbag was in her left hand, dangling behind the folds of her gown.

She made one deft, swift snip.

The ring was hers.

Girding herself for a sudden outcry that never came, Mystere made a straight but slow-paced beeline through the open side of the gallery. In mere moments she was on the side lawn of the Addison mansion, safe so far. Of course, her quick departure would be associated with the theft, but she meant to be in hiding by then.

Exposed to the wind, she realized the night had turned surprisingly chilly for late June. A sudden, whipping gust sent a knife edge of cold cutting into her exposed skin and made her wish she had brought a cloak. She saw a footman standing under a gaslight and called to him.

"Yes, ma'am?" he replied, trotting over to her.

"Please summon a cab for me. I don't feel well and I'm leaving early."

"Right away, miss."

He hurried out toward the avenue. Mystere knew she still faced plenty of difficulties with Rillieux. The cry would go up at any moment, as soon as Antonia missed her ring. But with a bit more luck, she could return for her escape trunk, pay the cabbie to carry it down for her, and be in her new room on Centre Street before she had to face Paul.

In the midst of these thoughts, a shadowy form suddenly emerged from the nearby shrubbery. She thought it might be another footman, but suddenly she was staring at a policeman, his pistol outstretched toward her as she stood holding her own purse—and the damning evidence of Antonia's cut one.

"So this is our notorious little thief. Let me take a good look at you under the gaslight so I can tell Inspector Byrnes who you are." He pulled out of the shadows as she drew back.

A rush of panic filled her. Her ears pounded with the sound of her own blood seeping from her cheeks. She had been caught. Her worst nightmare was now going to come true.

"Come along here," he said, giving her a menacing wave of the gun. "Give me your name so I can take you to the inspector."

She took an instinctive step backward.

"Here now, no trickery. I never shot a lady before, but there's always the first time for everyth—Hey!"

A wild passion to survive gripped her. Blinded her. Irrationally, she picked up her skirt and took off like a wild mare running from a fire. She ran in the direction of the front and the carriages. Perhaps in her staccato thoughts she meant to find a cab. Perhaps Hush would be there and help hide her. She didn't know. All she did know was that she ran as if the devil was at her heels, and amid the deafening noise of her own heartbeat, she barely heard the policeman's whistle; nor did she hear the outcry within the ballroom when one lone report came from the policeman's revolver.

She had heard of shot dogs running for miles to find their masters, then dropping dead at their masters' feet. The burn in her upper arm was probably not life threatening, but the pain was excruciating. Still she ran, even shot like a dog. Even stumbling under the weight of the heavy mint-colored satin of her gown, she ran.

Until a strong pair of arms reached her in the darkness and pulled her inside a waiting carriage.

Wounded, her pale mint gown drenched in a widening ripple of scarlet, she struggled against her captor. Viselike, callused hands held her down against the button-tufted seat. Then his words told her the game was lost.

"Caught you, Lady Moonlight," Rafe Belloch gloated.

Chapter 19

At the sound of Rafe's voice, Mystere's heart sank like a stone. "Let me go," she pleaded, making a futile effort to free herself from his grip. "Let me *go!*"

"I think not," he said drily, then knocked on the front wall of the carriage. They took off at a gallop.

He settled on the seat in front of her, eyeing her in the dim lantern light.

She scrambled to the door latch, but her ebbing strength couldn't get it released before he pushed her back on the seat once more.

"You're damned lucky a norther is blowing in from Canada," he told her. "The reporters have left. This little scene won't end up in the gossip rags. But of course, they'll have a bigger story, won't they?"

He waited for an answer, his silence taunting her.

She refused to even look at him.

A strong but gentle grip pulled back her hand from her wound. Tersely he examined it, then tied it with a handkerchief from his jacket pocket. "You're due for a pretty fine scar, Lady Moonlight, but I doubt you'll die. The bullet just grazed your arm."

He sat back on the opposite seat and studied her for several long, torturous moments. "So what did you steal?" he asked bluntly. "I'm guessing you somehow got hold of Antonia's emerald."

She said nothing. There was no point. So she balefully stared at him, one hand cluching her tied-up arm, the other Antonia's precious silk bag with the emerald.

His mouth twisted in a derisive smile. "You've really made a mess of things, Lady Moonlight, now, haven't you? I suspected you'd try something. I watched you all night. Imagine my surprise when I saw you outside with a gun being held on you. Now look at you. You're hurt and you're captured. Things couldn't get worse, could they?"

"Let me go," she demanded, summoning all her bravado.

"Let you go?" He abruptly stopped as if an idea occurred to him. "Tell you what, I'll give you the choice. Either come with me, to face God knows what, or we'll return to the ball and face *them*. Perhaps I'll announce that all ladies inventory their valuables. What say you? Make good your escape with me, or go with Inspector Byrnes and the fine gentleman who shot you?"

The monstrousness of his offer struck her full force. Her damning silence coaxed another laugh from him.

"Just as I thought."

She had begun to tremble, not from the chill or the pain in her arm, but rather from acute fear. There was nothing worse to face than the unknown, and with Rafe Belloch, there was no way to predict the outcome.

Studying her, he slowly took off his jacket and flung it over her shoulders.

"Now then," he said with smug satisfaction as he took hold of Antonia's bag, "hand me your prize."

Feeling utterly helpless and doomed, she watched him open the clasp of Antonia's purse and dump the contents into his lap. He opened one of the leather curtains, letting the lurid illumination from the gaslights on the street seep in.

There, nestled among a lace handkerchief and the small party favors that had been given to the women, lay the object of her desire: the astonishingly large emerald ring encircled by diamonds. Even in subdued lighting its translucent green glimmer was breathtaking.

"Well, look at that," Rafe muttered in an almost reverent hush.

He picked up the ring and studied it as if unable to comprehend a

gem so huge and skillfully cut. Each perfect facet was clearly delin-
eated.

His gaze lifted from the ring and bored into her. "So. Our little innocent has been a wayward all this time, just as I knew she was."

"If you were so sure of it, why do you now act so surprised?" she
replied coldly.

"It's not surprise," he assured her. "Just a certain amazement. It's
always impressive to see a theory become a fact. What were you planning to *do* with this stone? Purchase France?"

She opened her mouth to somehow defend herself, but suddenly
the remark got stuck in her throat as a shock wave slammed into her.
She couldn't believe what she was seeing.

A little cry escaped her throat. Her hand shot out.

"Oh, no you don't," Rafe taunted, pulling the emerald out of her
reach.

But she wasn't after the emerald. Instead, she snatched up one of
the party favors scattered from Antonia's purse—it was a silk-and-lace
fan dotted with gold sequins.

Mystere had not even glanced at the fan when she put her own
favor in her purse earlier that evening. But Antonia's had come partially open when it fell out into Rafe's lap. Now, unable to believe her
eyes, she stared at the strange motif that had plagued her since her arrival in America.

Printed on each side of the fan was the split image of half an eagle
and a man's arm holding up a dagger. The exact same motif that was
embossed on the top of the letter that alluded to a will which included her and Bram—the very reason they had been sent to New
York by their dying mother. Only this time another insignia was added
just under the arm: a stag wrapped by laurel leaves.

"What . . . ?" She had to pause and swallow, for her voice had nearly
deserted her. "What is this?" she demanded of him.

Rafe, eyes narrowed speculatively as he watched her, said solemnly,
"Don't think to pretend madness; it won't work. You're about as calculating as a pair of crows, and this jibberish won't sway me—"

"No," she gasped, still transfixed upon the fan, "you don't understand, I know this—"

"Back to the subject at hand, baggage," he growled, ruthlessly tossing the emerald in his hand. "Not only are you the Lady Moonlight,

but it *was* you who robbed me at Five Points. I want a confession. That's the first bill that's come due here."

A few moments ago she would have admitted it—and why not? Her plight seemed hopeless. But seeing the strange motif again, so unexpectedly, had filled her with new will to resist, to lie, to do *any*thing that might permit her to remain free to explore the unexpected revelation.

"I'm not the Lady Moonlight," she retorted. "I found Antonia's bag on the floor of the ballroom and went into the garden thinking she had gone there with the young soldier. Then the policeman frightened me by surprising me in the shadows, and when I turned to go back to the ballroom, he wounded me. So of course I ran. I was terrified."

His jaw dropped in astonishment at her brazen lies and accusations. "Oh, how could this be? You mean it's all been a terrible mistake?" he played along sarcastically.

"Yes," she whispered, weak from her still-bleeding wound. She distractedly opened the fan, and then studied it as if it were a sacred relic.

He stared at her, strange conflicting emotions riding across his hard face.

"What does this symbol mean?" she asked, her eyes earnest.

He leaned closer to study her face. "You aren't acting, are you? You really do want to know?"

"Please. Do you know what it means?"

He seemed somewhat nonplussed. "Look, you have more important problems than—"

"Please. Do you know?"

"The fans were given to the ladies by the Duchess of Granville, who as you surely know is visiting from London. That primary motif on the fan, I learned just this evening from Carrie, is from the shield of Connacht where the duchess has roots. The stag and laurels are from the Granville coat of arms. Why are you so taken with it?"

Instead of any sense of enlightenment, however, his reply left her feeling devastated and emotionally drained. Now she had been caught thieving, and the first time in all her years of trying to find answers to the riddle of her past, the answers stumped her more than ever.

She and Bram were from Dublin, a city on the opposite side of Ireland from the province of Connacht. And they surely had no indication, in the letter from New York, that they might find their relations connected to London and the British peerage. The Duke and Duchess of Granville were in no way linked to two orphans trained in thievery—she could have laughed at the very idea. Rafe's answers only seemed as useless as her questions.

"Why are you so taken with it?" he repeated impatiently.

"I'm not," she finally replied in a hopeless, defeated tone. She slumped in her seat, discouraged and in pain, resigning herself to a terrible fate at the hands of Rafe Belloch.

"Are you taking me to the police?" she asked him, her voice dead.

"Since you so loudly protest your innocence, would that be a problem?"

It would be, she thought. In truth, however, she worried more about Rillieux. He would kill her now that he knew she was working on her own. His wrath would be worse than anything the authorities might do. He might appear to be the kindly gentleman, but she knew for a fact the man had performed intense cruelties, especially to those who showed him disloyalty.

Belloch gave a harsh laugh. He held the ring up under her nose, forcing her to turn her head away like a child refusing its lunch.

"You professional thieves fight from instinct, don't you? Well, never mind the police, Lady Moonlight. I have no interest in letting an inept government settle my personal scores. Remember, it was me in that alley in Five Points. I've never forgotten it."

Alarm tightened her throat. "What do you plan on doing, then?"

"I have my own punishment in store for you. You are going to board my yacht in just a few minutes. Then I'm taking you to my house, where you will be subjected to the self-same humiliation *I* had to endure in the alley at Five Points."

Stunned, she nontheless managed to whisper, "What humiliation?"

"Still playing the innocent little cherub, eh? Well then, let me spell it out plain." His face turned hard, his words harsh. "I'm going to have that wound of yours treated. Then when you're good and well, I'll see you undress in front of me—stripped right on down to that lovely 'Creole' skin of yours. And then, if the whim takes me, I'll let you leave my house, but you'll leave with nothing more than I had on when you finally left me in the shadows."

Chapter 20

Traffic was almost nonexistent at the late hour, and Rafe's coachman let the horses out, their iron-shod hooves striking sparks on the cobblestones. Within minutes they had reached the silent, nearly deserted Battery. The night had turned chilly and gloomy, with a dank mist clinging to everything.

The day's last ferry to Staten Island had already docked until morning. But Rafe's steam yacht, the *Courageous Kate*, waited in a nearby slip, crew on standby and boilers at cruising pressure. A few other private yachts were moored nearby, including one belonging to the Astors.

Mystere, still numb with shock at Rafe's pronouncement of her punishment, was almost docile as he led her up the gangplank.

"A bit brisk tonight, eh, Skeels?" Rafe greeted a crewman waiting to secure the plank and cast off the mooring rope.

"Colder than a landlord's heart, sir. Your stove's been lit below-decks," Skeels replied, his eyes raking quickly over Mystere in the flickering glow of a kerosene running light.

Mystere still shivered despite the added warmth of Rafe's jacket. She took heart at the mention of a warm stove. But as if seizing that thought from her mind, Rafe replied, "Thanks, but I think we two will tough it out on deck."

More of his deliberate cruelty, she thought, *for he sees I'm chilled. So is he, but he'll gladly suffer if it means more misery for me.*

But even her irritation at him could not long quell a growing nausea caused by fear. She didn't know how she would ever survive the night.

The crew hoisted anchor, and the yacht hove to, her bow pointed southwest for the brief trip across the Upper Bay to Staten Island. Keeping one hand firmly on her arm, Rafe guided her to the gunnel and leaned against it, watching her as they cut through the water.

"You're making a terrible mistake," she told him in a small, helpless voice, her teeth actually chattering a little from the brisk northern gusts.

He patted his shirt pocket, which now contained Antonia's ring. "*You* sent out the first soldier in this war," he reminded her, "when you robbed me at Five Points."

"Damn you, I did *not* rob you!"

"The cursing is a nice touch. Very ladylike," he assured her.

A sickening misery filled her as if she were a glass under a tap. Desperately, she tried another tack. "Even if I were in fact Lady Moonlight," she reasoned, "that wouldn't mean I robbed you at Five Points, would it?"

"We both know it was you who robbed me. And soon we'll prove it. As for your Lady Moonlight persona—I harbor no great grudge toward her. In fact, I've actually enjoyed watching her—you—rattle the Four Hundred." He stared at her, studying her, a cloaked expression on his face. "I suppose that explains my obsession with catching you . . . with having you."

The yacht eased past Governors Island and steamed steadily closer to Staten Island, where a few solitary shore lights winked like fireflies. Mystere felt the engines thrumming through the soles of her shoes. A deep, defeated sadness gripped her. Again she felt her joyous surprise at seeing the insignia from the shield of Connacht—and then her bitter despair that the answer to her quest answered nothing at all. Perhaps if Rafe hadn't been holding her so tightly, she might have leaped over the gunnel and ended it all.

For a moment the moon emerged from a scud of dark clouds, illuminating the bay in silvery light, and she witnessed a sight off the port bow that only sharpened her sorrow. Every two weeks, under the cloak of night, the Charity Commission's boat made the trip to Hart

Island, a desolate spot in Long Island Sound where the city buried the poor in anonymous mass graves.

She glimpsed the boat now, loaded down with cheap coffins and steaming toward the mouth of the East River. Suddenly a chance remark Lorenzo Perkins had made about Bram echoed in her mind: *He may be buried in Potter's Field by now.*

She turned away from the sight, overcome.

"The death boat is a sad sight," Rafe remarked with a rare trace of sympathy in his voice.

"You don't know what it means to be poor and friendless," she bit out.

"I give as good as I get," he told her coldly. But then his voice changed. A strangely wistful note came to his words. "That night I kissed you in the gazebo—I was planning on giving more. I would have wanted to give you more had you—reciprocated."

She averted her face, refusing to even look at him. But that only egged him on to further torment. He took the hand off her arm and used it to cup her chin and force her to look at him.

"That's a full moon behind those clouds," he reminded her. "Widely known as a lunatic moon because of the widespread belief that the mind is affected by the phases of the moon—that the insane are literally 'moonstruck.' Tell me, Lady Moonlight, is that *your* defense? It might play well in court: 'The moon makes me do it, your honor, I just can't help it.'"

He laughed again, his eyes mocking her, and in that moment she was filled with a bottomless hatred for him.

"In court? I thought you weren't taking me to the authorities," she reminded him. "I thought this torment was a way of avoiding jail."

"If you continue on this wayward career, someone will see you go to jail. You thieving types are too clever by half and inevitably get caught. However, I plan to take this night and the next and the next to see that you reform."

She stared at him, sickened, speechless, and wondering if she had just made a bargain with the devil.

The *Courageous Kate* docked within easy walking distance of Rafe's house. From the shore of the island, the dark building hunkered atop its small rise in menacing profile, reminding Mystere of some ancient Rumanian castle in a gypsy folk tale. The moon appeared briefly from a cloud bank, and she also glimpsed a coachhouse nearby, grown over with wisteria.

During their brief walk Rafe remained silent, and the clouded moonlight did not reveal his face. Her instincts raged, in spite of her growing despair, to protest her innocence to the last. But it was quite possible, however, that he had finally heard something—perhaps from New Orleans—that explained his total confidence in her guilt. She had no doubt she would know his thoughts soon.

They drew up at a stately fieldstone gatehouse topped with cast-iron pillars.

"Jimmy!" Rafe called out, and a moment later somebody uncovered a lantern only a few feet away. Mystere shrank back, intimidated by the massive gatekeeper of big-boned Ulster stock who emerged from the gatehouse. She stared at the sidearm tucked into his belt.

"My male domestic staff are all armed, well-trained marksmen as am I. You're not the only one who hates me, Lady Moonlight," Rafe muttered as Jimmy unlocked the heavy gate and swung it open. "The pops and the Wobblies are also howling for my robber-baron hide."

She had no idea who the Wobblies were, but she had heard Abbot Pollard damning the pops—populists—plenty of times. Jimmy secured the gate behind them as Rafe, using merciless force now, literally dragged her up to the front entrance of the nearly dark house.

He tugged a bellpull beside the massive doors. Soon a woman in her middle years, dressed in crisp white linen, admitted them. Mystere took a quick glance behind her and saw a stately central hallway with an English oak tall-case clock. But the only light, barely adequate, came from a brass, six-candle chandelier.

"Gas is available out here now," Rafe explained, seeing her look of astonishment, "but I hate the smell of it and only use it in the study where I work. I'll wait for electricity."

He turned to the servant. "Good evening, Ruth. This is Miss Rillieux. She'll be visiting tonight."

"Ma'am." Ruth sent her employer a discreet, questioning glance. "Shall I ready up a room for her, sir?"

Rafe's lips parted in a wolf grin. "I think not. A *guest* deserves a room. But a criminal deserves a cell."

The woman was obviously startled at this news as if the last thing the young elegantly gowned woman seemed to be was criminal.

"She's had an accident, however," he added, removing his jacket from Mystere's shoulders. "Do you think one of your witch's unguents can cure it or should I send for a physician?"

The housekeeper Ruth studied the flesh wound after Rafe untied the handkerchief. Confidently, she said, "I can tend to it, sir. No need to call the butcher."

Rafe laughed. "I'll let you take over from here, then, Ruth," he added. "Is Sam still awake?"

"Reading in his quarters, sir. I just took him in some cocoa."

Ruth cast a last, dubious glance at Mystere, then disappeared somewhere in the dark interior of the big house. Rafe, holding Mystere's wrist so tightly it ached, led her to a narrow, descending stairwell off a smaller hall that evidently led to the kitchen.

"Let me show you your eventual quarters," he mocked in a proper and polite tone, as if he were an innkeeper and she a guest. He borrowed a four-branch candlestick from the stand beside the stairwell door.

Holding the light out before them, he led his reluctant captive downstairs into a damp, gloomy chamber she could only call a dungeon. The light cast shape-changing shadows on walls of cold gray stone. Cobwebs clung everywhere, and she shuddered at the clammy tickle when one brushed her cheek.

"Watch out for rats, too," he warned her, grinning when she actually drew closer to him and his circle of light.

He stopped in front of an iron door with a covered judas hole. He thumbed the cover back.

"Peek inside," he invited her cheerfully. "There's a grate near the ceiling that lets moonlight in. Won't that be cozy for a nocturnal predator such as yourself?"

"You would not dare lock me up," she protested, covering her fear with boldness. "You have no authority whatsoever to do so."

"Oh, it won't be necessary if you cooperate. Otherwise you'll spend the rest of the night down here—some house-arrest time, so to speak, to examine your conscience. But if you fail to cooperate, you'll remain here much longer, 'authority' be damned." He chuckled and motioned to the judas hole. "Go ahead, look inside."

She lowered one eye to the hole and glimpsed a bare stone cell with only a thin rug braided out of shoddy scraps covering part of the rammed-earth floor. The "bed" was a narrow wooden shelf jutting out from one wall.

"I suppose you can guess what the bucket in the corner is for," he remarked, and she shuddered, looking quickly away.

"This place held rebel espionage agents during the war," he explained. "Female spies, mostly, sent here for . . . special interrogations, you might say. Perhaps not unlike what you're about to experience."

"You cannot do this," she spat at him in contempt, although fear still made her knees tremble like rain-soaked kittens.

"No?" he beckoned, leading her back toward the narrow stairwell. "Then, convince me otherwise. I'd much rather see you in silk sheets than in this low and dangerous dungeon."

Her spine tingled at the reference. "And what of mercy, Mr. Belloch?"

"I haven't informed the police about you, have I? Nor the press. That's mercy. Your . . . indiscretions remain our little secret."

"I see."

He grinned. "I'm not quite the mad lecher you think I am. Ah, here we are."

He flung open the oak-paneled doors of a magnificent drawing room with tall, narrow windows and woolen draperies. She glimpsed Jacobean-style carved furniture, carved rosewood bookcases lined with leather-bound volumes, and friezed walls displaying French watercolors from the early nineteenth century framed in gold scrollwork. A cozy fire crackled in a wide fireplace of Italian black marble. Its flames reflected in the polish of the floor and furniture, making them glow like rubescent embers.

"Cozy and warm," he remarked as he pulled her in, closing the doors behind them. "You'll feel better once Ruth has tended to your arm."

As if listening at the keyhole, the housekeeper appeared with bandages and a strong, volatile green ointment. After Mystere's arm was cleansed and dressed, Ruth poured her a warmed brandy. Mystere wanted to take it in two gulps but was afraid to do so might show her fear.

Ruth excused herself for the night. It was then that Mystere decided to begin her plea. Her voice had lost its proud formality. "So what exactly do you want from me? Is it a take of the loot you're after? Or is this just some game in which you want to be declared the winner?" She was completely honest now, her head swimming with fear, fatigue and warmed brandy. "If that's what you desire, know that I declare you the winner and let this Inquisition be over."

"*Inquisition*, is it?" He tossed back his head and mocked her with laughter. "No, Lady Moonlight, tonight I am not Rafe Belloch. Since you have accused me of being an inquisitor, tonight I am Tomás de Torquemada, First Inquisitor General."

He stepped behind a lift-top desk and raised the mahogany lid. She felt her blood run cold when he removed a sharp silver knife.

"As Inquisitor General," he announced, teal eyes pinning her to the spot, "I have learned that the cowl does not make the monk. So disrobe, my lady, and let me see how holy you are."

He crossed to where she stood, then moved around behind her. "I'm going to get you started. No need to hurt your arm all over again."

An involuntary shudder, very different than fear, moved through her as she felt his fingers unlooping the stays of her gown in back.

"From the outside it seems you don't wear—or need—a corset. But I think you are too modest in displaying your charms. Let's have a look, shall we?" He ran his warm, rough palm between the satin lacings and her bare skin. His fingers stopped at the linen bindings that held her bosom.

Deftly, he slipped the blade of the knife between the straining linen. She heard it rip like the tattering of a sail.

Her breasts bloomed forth, betraying her, spilling into the front of her innocent satin gown. She clutched her front with her one good hand, desperately trying to keep the gown up despite its unlacing.

He leaned down from behind, capturing her jaw with his hand and turning her head to look at him. The sudden glint in his dark eyes told her that any final doubts were now removed: he was sure he had nabbed his highwaywoman.

He was so close, she felt his breath like the devil's hot caress upon her temple. "So wicked, so deceiving. Confess now, my lady. Why do you do it?"

"I cannot tell you," she whispered, her eyes suddenly filling with helpless tears.

An unnamed expression crossed his face as he held her gaze. His mouth grew hard. "Does your 'dear' uncle make you do these things?"

She ripped her jaw from his grasp, the pain of her arm unmatched to the pain in her heart. "I will not tell you," she said coldly, convinced of Rillieux's wrath if she did.

His voice softened to a whisper. "A very thin line separates the madman from the hero."

"And which are you, sir?" Never one to weep, she shocked even herself at the unexpected tears that slipped silently down one cheek. She was at the cracking point.

He held up the knife to her eyes. It glistened in the orange fireglow. "Tonight I confess I'm not sure. I've never kidnapped a woman before. But then, I've met very few women who've managed to rob me—twice."

Straightening, he moved to the nearest windowsill and sat on it, watching her with the intensity of an unrequited lover.

"You may have the ring if you let me go. I can get you more, too, if you like," she offered, her face proud and defiant, her eyes dark with unspeakable sadness.

"It was you who robbed me at Five Points. Was that some kind of training for the bigger thievery?"

She took a deep, wretched breath and confessed, "It was shameless the way I behaved that night. I never dreamt I'd see you again."

With his uncanny insight he goaded, " 'I'll always be wondering, Mr. Belloch.' "

Warmth flooded into her face. "If the only way to appease you is to see me suffer the same humiliation, then so be it. If only you'll let me go afterward." She whisked away the moisture still clinging to her lashes. Defiantly, she stood, shrugged the mint satin gown off her shoulders and let it fall in a puddle around her feet. The bindings scattered across the costly carpet. Only a whisper-light pink silk chemise and lacy pantaloons covered her nakedness.

Rafe nodded. His next remark proved he had a merciless memory for details: " 'The preamble has been pleasing, indeed. Don't disappoint me now.' "

Again, she was slapped by her very words to him on that shameful night in the alley. She hated him, but he had only spoken the cruel truth when he said *I give as good as I get.*

Her shame and hesitancy was clear. She wanted to cover herself with her hands and run from the room. The sheer chemise left nothing to the imagination. Even she could see her chilled nipples through the pale pink silk. Her heavy breasts belied any claim of childish innocence. She was a woman in full.

"Any more denials?" he whispered, his gaze clouded by dark hunger as he looked at her chest.

"It was I who robbed you," she confessed, neither her face nor her tone remorseful.

"You beguiling little wretch," he said, his gaze finally holding her own. "Our flat-chested chit of a girl proves to be a buxom woman after all. So continue. I swear I'll not stop until I'm satisfied."

The ambiguity of his last sentence terrified her, but defiant anger burned in her veins like hot acid.

"You've had payment enough. Now go to hell, Rafe Belloch!" She turned from him and hid her chest with her crossed arms. "I am a thief, not a prostitute," she informed him with cold, determined precision. "If you want me naked, you'll have to shoot me first. Since you plan to rape me anyway, I'd prefer the bullet."

"You shameless hypocrite. All this 'noble virtue' now—where does it go when you rob and steal, when you live a lie about who you really are?"

Her small shoulders trembled from fear and exhaustion, but her face was a calm mask of strength. "I don't live a lie. I know what I am," she said, her insides raw from the honesty of it. "But it's you, the Four Hundred, who lie. You pretend there is no vulgar poverty, no starving children. I'm like so many others of my kind, a product of the famine in Ireland. At the tender age of eight I was left on the streets of New York to fend for myself. Rillieux saved me from death and prostitution. He is, at heart, an evil man, but I'll be indebted to him forever for his salvation. And believe it or not, Rafe Belloch, I pay back my debts."

At her remarkable confession, the hardness in his eyes seemed to soften. A muscle bunched in his jaw as if he was contemplating something distasteful. "I've told you before, my lady, that you and I are alike. I have no love lost for the Four Hundred, though I may be counted among them. They are nothing but the pampered purveyors of hypocrisy. And I scorn them above all others."

"And yet you look through me now as if I were a pane of dirty glass," she said softly.

His gaze flicked down at her near nudity. By his expression, he almost seemed to chastise himself. Gently, he asked, "Who are you, really? Is your name in fact Mystere Rillieux?"

"My name is Mystere, yes, but—but Rillieux is assumed."

"And the old man—he's no relation?"

She shook her head.

"So what *is* your last name?"

"I don't know. I've either never known, or have long since forgotten, my family name."

He shook his head as he stood up and crossed to his desk, putting the knife away. "You live up to the name Mystere." He turned to her. Almost begrudgingly, he tossed her a paisley cashmere lap blanket from a nearby chair. "Cover yourself, then, but bare more of your past."

She wrapped the lap blanket over her shoulders and clutched the ends to her chest. Slowly, she offered him her story, from her earliest memories in Dublin to the horrible years in the Jersey Street Orphanage, and on to losing Bram and her ignoble "rescue" at the hands of Paul Rillieux.

He asked constant questions, obviously looking for holes in her story. When she was through, he was silent for a very long time, just staring at her, studying her as if she were some kind of thing he had never laid eyes on before.

Slowly, he murmured, "You intrigued me from the first moment of your entry into society. The insignia in your letter—you may be placing too much store in it. But whoever wrote it could have been a domestic servant who purloined some of his employer's stationery—that's quite common. Also, printers often usurp armorial insignias without authority, for it is not illegal and makes their stationery more appealing to the masses. Remember, the Granvilles are an old, established family, and it is highly unlikely there would be any unknown claimants on their name."

His offhand remark crushed her hopes even more, for clearly he spoke with great authority and good sense. But she could hardly continue to stand, let alone gather her thoughts. The night's ordeal had taken a harsh toll on her—she was trembling visibly, and not from cold.

"Come closer to the fire," he murmured, taking her by the hand. He sat her upon an ornately carved Jacobean daybed that flanked one side of the hearth, then took the place next to her.

"You know you can't continue being Lady Moonlight," he said. "It's too dangerous."

She released a bitter laugh. "You sound almost as if you care."

"I don't want to care, but you keep making me do so."

She met his gaze. "I took Antonia's ring so that I might be free of Rillieux. If I now must escape you—"

"You need not escape." His eyes warmed.

She shook her head. "Rillieux will demand marriage." She stared at him steadfastly. "And so will I," she whispered.

He tossed his head back and laughed.

Anger shot through her veins. "Is it so ridiculous, then?"

He could hardly answer, he was laughing so.

She turned away from him. "You claim you hate the Four Hundred, but look at you; you're just as haughty as the rest of them. And why shouldn't you be? Though you spurn them—and perhaps with good reason—your upbringing was far superior to mine. Why, if you hadn't had the misfortune of your parents' deaths, you'd have no feeling whatsoever. You ought to be beaten soundly for not having turned out better considering all the privileges you've known."

"I have feeling," he said, his voice holding no mockery now.

She turned back to him, tears glistening in her eyes. "Then, show some."

"You want marriage—but what about love? Shouldn't that be a part of it?" he demanded.

"I've known little love in my life, but I believe I would recognize it. You're an arrogant beast, I admit." Her voice softened. "But there have been moments when I think I could love you."

He was deathly silent for several long moments. Finally he said, "You know, if this is some kind of new con, I have to say it's brilliant. It's almost working."

Disheartened, she shook her head, convinced she would never reach him.

"You need protection, Mystere. I would like to provide that."

"I can protect myself."

"Yes, your claws are sharp, but I daresay your heart is not." Slowly he lifted his hand to her chest and placed his palm over her fast-beating heart. "You talk of love, but I see very little of it in you."

"I can love," she vowed. "No one has taken that away from me."

"Then, show it," he whispered, his eyes holding hers.

She took a deep, wretched breath and gazed into the distance. It was against all her instincts to kiss him; it would only lead her down more treacherous paths. But suddenly the future looked so bleak, she wondered if she was a fool not to fall into his arms. Nothing awaited her but jail and loneliness. If she grabbed some happiness now, she would have some comfort in her memories. She knew he would never ask her to marry him; she knew also she could never be his mistress. But one night of love—it didn't seem so wrong with him near, and the fire warming them, and brandy inside her giving her courage. . . .

Her heart quickened. She turned her head toward him and met that infamous teal gaze. Slowly, she put out her hand and ran her soft palm down his beard-roughened cheek. She might have quit there had he not closed his eyes as if savoring the caress, had he not grabbed her hand and placed an achingly grateful kiss upon her sensitive palm.

Everything moved very quickly after that. It was as if they were dancing a waltz that she knew even without lessons. Her shift and pantaloons slid to the thick carpet with the paisley lap blanket. His lips hungrily took each of her breasts, licking them, nibbling at them until the warmth between her legs became a fire.

He stood over her and unbuttoned his shirt.

With an almost drugged gaze, she watched him, instinctively covering herself with her hands. His chest was magnificent, hard and ridged with muscle, lightly sprinkled with dark hair. She longed for it to cover her and take away the chill.

He slid off his trousers and underdrawers. As she already knew, his legs were long and well-formed. In full regalia, he returned to the daybed, pulling away her arms from her body, silently forbidding her to hide from his view.

"I don't want to hurt you," he whispered, taking her lips in a deep soul kiss.

"Then, don't," she answered simply as he slid between her legs.

He filled her mouth with his tongue and thrust inside her. If there was any pain, she lost the sensation in his kiss and the sweet, exquisite fullness of him. Gently, he sucked on the white skin of her neck and coaxed her into following his rhythm. He thrust harder and harder, his greed for her increasing until it seemed to swallow them both.

The sensation drifted through her like a wave. It swelled and swelled until finally it peaked and broke over her. She moaned with pleasure, tears of joy squeezing from her eyes and mixing with their kiss. His pounding body brought her to another spasm of pleasure, this one sharp and drawn out, until he groaned and she felt him pour inside of her, sated and spent.

Panting, he fell on top of her and held her, his warmth and hardness comfort against the cold rainy night. Sleep seemed to tug at both of them, but she knew she wouldn't sleep. Her mind raced with the fear of the pain that she knew was to come.

It came much too quickly.

He stood and gathered his trousers, pulling them on.

Naked and cold on the daybed, she fumbled for her chemise and pantaloons, wondering how she had succumbed so quickly. Spots of blood from her maidenhead dotted her pantaloons, evidence of her surrender.

Dressed, he looked down upon her, studying her, gauging her. Hesitantly, he began, "I suggest a truce of sorts between us."

She said nothing; she merely stared at him, holding her raging emotions in check like the lap blanket around her shoulders.

"I'll contemplate sending you back to your uncle. In the meantime I'm sure Rillieux can dodge the scandal of your disappearance, especially if there is no evidence it was you who was shot by the policeman. I'll do my part by squelching the story of Antonia's missing ring. By the time I'm through, the policeman and Antonia will believe they imagined the entire night." He paused and stared hard at her. "But I must tell you one thing: you do need a protector, Mystere. Rillieux is only hungry for the riches you can steal for him. I, on the other hand, find myself hungry for something much more pleasurably provided."

By now, only inches separated them. He reached out and stroked the smooth skin of her cheek. The touch confused her, and strangely left her aching for more.

"I'm not a whore. I told you that," she said, her stare shadowed with misery.

"I know. The evidence is between your legs." He outlined her lips with one strong finger. "Besides, mistress is a much prettier word."

"But I won't—"

The finger silenced her. "Rillieux has obviously not kept you, but it's time someone does."

"You cannot do it," she whispered harshly, heartbroken. "Besides, Rillieux won't let me go easily."

He laughed. "You forget the old adage about beggars, love. But this time it's robbers who can't be choosers."

"If you force me, there will be no love between us."

He took her face in his large hands and studied her. "It will not be loveless, Mystere. No, it must be seduction. Nothing else will do for my mistress." He noticed her trembling again and dropped his hands. "But for now the first seduction is to see to your care. I'll have Ruth show you to your room, and she'll see to it that your wound bothers you no more."

"I cannot stay here—Rillieux will—"

"Shall I see to it he bothers you no more?"

Helpless and bewildered, she stared at him while he rung for his housekeeper. Desperate to save herself, she said, "Your offer is tempting, Mr. Belloch—"

"Rafe."

"R-Rafe—" she stammered, "but all my things are with Rillieux. I *must* return there. The letter is with him. It's all I have of my past, and I will not let it go. So I must refuse your offer, chooser or not, because as much as it would be nice to be protected and cared for, I know better than anyone else such things come at a cost."

"Hardly any cost at all," he tossed out, a wicked smile curving his hard lips.

"I shall give you the emerald. I'll do anything you want, but I cannot stay here—"

He only smiled and rolled Antonia's emerald between his hands. "You forget, love, that I already have the emerald."

"Yet there must be something else you want that I can get for you. Are none of Mrs. Astor's jewels temptation?"

Unexpectedly, he tossed her the emerald. "As you can see, my lady, I'm no pauper and do not have to steal to make my living." His eyes narrowed. An idea seemed to be eating at him. "However, I can make you this bargain: You stay here and heal your arm. If you still object to the role of mistress, I may have a nice little job for you after all. There is one piece I covet which has long been out of reach."

"Tell me and I'll work for it this very night," she said desperately.

He grimaced a soft smile. "Your face is white from loss of blood; you're trembling from shock. I daresay you won't be doing anything tonight but taking Ruth's cures and sleeping."

With that the housekeeper knocked on the door and let herself in.

"N-no. I can't stay here," Mystere stammered, backing away from both of them.

"Ready the Venetian suite, Ruth."

The middle-aged woman nodded. Her frilled cap bobbed.

"No—" Mystere moaned. Weak and unsettled, her legs tangled in the tasseled points of the lap blanket. Before she could steady herself, she was in his arms, being carried up a handsome mahogany staircase.

"I cannot do this," she pleaded with nearly her last breath.

"I like the fight in you, my lady. Use it to heal, not to go against the one who cares for you."

"But you do not care for me," she nearly wept.

He placed her on a French bed in a glorious bedroom painted Venetian pink. Before he left, he swept away a lock of her dark hair and held her gaze for several long moments. "If you fear I do not care for you, do nothing to make that your fate. Now sleep and do as Ruth says."

"I'll do anything you want. Anything, but not—" Her words were drowned by a glass of laudanum. Her last memory was that of the kindly housekeeper fussing over her bedclothes, and the fierce stare of Rafe Belloch as he gave emphatic instructions to Ruth as to her care.

Chapter 21

There were horrifying moments when darkness seemed to crash over Mystere like a liquid shroud. In her drugged sleep, her body awash in heat, she tossed and turned in the satin sheets, moaning, pleading for mercy. Lost in shadow, she was unmindful of the cool cloth held to her brow; blinded to the strong, masculine hand that ministered.

But blessed daybreak arrived. Slowly, fluttering, her eyes opened to a golden shaft of sunbeam that fell across the coverlet. Her arm still throbbed in pain, but it was a dull ache, not the sharp, exquisite pain of the night before. She rose to a sitting position and looked around the unfamiliar room. The sun lit the Venetian velvet draperies until they flamed pink gold. On one Louis XVI bergere was her ruined mint green satin dress, its side drenched in ugly dried blood. On the other bergere was a man, his long legs stretched out before him, his arms held tightly across his chest. Rafe was fast asleep in his clothes. He still wore his trousers from the night before and had stripped down to only his fine batiste shirt.

Nervously, she assessed him. She was caged with the lion, and her options were few. Even if she could dress and sneak away, she still had to get back to Manhattan on her own. Her things were at Paul's, and he would not be pleased at her return. There seemed no way out.

His hand came up and rubbed his face. Teal eyes now stared at her.

"Sleeping beauty awakes," he said, straightening in the chair. "How do you feel?"

Unsure and stammering, she said, "F-fine, but I-I'd like to go home."

"You have no home to return to." The statement was made like a death sentence. She had no real way to refute it.

He stood and stretched. His chest was visible through the thin batiste. The muscles she had come to know beneath her fingertips rippled; the fine sprinkling of black hair showed through the unbuttoned front. With his face still wearing sleep, he looked impossibly relaxed and handsome. Not at all like the demon who was bent on chasing her to her doom.

"If I'm to be held captive here, I should at the very least like to request that I get my things. My letter is still at Paul's house."

"You'll get whatever you desire," he answered gruffly. "But in good time. First I'd like a few days to see how biddable a mistress you prove to be."

She stared at him, silent, thinking.

He stared back, then laughed. "I see you're still plotting my demise." He walked to the bed. Taking both her arms, he held her down upon the mattress and said, "I assure you, I've never been kicked out of a woman's bed, and I don't plan on having you be the first one to do it."

She was nearly naked beneath the fine silk sheets. Her filmy blush-colored chemise provided no modesty at all. When he sat on the edge of the bed, his weight pulled away the sheet that covered her chest. Cold and vulnerable, her breasts seemed to entice his hand, but he restrained himself, brushing the tip of one hard nipple with his palm before he caressed her face.

"I can see you're not up to bedroom play yet, so come downstairs with me. We'll eat and discuss our new"—he smiled—"our new 'alliance.' "

A knock came to the door. "Is the young lady up?" Ruth popped her head through the door. The housekeeper entered with a silver tray, apparently not even noticing the impropriety of the master of the house sitting on the edge of a guest's bed.

"I'll leave you to Ruth's good care. It's cold this morning, so we'll break our fast in front of the library fire." He stood and went to the door.

Mystere stared after him, helpless to fight, unable to surrender.

"This is already healing nicely," the kind housekeeper said as she unwrapped Mystere's arm. "It shouldn't leave too fierce a scar, I wager."

"I'll always be indebted. Thank you," Mystere murmured, her heart too heavy to utter anything more.

Two hot cups of coffee by the fire and Mystere felt herself begin to rally. As she faced off against Rafe, she realized escape of any kind was her only path to salvation. But the more she plotted in her head, the more his stares became pointed and intrusive. He would be a difficult predator to evade. She didn't delude herself.

"Come here," he finally said when they were through and Ruth re-moved the breakfast tray.

Warily, she stood up from her chair. She tightened the black silk tasseled cord that held together his robe. The black vicuna dressing gown was more than a foot too long for her, so she almost tripped on the hem.

When she stood in front of him, she watched in horror as his hands went to the silk cord.

"I could pull this away and then feast my eyes." He locked gazes with her. "But I would far prefer you undo the cord. I like you to be the one to come to me. To undress for me."

"I won't," she whispered harshly.

He nodded. His hands lowered to her hips and he dragged her down into his lap. "You won't because you so quickly forgot the re-wards, my love." His mouth found hers. She wanted to struggle, to flee, but the warmth of his lips, the comforting strength of his un-yielding chest, made her succumb.

The satin kiss deepened into velvet. His hot tongue thrust into her, branding her with possession. Without any manipulations on either side, the robe loosened. It parted at the top revealing the lush swell of her breasts. Worse, it parted between her legs, leaving invitation for a caress.

His hand stroked her. Masterfully.

Her breath froze in her chest.

A melting sensation seeped between her legs. Her breathing returned, this time quickened. She was grateful the robe hid the wickedness of his actions, for even she herself couldn't bear to see.

It was as if he was a spell caster and she the unwary victim. Paralyzed, she sat half-naked upon his lap, accepting his wicked caress like a purring kitten. The spell seemed complete as his finger sought her most holy spot, and she could think of nothing more than how empty she was there, and how she longed for him to fill it again.

"God in heaven!" came the voice from the door.

Drugged by their own loveplay, neither Rafe nor Mystere had heard the door open.

There, with jaws agape, stood Mrs. Astor and Ward, and a very upset housekeeper Ruth in their wake.

The master of control, Rafe made a concise effort to maintain Mystere's modesty. He closed up the parted robe and slowly allowed her to get to her feet. Joining her, he watched as Caroline entered the library, Ward like a sniffing dog behind her. Ruth moaned several apologies before he nodded her out the door.

The entire proceedings were a confused blur to Mystere. She snatched the shawl collar of the robe and clutched it to her neck, utterly mortified, praying she could wake up and find the last twenty-four hours nothing but a bad dream.

Rafe, however, recovered his aplomb quickly after the initial shock. A grim, cynical, tight-lipped smile divided his face, reminding Mystere of a soldier who had resigned himself to dying well for a lost cause.

"Caroline, Ward," he greeted them cordially. "Won't you take off your things?"

Mystere couldn't believe the audacity of his bad joke. Nor did it improve Caroline's mood. Her expression was as jaundiced as the mustard yellow taffeta of her dress.

"You callous, unprincipled scoundrel," she pronounced coldly. "You base seducer and defiler of innocence. You have led this lamb to the slaughter."

"Wait, Mrs. Astor," Mystere tried to protest, "you—"

"Be quiet, child," the matron cut her off with decisive finality. "I am not all that surprised by your lack of . . . self-control. Rafe is highly attractive, and you've had no motherly hand to guide you. I do not consider you the villain in this sordid drama. You have been beguiled by a master. But do *not* presume on my goodwill, for it has its limits."

Mrs. Astor turned her wrathful eyes toward Rafe again.

He spoke before she could. "Just curious, Caroline—why are you and Ward here? What could have inspired you to desert the noble rock of Manhattan and cross the bay so early on a cold morning? Just to see me," he added in a sly undertone, and she seemed on the verge of slapping him.

"Misplaced concern, that's what. You disappeared so suddenly last night, a rumor sprang up that you were taken ill. To think I went to all the bother of rousing our boat crew only to discover *this*. Have you anything to say for yourself?"

Here it comes, Mystere warned herself, trying hard to overcome the trembling weakness in her legs. *He's going to tell her everything, and I will be ruined.*

Instead of addressing himself to Mrs. Astor, however, Rafe's eyes cut to Ward, whose own eyes were absorbing the striking image of the scantily clad Mystere.

"Move toward the back wall, old sock," Rafe suggested, "and you'll have a much better view."

McAllister flushed and started to protest, but Caroline's voice overrode his.

"This is not a game," the iron-willed woman snapped. "There can be no way to prevent a scandal, Rafe, do you see that?"

"Sure there is," he gainsaid calmly. "You and Ward just keep your mouths shut."

Mrs. Astor was suddenly on her full dignity as she glowered at him. "I do not 'conspire' in shameful activities. You may think I am nothing but a snob; however you are wrong. I hold our strata of society to a high-minded code of conduct."

"A high-hatted code, you mean," he corrected her.

"This is not the time for your insolence. I can ruin you, Rafe, you know that. One word to the right man on Wall Street, and your company stock will be wrapping fish. Do you doubt I could do that?"

"Caroline," he confessed with weary candor, "I honestly believe your influence could make the sun rise in the west."

"Good, it seems that at least we understand each other. This is not just a scandal—it is a scandal that now includes me if I choose to keep it quiet. There has never been a mark against my name, and there never will be."

Mystere simply could not believe that Rafe was protecting her secret in the face of this threat to himself. Nor could she understand where all this was going. All was made horribly clear, however, when Mrs. Astor turned to her social director.

"Ward, what we have seen here never happened. Tonight I will compose a message that you will take to Reverend Lowell early in the morning. He is to immediately post the banns so that Mr. Belloch may marry Miss Rillieux and vanquish any rumors of scandal."

The room seemed to spin dizzily for a moment, and Mystere saw a gray pallor settle over Rafe's handsome features. She opened her mouth to protest, but she simply had no power of utterance. Caroline's pronouncement had literally stunned her.

"Those are my non-negotiable terms," the matron added resolutely. "Do you object, Rafe?"

"Of course I object."

"Yes, but will you comply?"

"If I don't, it will cost me a corporation, am I right?"

"Among other things. Do you doubt I'd do it?"

For the first time since she had arrived, a trace of anger hardened his tone. "Why should I? You and your ilk didn't hesitate to kill my father, did you?"

"My 'ilk,' Rafe, includes you," she rejoined without missing a beat. "As to your father, he dug his own grave. Just as you appear to be doing. Now come along, Ward, I have a splitting headache."

They left, not wasting a backward glance.

Rafe expelled a long sigh and wearily lowered himself into a Queen Anne mahogany armchair behind his desk. Uttering a little cry of despair, Mystere grabbed up the hem of the robe and made a dash for the doors. Rafe, however, surprised her with his quick athleticism, leaping up and grabbing her by the arm once more before she could escape.

"Damn you," he muttered, "you've cost me enough trouble. Now stay put a moment until I think this thing through."

"Rafe, please let me go! I promise I'll pay back every cent I stole from you, I—"

"Pipe down. Right now I've got bigger fish to fry. She means it; she will destroy my corporation. *I* could survive that blow—I'm diversified enough. But do you realize how many of my employees will be plunged into utter destitution? I have an obligation to them and their families, and I don't take it lightly. Besides, did you hear what she told McCallister to do?"

"She—she can't really force us to get married. I mean, she won't really post the banns once she settles down a bit. Remember how she vowed to ruin Abbot but didn't?"

Rafe laughed and shook his head. "In some ways, at least, you *are* still innocent, Lady M, and I confess it's charming. Forgiving Abbot was not a serious blow to her pride. Forgiving me would be."

"Why?"

"Why?" he repeated, anger spiking his tone. "Because she had no plans to make Abbot her illicit lover, you little simp."

Mystere stared at him in wide-eyed disbelief. "You mean she . . . and you? You can't possibly believe that of Caroline!"

"She's not the Virgin Mary, you know. Why in hell do you think she got on her high horse and gave me that lecture about her high-minded morals? It was guilt over what she wanted to do with me. And do you really believe she came out here to see if I was ill?"

"Ward was with her."

He snorted. "She trusts Ward absolutely; he's as loyal as the Swiss Guard. And I'll tell you quite frankly: Had I not begun wasting so much time on *you,* the seduction of Mrs. Astor would be a fait accompli by now. And known to all by my own efforts."

His smug, bragging tone made her bristle, as did the distasteful topic. "Well, I knew you were conceited. But *this* is preposterous. You heard her just now, boasting how there has never been a mark against her name."

"Caroline is talking about *being caught,* not about avoiding transgression. You see, I had it all worked out. I was just waiting for the day when Caroline Astor would succumb to her inner temptations. Now, thanks to you, that day will never come."

"But . . . but you clearly despise her. Why in God's name would you plot the seduction of a woman you—"

" 'The heart has its reasons,' " he cut her off, " 'which reason may never know.' "

"Your father," she said quietly. "That's why, isn't it? I heard what you said, and Abbot mentioned some 'grudge' of yours. What did she do to your father?"

"Nothing," he replied bitterly. "And that nothing was everything. But it's none of your damn business, never mind all that."

With a visible effort he shook off his anger and met his captive's eyes. He said, perhaps thinking out loud more than talking, "Well, today is Sunday; we may not have to wait long to see what Caroline's next play will be. Right now she holds all the cards."

He aimed a low-lidded gaze at her, and she paled slightly. "But I still have a proposition for you."

The sudden fear in her face made him laugh harshly. "Not that kind of proposition, you little coward, although I confess, after what I've seen of you this morning, it will be on my mind. No—I want you to do what you do best, Lady M. I want you to steal something for me. Steal it back, actually."

"I don't understand," she blurted out, numb and afraid.

"Think back to the middle of March and a soiree hosted by John and Joanna Strahan. It was shortly before the Vanderbilt ball, and before you had been dubbed Lady Moonlight by the press. You stole a diamond-and-sapphire tiara from a dizzy old matron named Louise Blackburn."

Mystere recalled it immediately, for it was one of the prizes she had glimpsed in Paul's wall safe.

"It wasn't stolen," she said very quietly. "It was arrogated."

"How's that?" he demanded, impatient at the interruption.

"Nothing. What about the tiara?" she inquired reluctantly, for even now—fully exposed as Lady Moonlight—it was unpleasant to acknowledge her crimes.

"It was my mother's, that's what. An item she prized dearly in her lifetime. It was auctioned off as part of our estate sale after she died, all the proceeds going to creditors. And I want it back."

"That's impossible."

"Too bad for you, then. Because I was planning to make you a very fair offer. Get that tiara for me, and I'll consider my score against you settled. No time down in the cell, and no more threats of exposing your crimes. Plus . . ."

He dipped one hand into his shirt pocket and retrieved Antonia's ring. It caught some light from the fireplace and glowed the radiant green color of sun-pierced seawater.

"This will be yours. The ring for the tiara."

Considering everything, Mystere thought, it was, indeed, a fair offer. The idea of stealing from Paul terrified her, but the trouble Rafe could stir up terrified her even more. Besides, even if he was bluffing about exposing her—she needed that ring.

"It will be very difficult," she finally replied. "Nor can I guarantee success. But I will try."

He nodded. "If I were you, I'd try very hard. I'm damned if I know why I protected you today by keeping my mouth shut." His voice turned dark and threatening. "Remember, all I need do is sit down with Caroline and explain this entire sordid mess. Once she learns who—and what—her 'lamb' truly is, you will find yourself in a world of suffering."

Chapter 22

As part of his elaborate masquerade, Paul Rillieux often attended Trinity Church on Sunday mornings along with many others in the Four Hundred, forcing Mystere to go with him. She knew he secretly delighted in the irony of a devout Catholic awash in Anglicans.

However, this Sunday he was in a terrible mood and skipped church in order to confront her about the events of the night before at the Addison ball. Unpleasant as that was, Mystere preferred Paul's bad temper to the possible shock of hearing Reverend Lowell publicly proclaim her engagement to Rafe Belloch. She could only hope against hope that Mrs. Astor, having calmed down, might rescind her drastic order. She would have perhaps gladly married Rafe if he had asked her, but to find herself chained to an unwilling groom, especially the lion Rafe was, seemed like an unimaginable nightmare.

"Have you seen the late edition newspapers, young lady?" Paul demanded the moment Mystere entered the parlor.

She looked pale and distracted, almost frail in her linen wrapper. Dark circles under her eyes testified to a bone-tired exhaustion.

"You know I only read the *Times*," she replied, taking a seat across the alabaster table from him and pouring herself some brandy from the decanter. "And they don't keep people like Lance Streeter on their staff, if that's what you mean."

"I'm not talking about gossip," he snapped. "And for your information, what I'm alluding to *is* mentioned in the *Times*. On page one, as it is with every other paper."

He shook the creases out of the *Herald,* his personal favorite, and began reading aloud: " 'Once again the elusive society thief known as Lady Moonlight has victimized the city's wealthy elite, striking sometime last night at the annual ball hosted by James and Lizet Addison. This time the mysterious purloiner of jewels has captured a true prize: a beautiful, one-of-a-kind emerald ring, its value undisclosed to the press, belonging to Miss Antonia Butler.' "

Paul closed the newspaper and cast it aside, glowering across the table at her. "Where is that ring?" he demanded. "It's one thing for you to whore all night for that bastard Belloch; it's another for you to provide for him."

Normally, Paul's wrath cowed and terrified her. However, the new crisis that she and Rafe both faced with Mrs. Astor tended to dwarf all else. Yet again she fretted, wondering if the vengeful matron would actually hold them to a forced marriage. If Rafe's back was to the wall, he would expose her; she had no doubt of it. Now she also faced the thorny problem of somehow getting into Paul's safe to retrieve the tiara for Rafe.

"I stole nothing last night," she informed him in a bold, bald-faced lie, feigning surprise at hearing the news. She added truthfully, "*I* don't have that ring."

Clearly Rillieux did not expect a denial. After a moment to collect himself, he went on in a chillingly quiet tone, "What have I told you, Mystere, about disloyalty to the family?"

"I don't like your tone," she snapped.

"Goddamnit, I don't give a hang *what* you don't like, you ungrateful little witch. If you didn't steal it, *why* did you disappear so suddenly?"

She stared into the dark depths of her coffee, saying nothing. She flinched when Paul smacked the tabletop so hard it rattled the cups.

"Why did you disappear?" he repeated. "And where did Belloch take you? You obviously did not return here until just an hour ago."

She met his eyes and played the one card she knew would calm him down. "Perhaps," she said quietly, "I have my own big plans for our prosperity."

For a moment her words only irritated him, and he was about to snap at her again. Then, abruptly, a look of enlightenment seized him.

"Do you mean marriage?" he asked.

She nodded, flushing slightly. "I . . . I went with Rafe to his home. There was talk of marriage."

As understanding set in, hope worked into Paul's seamed face, replacing the anger. "Well, I'm a Dutchman," he said in a tone of wonder. "But you weren't so foolish as to let him . . . ?"

She shook her head, genuinely embarrassed. Paul, if not quite completely mollified by this turn of events, had certainly calmed down.

"I see. Well . . . that *is* interesting. So you've taken to heart some of the things I've told you? But if you didn't take that ring, who did?"

He paused to reflect, pulling at the point of his chin. Mystere's unexpected news had put him in a much better mood.

"You know," he finally said, "it *is* quite possible that some clever, enterprising thief took advantage of the Lady Moonlight's publicity, knowing the crime would be attributed to her. There was the shot fired. The policeman thought he hit the mysterious woman."

He looked at Mystere and studied her in the linen wrapper. "But she couldn't have been you. You look too fit to have been shot." Then he actually smiled. "Well, I guess *we* don't have exclusive rights to rob the wealthy, eh? The ring will hardly matter if this new development between you and Rafe bears fruit—so to speak. I'm sorry, my dear, that I was so snappish with you. I should have known that a good, obedient girl like yourself would not let the family down."

"You needn't act as if our future is now secured," she demurred. "Rafe is still his own man."

"Well, yes . . . of course, of course. And I don't mean to be indelicate, Mystere, but what about . . . the bindings? How did you explain that part of it to him?"

She blushed again, dropping her gaze from his. But it was feigned to buy a little time. Rapidly her mind searched for a convincing lie.

"You *are* being indelicate, Paul. I told him . . . I said that I felt self-conscious about the . . . the fullness of my figure, that it bothers me to have others notice it. He must have believed me, for he teased me about it."

"Teased you, did he? Good, good." Paul's mood was getting better and better as the possible implications of all this began to register with him. "Have the two of you reached any, ahh, understanding? Is the relationship to continue?"

She had to be cautious here. She dared not say no in case Mrs. Astor had, indeed, announced the banns. Then again, if she had relented, Mystère did not want to build Paul's hopes too high—his wrath would truly be terrible once his hopes were dashed.

She opted for tactful ambiguity.

"The relationship will continue," she replied, "although on what footing, I'm not completely sure at this time."

"Well, that's certainly better than a poke in the eye with a sharp stick, eh? Tell me one more thing: how definite was he on the subject of marriage?"

The irony of this question almost coaxed a smile out of her despite the problems weighing so heavily on her mind. "He was," she told him, again truthfully, "very definite."

"Hmm," was all he replied, but his ear-to-ear smile spoke volumes.

Rafe Belloch was not a religious man, and although his domestic staff received Sundays off, the Sabbath was merely another working day at Garden Cove for him and Sam Farrell. At nine A.M. both men met in Rafe's study-cum-office for their usual weekly conference.

"This arrived by late post yesterday," Sam informed him first thing. He handed his employer a letter postmarked New Orleans. "I looked for you, but Ruth told me you were to stay in town yesterday."

"Ah, finally. Our report from Stephen Breaux," Rafe said, using a solid gold letter opener shaped like a railroad spike to slit open the envelope. "It may prove a bit anticlimactic, Sam, after the dog-and-pony show that took place here last night. Still, I've been curious."

Rafe's gaze quickly fell over the cordial greeting from Breaux, then slowed as he reached the meat of the report.

> *We have unearthed no trace whatsoever that Paul Rillieux had a niece living with him, or any other relative for that matter. Nor do any city records record the name Mystère Rillieux. As for Paul Rillieux himself, he was quite active in what is known locally as the Lafayette Circle, i.e., the wealthy class who live "uptown" on the streetcar line from the Vieux Carré, the old French Quarter heart of New Orleans.*

I never personally met him, but all reports indicate the man was quite popular with some of our leading citizens, and apparently pursued no profession. Reportedly he lived quite comfortably, though not lavishly, on income derived from land holdings in France. However, after his departure (back to France, he claimed) an interesting development occurred.

A young man who once served as Rillieux's valet was caught stealing an expensive gold watch from a visitor to our city. When remanded to parish court for the offense, he claimed to have been trained in the art of theft by his former employer, Rillieux. He told an incredible tale (too incredible, in the judge's opinion, for it was dismissed out of hand) of a "master thief" who recruited denizens of Gallatin Alley, set them up as servants in his home, and lived well off the sale of their plunder.

Rafe glanced up at Sam after reading the letter, a smile pulling at his lips. He handed it to Sam, who quickly read it.

"So the old scoundrel is up to the same tricks," Rafe remarked. "Well, it's damning, all right. Especially as it concerns Paul Rillieux. In fact, this is all we need to turn his cake into dough. He'd spend the rest of his life in prison."

"I assume it could also go very hard for Mystere," Sam put in quietly.

Rafe nodded. "Yes, damn it. Perhaps harder than she deserves, which is why I won't go to the authorities. I see now that she most likely told me the truth last night. She claims Rillieux recruited her from an orphanage and trained her to steal just as you might train a yearling horse to pace."

"Consistent," Sam pointed out, "with his modus operandi in New Orleans."

"Yes, and that mitigates the girl's guilt somewhat. But no amount of pity makes me want to *marry* the charming little thief."

"Marry?" Sam repeated, a rare look of surprise widening his eyes.

"Yes, my reaction precisely."

Briefly Rafe outlined the situation in the drawing room that had culminated with Mrs. Astor's merciless ultimatum.

"No," Sam agreed when he had finished. "Pity is certainly the wrong motivation for wedlock. Assuming, of course, that's *all* you feel."

Sam seldom pushed into his employer's personal affairs; so seldom, in fact, that Rafe did not resent it now. Nonetheless, he sent Sam a sharp glance, eyes narrowed.

"Well, of course she's a beauty," Rafe conceded. "Especially when she isn't . . . shall we say, downplaying her full charms. But lust is no better reason to marry than pity."

Sam had a rare knack for using silence to great effect, and he did so now.

"You think I'm in love with her, is that it?" Rafe demanded.

"I have no idea. But there's more than lust and pity that's been causing you to be preoccupied with her these past weeks."

"I can't deny that," Rafe begrudged. "But don't forget, old son—there's also the small matter of Caroline's threat to the solvency of Belloch Enterprises."

"Would she follow through on that threat?"

"To quote you just now, I have no idea. If you're asking me if she's capable of following through, absolutely. The woman is solid iron."

He lapsed into silence, and the pleasing image of Mystere's near nakedness recurred unbidden to his mind. Lust might not justify a marriage, he reasoned, but neither could he deny its compelling allure—especially in her case. He had spent much of the past few weeks tossing sleepless in his bed, and it wasn't the threat of bankruptcy that kept him sweating into the sheets.

On the heels of this reaction, however, followed another: intense irritation at his own weakness. Why in God's name did he protect her secret from Caroline? It would bollix up all his plans if he *did* let himself fall in love with this treacherous little thief.

He could no longer deny that his frivolous adventure with Mystere had distracted him from his primary goal: to make Caroline his greatest coup by embroiling her in a nasty scandal. Mystere had lost him that goal forever. There were still plenty of eligible socialites, of course, Antonia Butler included. He must not let himself get trapped in a marriage with some deceitful little beauty who, for all he knew, might poison him for his own fortune.

"In any event," Rafe finally resumed, "I won't be able to plan my next move until I find out if the banns have been announced. That news could come at any moment now. In the meantime . . ."

Rafe handed the letter back to Sam. "Type out a copy of this, would you? Then file away the original and mail the copy to Mystere Rillieux. You'll find her address in the Manhattan phone directory."

Just a bit of incentive, Rafe told himself, *to remind her I'm dead serious about getting that tiara.*

Chapter 23

Less than an hour after church services ended at Trinity, the telephone in the hallway of the Rillieux residence suddenly shrilled. Mystere, busy in the parlor repairing the rickrack braiding on one of her gowns, started at the sound, pricking her finger with the needle.

She felt like the condemned who had just heard the executioner testing his scaffold. Mrs. Astor and Ward had escorted her back to Rillieux's as though she were a prisoner. Few words had been exchanged. The only admonition Caroline had given Paul was, "Do not let her out of your sight."

What Mrs. Astor wanted, Paul Rillieux was sure to do. Now he watched her from his leather chair, like a cat on a canary, waiting patiently for her to confess or explain. But so far, she had chosen to do neither. She still wanted her options open, and she didn't yet know when the other shoe was to fall.

But by the sound of the ringing in the hallway, the boot was coming down fast.

Even though Hush had the day off and wasn't present to answer the phone, Mystere made no move for it. She remained frozen in her chair. However, Baylis was just then in the hallway and picked up the phone. She heard the brief drone of his voice, the words indistinct at this distance. A moment later he poked his head inside the room.

"Telephone, Paul," he informed Rillieux, who was on the opposite side of the parlor from Mystere. "It's old lady Astor."

"*Mrs.* Astor," Paul corrected him with an angry frown. "Show some respect for your betters."

Baylis sneered while Paul, using his walking stick for support, rose from the chair and limped out of the room. When Rillieux was out of earshot, Baylis winked at Mystere from beneath the brim of his feathered derby.

"Hell, the old bag never bought *me* a beer," he told her in a low voice.

Mystere tried to smile politely at his poor joke, but she was suddenly overcome with a paralytic dread. *Please,* she prayed silently, *let it just be an invitation to a Sunday outing.*

It became clear the moment Paul returned, however, that her prayer had not been answered.

"Mystere, you little imp," he said from the doorway of the parlor, beaming fondly at her. "You kept your great secret all morning, didn't you? Letting me scold you as I did, shame on you!"

Baylis, about to exit through the front door, returned to the parlor. "What secret?" he demanded curiously.

"Baylis," Paul announced grandly, barely able to contain himself, "our little girl has trumped us all. Mrs. Astor called just now to congratulate me on Mystere's official engagement to Rafe Belloch."

"Well, by the Lord Harry! *The* Belloch? That rich toff we heisted at Five Points? The Mountain Mover himself?"

"The very man," Paul confirmed, still beaming proudly at his "little girl." "And to think I questioned her loyalty to the family. Will you forgive me, my dear?"

But Mystere hardly heard him. For a long moment the room seemed to be a rapidly spinning top, and she clutched the arms of the chair as if afraid she might be flung off.

"Belloch's a reg'lar Vanderbilt!" Baylis exclaimed.

"Not quite," Paul corrected him. "But without question he's one of the wealthiest men in the nation. And to think our girl is to be his wife."

"Our ship has finally come in," Baylis gloated. "Look at her, boss— the great lady. Ain't *she* silky satin? When's the wedding, hon?"

Mystere tried to speak, but it felt as if a hand was choking her throat.

"The poor thing's overcome at the thought of it," Paul effused. "The date's not been set yet, according to Caroline. But the sooner the better, I say." He winked at her, looking for all like Satan himself. "Just to let you know, Mystere, I reassured Mrs. Astor that I would not let you out of my sight, and I mean to stick to that promise. You've had way too much freedom for an unprotected debutante, and that's what's gotten you into this mess." Paul laughed. "We don't want the goose to fly the coop before she lays the golden egg, do we?"

Staring at him, Mystere knew the end had come. If she couldn't flee, she would be forced to marry Belloch for their profit. She couldn't predict how it would all end, but she saw a funeral much too soon into the marriage.

"When *this* kind of opportunity presents itself, best to strike while the iron is hot," Paul continued.

"Or while Belloch is," Baylis punned, and both men laughed coarsely.

Still numb, Mystere was suddenly desperate to be free of their barracks-room joviality. She gathered up her gown and somehow willed her legs to support her when she stood up.

"I . . . I think I'll work on this upstairs," she managed to say.

"Oh-*ho!*" Baylis teased. "See how it is? She's already too good for our company."

"Now, now," Paul admonished him. "You've embarrassed her. Don't be twitting her so much; the poor thing must be feeling over-whelmed right now. I certainly am, and I'll only be giving away the bride."

Both men stepped aside as she approached the doorway, beaming at her as if she had just saved Western civilization. She was halfway down the hall, aiming for the spiral staircase, when their excited voices from within the parlor arrested her.

Quickly and quietly she retraced her steps, stopping when she was close enough to the doors to make out what they were saying.

"Yes, well, no doubt," Baylis was pointing out, "Belloch plans to hang on tight to his fortune."

"Of course, wouldn't you? But you know, I've begun to think Mystere looks quite fetching in black."

"We must *all* go home to God someday," Baylis quipped, and both men laughed.

An icy finger touched her heart. She would have to protect Rafe. The words now only steeled her resolve to refuse his hand as resolutely as Rafe protested taking hers.

Choking back a sob of despair, she hurried toward the staircase.

Mystere had no idea how long she lay on her bed, crying into her pillows and repeating Bram's name over and over. Even now he was first in her thoughts, and she despaired of ever seeing him again. She could never hope to find him when one awful complication after another prevented her from even searching.

It struck her now, more forcefully than ever, how she had grown up the child of two extremes. One extreme was the overwhelming urge to solve the enigma that had become central to her existence, the enigma of her very identity—an urge literally self-centered; the other extreme was the collective memories of those early years, the hopeless existence on the streets and later at the orphanage—that part of her, in short, that was just the opposite of self-centered. The candid part of her that knew full well her existence mattered to no one, that she could be snuffed out in a heartbeat.

Gradually, however, her personal despair gave way to thoughts of Rafe.

Despite all his horrid words and behavior toward her these past weeks, she couldn't help a growing feeling of gratitude at the way he had borne the brunt of Mrs. Astor's wrath, all to protect her from exposure. Her gratitude made her wonder again about Rafe's "grudge," as Abbot called it. Rafe had flatly accused Mrs. Astor of killing his father—if that was even remotely true, it certainly helped explain Rafe's cynical attitude and harsh manner.

A sudden knock at her bedroom door startled her thoughts back to the present. "Mystere?" Rose's voice called to her.

She quickly sat up on the bed, using one corner of the counterpane to dry her tears. "Come in, Rose."

Rose, too, had Sundays free. However, she often insisted on working a few hours to keep the house tidy. She smiled affectionately at the younger woman as she stepped inside and crossed to the bed, sitting down beside Mystere and taking both of her hands in hers.

"I don't mean to butt in," she apologized, "but earlier I heard you crying. That seems a peculiar response to one of the most joyous days of your life."

Joyous. The word seemed to mock her, but Mystere stoically kept her feelings from her face.

"You've already heard?" she asked.

"Heard?" Rose laughed. Her bright red hair hung in thick plaits. "Baylis is like a newsboy with it, hawking the word to everyone he sees. You'd think *he* was getting married."

A rogue tear spilled from Mystere's eye, but she kept her voice firm. "Yes, Paul acted the same way. But they—"

She caught herself in the nick of time, remembering that Rose was, after all, trained in loyalty to Paul. She would never intentionally hurt Mystere, and she could be counted on to keep some things secret from Paul and the others in the name of female camaraderie. But it would be indiscreet, and needlessly risky, to tell Rose she was *not* marrying Rafe Belloch come hell or high water.

"But they only see the gain for themselves," she amended.

"Yes," Rose agreed. "Frankly that's all they've ever seen in you—a source of profits. When in truth there is so much more to you."

Mystere embraced her for a long moment, hugging tightly. "*You* should talk. I'm afraid we're both in the same leaky boat."

"Yes, but before Paul we were drowning," Rose reminded her dutifully. "So a leaky boat is an improvement, I s'pose. Why are you crying, hon?"

Reluctantly, Mystere forced her mind back to more pressing matters—namely that tiara Rafe had demanded. She knew there would be the devil to pay once Paul missed it. But she couldn't expect to get out of her terrible predicament without some cost.

Nor did Rafe's apparent gallantry last night fool her into forgetting that he was a cynical, dangerous, unpredictable man. She must try to do his bidding—and after all, it *had* been his mother's possession. She could hardly fault him for wanting it. Rose, as their resident maid, knew more about Paul's secrets than anyone.

She decided to just be honest and throw herself on Rose's mercy.

"I'm in a nasty dilemma," she finally replied. "Rafe Belloch very much wants a silver tiara that I stole this past spring. You see, it was his mother's, and she's passed away now."

"But it will have been sold to Paul's fence by now," Rose pointed out. "Lord knows where it is."

"No, I think I saw it once in Paul's wall safe. You know how he holds back some things."

Rose nodded. "So you've tumbled to that fact, too? I thought only I knew."

"Yes. But you see, Rose, Rafe *truly* wants that tiara. He's told me that if I don't get it for him . . . well, suffice it to say things will go hard for me. Very hard."

"This from the man who is going to marry you?"

Mystere frowned, a sadness entering the depths of her forget-me-not eyes. "Rose, it's very complicated. You mustn't mention this to anyone, but—you see, Rafe didn't *ask* me to marry him. Mrs. Astor's forcing his hand under threat of financial ruin."

"Oh, good heart of God," Rose breathed. "So *that's* why you're crying, you poor thing."

"Yes. I know I'm asking a lot of you, but I'm in a terrible bind. Can you . . . do you know where Paul keeps the key to his safe?"

Rose paled slightly at what was being asked of her. Yet clearly her heart went out to Mystere, who had always treated her like a big sister, not a menial servant as did the others.

"You know he'll be in an awful wax, Mystere, when he misses it."

"Yes, and don't worry, I'll confess to it when he discovers it."

"It's not just the value—he'll be outraged that someone snooped into his safe. You've heard his speeches about loyalty."

Mystere nodded. "I know. But I'll have to count on his new good mood caused by the engagement announcement."

Rose brightened a little. "Yes, there's a point. He wants to keep on your good side now. Well . . . I think I know where he keeps one of the keys. Have you ever seen that old, battered Gladstone bag of his?"

"The green one with rusty brass clasps?"

"That's it. I once saw him take a key out of a little manila envelope he keeps in that bag. The bag itself, unless he's moved it, is somewhere under his bed."

Now that she was committed to helping, Rose was all business. She stood up, smoothing her cotton skirt. "This is a good time, dear. Evan and Baylis have gone to the tavern, and Hush is off God knows where. I left Paul writing letters in the parlor. I'll go back down and keep him occupied. Hurry now."

"*Thank* you, Rose," Mystere said, hugging her again.

"Hurry," Rose repeated, leaving the room.

Now that the moment to act was at hand, Mystere felt a nervous stirring in her stomach. She rushed out into the long hallway that led to the opposite upstairs wing, Paul's quarters.

She hesitated for a few moments outside the door to his bedroom, trying to hear any sounds above the surf-crashing roar of her pulse in her ears. The hinges creaked when she opened the door, and though no one else was even remotely close enough to hear it, she winced at the sound.

The large room was nearly dark, for Paul was a human bat and hated sunlight. Drapes made of heavy monk's cloth covered both windows. She switched on the newly installed electric light, revealing a walnut half-tester bed and a three-door carved walnut armoire with a beveled mirror on the center door. The old grifter was vain, despite his age—a second looking glass, a French Empire gilt bronze dressing mirror, was mounted on the lefthand wall.

She hurried to the bed, kneeled, and quickly spotted the battered old Gladstone bag. Mystere dragged it out and unsnapped the clasps, exposing a confusion of old letters, newspaper clippings, and photographs, mostly from his younger days in New Orleans. Almost immediately she found the small envelope Rose had mentioned—and there was, indeed, a brass key inside it.

The safe was located on the back wall behind a western landscape painted by Albert Bierstadt. With trembling hands she removed the framed painting and set it aside, admonishing herself to hurry. Despite her urgency to get out of there, however, she was startled into momentary immobility by the sight of the contents when she opened the iron door of the safe.

The tiara was there, all right, its pure silver offset by oval blue sapphires. She also saw a solid gold cameo brooch, a gold filigree cross encrusted with mine-cut diamonds, a pair of sapphire-and-diamond drop earrings, and other high-price sparklers as well as cash—more cash than she had time to count.

Mystere recognized items she had stolen as well as contributions from Hush and the others. She had just reached inside for the tiara when she heard Rose's voice out on the stairway, and her heart leaped into her throat.

"Yes, there will, indeed, be many preparations for the wedding. But Mystere and I will handle it easily, Paul, don't you worry."

Rose, her voice deliberately raised to warn Mystere that Paul was on his way up. A blind panic almost overtook her, but she forced herself to act without delay. Paul's lameness made him quite slow going up steps, so there was still a slim chance of escape. However, taking the tiara now was out of the question—not when he might well catch her in the hallway with it.

She slammed the safe shut, hung the painting again, returned the key to the bag and kicked it under the bed. She switched off the light and escaped from his room just in time, encountering Rose and Paul when she was safely out of range of Paul's door. It appeared that she had just left her own room.

"There's our wedding girl." The old con man beamed at her. "Has it finally sunk in that you're going to be one of the wealthiest women in America?"

"No," she managed to reply in a steady voice. "Right now it all still seems like a dream."

By the time Hush finally spotted Lorenzo Perkins exit his house on Amos Street, only a couple hours of daylight remained. The man's shadow was long and thin and sinister in the setting sun as he bore toward the saloons scattered throughout Tin Pan Alley, a busy block of Twenty-eighth Street between Broadway and Sixth Avenue, home of the music-publishing industry.

Hush was spying on his own initiative now, watching Sparky and Lorenzo whenever he could. For he was determined not to let these two double-poxed hounds ruin Mystere. So he had decided to find out what they were planning.

The Sunday shift ended at a nearby tannery, and the weary workers emerged into the dying light, looking like damned souls escaped from hell. They provided good cover as Hush moved up closer to his man, who abruptly ducked into a brick building with iron shutters— the C-note Bar, a favorite with local songwriters and performers.

Since Tammany politicians had managed to repeal the unpopular "blue laws," bars throughout the city were packed on the Sabbath. This tavern was of slightly better class than those on the Bowery— Hush spotted Currier and Ives prints lining the walls, and here and there hung a few wooden cages with starlings inside.

At first, in the crush of noisy men and thick pall of tobacco smoke, he couldn't see Lorenzo. Then he spotted him at a table near the back wall, huddled close with Sparky.

Luck was with Hush today. The interior was dark, and he managed to wedge himself behind a hogshead filled with ice, only a few feet from the two men. Despite the din of voices and a player piano, he could hear them clearly.

"Are you sure of it?" Sparky demanded.

"I swear it on the bones of my mother."

"Your mother is still alive, you blockhead."

"Right, and hasn't she bones? I'm telling you, my wife heard it in church this morning. The preacher himself announced it."

Sparky absently scraped the mud off his right boot on a chair rung. One of his suspender loops had come unbuttoned, and his britches sagged on that side.

"Then, by God," he said, "let's win the horse or lose the saddle. I'm *sick* of being poor as Job's turkey."

Sparky took the clay pipe from his mouth—the universal mark of the dirt-poor—and held it out over the table. "Never mind any stinking, flea-bit monkeys. I dream of smoking from meerschaum like the toffs do. And this wedding, b'hoy, is our big chance. We'll go straight to Belloch ourselves and make him hungry to know what we can tell him."

"Just hold your whist," Lorenzo warned. "We must use caution with him, for the man has a good think-piece on him."

"No misdoubting that. Stupid men don't get filthy rich, do they? But any man can be stupid where a woman he loves is involved."

From his cramped vantage point Hush had a good view of Lorenzo's dull little eyes and stiffly waxed mustache. The man took down half a schooner of beer in one sweeping-deep draught, backhanding the foam off his mustache.

"This is fate, Sparky. Our destiny. The wheel of fortune has finally turned round to *us.*"

"Now you're whistlin'!"

"You know, I've always wanted to be a ward boss. I've felt it in my bones that I'm bound for greatness. Even the wife thinks so; that's why she goes to the rich man's church even though she must stand at the back."

"That's the gait. T'hell with this penny-ante game, eh? Why bust our humps to squeeze fifty bucks out of the woman—Christ, Belloch's going to *marry* her. Now it's out in public, we can threaten him with ruination."

Hush felt a jolt of shock. Hookey Walker! Mystere getting married?

"We must somehow arrange a meeting with Belloch," Lorenzo said. "Make it clear his money will buy our silence."

Unfortunately Hush was privy to no more of their plans, for at that moment an employee hauled him out from his hiding place and soundly slapped his ears before tossing the boy outside. But he had heard enough to realize these men meant to cause Mystere great harm. Even the sting of jealousy, when he heard she was getting married, paled in comparison to his fear for her safety.

Hush ducked into a dark alley for a moment to remove the money from the wallet he had just stolen off the man who threw him out. Only three dollars, but it might help Mystere. He had decided to defy Rillieux by giving most of what he stole to her—she needed it more than the old man did.

He tossed the empty billfold onto a heap of garbage and headed home, trying to puzzle out a plan to help Mystere. He meant to act on his own now, for the poor girl had so much on her mind lately. He had seen her crying when she thought she was alone, and the sight pained him worse than any beating. So did the fine little worry lines that seemed to be forming around her mouth.

How anyone could want to hurt her was beyond him, for she was as sweet as she was beautiful. He loved it when she read to him, for her voice must be the sound made by angels' harps. When he gazed into her perfect blue eyes he felt all funny inside—as if he could conquer nations for her sake.

He wanted to marry her. Why couldn't he be as rich as Rafe Belloch so she would love him instead?

At the back of his mind, however, Sparky's words echoed like the threat of distant artillery: *I say let's win the horse or lose the saddle. This wedding, b'hoy, is our big chance.*

Chapter 24

On Tuesday morning Ward McCallister called the Rillieux residence to announce that Mrs. Astor was hosting an engagement party for Rafe and Mystere at the Astor residence the coming Saturday.

As usual, Mystere noticed in a flush of impotent irritation, there was no polite attempt to make sure that date was convenient for her. Caroline had simply issued marching orders, and everyone else must get into lockstep.

Lance Streeter, too, had complicated her life with a gushing column on Monday, most of it purple tripe devoted to "the match of the season." The phone had not finally stopped ringing until well into the evening as well-wishers called, raising a litany of cliched congratulations that soon left her with a pounding headache.

Mystere felt the full irony of her situation. Not too long ago, during her last cab ride through Brooklyn, she had made a determined vow to "become her own woman." Now, only look—a highly public pseudoengagement, completely forced on her, that made her feel as if she was living in a glass cage, her every action visible from any angle. Under such conditions she had no more chance of finding Bram than she had of going to the moon.

As if she didn't have enough to contend with, she had still not managed to get the tiara out of Paul's safe. That goal acquired a new urgency with the arrival of the Tuesday afternoon post.

"Letter for you on the stand," Rose informed her when Mystere came downstairs around one P.M. "The return address is Staten Island," she added, and Mystere felt apprehension quicken her pulse. Where Rafe Belloch was concerned, no news was good news.

She took the neatly typed envelope from the marble stand and opened it with trembling fingers. The likewise neatly typed letter inside—marked "original on file"—needed no explanation. While it barely mentioned her, the letter from Stephen Breaux's law firm in New Orleans was potentially damning to Paul and his entire "family," herself included. She did not require a tutor to understand why Rafe had sent it.

Rose worked nearby as she read it, busy running a feather-duster over the hallway furnishings.

"Mystere! What is it!" she demanded, for the younger woman suddenly paled as if she had lost half her blood.

"That stupid tiara," she replied, close to tears of frustration. "Rafe is pressuring me to get it."

"You'll not likely have a chance to grab it today," Rose fretted. "Paul told me to cancel all his appointments today, for he's under the weather. He'll most likely lay abed all day."

Paul . . . Mystere tore the envelope and letter into bits and dropped them into the nearby litter can, shaking it to make sure they dropped out of sight. One reason he was happy as a clam about the engagement, of course, was that he expected Rafe's money to cover his bad investments. He would be terrifying in his rage against her if she ever jeopardized that. But even worse if he ever learned that Rafe had discovered the old thief's modus operandi.

It's the attention from Mrs. Astor, she reminded herself. *It's turned his head more than anything ever has, for it's not only certified approval of his worth, but top certification. So even more than poverty he fears exposure, for it will cost him his prize.* And that made him, age notwithstanding, dangerous.

Rafe was clearly a strong and capable man, and probably quite safe when at home at Garden Cove. But when he left Staten Island, he carelessly placed himself in danger of attack—as her own robbery of him two years earlier proved. Evan or Baylis would not hesitate to kill him on Paul's orders—she was sure of that. They would do it all wrong and quickly be caught, probably, but Rafe would be just as dead.

In the midst of her troubled thoughts, the telephone shrilled. Rose answered.

"Yessir," Mystere heard her tell the caller. "It happens she's right here beside me. One moment please."

She held the earpiece out toward Mystere. "For you. It's your fiancé."

Your fiancé. Those two little words struck her like quick slaps to the face.

"Yes?" she answered curtly.

"What's this?" His distorted voice still managed to convey sarcasm. "No 'good afternoon, darling' for your sweetest love?"

"What do you want?" she demanded impatiently.

"Ouch, what has made our girl so peevish? Have you perchance received the afternoon mail?"

"You know I have," she retorted coldly. "Must you play everything to the gallery?"

"Oh, put aside your lah-de-dah, Lady Moonlight—I've seen you naked, and—"

"Damn you!" she blurted, shocked that he was saying it over a party-line phone, and Rose gaped in astonishment. "Tell me why you called or I'll hang up this instant."

"All right," he complied, dropping the mincing voice. "Consider this phone call a follow-up to the letter. Have you got the tiara?"

"Not yet. I've not had a clear chance to get it. You said nothing, when we reached our little agreement, about any deadline."

"Well, now I am. If you don't place that tiara in my hands this very afternoon, I'll call your 'uncle' this evening and read Breaux's letter to him."

A muscle twitched in her throat. "Rafe! That's impossible, I can't—"

"*That* shocked the sass out of you, eh? Listen here, you are the most accomplished thief in this entire city, and that's saying a lot. Don't go crying how you can't get it."

"You don't understand, Paul is—"

"This afternoon," he repeated with merciless insistence. "I'm working in my suite at the Astor House Hotel between two and five P.M. Room 511."

"Rafe, please, I simply cannot—"

"You will or face the consequences. Sunday I kept my mouth shut about you to Caroline, though God knows why. Don't forget I can get free of this entire mess by going to see her and explaining everything."

"Then, why don't you?"

"Where's the fun in that? I confess to a certain perverse pleasure in having some laughs at everyone's expense."

"Including mine."

He said nothing. His lack of a taunt seemed to mean something, but what she couldn't tell. He finished with, "I'll look for you between two and five. Until then, *darling.*"

He hung up before she could plead further. In her anger and frustration she slammed the earpiece into the wall unit so hard that she made the bell ring for a moment.

"I heard your end of it," Rose apologized. "And I think I have a plan to help you."

"Anything," Mystere grasped desperately. "He's adamant."

"You know how Paul never refuses to come to the phone when called? Hush is out in the carriage house right now repairing harness. You'll go on up to your quarters and listen for the phone. I'll send Hush to the exchange and have him request our number of the hello girl. He can hang up once I've answered."

Mystere had forgotten about the nearby telephone exchange, where the general public could place local calls for the astronomical price of five cents.

"Yes, of course." She felt a nubbin of hope work its way into the core of her despair. "You'll call upstairs for Paul. He takes forever to get up and down the stairs."

Rose nodded, already fishing a nickel out of the household-expense drawer and heading for the front door. "I'll say it's . . . some woman named Sandra. He'll think the connection got broken. But be quick, hon. God help us all if he catches you in the act and figures out how we foxed him."

"Oh, *thank* you, Rosie," Mystere called as she started up the stairs. "And don't worry. This time I'll get it."

Rose's plan went off without a hitch. By the time Paul returned upstairs, swearing profusely about the needless climb, the diamond-and-sapphire tiara was safely tucked into Mystere's handbag. As soon as Paul shut his door again, she demanded Baylis take out the carriage for her to go out for a ride.

The brief ride to the Astor House, a massive structure of six stories and three hundred rooms located across the street from City Hall Park, gave her some welcome time to collect her thoughts a bit.

It was a gorgeous July afternoon, hot but with a steady, cooling breeze. However, the sunny streets and shimmering green park lawns were wasted on her today as she began to worry if Rafe would really give her Antonia's ring, as he had promised, in exchange for the tiara. He hadn't given her a chance to mention it before he had rudely hung up on her.

Rudely . . . that was the only way he seemed to know how to treat her. And by now it should have taught her to despise him. Instead, she caught herself remembering, with shameless frequency, the dangerous excitement of his kisses, the illicit fire in her loins, when his hands touched her in a way—and in places—that *should* have enraged her.

And for all his surface rudeness, she knew he, too, felt a powerful sensual attraction to her. Indeed, his rudeness might well be his masculine defense against admitting that attraction.

But lust, she lectured herself, was an animal response. How could she possibly sanction a lust devoid of affection? His constant cruelty toward her would obviate any possibility of her actually caring for him. As for Rafe—his rudeness was directed toward almost everyone, not just her. She feared that he was simply incapable of affection for anyone, his heart as hard and unbending as Caroline Astor's will to power.

Baylis's voice scattered her thoughts. "Here we are, ma-dame," he taunted in a self-satisfied tone.

He reined in his horse in front of the gray masonry facade of the Astor House, leaping down to hand her out. She tried to tell him to stay with the carriage, but there was no getting rid of him. Ignoring the amused eyes of the liveried bellhops, she hurried across the lobby toward a bank of pneumatic elevators, Baylis glued to her side. The elevator boy took them up to the fifth floor, watching her with a knowing smile no doubt reserved for women without luggage. He made her wish she had taken the stairs.

Suddenly, at the prospect of entering Rafe's hotel suite, a fist seemed to clench in her chest. She told Baylis to wait outside, then took a deep breath to steady herself as she clapped the brass knocker on the door of room 511.

"It's open," Rafe's strong, commanding voice called from within, sounding a bit impatient at the interruption.

Her eyes rushed over the plush interior of the outer room, which he had managed to turn into a drab, cluttered, workaday office space. The textured walls were covered with a hodgepodge of charts and graphs and maps, and every available piece of furniture was piled high with notebooks and binders and thick reference manuals with scintillating titles such as *Subsurface Sedimentation in the Cumberland Valley.*

Rafe sat studying something at a wide, pecan-veneer desk dotted with deep gouges. He wore a pair of horn-rim reading glasses which he took off as she entered, tucking them into his shirt pocket. He stood up, making his action seem more pro forma than courteous, even as the usual cynical smile flitted over his lips like an ingrained reflex.

"Ahh, my lovely bride-to-be," he greeted her. "Come kiss me hello, darling."

She stoically ignored his sophomoric taunting. "I have the tiara," she announced in a cold, businesslike tone. "Do you have the ring here?"

He feigned puzzlement. "Our engagement ring, do you mean? Darling, I've hardly had time—"

"You know very well which ring I mean, Rafe. Do you have it here?"

Clearly enjoying himself, he perched on the edge of the desk. His eyes never once leaving her, he picked up an obsidian paperweight from the desk and began tossing it from one hand to the other.

"I have it," he assured her. Instead of pursuing that topic, however, he suddenly demanded, "I take it you already know there's to be an engagement party for us this weekend?"

She nodded. "What do you propose we do?"

"Do? What would any two people madly in love with each other do? We'll dress up and be gracious and smile into each other's eyes all night. What else can we do? After all, we're to be married."

"You can't be serious."

"What, about marrying you?" The amusement still laced through his voice. "Your beauty, grace, and intelligence are nothing to the matter when the only proven way to reform a hardened character like you is with the lash. And I would have no taste for beating my wife."

He pointed toward a door in the rear wall with his chin. "However, I *would* very much enjoy making you my mistress. That's the bedroom there—shall we skip the wedding and go directly to the honeymoon?"

Anger stung her like hot acid. "You're a cad."

His arrogant smile made her almost strike him, but she recovered her dignity in only moments. "I brought what you asked. Are you to keep your side of the bargain?"

His jaw tight, he snipped, "The moral high ground does not suit you, Lady M, so best to surrender it."

"I'll surrender nothing to you but my part of the bargain."

"No matter. As Caroline has already warned you: I get what I want, one way or another."

His gaze dropped from her face to the lace-trimmed bodice of her rose damask dress. "What's this? That flat-chested look of a *jeune fille* again?"

She felt herself blushing to the roots of her hair. "I can hardly develop a full bust overnight, can I?"

"Why not? It only took about two minutes on Saturday night. I assure you Ward McCallister will never look at you the same again. What about Caroline? Surely she noticed, too. What if she—"

"May we drop this subject?" she interrupted him sharply. "I came here to trade the tiara for the ring, not to endure your insufferable boorishness."

"All business, eh? All right, let me see it."

"First let me see the ring."

"Whence all this mistrust? I am a gentleman, a Patriarch of the Four Hundred. *You* are the common-born criminal who can't be trusted."

"Yes, I heard your 'gentlemanly' filth only a moment ago. First show me you have the ring."

He stood up again and slid open the wide top drawer of the desk, producing the ring. But when she reached for it, he pulled it back from her.

"Restrain yourself, Lady Moonlight. First the tiara."

She hesitated, trying to read the intention in his face. Then she took the tiara from her purse and handed it to him. A sea change seemed to come over him, a new softness moving into his face for a few moments. Even his voice lost its scalpel edge.

"Yes, that's it, all right. I'd forgotten how pretty it is. No wonder my mother loved it best among all her possessions. She used to positively glow when she wore it."

His altered mood affected her own, and suddenly she felt less combative. The only time he seemed to lose his cynical shell was when he talked about his parents.

"What did you mean," she asked him in a quiet tone, "when you accused Caroline of . . . killing your father?"

Immediately she realized she had blundered. His face was instantly hard as granite again.

"They're both dead—no point in throwing salt into the wound."

He put the tiara in the drawer but kept Antonia's ring in his clenched fist.

"May I have the ring now?" she reminded him.

"But why, darling? The emerald is so big it's vulgar, even if I rather like the encircling diamonds."

Shock thrummed in her veins like a narcotic. Sputtering, she blurted out, "You promised!"

"You stole the tiara, after all. Twice, as a matter of fact."

"But I gave it to you, didn't I?"

"So what do you want, a gold medal from Congress?"

"No, I want the ring. It's not yours by law, either."

He gave her a long, hard stare. Something softened in his eyes—something almost like empathy—but the straight-seamed grin registered his point. "Yes. Yes, you're right. Technically speaking, I'm receiving stolen property, aren't I? I suppose that makes us accomplices. The Mountain Mover and the Lady Moonlight—sounds like a strange new minstrel show, doesn't it?"

When he still made no move to give her the ring, sudden anger tightened her face. She lunged at him, grabbing his fist and trying to force it open. But it was like trying to pry open a rock. He made no attempt to stop her, merely laughing in great delight at her useless efforts.

The struggle had forced him back onto the desk, and suddenly she became aware that all of her weight was leaning tightly against him. She was breathing heavily from her exertion, and her face was only inches from his.

Their gazes locked, all struggle ceased, and she saw the mirth bleed from his eyes as some very different emotion took over his being. She could smell his masculine scent and feel the power and danger coursing through him. She could not deny the abrupt, pulsing desire low in her belly, but also the fear that left a bitter metallic taste in her throat.

She placed both fists against his broad chest and pushed herself back, turning away from him.

"You *promised,*" she repeated, so frustrated now that hot tears welled in her eyes. She thought of how Baylis was watching her like a prison guard, and of her rented room on Centre Street, the last possibility of her salvation. The ring was her last resort. Even if she could escape from this new trap of Caroline's, she could never hope to survive on her own without that ring.

Rafe watched a crystal teardrop gather on one of her eyelids, quiver for a moment like quicksilver, then splash zigzag down her cheek.

"Why is it so important?" he relented. With a grand gesture, he finally handed her the ring. "Will old Rillieux beat you if you don't give it to him?"

Mystere held the emerald in her palm, staring at it as if giving a silent prayer. She then tucked it into her purse and said, "He doesn't know I took it. I told you on Sunday, I need money to search for my brother."

"Yes, and I told you that no doubt you're wasting your time. If an impress gang grabbed him and forced him to sea that long ago, he'd stand little chance of being alive now."

"Fine. You've said it twice now. It's *my* time; I can waste it if I choose."

She made a movement toward the door, but he grabbed one wrist, detaining her.

"Are you still stealing for the old man?" he demanded.

"No."

"Yes you are."

"Why bother to ask me if you're simply going to call me a liar?"

"Liar? Well, if that offends you, allow me to phrase it more delicately: I would call your answer remote from the truth. After all, you obviously have a great talent for deceit."

She tried to pull her arm away. "You must be sure to search the place after I leave. Let *go* of me!"

He ignored her. His cynical veneer was back now in full force.

"No more of this damned stealing," he ordered her. His tone heightened ironically as he added, *"My* future wife must be pure as the driven snow."

For the moment she ceased struggling, his tasteless remark reminding her again of the terrible trap Caroline had set for them.

"Rafe, seriously—you seem to find this matrimonial charade highly amusing. But don't you realize the longer we pretend, the harder it will be to extract ourselves from it? And have you stopped to realize how Caroline will seek retribution when we cross her? You stand to lose more than I, for she's vowed to ruin you financially."

This time her words, and earnest tone, actually seemed to sink through to him. For a moment he looked serious but not quite so overbearing.

"We're in a dirty corner, all right," he conceded. "Both of us. I meant to teach you the lesson of your life, and damned if I didn't end up hoisted on my own petard. How appropriate," he added bitterly, "that a man in my business ends up *railroaded* to the gallows."

Despite her gratitude that he hadn't revealed her secret to Caroline, his comment made her bristle with sudden anger.

"Gallows?" she flung at him. "Gallows? It's I who face the true gallows. Marriage is nothing compared to that, and for your information I'd rather join a nunnery than marry you."

"Why? So you could steal all the crucifixes?"

"Rot in hell, you self-adulating tyrant!"

Again she turned toward the door, and again he detained her. The last thing she wanted to do right now was cry again, but she had been too emotionally keyed up these past few days. She felt the warmth of tears filling her eyes.

"There, there," he soothed in an even tone, "that's a tough old soldier."

It surprised both of them when she suddenly slapped him so hard it left a red imprint of her hand on his cheek.

Now the anger shifted to him, and she nearly quailed at sight of the sudden fury in his blue-green eyes.

"So you want to make it physical," he told her in a dangerously quiet voice. The next moment his strong hands cupped her face, and he crushed his lips to hers with almost bruising power, forcing her mouth open. Just as she had done that night in the gazebo, her body reacted hungrily to his demanding need. One of his hands slid down to the small of her back, pulling her against him, and for a long moment their two bodies seemed to meld into one.

She finally managed to pull away, every sense in her body acutely enhanced. It shamed her that she was practically panting. He wasn't holding her trapped now, and even though she had trouble meeting his eyes, neither did she escape to the door. It was as if the kiss had destroyed her will.

"What kind of con are you up to now?" he demanded harshly.

"None."

She placed the back of her hand on her burning lips and turned toward the door, but his voice arrested her. "It's understandable that I wouldn't want to marry a criminal. But satisfy my curiosity on one point. Why are *you* so opposed to marrying me? I think you actually mean it, yet just now when I kissed you, I think you felt something else for me entirely."

She looked back over her shoulder at him. "My rejection wounds your vanity, does it?"

"You stand to gain everything."

"Your modesty and humility included?"

He gave that a contemptuous little snort. "I'm an honest man. Why should I fake common virtues when I have none? Tell me—why do you so oppose this match?"

She might have told him the truth, because there was something frightfully dangerous about him, a kind of self-destructive, self-loathing recklessness that made being close to him feel as if she were balancing on a tightrope over boiling rapids. And only look how he played with human hearts like a boy pulling wings off flies for sport.

But even that truthful answer didn't completely explain her motivation. For she was compelled to protect him from Paul's treachery. She would not see him harmed from her actions. No matter what.

"Why not at least become my mistress?" he demanded when she turned silently away and placed her hand on the porcelain doorknob.

"Because, Mr. Belloch," she replied coolly just before she left his suite, "I personally find more honor in being a thief than a concubine. Nor would I ever feel comfortable enjoying the caresses of a man I so thoroughly despise."

Chapter 25

Because the thieves who masqueraded as Paul Rillieux's servants were not fairly compensated for their domestic servitude, Mystere had steadfastly insisted they must be allowed free time whenever their services were not immediately required. Rillieux carped about this constantly, complaining that such liberties jeopardized the illusion he had so artfully constructed. But on this one point Mystere had stubbornly put her foot down, and the old man grudgingly relented.

Thus it was that Hush found time, early on the Saturday afternoon of Mrs. Astor's party, to take the ferry from the Battery to Staten Island. He was free until six P.M., when he had to again don his monkey suit, as he called it, and be ready for the trip to the Astor residence.

He had used the new reading skills Mystere taught him to look up Rafe Belloch's name in the phone directory. There were two addresses listed for him, one at the Astor House Hotel and another on Staten Island. But when he went to the hotel, the desk clerk told him Belloch would not return there until Monday. So Hush decided to try the Bay Street address.

Only a few other passengers disembarked with him at the wooden slip, mostly island residents returning from shopping trips or their jobs in the city. It was a hot, windless day, a few ragged tatters of cloud strung thinly across a sky as blue as a lagoon. Hush tramped along the crushed gravel of Bay Street, which followed the curving sea wall, south toward a huge white house that sat atop a low rise, offering a commanding view of the Upper Bay.

"Jiminy!" he said under his breath as he approached the impressive gate of fieldstone and wrought iron, its cast-iron pillars thrusting into the sky like artillery guns. He was even more impressed—and intimidated—by the huge gatekeeper who stepped out of the gatehouse to greet him.

The man smiled down at him in a friendly manner. But Hush could barely take his eyes off the ivory-grip pistol tucked into his belt.

"Hey there, lad," the giant greeted him in a thick Irish accent. "What's on your mind besides your hat? Be you lost?"

"No, sir. I've come to see Mr. Belloch, please."

"Oh, you have, eh? Is he expectin' you?"

"No, sir."

"Sonny, this ain't a penny arcade. Mr. Belloch is an important man. He generally sees visitors by appointment, y'unnerstan'."

"Yessir. But—but it's very important that I see him."

"Important, you say?" The giant mulled this for a few moments, watching the boy through the gate from amused, curious eyes.

"How old are you, tadpole?"

"Twelve, sir."

"And the nature of your visit?"

"It's . . . quite private, sir, no disrespect to you. I can only discuss it with Mr. Belloch himself."

By now the guard's curiosity seemed to overcome his hesitation. He glanced toward the house, and Hush followed his gaze. In a fenced-off paddock behind one corner of the house, he could see a distinguished-looking man in tan riding breeches and tall oxblood boots. He was currying a sorrel horse that was stripped down to the neck leather.

The gatekeeper turned around to pull a bell on the gatehouse door, getting the man's attention. Hush watched him hand the brush to a stable boy and stroll across the green, sloping lawn toward them, his step purposeful. He wore his chestnut hair short and swept straight back. In this better lighting, Hush liked the man's face even though he felt a little inner stab of jealousy—this was Rafael Belloch himself, the man Mystere was going to marry.

"What's up, Jimmy?" the man asked, nodding at the visitor as he drew up at the gate.

"This young fellow says he's come to see you on important business, Mr. Belloch. Says it can only be discussed privately with you."

By now Rafe's curiosity was piqued. He looked at Hush. "Private business, you say? What's your name, son?"

"I'm called Hush, sir."

"Hush." Rafe studied him a few moments in silence. "Hush, is it? Well, young Master Hush—what business could you have with me? Or have you come to dust my doublet?"

Hush grinned, embarrassed. "No, sir."

He glanced up uncertainly through the black wrought-iron bars at Jimmy. "It's about Mystere Rillieux, sir. Sorter private like."

Rafe's eyes narrowed in suspicion. "Mystere? Tell me straight-arrow now, did old man Rillieux send you here?" he demanded.

"No, sir. I've come on my own."

"Is that the truth?"

Hush placed his right hand over his heart. "God strike me down, sir, if it's not."

The solemn earnestness in the boy's pale face softened Rafe's features. "Let him come in, Jimmy."

When Hush had come inside the grounds, Rafe Belloch offered his hand and both of them shook.

"Well, sir," Rafe said in a brisk, businesslike manner. "Shall we go inside and discuss this man-to-man over coffee and cigars? Or perhaps you'd prefer brandy?"

Hush fell into step beside him, practically running to keep up with Rafe's long stride. "No, sir, coffee is fine."

"Then, coffee it shall be. I like a man who avoids spirits during the daytime. Show me a daylight drinker, sir, and I'll show you a man who does not take proper care of his family."

"Yessir," Hush said, feeling pleasantly overwhelmed by Rafe Belloch's reception. He was treating him like a man, not some snot-nosed brat. Hush had come prepared to dislike this man who was marrying Mystere; now, however, he could not blame her one bit for liking him.

A pleasant-looking older woman admitted them to the house, and

Rafe requested that she bring them coffee in the library. When Rafe flung open the oak-paneled doors, Hush gaped in astonishment at the luxuriously appointed room.

"Have you read all them books, sir?" he asked, awed at the hundreds of leather-bound volumes with gold-embossed titles on their spines.

"Many of them, and I'm working through the rest. Some are pure drivel, but others are quite good. Do you read?"

"I've just started, sir. Mystere taught me."

"She did?"

"Yessir. Mystere says a man must be a reader to get on properly in this world."

"I heartily agree," Rafe approved, watching Hush from thoughtful eyes. "Do you have a mother and father?"

Hush shook his head. "I never knew my father. I'm told the white plague got Mother, sir. I don't hardly remember her, neither."

Rafe nodded. "When a man has lost his parents," he told Hush, his tone matter-of-fact, "he can sometimes feel alone even in a big city surrounded by people."

"Yessir. Have you? Lost your parents too, I mean?"

Rafe dropped into a mahogany armchair and waved Hush into another nearby.

"Yes," he replied. "And everything you see around you, Hush, I earned after their deaths and with no one's help. Don't ever think that being an orphan is a crippling strike against you, do you understand me? Ours is not a perfect nation by a long shot, but it *is* a land of opportunity for those who roll up their sleeves."

Hush nodded. "That's sorter like what Mystere tells me, too. Study hard and learn an honest trade instead of—"

He caught himself just in time, and Rafe gave him another thoughtful glance. Ruth saved Hush by arriving just then carrying a silver coffee service.

"How do you take your coffee, young Master Hush?" she inquired, beaming at the awestruck lad.

Unsure, he glanced over to see how Rafe had taken his. "Black, please," he replied.

"That's the lad," Rafe encouraged him. "They say the man who drinks black coffee will rule Ireland."

"I wouldn't care much for that job, sir," Hush replied with a straight face. "You see, I want to drive trains when I'm older."

Ruth and her employer exchanged discreet, mirthful glances. Then she left the room, and Rafe crossed to a nearby lift-top desk, returning with a box of cigars. He used a small silver cutter to snip the ends off two, handing one to Hush. Rafe struck a match to life and lit first his, then Hush's.

"Good Cuban hand-rolleds," he remarked between puffs. "I like a good cigar now and then."

Hush had smoked only a pipe in his time, but felt foolish admitting it. "Me, too," he fibbed just before a coughing fit silenced him.

"Don't inhale it," Rafe advised him casually, barely restraining a grin. "Now then, Hush—what is it you wish to discuss with me?"

"It's about Mystere, sir."

"Mm, you said that already. What about her? You don't mean to challenge me to a duel for her hand, do you?"

Hush's mouth fell open, and he almost lost his cigar. Then he saw Rafe grinning and smiled a little himself. But now that the moment was at hand, he found himself at a loss for words.

"It's just that . . . well, I mean . . . you see, sir, she's in deep soup. And I *won't* let anyone hurt her, Mr. Belloch, sir."

"Do you think I mean to hurt her?"

"Oh, no, sir. You're going to marry her, ain'tcha?"

Rafe took the cigar out of his mouth and studied it a moment, a thin, bitter smile touching his lips. Or did he just have smoke in his eyes? Hush wondered.

"So it would seem," Rafe finally replied. "Does she seem happy about that?"

Hush had trouble fibbing to people he liked. He was suddenly embarrassed and feigned interest in a world globe standing near his chair.

"Not like you'd expect, sir," he admitted. "She . . . cries all the time now."

"She does, eh?"

"Yessir, but only when she thinks no one is looking. And Mystere ain't no bawl baby. For a girl so pretty and sweet, she's a tough one."

Rafe pondered this a moment, his eyes going distant.

"Women are often difficult to fathom, Hush," he finally replied.

"And their tears are seldom a clear clue to anything. But what do you mean about not letting anyone hurt her? *Is* someone hurting her?"

Hush nodded. "Yessir. Or trying to anyhow."

He paused, obviously reluctant to continue. Rafe guessed why.

"Just between me and you, Hush," he confided, "Mystere has already told me the truth."

"The . . . truth, sir?"

"Yes. About the old man, Rillieux, and how he sets up school to teach youngsters to steal for him. He's taught her, and he's taught you, hasn't he?"

Hush remained perfectly still for perhaps ten seconds. Then he nodded.

"Yessir. You see, Mystere had no choice about it. Mr. Rillieux, he has this sorter . . . power. Power to make you do what he wants."

Rafe flicked his cigar ash into a ceramic ashtray. "I see. Is it the old man you mean when you say someone is trying to hurt her?"

"No, sir. It's two other men."

Feeling uninhibited now, Hush explained everything he knew about Lorenzo Perkins and his partner, Sparky.

"And now," he concluded, "they've decided to come see you, sir. They haven't beat me here, have they? I come quick as I could."

Rafe shook his head. "I'm not an easy man to catch during the week. They might have tried and missed me."

"They mean to get a lot of money from you, sir. And if you don't pay them, they mean to . . . humiliate you, I think is how they said it. You and Mystere."

"That's quite interesting. Just how do they mean to do this? What do they know—or think they know?"

Hush shrugged one shoulder. "I ain't sure, sir. Something about how Rillieux ain't really Mystere's name, how she's a big fake. They mean to go to the police and the newspapers if you don't pay them."

"I see. And so you've come to me on your own to warn me, is that it?"

"Yessir. I daren't say anything to Mystere, for she has so much on her mind now."

"Yes," Rafe muttered, pulling on his chin. "I suppose she must."

After a moment he shook off his pensive mood.

"Well then, Hush," he said in a brisk tone, smiling at his visitor. "You and I are going to become partners. Would you like that?"

"Partners, sir?"

"Of course, for this woman is my fiancée. And it certainly appears to me that you have more than a casual regard for her or you wouldn't have come here like this."

"Oh, yessir. She's the specialest person I've ever knowed. I'd do anything for her."

"I see that. And I'll be counting on you to serve as her chief protector when I'm absent. Are you willing?"

Hush visibly swelled with pride and determination. "You bet! You can count on me, sir."

Rafe leaned over and patted the boy's shoulder. "I know I can, for you have the look of a stout fellow. Don't you worry. I'll be ready for this Lorenzo and—who?"

"Sparky, sir. A big, dumb galoot."

"Yes, this Sparky. I'll have a little welcome ready for them, and don't worry—I'll not mention your name."

Hush suddenly coughed again, turning a bit pale from the cigar. Rafe, covering a grin by averting his face, offered the box. "Care for another?"

"No thanks, sir. One is my limit."

"Ahh, a disciplined man, too. I like that. Well, I have some work to do, Hush, so I hope you'll excuse me. Have we covered everything to your satisfaction?"

"Oh, yessir."

"Good, good. How are you getting back to the city—by the ferry?"

Hush nodded.

"I take it sometimes, too, but it's a long wait on the weekends," Rafe pointed out. "I'll walk you down to the slip and have my crew take you across on the yacht."

Hush went wide-eyed with surprise. "You will?"

"Of course. You've done me a service, have you not? Turnabout is fair play. How'd you like to take the wheel?"

This time his boyish excitement made Hush forget to be formal. "Boy, would I! Man alive!"

Rafe laughed, enjoying his excitement. "One more thing, Hush," he said as the two of them started out of the drawing room. "Not a word to Mystere about this visit, eh? Mum's the word?"

"Mum's the word, sir."

"Good man. Remember we're partners now in looking after her. If we play our cards right, no one will hurt her."

As he was about to close the doors to the drawing room, Rafe thought of one last thing. "Hush, wait for me a few moments outside with Jimmy, will you? I'll be right out."

Rafe went back into the room and took a sheet of stationery from the desk. Dipping a steel nib into a pot of ink, he wrote only one sentence: *Get some relevant information on Lorenzo Perkins, who lives on Amos Street, and a dock laborer called Sparky, friend of Perkins.*

On his way out front to join Hush, Rafe gave the note to Ruth.

"See that Sam gets this tonight. And when you give it to him, tell him the sooner the better."

Sam would know full well what Rafe intended by "relevant information." And Sam also knew at least a dozen private detectives who had worked for Belloch Enterprises at one time or another. Rafe had learned long ago that any person was guilty of something if one looked closely enough. Let the two would-be blackmailers come—he would be ready for them.

Chapter 26

Dread lay heavy in her stomach as Mystere prepared for her first "engagement party."

Since Mrs. Astor herself was hosting it, Mystere knew full well that the night's gala would be only the first of many, for any marriage among the Four Hundred was always treated as an historical event ranking with the coronation of kings. How she could ever hope to maintain the deception was beyond her.

But she had pondered Rafe's motivation, his seeming eagerness to indulge this dangerous hypocrisy, and she had hit upon a suspicion that deeply troubled her. The first chance she had to get him alone, she meant to confront him about it.

Rafe might not care about the ultimate consequences of building false expectations, but *she* could hardly ignore them. Paul's new "affection" for her would turn ugly in a heartbeat once the engagement was broken off. And Evan and Baylis had suddenly become solicitous toward her in a manner that indicated they, too, had great expectations of personal gain. Baylis had even shaved off his ridiculous Newgate fringe, declaring it unworthy of a great lady's coachman.

Only Rose and Hush seemed to understand and sympathize with her latest dilemma. While drawing Mystere's dark coffee-colored hair into a chignon, late on Saturday afternoon, Rose offered some encouragement.

"Things may seem terrible now, hon, but you must not give up hope. When we brood, we create a picture of hell that fate may not have in store for us. Worry only about that which you can control, and let God handle the rest."

It was fine advice and did serve to cheer her mood considerably. So did Hush's whispered remark as he handed her into the carriage that evening.

"Don't you worry, Mystere, no one is going to hurt you on *our* watch."

The lad seemed so confident that she had to smile—her first in some time.

"Our?" she repeated. "Have you joined forces with a guardian angel?"

Hush only sent her a mysterious wink as he closed the door. It was but a brief ride to the Astor residence, located on upper Fifth Avenue.

"Remember, m'love," Paul said just before Baylis reined in the team out front, "you will be expected to join Rafe the moment you see him. This night is intended as a showcase for the two of you. Caroline told me she has even taken the unprecedented step of actually inviting newspaper people. Lance Streeter himself will be here, nibbling canapés alongside the Vanderbilts. No more of your caustic glances and cold shoulders—be radiant and submissive. This is theater, and the lights must come up, so to speak, the moment you and Rafe are together."

He took both her hands in his and leaned close, his sharp features sinister in the flickering gaslights from outside. "This tonight, why it's nothing. Your preparation and training will see you through it. The Lady Moonlight will soon be no more, and tonight you are under no pressure to steal sparklers under the noses of the rich. You are Mystere Rillieux, an accomplished Creole miss from New Orleans. Soon to become Mystere Belloch."

Except, she thought silently as Hush handed her out, *that Rafe knows precisely who—and what—I am. And being a man with secret, bitter, destructive motives, he might well turn Paul's "theater" into a farce, his "showcase" into a travesty.*

Hundreds of Chinese lanterns showed that many of the guests had already arrived, mingling in twos and threes in the lush gardens that wrapped the house on three sides. A servant led them along a slate pathway, setting a slow pace to accommodate Paul.

Despite Paul's reassurances just now, Mystere felt a nervous tickle in her chest like cobwebs brushing her heart. She mentally cataloged the guests she could recognize as she approached: Garret and Eugenia Teasdale, James and Lizet Addison, Sylvia Rohr, the Vernons, Antonia Butler with her parents, Dr. and Mrs. Sanford, and of course the Vanderbilt sisters, social fixtures who prized Mrs. Astor's invitations much more than did the male Vanderbilts.

"There's Trevor Sheridan and his sister," Paul remarked, visibly impressed that the Duchess of Granville had deigned to attend. "Caroline told me the duke, too, would have been here except that he is upstate on a hunting expedition."

The Duchess of Granville . . . Mystere thought again about the armorial insignia that she had so foolishly clung to for so many years. And for a few fleeting moments she wondered if somehow, despite the apparent absurdity of it, there *was* some kind of real link between the British peerage and two children of the Dublin slums. Or, more likely, at least some logical reason why someone would write to her family on stationery bearing the Connacht coat of arms.

However, she had no time to dwell on anything, for she had just spotted Rafe standing near the orchestra dais and talking animatedly to Mrs. Astor and Carrie.

"This way, miss," the servant said deferentially, surprising her by taking her hand and leading her up three marble steps that led to a broad, well-illuminated garden terrace.

As if on cue, Paul stepped aside for the moment. As she moved from shadow into light, Mystere realized this was deliberately choreographed by Caroline as the bride-to-be's grand entrance. The orchestra struck up a soft rendition of Liszt's "Beauty Triumphant." The hubbub of conversation and laughter abruptly abated, and men seemed to shed their slouches as she passed. She had chosen her finest gown, full-length and sleeveless, of emerald green satin with a double-ribbon tie at the waist, no jewelry except a simple pair of pale moonstone earrings. Even Rafe seemed genuinely transfixed at first sight of her.

He stepped forward as she approached, gallantly bowing and touching his lips to her hand. "Darling, your loveliness puts the Vestal Virgins to shame," he greeted her, his eyes silently goading her.

"They were selected for their chasteness, not their beauty," she reminded him, poking right back.

"Better chased than chaste, eh? Besides, this maidenhead business is vastly overrated."

Outsparred again, she managed a cold, withdrawn smile as he took her arm in his and led her to Caroline and Carrie.

"Oh, Mystere, I'm so happy for *both* of you," Carrie effused with genuine sweetness, hugging her close. Unlike her astute and jaded mother, Mystere realized, Carrie accepted this engagement at face value, and her deluded gushing hurt almost as much as Rafe's secret cynicism.

Caroline bussed her cheek, a bit more reserved than usual but keeping up a good front. Rafe, however, had evidently decided to show Mrs. Astor that he was not entirely her puppet.

"How do you like Mystere's gown, Caroline?" he asked in a pointed tone. "Don't you agree it *brings out* something in her?"

He meant just the opposite, of course, for Mystere had again carefully bound her breasts. But if Mrs. Astor was at all curious about the girl's adjustable bustline, she had decided to keep any questions to herself—no difficult matter for a woman who dealt almost exclusively in appearance over substance.

Refusing to be baited, she sent Rafe a quelling stare. "Heel, Mr. Belloch," she muttered, "or I'll bring out *my* artillery. Do I make myself clear?"

"Implicitly," he surrendered.

Caroline turned away for a moment to speak with the orchestra leader. Rafe seized the opportunity and led Mystere away from the throng, bearing toward a cast-iron footbridge that arced across a lovely, lily-covered pond.

However, before he could get her alone, Abbot Pollard, emitting a reek of whiskey, suddenly ambushed them from behind a clump of oleander shrubbery.

"Permit me to congratulate the happy couple," he slurred in his nasal baritone and affected enunciation, the words obviously ringing a false note.

He leaned close to whisper in Mystere's ear, "But *entre nous*, my dear, the pearl is being cast to the swine."

"Say it out loud, Pollard, you drunken sot," Rafe snapped impatiently. "Or has Dutch courage replaced your spine?"

Abbot raised his sweat-beaded cocktail glass in a mock salute. "Oh, come now, Mr. Mountain Mover, you are a friend of the laboring man. Don't you realize that drink is the work of the cursing classes?"

"Abbot," Mystere admonished him gently, "you *are* drinking too heavily. And what are you doing hiding over here all by yourself?"

Again he raised his glass, this time pointing in Caroline's direction with it. "Blame that humorless shrew. She's miffed at me again. I merely referred to the Astor Place riots as 'Disastor Place,' and she did not appreciate my taking her name in vain."

This confession actually evoked a chuckle from Rafe. "An old joke, but quite brazen right in front of her," he admitted with grudging admiration. "Perhaps I've underrated you a bit, Abbot. *Just* a bit."

Rafe led Mystere toward the footbridge again.

"Well, as long as we're being mawkishly sentimental," Abbot called out behind them, "you two really do make a fine-looking couple even if Mystere does deserve far better."

Rafe led her out onto the footbridge. They suddenly found shadowed solitude amidst the many, with a wonderful view of everything and everyone. Now and then violins rose above the muted hum of the guests, and a few couples had begun waltzing on a wooden dance floor constructed in the middle of the terrace.

"We must give the gossip merchants some juicy items," Rafe remarked, all the time studying Mystere as if she were a curious museum exhibit.

"I noticed you looking at Caroline's ruby bracelet," he remarked, still watching her closely. "A fine addition to your trousseau, eh, Lady Moonlight?"

"Lady Moonlight is no more now that I have the emerald." She didn't look at him.

"Yes, the ring. Your price of freedom. How is the search for that brother of yours going—this missing brother of yours, Brad."

"Bram."

"Right, Bram. You said he's eight years older than you. Do you seriously expect me to believe *he* never mentioned your last name to you?"

"My mother made him promise not to divulge it to others. I think she made such a point of that, and he was afraid I, being younger, would tell someone if I knew it."

"All right, but why would your mother do such an odd thing?"

It surprised her to realize that Rafe seemed genuinely curious to know the same answers she herself had sought for so long. She was about to mention the letter to him again, but his next question interrupted her.

"How do I know all this lost-identity business is not just concocted to hide a shadow on your name?"

Although the question angered her, she realized again that his tone implied genuine curiosity, not just his usual bullying sarcasm.

"It's no concoction," she assured him. "Rather, my name *is* a shadow, and I'm trying to throw light on it."

He digested her answer in silence, leaning both forearms on the handrail of the bridge and watching the dancers.

He truly is a handsome man, she thought, studying his swept-back chestnut hair and the strong patrician nose. Perhaps his claim that Caroline had intended to seduce him was not so absurd after all.

Thinking about this, however, also reminded her of the question she had determined to ask him.

"Rafe?"

"Hmm?"

"Your decision last Sunday to play along with Caroline rather than expose me—at first I flattered myself that you chose to protect me. But I have another theory."

He glanced at her, eyebrows raised in bemused inquiry. "Then, by all means, expound it."

"I think you meant it when you said you feel obligated to protect your employees from deprivation. But I also think you *are* perhaps willing to risk financial ruin—that you're doing all this to somehow eventually humiliate Caroline."

"Oh? And why would I want to do that?"

"Because more than anything else, you want to hurt her, hurt her entire social class, in fact, for what you think they did to your parents."

Instantly she realized she had touched a raw nerve. His face tightened, jaw muscles bunching, and he turned to face her. The comingling of great hurt and great anger in his face made her deeply regret being so blunt.

"You fight your battles and I shall fight mine," he lashed out, his voice barely under control. "And 'think' hasn't got one damn thing to do with it. It was a bullet my father fired into his own brain, not my opinions. It was *grief and shame* that took my mother early from this world, not my thin-skinned perceptions. . . ."

But his voice broke as powerful emotions overwhelmed his careful defenses. Mystere felt as though a dagger had been thrust into her heart when she thought a tear escaped one of his eyes, but he turned away from her as if hiding his weakness.

Overcome, she clutched his arm. "Oh, Rafe, I'm so terribly sorry. I didn't know anything about—"

He wrenched his arm away. "That's right, you didn't know, so keep your shallow theorizing to yourself, do you hear me?"

For the first time since she had known him, his cold words did not anger her, so overcome was she by remorse. She wanted, more than anything, to find something that might comfort him. But their brief time alone had come to an end. With the worst possible timing, Carrie Astor now joined them on the bridge.

"Forgive the interruption, you two lovebirds," she greeted them with an apologetic smile. "But Mother has requested that the two of you come dance a waltz for us. She has even cleared everyone else off the floor. It's your own fault, you know, for being such stunning dancers at the Addison ball."

"Anything for dear Caroline," Rafe responded, his old self securely back in place. "Come along, Lady M," he added in a lower tone when Carrie was far enough ahead of them, leading the way off the bridge. "Let's give Lance Streeter something to gush about."

Aware of all the eyes watching her, Mystere carefully made sure that her face mirrored nothing of her heart-pounding fear. But as the orchestra struck up "The Blue Danube," and Rafe led her out onto the dance floor, she mentally prepared herself for a repeat of his aggressive performance at the Addisons', when he had tried to turn dance into physical combat.

Especially after his angry, emotional outburst just a few minutes ago, she feared even her rigorous years of training could not help her control his turbulence, which always seemed to need release in physical action. But how wrong she was tonight.

With perhaps half of Mrs. Astor's elect ringed about them, not to mention a dozen or so mesmerized gossip writers, Rafe became a new man in her arms. Rather than *force* her to the very limits of grace and balance, he encouraged and joined her.

They seemed to become one person in mind and movement, sweeping round the floor so effortlessly and flawlessly that no seam existed between the dancers and the dance—"as if," Lance Streeter would later write in rapturous prose, "perfection were no longer an illusion of the artist, and Michelangelo's great *David* suddenly breathed life with the rest of us."

Again and again the music rose in a powerful shout of brass and percussion, then settled into a silken whisper of strings and woodwinds, and to a transported Mystere, it seemed that her heart kept the tempo, not the conductor's hand. But as she gazed up into Rafe's eyes, which now looked back at her in a new tenderness, she had to force herself back to the solid ground of reality.

He is only playacting, her mind lectured. *Do not confuse appearance and reality where he is concerned; this is not the storybook romance you have always pictured for yourself. He is a cruel and dangerous man, and while there may be just causes for his cruelty,* you *must fear only the results of it.*

When the musicians had reached their final flourish, Rafe, still holding one of her hands, stepped back and bowed gallantly to her. The spellbound audience erupted in a cheering ovation that no one could ever have expected from such a normally staid and reserved group. Mrs. Astor herself, whom Lance Streeter once described as "possessing no more emotion than a stone lion," was forced to blink back tears of feeling.

"I confess," she whispered afterward to Mystere, "that I had second thoughts about my decision to compel this marriage. But no two persons were ever more intended for each other than you and Rafe."

Mystere somehow managed a smile to that, but each word was a nail in the coffin of her hopes. And Rafe, as if sensing that his little performance had only plunged her deeper into despair, was now truly enjoying his ironic game for the public's consumption. He was tender, attentive, gallant, never once leaving her side for the rest of the evening.

Nor was everyone present completely captivated by this "perfect romance." Even as Mystere watched, Antonia Butler stared in her direction and made some obviously barbed comment that caused the women around her to laugh. Antonia's venom made Mystere almost glad she had stolen her ring, which was now carefully hidden in the same box that held the letter to her father.

She was actually grateful for Antonia's animosity, for it burst the illusive bubble of this night and reminded her of the threats she must not underestimate. Threats such as Lorenzo Perkins and Sparky. They had not bothered her since her fifty-dollar payment, but why had they been so quiet lately? She doubted that their greed could be so easily appeased. They were planning something, and she mustn't let a few minutes of waltzing fool her into a false sense of security.

"Why so despondent, darling?" Rafe's voice startled her back to the present. "You look like you're being led to the guillotine. Is my girl unhappy about something?"

His sarcasm was back, and he had managed to lead her aside for a moment, a shimmering fountain hiding them from the others.

"The splendor of the moment won't last, and you know it as well as I," she whispered intimately to him. "We each must strike out upon our own path. The folly of this becomes ever more like a knife through the heart."

He suddenly brought both arms around her and pulled her close before she could prevent him. She felt his strength, the solid form that felt like a coiled spring about to release. It attracted, yet frightened her, and even as she felt the inner stirrings of sexual response, her mind recoiled from the sheer danger of him.

"All right, then," he said close to her ear, his breath moist and warm as the response within her, "let's change this statas quo you cannot abide. I meant what I told you at the hotel—I want you."

This time, however, she turned her face away when he tried to force a kiss on her.

"Why should I?" she shot back angrily. "So that once your passion is spent, you can shove me out of your bed and go back to your ledgers and maps as if you'd just finished a cup of tea? I've told you before that I have no desire to become your whore."

"Some would say that Lady Moonlight has already made a whore of her soul. Why not bring your body into harmony with it?"

"Perhaps that's true, but at least I *have* a soul, however tarnished. You have willingly banished yours and allowed an unreasoning hatred to take its place. Let me *go!*"

Rafe laughed harshly, easily forcing her even closer despite her best efforts to get free. "I keep seeing you as you looked that morning in my library," he said, his voice a low husk as desire tightened his throat. "And I feel my body on fire, a fire only you can quench."

"Gracious God, what's this?" exclaimed a mocking, slurred voice behind them. "Have I caught the lovebirds in flagrante delicto?"

Abbot, so drunk by now that he seemed to be walking on sea legs, had come around behind the fountain. One hand held his latest cocktail glass; the other wagged a shame-on-you finger at them. "Naughty, naughty. I shall run and tell the Shrew, and you'll be forced to do pennance."

Reluctantly, cursing under his breath, Rafe was forced to let her go. Mystere quickly turned to Abbot, managing a smile for him. He had suddenly become her unlikely knight.

"I see you've raided Caroline's prize flower beds," she said lightly, for now there was a fresh chrysanthemum in Abbot's lapel. "Perhaps I shall tell on *you*."

Taking one quick backward step to retain his shaky balance, Abbot lowered his nose to sniff the purloined flower.

"It covers the stink of all this new money," he confided, thick-tongued. "So many minks, so few manners. And Caroline actually *invited* them, the traitorous bitch. Lovebirds, I ask, 'If gold will rust, what then will iron do?' "

Rafe snorted but seemed quite amused at the spectacle of a drunken, disheveled Abbot Pollard acting as a lone crusader for New York's embattled Old Guard.

Mystere moved away from Rafe and took Abbot by the arm. "Come along, we're getting some coffee into you. You've always been a scratchy old grump, but now you're becoming downright mean."

"So what?" he slurred belligerently, although he allowed himself to be led. He looked at Rafe, who had come up on his other side to help support him. "Some men mellow with age. Others, like myself, harden and narrow. So? Who's to say which group is right? I ask you, Mr. Mountain Mover—who's to say?"

"Who, indeed?" Rafe replied, his invasive teal eyes leveled at Mystere—as was his next remark. "One man's 'unreasoning hatred' is often the next man's reason for being."

Chapter 27

"It's now or never, Sparky," Lorenzo Perkins announced, glancing nervously across Broadway toward the massive structure of the Astor House Hotel. "We played hell tracking him down; let's not botch it now."

He and Sparky occupied a wrought-iron bench in City Hall Park, killing the few minutes left before their eleven A.M. appointment with Rafe Belloch.

"Tell you the honest-to-Christ truth," Sparky replied, "I'd feel better about this if we had more to spill about the girl."

"You're not getting icy feet on me now, are you?"

"You fool, you know damn well I'd kiss the devil's ass if it meant a quick profit," Sparky assured his partner. "But you never shoulda made no appointment until we had more solid goods on his woman. *You're* the one alla time bragging how you was once a Pinkerton. I've heard that's just a lie; all you done was type up surveillance reports for them."

"You just don't grasp it, do you? The details ain't so important. It's the fear of what we *might* know or find out; that's what we have to plant inside Belloch's mind. We paint a picture for him, see? He's engaged to this woman; the last thing he'll want is any dirt coming out about her now. Am I right 'r not?"

"I s'pose you've got a point."

"All right, then." Lorenzo stood up, slapping the dust off his trousers. "Let's go. Just let me do the talking, and you watch how quick our boy Belloch reaches for his billfold."

Rafe, seated at his work-cluttered desk, watched his visitors from eyes as hard as gems. The two men stood just inside the open door of room 511, for Belloch had not even asked them to have a seat.

"No one asked either of you to stick your oar in my boat, gentlemen. Now that you have, please get to your point. I have a business to run."

"P'r'aps you should keep a more civil tongue in your head, Mr. Belloch," Lorenzo replied boldly. "We're the ones holding all the aces."

Rafe cast an amused glance toward Sam Farrell, who occupied a corner sofa at the rear of the room, idly scanning the *Times*.

"All right, then," Rafe countered. "Let's go with your metaphor. I call. Let's see these aces of yours."

"For starters, your fiancée is not who she claims to be," Lorenzo stated with melodramatic triumph.

"Who among us is? All the world's a stage, Mr. Perkins."

"This ain't philosophy I'm talking," he persisted stubbornly. "I'm telling you she *claims* her last name is Rillieux, but it ain't."

"No? Then, what is it?"

Lorenzo failed to respond quickly, evidently taken aback by the blunt, practical way Rafe posed his question.

"Well, it sure's hell ain't Rillieux," Sparky chimed in, sending a warning elbow into Perkins's side.

Rafe laughed, shaking his head. "I'm dubious, gentlemen, to say the least. You march in here boasting how you're 'in the know,' but frankly I think you have less than spider leavings. I ask you again: If Rillieux is not my fiancée's last name, what *is* her real name?"

"She don't know that fact herself," Lorenzo volunteered. "For I was hired to locate a brother of hers, and she admitted to me she didn't know his last name."

"Did you find the brother?" Rafe demanded.

"No," Lorenzo admitted.

"But got paid plenty for it, I'll wager."

Lorenzo ignored that. "What else could that mean except she don't know her own name?"

Rafe drummed his fingers impatiently on the desk. "Mere mental vapors, gentlemen. For your information she's told me all this already. Did you ever find out anything at all about this brother?"

"Some things," Lorenzo replied cryptically.

"Such as . . . ?"

Lorenzo's turtle eyes slanted away from Belloch's probing stare. "This. That."

Rafe laughed again, looking from one to the other. "I figured as much. You took the girl's money and lied about trying to find the brother. Simply exploited her love and concern to make an easy buck."

Neither man responded. Rafe slapped the desk. "Well, come on then, boys—*one* of you had better quit scowling at me and pull a rabbit from a hat."

"Listen, Belloch," Lorenzo protested, "I worked for your fiancée, and I'm saying it would've been obvious to a blind man she's hiding plenty of secrets about her past and who she is."

The two blackmailers were mostly engaged in stalling tactics. Nonetheless they did know just enough to perhaps cause Mystere some trouble somewhere down the line; Rafe could see that. That might interfere with his own plans. He looked at Sam and nodded once.

Sam, sighing as if bored, laid his newspaper aside and produced a file folder from the leather briefcase leaning against his legs. He opened it and took out a hand-written letter.

"Mr. Perkins," he announced, "I have here a letter written by Miss Laura Driscoll of 17 Washington Street. Your mistress of nearly two years now by her own admission. You may examine the letter if you wish. No? Well, in summation, she agrees to testify in court how you have given her money that by your own admission, should have been used for an operation your wife requires. I think you know what a dim view the city courts take of adultery. You can expect a few years at hard labor on Blackwell's Island."

Rafe watched Perkins remove his derby to mop the sweat from his brow with a limp handkerchief. His heavily pomaded hair had a part down it straight as a pike.

"As for you, Sparky," Sam continued in an efficient drone, "your penchant for carnal knowledge of juveniles may not much interest the city courts, for your victims are, like you, from the dregs of society."

Sparky frowned, his big nose wrinkling at the bridge. "Careful, you little barber's clerk," the big man interrupted angrily. "I'll make you swallow back them insults."

Sam's right hand disappeared inside his suit jacket and reemerged cocking a .38-caliber derringer. Both of the visitors paled noticeably. Sam continued reading from his notes.

"But one of your favorite victims is a girl named Sissy Folam, only fourteen. And her brother is Terrance Folam, leader of the Five Points gang known as the Plug Uglies. Terrance is said to be a hard, ruthless man with only one soft spot in him, and that's for his kid sister. Tell us, Sparky—Terrance doesn't know yet what you've done to the girl, does he?"

A radical transformation had come over Sparky. His cocky beligerence had become cunning servility. "I . . . no, sir, I 'spect he don't, at that. And I'm after keeping things that way, for a fact I am."

Rafe looked at Lorenzo. "Is that how you see it, too, Perkins?"

Lorenzo gave a surly frown, but he also nodded.

"You two bungling fools should stick to the Bowery," Rafe advised, his tone bristling with impatience. "On Wall Street you're just chum among sharks."

He took a jade-inlaid teak box from his desk. "Nothing is owed to you by law or morality. But here's two hundred fifty dollars for each of you. I do this for my fiancée's sake, not my own, so you'll have no cause to victimize her in the future."

Rafe handed each man his share, forcing eye contact before letting go of it. "Now you'll have no claim to any grudge against her, neither of you, so leave her alone, I warn you. Mark me, men, for I keep my word: Every man who works for me is an armed marksman, as am I. Show your greedy faces here, at my Staten Island property, or at my office on Wall Street ever again, and you'll be arrested on sight. I have a witness here that you are blackmailers, a serious felony. You've both been warned, now good day."

When both men had hurried out, Rafe crossed to the door and shut it. Then he went into the bedroom, where he could lean out an open window and verify that Lorenzo and Sparky had emerged on the sidewalk below. He went back to the outer room and looked at Sam. "Think we adequately neutralized the risk?"

"No question. The charges we have against them are strong, and they both know it. You gave them enough money to quench any thirst for revenge. But not so much that you appear desperate to muzzle them. By the way—that 'chum among sharks' business almost got me up laughing. Scared them, though."

"I hope," Rafe said absently. "You know, Sam, I really was hoping to learn something from them. About the woman, I mean."

"I noticed that. I was, too, actually."

"See? See how she is? She does that to people, gets under their skin quick, but she doesn't try to—it just happens." Rafe put the box back in the drawer, then began pacing slowly between the desk and the bedroom door.

"Damnit anyway, Sam, but I'm letting her get *to* me."

"There's a bold theory," Sam remarked drily, and Rafe grinned quick, a brief apology for being so obvious.

"I understand now," he continued, "why the Roman generals considered women such a bad influence on the warrior. They give men too much to think about, and men with naked women on their minds do not boldly face death."

Rafe knew he was waxing dramatic, yet he truly resented Mystere for weakening his resolve of destruction in the interest of vengeance. To Caroline Astor and her cohorts, the deaths of John and Kathrine Belloch were not simply forbidden topics. In a sense they were less than that—utterly insignificant. So what if his father had kept many of them solvent during the sluggish days before the War of Rebellion? Not even one of them had shown up to give a decent man a decent burial.

When his mother died soon after, Caroline and a few others did send condolences. But her funeral, too, was an ostracized event, attended only by a few relatives. Those final slights had remained with Rafe all these years—cankering.

All right, then, a sickness, he admitted to himself. *Perhaps we are only as sick as our secrets.*

And that was probably the lure of Lady Moonlight, he thought with a dark smile. No one, it seemed, had more secrets than her.

"You're being too hard on yourself," Sam assured him as he packed everything back into his briefcase. "I've not met her yet, but from all indications the woman truly is remarkable. I think you've discovered that her captivating personality is not all an act."

"No, you're right, she really is a mystery, just like her name. But this is one time when I'd rather handle the fact-finding myself, Sam."

Farrell flashed his snaggled grin. "I wasn't aware that I'd offered my services. I'm glad you feel that way about it, though."

"I believe most of her story, and no matter how lowly her beginnings in Dublin, there's no denying her accomplishments now. The woman is a superb dancer, and in one eyeblink she can leap from the subject of French laces to the battle acumen of Julius Caesar."

But never mind all that, he urged himself desperately. *You're foolishly making room in your one-track mind for her, and it's partly the fault of that boy, Hush. Unless the lad, too, is a cynical, first-rate actor, that visit on Saturday was genuine.* And the boy's notions about Mystere fit Rafe's unwilling view of her, too. Still, he mustn't dwell on her like this; he must defeat this unwanted attraction.

Because in cold, hard truth, *she* had become his best possible instrument of revenge. Sickness, unreasoning hatred—maybe so. But wasn't Caroline's pathetic, last-gasp aristocracy also sick in its own way? As Pasteur had proved, the best way to cure sickness was *with* sickness.

He suddenly stopped pacing and looked at Sam, who was patiently awaiting his employer's orders.

"At one moment, Sam, I think I've grasped everything. The next moment my insight is gone, like a fist when you open your hand. The truth about women, I fear, abides someplace where language can't quite reach it."

"A mystery," Sam summed up, smiling apologetically for the obvious pun.

Rafe nodded, his eyes clouded with conflicting ideas. He saw her again in the burnished gold candlelight of his drawing room, how the lines and form of her nakedness were so clear in that thin chemise. The dark, plum-colored circles where her nipples prodded the fabric, the dark and mysterious shadow between her legs . . . suddenly his blood was pulsing in demanding, needful surges, and only reluctantly he picked up his own briefcase.

"Yes. Mystere," he finally replied. "Now let's find Wilson and head back to the offices. She's cost us enough time."

Mystere knew she was in trouble, and why, the moment Paul called for a family meeting after lunch on Wednesday.

The quarterly payment on his "sure investment" had recently come due, and she knew, without being told, that he had gone to his safe and discovered the tiara was missing. With Mystere, Rose, Evan, Baylis, and Hush all assembled in the downstairs parlor, he drew himself up in a fearfully pompous huff and announced, "There has been an intolerable invasion of my privacy."

Before he could even find his verbal stride, Mystere spoke up boldly: "It was I who invaded your privacy, Paul. I took the tiara. The rest of them had nothing to do with it."

She knew she was taking a dangerous chance. It was true that she was his meal ticket now, and Paul's greed made him a calculating man—but only to a point. He had become insufferably self-important since he had been absorbed into Caroline Astor's inner circle. He saw the entry into his safe as an absolute affront.

So his rage now was immediate and terrifying. His face went splotchy with choleric blood. He rose unsteadily from his chair and hovered in front of her, raising his cane as if to strike her.

"Paul!" Rose exclaimed. "No!"

Evan moved quickly for such a big man. With one hand he collared Hush, who was about to tackle old Rillieux; with the other he gently, respectfully stayed Rillieux's hand.

"Nix on that, boss," Baylis reminded him. "Hand that feeds us and all that."

The hint was clumsy, perhaps, but Rillieux was crafty enough to heed it. This defiant young woman was his best hope of financial salvation, and he knew it.

But even as he calmed down, his petty tyranny only made Mystere all the more defiant.

"Paul, we're *all* sick and tired of your heavy-handed manner," she berated him. "You go too far in what you call 'loyalty.' "

"All of you?" he repeated, making it a demand as he looked round at the others. "Is this a rebellion, then?"

She, too, looked from one to the other, but even Rose and Hush glanced away, refusing to side against Paul.

"Baylis," she pleaded, "won't you at least be consistent? Every Thursday evening you attend the workers' free lectures. Where's that 'surplus labor value' talk you spout all day long?"

Baylis shrugged awkwardly. "Talk's cheap. I got no real kick, hon. Hell, it was a lucky night for me if I had a haystall to sleep in before Paul took me in. If not for him, the eye-ties would've gutted me by now."

"That's it." Evan nodded. "It ain't so bad, what we all got here. It ain't so bad at all, Mystere, and once we fit Belloch for a pine box—"

"That's enough," Paul interrupted hastily. "The rest of you can go now. I wish to speak with Mystere alone."

Having refused to support her courage, they were now slow in dispersing, as if to warn Paul against turning his temper on Mystere again. She was forced to accept it: Paul had given them, or so they viewed it, the only way they knew out of a miserable existence. Having tasted this new life, they were all justifiably frightened of returning to the old. She was on her own in resisting Paul's despotism. And she realized Rafe would almost surely be in danger if by some unlucky stroke of fortune or his sick will, this match between them actually resulted in marriage.

She couldn't be sure if Rafe would actually push things that far, even to satisfy his spite. But he might, and if it went that far *she* had to prevent marriage by disappearing. But it was going to be difficult to escape Paul's watchful eye. It was as if he knew she wanted flight. She could go nowhere without escort. Even the room on Centre Street, she now realized, would not prove the safe haven she had hoped. It might give her a few days at best—her disappearance would be a windfall for the daily papers, and even disguised she could not long maintain the fiction of Lydia Powell, bereaved young widow.

But if she hurried, she could sell the emerald ring and make arrangements to leave the city—perhaps by steamship to Europe, where it would be easier to get lost among the faces. She could give lessons in English, perhaps, or find some minor theatrical work.

When the others had filed out, Paul's cold, precise words nudged her back to the moment.

"Mystere, it's sufficient to tell you I cannot possibly countenance what you did. But at least you own up to taking the tiara. Will you also honestly tell me what you did with the money you got for it, for I assume it's sold by now?"

At least, she comforted herself, *he doesn't know the real reason I took it.* However, if Paul ever did find out somehow just how much Rafe knew about him, Paul's desperation would be unpredictable. Thus she must deflect his rage onto herself.

"I've used it to search for Bram," she lied in a clear, quiet voice.

Her answer didn't seem to surprise him, but he barely restrained his anger. "And have you found him?"

She shook her head. "Not even a trace of him."

"Did you also steal Antonia's ring for this purpose?"

"Someone else took it."

His questions answered, he allowed his rage to erupt. "I have repeatedly ordered you to give up this ridiculous search, have I not?"

"Yes, but why? Why does it anger you so inordinately that I search for my only blood relative?"

"You ask why? Mystere, have you gone insane? *Why?* Tell me, how much money has it cost me already?"

"Cost you? Only you?"

"All right, cost the family, I mean. Mystere, I trained you. I rescued you from that roach pit on Jersey Street and gave you all this. Not just table scraps, either! Look how you live here, privileged, with servants and—"

"Those servants include myself. Paul, even when you took me around the Continent, you had me stealing. Rose makes your bed and must still go out to pick pockets. It's our efforts that keep you in tailored clothing."

But her tone as she said this was almost mild, for a new suspicion had begun to poke at her. She didn't believe his implication that only the wasted money was behind his anger. She had begun to wonder if Paul had another reason why he didn't want her looking for Bram. Curiosity to know made her less eager to leave the city just yet.

"Paul, what is it you know about Bram that you won't tell me?"

"Nothing," he snapped. "Except that only a fool would waste good money searching for a man who's most likely long dead."

"You have proof Bram's dead?"

"Proof? We aren't talking about Jesus Christ here! Your brother no doubt became a common sailor. Especially if they're impressed into service, common seamen often die without record of the event."

She could say nothing to refute that, and Paul seemed eager to change the subject.

"Mystere," he began, his face grimly calm now, "with astute management and great personal hardship, I have managed to make the quarterly note on my—that is, the family's investment. Another payment comes due in November. In the interim, we have plenty of additional expenses. Especially now that you're engaged."

"Meaning . . . ?"

"Meaning it may prove necessary for Lady Moonlight to strike again."

Reflexively, she shook her head no.

"Better think a moment," he cajoled. "It's starting to look a little suspicious already."

"What is?"

"Why, the naked facts! The moment your engagement, to one of the wealthiest men in the city, is announced, no more Lady Moonlight. Even the stupid newspaper hacks can deduce a story from that."

Paul saw that his logic was at least making her think. His tone became even more ingratiating.

"Mystere, I saw the pained look on your face when Evan stupidly alluded to fitting Rafe for a coffin. You know how that big blowhard likes to shoot off his mouth; it's all that gutter bravado he grew up with."

But his sincere assurances did nothing to assuage her doubts. *You're lying,* she thought. *I've heard you and Evan gloating, and I know you mean to kill Rafe.*

"There would be no need whatsoever for violence," he continued, "if Rafe were generous and forthcoming with you, financially speaking. All you need do is catch him at a . . . close and personal moment. You know, mention how beastly the expenses are becoming, that sort of thing."

"And if he were not forthcoming?"

Paul shrugged, giving her a ruthless look that chilled her spine. "Needs must," was all he replied.

"Suppose it's not him," she challenged. "What if I refuse to cooperate?"

She had deliberately pushed him to confirm what she already feared.

"You don't have the option to refuse," he replied in a voice entirely devoid of humanity. "You'll do what I tell you to do."

"But if I don't?"

"Then, I'll kill you myself," he declared unflinchingly. "I created you, and I can damn well destroy you."

Chapter 28

As he frequently did after using deadly threats against Mystere, Rillieux tried being affable and contrite during afternoon tea, but she merely retreated behind the distant, forced smile she had perfected over the years. Paul's most recent tantrum had left her feeling more than ever how *she* was the key to avoiding bloodshed or prosecution on either side. Despite her increasing fear of Paul, and her loathing for his "art of arrogation" as he called thievery, this was her family of sorts. Rose and Hush especially. She must do the best thing for them, too, not just herself and Rafe.

But she did not want to flee the city forever without first satisfying her latest doubts about Paul, for the conviction was growing within her that he was part of a conspiracy surrounding Bram's disappearance. An incident right after tea only increased her conviction.

The afternoon post had arrived during tea, and Hush had dutifully sorted it out on the letter stand in the hallway. Mystere's little pile held only a note from a former school friend now vacationing in Greece.

On the top of Paul's pile, however, she spied the familiar gold-embossed insignia of the Granville line, with Sheridan's arm-and-eagle joined to it. Paul picked up his mail without comment, turning toward the stairway.

"Aren't you going to open your mail?" she called out behind him. "Usually you can't wait and tear it open right here."

"I'm tired," he called back without turning around. She couldn't be sure if he was exaggerating his lameness for pity's sake, but he really did sound tired. She hated the twinge of sympathy she felt for him; after all, he was an old scoundrel who deserved his troubles.

Hush saw her getting her pongee parasol out of the umbrella stand. "Shall I hitch the team to the traces?" he asked, eager to be in her company.

"I'll not be using the carriage today," she told him, fondly tousling his thick shock of coal black hair. "But I still want to hear you read some Wilkie Collins for me. Perhaps later."

Hush glanced quickly toward the staircase and saw that Paul was only halfway upstairs, the spiral turn giving him an excellent view of everything below. He followed Mystere out onto the front steps and quickly tucked something into the pocket of her ivy silk dress.

She glanced down and saw an impressive wad of banknotes.

"Almost a hunnert bucks," he boasted before she could speak. "And Paul don't know I got it. It's all yours."

"Hush, I—"

She wanted very much to ask him to stop stealing for *any*one. But she couldn't be such a hypocrite, for if she could manage it under Baylis's constant watch, she herself would be all too happy to sell Antonia's ring. And she really did need Hush's gift, for disposal of the ring had become problematic. Some stolen items were always "hotter" than others, and word was out on the streets how the police especially wanted this thief. There was a rumored reward, too, which made it dangerous to even discuss the ring with potential buyers.

"You shouldn't worry about Sparky and Lorenzo no more, neither," he added.

"And why shouldn't I?"

"You just shouldn't, that's all," he eluded her. "You got enough on your mind, forget them."

"Hush, thank you for the money," she finally settled on saying, giving him a quick hug. "I only hope we both can stop being thieves," she whispered just before she let him go and Baylis appeared at her side.

She spotted Rafe's carriage almost immediately, parked tight to the slate curb of Great Jones Street, perhaps fifteen yards back from the stone-paved cul-de-sac of the Rillieux residence.

She turned around. "Did you know he was there?" she asked Hush, who still stood on the front stairs. A little flush of annoyance warmed her face when the boy only grinned and defiantly closed the door against her.

After her first hesitation, she gathered her skirt with her free hand and began walking briskly toward the carriage, anger tightening her face. She wondered how long Rafe had been lurking there, spying on her in broad daylight.

Under Wilson's bemused scrutiny, she marched straight up to Rafe's side of the carriage. "Why don't you just fit me with a collar and leash?" she demanded.

"Oh, I think you're already restrained enough," he managed, eyes hovering pointedly at the level of her subdued breasts. "Get in. Take a ride with me on this beautiful day like the good fiancée you are."

"I will not."

She started walking quickly along the bluestone sidewalk, using her parasol to block him from view. Wilson needed no orders; he unwrapped the reins and gave them a little snap, the team beginning to pace Mystere at a walk.

Rafe swung the door open and kicked the step down. "I said get in."

"And I said I will *not*. I'm not one of your employees; I needn't jump at your commands."

"Lofty, are we?" He seemed in no mood for her high-hatting manner. "Wilson, hard right," he shouted, and the well-trained coachman instantly veered them toward the sidewalk. Mystere hardly had time to react before Rafe leaped athletically out, carriage still rolling, and seized her under each elbow with his powerful hands.

He literally manhandled her inside and landed against her in the same seat.

"Get off me," she protested, pushing against him with little effect.

He laughed, enjoying her futility like a young boy with a bird trapped in his hand. "Pipe down. Will you cry rape next?"

"No, for that would only excite you. Please get *off* me!"

"Wilson," he called out past the open leather curtain. "Take the long way to the park."

"The park?" she echoed, her struggles ceasing for a moment. "Why not be honest about it and command him take us to your hotel?"

He laughed again, his face only inches from hers. Much of his body was pressed tightly against her, including some pressure that made her intimately aware of his gender.

"Because not even Wilson would believe I asked you to my hotel for your advice on an engineering problem."

Before she could say anything, his mouth took possession of hers.

She couldn't deny his need to use her in a quest for revenge, but his kiss also assured her of his lust to bed her. And for a few fatal moments, her own physical desire rose to match his, complicating her plight as the fire within her threatened to destroy all her plans.

"Why this again?" he demanded, breathing in ragged gasps, when she finally managed to turn her face away.

She suddenly moved over to the empty seat, trying to get her own breathing under control. From the window, she could see Baylis running to the front door to tell Rillieux she had been "kidnapped." If she had had Antonia's emerald and her letter on her, she would have taken just such an opportunity to disappear.

But timing, once more, was against her.

"Perhaps a prostitute might be more expedient," she clipped.

"Believe me," he assured her bitterly, spearing his fingers through his hair, "I would if I thought it would help me."

"Rafe?" she said after they had ridden in strained silence for perhaps two minutes.

"What?" He sounded vaguely annoyed, like a harried parent who needed a quiet moment to think.

"What kind of man is Trevor Sheridan?"

He narrowed his eyes as if to ask her something. Instead, he only replied absently, "The usual kind, I suppose, of his type—walks on two legs and never stops scheming. I don't know him that well, but one hears things from reliable sources."

"Things such as . . . ?"

He frowned harshly. "Look, he's too old for you, if it's seduction you have in mind. Also he is happily married to Alana Van Alen, a great wit and beauty. Nor is he any man to champion a calculating social climber, though it's been said was once one himself. Indeed, he has acquired a nickname among the social clubs, the Predator, so you'd also be a fool to rob him."

"Why is he called—"

But he raised a peremptory hand to silence her. He looked intensely curious all of a sudden. "If it's about that unsigned letter of yours, I warned you before not to spin grand ideas from little threads. What's got you all worked up about Sheridan?"

She said nothing at first, only studying his face closely as she decided whether or not to trust him.

"Is this some voodoo hex?" he complained irately, averting his gaze from her close scrutiny.

She made up her mind and told him about the letter that arrived today, how she had spotted the Granville-Sheridan crest and Paul's refusal to open it in front of her.

"I can tell you exactly what it is," he interposed, "for I received one also. No intrigue involved, it's just an invitation for a soiree this weekend at the Sheridan mansion, in honor of the duke and duchess. Rillieux surely knew it was coming, for he's tight as ticks with Mrs. Astor."

"Well, he certainly doesn't want me to know about it," she pointed out. "And he became almost violent earlier when I told him I'm still searching for Bram. When I pressed him to see if he knew anything about Bram's disappearance, he lied to me. I could tell."

She was silent perhaps another thirty seconds, brow furled with the effort of concentration.

"It's Evan," she said abruptly, thinking out loud.

"Evan who?"

"The man who serves as our butler. He's always been civil toward me, even kind. But I seem to remember him somehow from the days before Paul snatched us away from the orphanage. Remember seeing him briefly."

"Us? So Rillieux did take your brother, too?"

"Yes. One afternoon each week the orphans were sent out to beg for their keep. Paul caught us on a little alley off Lexington Street, I think it was. I forget where, exactly, but there were tenements on one side of the alley, restaurants and groceries on the other. I think it was he and Baylis who approached us. They were never violent; there was no force or threats. They bought us a fine restaurant meal, and treated our escape from the orphanage as a great adventure with our new 'family.' They all spoiled us terribly and seemed genuinely grieved when Bram was taken."

" 'Seemed' may be the operative word," Rafe tossed in with mild sarcasm. "Could you or your brother have inadvertently said something to suggest you had people with money here in America? Anything that could've gotten back to old Rillieux?"

"It's certainly possible, although we were both tight-lipped by habit; my mother saw to that. It's more likely someone could have seen the letter at some point. But Bram was always careful with it."

"Careful for a boy, sure. But there had to be times when it was left unguarded. By the way, I'd like to see this letter sometime myself."

Sudden alarm tingled her skin as she realized she was taking a dangerous risk with the one secret her dying mother swore her to protect. This man with her now proved that "close" did not always mean affectionate, and she was a fool to forget *he* might be one of the dangers her mother had foreseen. As for all his questions and apparent curiosity, he was a general collecting intelligence for a war, that's all, not someone concerned to help her.

"Anyhow," he added with brusque dismissal as the Astor House began to appear a few blocks ahead, just in glimmers through the trees, "you're almost surely reading too much into this supposed nexus to the house of Granville. All due respect to your mother, but she was leaving life feeling desperate to help her children survive. She—say, that's all right, then, stop that. I'll shut up."

She had surprised both of them when his description of her mother evoked sudden tears, just two, one clinging to the high promontory of each curved cheekbone.

"You women agitate for suffrage," he groused, "yet look how weepy and weak you are."

"This woman agitates for nothing," she declared in a rush of defensive anger and hurt. "Shall we casually discuss *your* mother's last moments? Or is her death more tragic because she was wealthier? Believe it or not, Rafe, a poor heart breaks as deeply as a rich one."

"She was poor when her heart broke, too, you forget." He leaned closer to her side of the carriage and kissed her on the lips again, this time not so forceful but no less passionate. Again she felt the heart-racing, pulse-shaking demands of her physical desire for him.

"Here's the park," he urged in a strained whisper. "Shall I have Wilson rein in?"

"At least you're asking now," she said, grudging him a brief smile.

Chapter 29

All week long Mystere waited for Paul to mention the upcoming soiree at the Sheridan mansion, honoring the Duke and Duchess of Granville. However, he made no reference to it. He kept to his room often, complaining, "My damned *age* is what I've caught." Overall he was civil but distant with everyone. Even when he overheard Rafe calling on Thursday, arranging to stop by for Mystere on the night of the Sheridan affair, Paul still acted as if nothing were happening.

It made no sense to Mystere. By now Paul had become such a fixture at Caroline's side he was jokingly referred to as Ward the Elder. When he had still said nothing by Saturday morning, she decided to brooch the topic with him.

She found him seated at a little escritoire in the downstairs parlor, still in his robe.

"Paul?"

Slowly he looked up from whatever he was studying under an electric reading lamp. One corner of the bright light beam caught his face, revealing an ashen pallor that shocked her. He had been feeling poorly all week, and now she realized it wasn't just his usual hypochondria.

"You'll have to speak up, my dear. I've just taken quinine, and the damnable stuff makes my head ring."

"I just wondered if, assuming you feel better, you have plans to attend the Sheridan affair this evening? If so, you can ride with me and Rafe."

She had no idea if Rafe would tolerate that, but it didn't matter. She only wanted an excuse to gauge Paul's response. But instead of mentioning the soiree itself, he focused on Rafe.

"Mr. Rafael Belloch," he mused in a distracted tone. "And I always wondered why the man will barely nod to the uncle of his fiancée."

The answer worried her. She wondered how much he suspected of Rafe's knowledge. Cautiously she inquired, "What do you mean?"

"Never mind. No, I'm not going," he finally answered her. "Caroline has agreed to give my regrets."

"But . . . why didn't you at least tell me about the soiree?"

"Why? You found out, didn't you?"

His cryptic answer further convinced her he knew something he had been keeping to himself. But she couldn't find the courage to ask him about it directly. He was not a man, even old and frail, whom she cared to corner.

"But why don't you want me to go?" she persisted.

"Go, don't go, I don't care. But has it ever occurred to you that it might be wise to place more value on your presence by *removing* it once in a while?"

He gazed up at her where she stood just inside the open doors. "Especially after that impressive performance you and Rafe put on at Mrs. Astor's last weekend. By the bye—Antonia, I'm told by Caroline, immediately planted the nasty rumor that you and Rafe secretly rehearsed for that apparent moment of dance-floor spontaneity. But Lance Streeter, romantic ponce-man that he is, has led the charge against such vicious snipes. You are winning the Consul of Plebians, my dear. You should be pleased."

"Immeasureably," she replied with scant attention, for she was still trying to understand Paul's new reasoning. "Since when have you become so strategic about public appearances? Your usual approach is simply to go out each time you're invited. What's different now?"

"I'm not the issue, goose. I am an old man on tottering legs. Addicted to wealth and power."

"Especially power," she reminded him, though with a disarming smile.

"Of course. Just look at me. I've developed a sort of compensatory adaptation to my decreasing . . . potency, if you will. I admit it. I've become a vampire bat, flitting about and sucking blood where I can."

"Paul, I only meant—"

"But you," he pressed on, "are not a predatory old man, cursed with my limitations. And I see now that I've pushed you too far in the wrong direction. Do you want to become like the Vanderbilt sisters, so *grateful* that you never snub an invitation? I've always said look to the old sayings, for there is where you'll find God's truth. Familiarity does, indeed, breed contempt, while a certain aloofness inspires awe and respect."

It was a good argument, she realized, but suspicious nonetheless. None of this had concerned him one whit until the Sheridan invitation.

"I'm glad to see you're suddenly a student of 'God's truth,' " she finally replied, her submissive tone softening the irony of her words.

"I'm a criminal," he insisted brusquely, "not a heretic."

That he had actually called himself a criminal shocked her into thoughtful silence. She had observed Paul closely for many years now, and she knew his infrequent attacks of conscience usually accompanied his darker deeds.

"Have you and Rafe decided on a wedding date yet?" he abruptly demanded.

"*I* and Rafe? You grant me more powers than I possess."

"Nonsense. You *use* fewer powers than you possess, and I don't mean psychic. At any rate you'd better settle on a date, the sooner the better."

"Paul, you've been acting oddly for days. What's bothering you?"

"Where do past years go?" he countered evasively, struggling to his feet. "Excuse me, dear, but I'm off to take a nap."

She watched him make his way unsteadily out of the parlor. The tiara incident, she reflected, seemed to have been a turning point of sorts, perhaps triggering his fear that he was losing control of her. That might explain his remark about having the wedding as soon as possible.

But the rest of it, his atypical behavior about the Sheridan affair, and that odd remark about how Rafe would barely nod to him—she could fathom no reason for it.

While she mulled all these impressions, she absently started across the room to turn off the light Paul had forgotten. She was perhaps halfway to the escritoire when something caught the corner of her eye, something on the blotter reflecting a bright, almost accusatory white. With no clear view of it yet, she nonetheless realized that Paul had not forgotten the light—this was left for her to see.

She leaned closer, body trembling all over when she realized what lay there. All her fretting about others, and *she* had become her own worst enemy. She and her stupid, stupid carelessness. Those little, torn scraps of paper meticulously reassembled and pasted to a sheet of stationery had been fished from the bottom of the litter can in the hallway: the letter from Stephen Breaux's law offices.

In a heartbeat her legs felt hollow and weak, and she was forced to sit in the chair still warm from Paul's body. "Mother Mary," she whispered, too stunned to even feel properly afraid.

"I swear this isn't hair; it's Persian silk," Rose praised, her tone as ebullient as her mood. She pulled a horn brush through the dark brown tresses, marveling at the mahogany hues where late-afternoon sunlight drenched Mystere's hair.

Mystere's eyes lifted to the vanity mirror for a moment, meeting Rose's as she smiled her thanks at the compliment. The older woman's good mood had actually begun two nights ago, when Rafe called and Rose took his message.

Rose knew her well by now and could guess Mystere's thinking at times.

"Oh, I know," she confessed as she deftly tied the hair and slipped a black net over it. "But life around here is usually quite unromantic. Now your gentleman's to be calling on us regularly, it's more exciting. More like a proper love story, it is."

A proper love story . . . the cruel hoax of those words blemished her smile, but Mystere had no heart to dampen Rose's spirits. "You seem to like Rafe Belloch," was all she said.

"He's dangerously good-looking," Rose giggled, "and they say his past is terribly romantic and sad."

"Why? What have you heard about him?"

"Well, there's . . . it's said how he was only a lad, perhaps the age of our Hush, when his father threw away the family fortune—some terrible gamble on the foreign banks, or some such. The old man, 'tis said, after being frightfully cut by Mrs. Astor's crowd, blew his own head off. He faced a prison term for his debts, and not one of them would loan him a cent. I s'pose he could not stomach the shame of it."

"Yes," Mystere said, amazed how the version spread by Dame Rumor got it all more-or-less accurately, assuming her own view of it was right.

"But we cannot lick old wounds forever," Rose pointed out, refusing to surrender her gay, hopeful mood. "I know everything seems so frightful and complicated to you, hon. But 'tis a long lane, indeed, that takes no turns."

Rose turned away and began humming to herself as she laid out Mystere's silk-and-lace gown for tonight, giving it a final inspection for flaws.

Mystere felt suddenly angry with herself. After all, if Rose could feel her spirits buoyed by the prospect of a marriage—"a *grand* marriage," she had called it—why was she herself immune to at least some share in Rose's hope? Perhaps play-acting was all anyone ever really did anyway, so why not act happy?

"Honey, what are you thinking about?" Rose asked, crossing back to the mirror and standing beside her. "Don't let my silly whistling keep you from complaining if you'd like."

"Rose, I'm sorry, I don't mean to be so gloomy."

"I won't allow you to apologize," she insisted. "This time *I'm* the one gets to be sorry. It's been troubling me since Wednesday."

"What has?"

"The way you spoke up for us to Paul's face, and we all just stood there like clothes poles."

"You don't need—"

"I can't speak for the boys, mind you, but *I'm* proud of what you said, saints preserve you. But I was also afraid, Mystere. Not just for me, but for you also."

"Afraid to encourage me, you mean?"

"Yes. Sure, Paul's too old and frail to seem very dangerous. Except that Evan and Baylis prac'ly lick his hand. They'll do his bidding, Mystere, never mind how stupid and wrong it may turn out. You *must* think of that, and fix your thoughts on any way out of here. So what if it's really Mrs. Astor's doing—can marrying Rafe Belloch place you in worse danger than you face here?"

"I don't know," she replied honestly. "I wonder, sometimes, if 'choice' is a word invented by the devil to drive us mad."

"No, it was men he invented for that," Rose corrected her, and they both laughed. "When men cannot refute us with reason, they find other ways to enforce their wills."

"I'm not so sure it's only men, Rosie. Mrs. Astor plays by the same rules and always wins. May I ask you something?"

The sudden change in her tone caused a slight tensing of Rose's features. "Shame on you for asking my permission first."

"It's just that . . . it's about Evan. You mentioned once that he spent six months on a jailhouse work crew. Years ago?"

Rose nodded.

"Perhaps twelve years ago?"

Rose knew where this was headed; Mystere could read the uncertainty and fear in her eyes. But she also saw resolve in the set of Rose's jaw.

"Yes," she replied, adding in a firm voice, "about the same time you ran away from the orphanage."

"And he was already working for Paul, too?"

"Yes." This time Rose hesitated only a moment, then quickly blurted the fact she knew Mystere was driving at: "Evan's crew often hauled donated furniture to city orphanages. Paul had him on notice to keep his eye open for 'likely waifs' as Paul called them. I'm sure that's how he first learned of you and . . . well, you and your brother."

Furniture . . . Mystere now remembered where and when she had seen Evan's face for the first time. He was with several other unshaven convicts in striped clothing and knit caps who had carried new wooden bedsteads into the top floor of the Jersey Street Orphanage. The children had all been chased out into the common room . . . and Evan, especially after Paul's training, would surely have been watching for valuables of any kind. He could also read, and Bram had sometimes kept the letter hidden under his mattress cover.

She looked at Rose. "You've known for some time about the letter I have, haven't you?"

"Yes. Not right off, nor have I ever read it. But Baylis told me about it."

Mystere started to speak; but her voice failed her for a moment, and she was forced to start over. "Rosie, what about Bram? Did Paul and the boys arrange for him to be taken?"

Rose took both of Mystere's hands in hers. "Mystere, I would not lie about that if I knew the truth. But I just don't. It's not below them, of course, but I can't see what Paul would gain except perhaps a bit of money from an impress gang. However, we both know a sharp child is worth far more than a bit of money, at least to Paul."

Mystere believed her. She was silent a minute, trying to grasp the meaning of all this; however, Paul's ultimate motives eluded her.

"Rose, I don't understand, what is Paul's plan? What does he know that I don't? He's had the information for years, yet apparently done nothing with it."

"Baylis tells me more than Evan will, but he's said nothing to me about it even if he knows. But, hon, you already found that pasted-together letter, didn't you? The one Paul sifted from the litter can?"

Mystere nodded, feeling a tightening around her heart at the reminder.

Rose clucked. "La, girl, I wish I'd seen you do it. You *know* he pokes through the trash, don't you?"

"Yes, I . . . oh, it's just there's been so much on my mind, I got careless."

"You did, indeed, and like you I have no idea what Paul means to do about it. He may see that Rafe has kept quiet this long for your sake, and count on your marriage to protect him in the future."

"Yes, for no doubt he knows that copies of that letter could hang him if he harms Rafe. Unless Paul can arrange an 'accident' so convincing that Rafe's estate will not suspect him."

"It's all in a frightful boil," Rose admitted, "and I can't blame you for being afraid, Mystere. But if Paul is placing his hopes on this marriage, you have even more reason to. It may be your new dawn, hon. Place all your hopes on that thought."

Chapter 30

"Sheridan residence, Wilson," Rafe called out, handing Mystere into the carriage.

"That's lower Fifth?" Wilson called back.

"Yes. I forget the number, but you'll see the traffic."

"Right. Be there in jig time, sir!"

The conveyance started forward, and Rafe opened the leather curtains on both sides, letting in the dim illumination of the streetlights. He had taken the opposite seat instead of crowding her. He studied her for some moments in silence.

"Old Rillieux gave me a dirty look," he finally commented. "What's going through his head?"

"He knows that *you* know—about him, I mean. He found the letter from Stephen Breaux."

"Ahh . . . careless, were you? Is that why he chose not to go with us?"

"I'm not sure. I suspect he originally planned on staying home in hopes I would also. I think he doesn't want me too near Trevor Sheridan or the duke and duchess."

"Then, why didn't he avoid the Addison ball? They were all present."

"Yes, but he hustled me away from them. And that was before I started asking him questions."

"Well, I'm glad the old reprobate found Breaux's letter. Let him sweat a little. He's had it too damned easy at everyone else's expense."

"You shouldn't underestimate him. He is old and ailing, yes. But his mind never stops scheming. He represents a very real danger."

"To hell with him. Actually, that letter is perfect. It serves to warn him, yet doesn't involve the police, nor is there any direct threat."

"As *you* interpret the phrase."

"Never mind him. Tell me, how much did you get for Antonia's ring?"

Resentment at his blunt, demanding manner filled her. In fact she had decided to let the ring lose a bit of its notoriety before she approached Helzer, Paul's usual fence, in person. She dreaded the thought of visiting his salvage yard on Water Street, a terrible rough area. But she had met him once at their home, and he had been quite kind and urbane with her. He had survived in an illegal business for many years through greed and cunning and, above all, discretion—she might be able to deal with him.

"Nothing yet," she answered truthfully.

His taunting laugh only irritated her further. "So. You're finding out, eh, that a hungry dog must eat dirty pudding. You can't get even a tenth of its true value, can you?"

"Don't you have an empire to run? Why are you so preoccupied with the ring?"

"That's obvious and you know it. I half expect you to disappear once it's sold."

She glanced out her window, ignoring him. "Thus breaking your heart, I'm sure."

"Oh, I'd miss you for a day or two, I suppose. But my heart isn't the point. Your disappearance would humiliate me publicly; that's the big problem. All that speculation as to whom my fiancée has dumped me for . . . not to mention that you'll only get caught, anyway."

"That's hogwash and you know it," she accused, still refusing to look in his direction. "The true reason you fear my running away is the blow it would deliver to all your sick plans."

"You, of all people, lecture on sickness—a robber and thief whose very life is a lie? Those cloths wrapping your breasts right now, hiding charms that ought to be proudly revealed—no sickness there, eh?"

"No! It's wrong and it's illegal, what I do, but it's not sick. My end is survival, not revenge. But you—you are going to ruin both of us, aren't you? All just to break another useless arrow on Caroline's hide."

"Caroline's alone, do you mean? No, I'm out to destroy the rank, not the woman. There are Four Hundred in my sights, though I confess she is center of the target and will take the most direct hit. And you're wrong; I don't have any special plan to destroy you. But . . ."

"But to continue your metaphor," she finished when he paused, "often there are peripheral victims in any great battle."

By now she was watching him again.

He smiled at her cynical phrasing. "Well said," he praised. "Besides, you've apparently got me down for one nefarious deed. But I did not go to so much trouble to become a gossip-page celebrity for nought. Now I'm front stage, and perhaps I mean to chip away at the edifice of respectability, one crack at a time."

His words stung, for she took his meaning immediately. The dancing, the stolen kisses, all of it calculated to hook reporters and acquire a mouthpiece and an audience for his plans. That answered Paul's question as to why a "man of empire" was so eager to get his name in the papers.

And she was being used like everyone else.

"Yes," she retorted, injured feelings making her raise her voice a little, "that's how you'll do it at first, for what's the point of cruelty if one cannot prolong and enjoy it. But when you see your main chance, you'll seize it."

Only part of his face was visible to her at the moment, but even in the shadow light she could see the anger that tightened his jawline.

"Leave all this thought reading to that charlatan 'uncle' of yours," he snapped. "My plans aren't spoken into my ear by a genie. I live my life as I go, like most."

"No. Despite all the opportunities of great wealth, you're simply a doomsday prophet, and your tale is doom from the opening. But your grand scheme of destruction will succeed only in your mind. You will topple the pyramids at Giza before you topple Mrs. Astor."

"And you? You who level *my* plans—what about your own quixotic quest for the Holy Grail? Not only a brother, who's no doubt a prince by now somewhere in Tahiti, but a fortune, too, if only she can find them. End of fairy tale."

His words struck like blows, both for their scorn and their accuracy. With great effort she fought back tears, knowing he would only mock her for a bawl baby.

"I said nothing about any fortune," she corrected him. "And I fail to see how my love for Bram compares to your overweening hatred."

After a moment's silence he relented a bit. "You've a point, I suppose. I don't blame you one bit for keeping up the search for Bram, especially given your cruel parody of a family with Rillieux's bunch. I'd want my real brother, too, even if he turned out to be Sheriff of Nottingham. But I advise you to gird for bad news after so many years."

This was an olive branch, of sorts, or at least a twig, she supposed. So she decided to extend one herself.

"You've talked to Perkins and Sparky on my behalf, haven't you?" she asked him. "Scared them away from me? You and Hush working together somehow?"

"I and Hush? Well, we did have a bit of conversation over a cigar, yes."

"A cig—you despise my uncle, but your own corruptions of youth don't matter much, I see."

"Corruption? That's harsh. I probably put him off stogies for life. Tell me, am I 'corrupting' you with my seductions; is that the coy hint here? For if I am, then, by all means I will stop and desist. The choice is yours."

His demanding eyes would not let her off the hook. Despising him even as she surrendered, she replied in a snappish voice, "No, you're not corrupting me. I'm a woman and know what I'm about. But Hush is only twelve."

"That's old enough to keep his word, yet the little scamp told you anyway."

"He didn't actually tell me. But I guessed from his behavior and certain remarks. I . . . anyway, thank you, Rafe. For chasing off Lorenzo and Sparky, I mean."

"You needn't thank me. I just don't want those two bunglers in my way."

"You can't ever appear human, can you? You snap if someone looks at you too long or only tries to be cordial. What are you so afraid of?"

"Afraid of," he repeated irritably. "Death, disease, poverty, the usual gang. Have you become an alienist now, charting people's psyches?"

"Oh, Rafe, stop it! How can a man so successful and brilliant fail to see that revenge is not a good enough reason to live?"

"Damnit, I've told you before to spare me your pious, Brook Farm sermons. I'll live for whatever the hell I please. You ought to read some history some time, not just all these foolish, sentimental love stories you women devour like bon bons. *Revenge* is at the heart of human events, Lady M. Men like Alexander the Great and Genghis Khan placed it above all else."

"It's no use," she surrendered. "No one can win against you, for you know everything and you're always right."

"Just keep that in mind," he advised her, "and we'll get along fine."

They finished the journey in a strained silence, Mystere staring out the windows at the well-lighted homes and superbly maintained lawns rolling past on either side. This stretch of Fifth Avenue, where the Sheridan mansion was located, had seen some flight of the rich lately as business interests were starting to squeeze in to capitalize on the prestigious address. But there were still plenty of grand mansions.

Rafe finally broke the silence, but only to be insulting.

"Look," he remarked, pointing out the window and up at the night sky. "A moon bright enough to make shadows. Are you succumbing?"

"In no sense of the word, Mr. Belloch," she assured him.

"You're daring me now. Daring me to *make* you succumb?"

"Here, do you mean? Along Fifth Avenue in a carriage?"

"It's done quite commonly in carriages."

"Quite commonly, indeed."

He laughed at her offended tone and manner. "Perhaps all that rocking on the braces only makes it—"

She tried to slap him, but he easily caught her wrist. Laughing to taunt her, he tugged her off balance from her seat and easily toppled her into his lap. Before she could even recover, his hungry mouth had opened hers, and his tongue was greedily exploring, teasing.

An unwilling moan escaped her, heat flared in her loins, and her anger at him became a resentful, aggressive passion matching his own and daring him to get hotter. Only Wilson's voice, commanding the team to slow, made her turn her face from his, gasping to find her breath.

"Still claim you're not succumbing?" he whispered, kissing her ear and giving it a little nibble that made her wish she was naked in his arms.

"Not of my own volition," she protested lamely as she struggled to her feet and sat down on the other side of the carriage.

"Blame it on the moon," he said innocently.

Wilson joined the queue of arriving conveyances before a high wall of alternating white and black marble blocks. Massive black-iron gates on the avenue side were now thrown open wide to reveal a well-lighted house with a mansard roof. French doors were thrown open, and Mystere saw guests mingling throughout the first floor and attached gallery, groups and couples spilling out onto the front lawn. Her eyes sought Trevor Sheridan, always easy to spot because of his ever-present ebony and gold lion-ornamented walking stick. But she could locate neither him nor the duke and duchess.

Nervous expectation left her feeling short of breath. She made up her mind to finally end, if she could, this long uncertainty. She would ask Sheridan outright if he might have some knowledge of her family—or at least of anyone else in New York who might have sent letters bearing the Connacht motif to Dublin.

But Rafe had evidently anticipated her decision. As he handed her out and Wilson moved to join the line of parked vehicles, Mystere tugged Rafe's arm to halt them in front of the gates emblazoned with the familiar half eagle and arm holding a dagger.

He studied her transfixed, purposeful face. Suddenly he cursed under his breath. "You damned fool."

With a burst of strength she didn't even try to resist, he pulled her perhaps ten yards away from the paved drive to a little niche in the surrounding wall.

"Lady M, I'm afraid your wick is flickering. You don't just approach a man like Sheridan at a social function," he admonished in an urgent tone of voice, "and blurt out a damned-fool lot of questions about possible connections to the peerage."

"That's easy for you to—"

"For one thing," he silenced her with commanding anger, "he'll be surrounded by lick-spittles and toadies, at least one of whom is bribed regularly by the yellow press. Do you want all of your precious secrets told in lurid headlines? *All* of them?"

The urgency of his anger made her think about his questions. In a few moments it became clear that he was right; she was being a fool. Let one gossip writer get hold of even a hint, and it would all come out in shocking, newspaper-selling detail.

"Then, how?" she pleaded. "I *must* talk to him."

"Then, you're a bigger fool than God made you."

"Why?"

"Because Sheridan is a man well worth fearing, that's why. He's ruthless."

"He has no monopoly on that market, has he?"

Rafe gave her an impatient little shake. "Listen to me. Trevor Sheridan is best avoided like the plague. In any event, you must realize that claims of 'family ties' are common—and commonly proved false. You would begin with Sheridan's attorneys, not with him."

"Yes," she agreed after a moment. "That's how I'll do it, you're right."

As Rafe led her back toward the front gates, she noticed a streamer of sparks ahead about a block away, shooting up into the night sky. A group of men surrounded some sort of big bonfire built right in the avenue. They were surrounded, in turn, by a line of policemen wielding shotguns and clubs. She could hear a confused hubbub of shouted taunts and curses, the words indistinct at this distance.

"What's all that?" she asked Rafe.

"Some longshoremen who blame 'the bosses' for bloody union-busting tactics. Of course, their own unions are run by honest, peace-loving angels. Look sharp—here comes Her Nibs."

Caroline and Ward had paused near the gate, seeing the two of them approach from the shadows. Rafe glanced at McCallister, who in turn couldn't take his eyes off Mystere.

"Easy, Ward," Rafe laughed. "You're leering. Get control of yourself and save it for your wife."

Caroline, however, was in no mood to let Rafe take charge.

"Have you two discussed a date yet?" she queried Rafe without preamble.

"Alas, Caroline, in our heady delirium of joy we—"

"Everyone likes a June bride," she rode him down, "but that's nearly a year off. This coming September might do quite nicely, don't you think? The frightful heat will have broken, yet you can fit in a lovely honeymoon trip before winter."

Rafe was no longer in a joking mood, for there was no trace of suggestion in Caroline's tone.

"But . . . September," Mystere managed to protest weakly in the face of Rafe's continued silence. "It's . . . only month after next, so— so soon."

Caroline fixed unblinking eyes on her. "Have you two noticed one welcome by-product of your engagement? We now hear of something besides the Lady Moonlight."

Mystere lost all strength, and only Rafe's support kept her standing as she feared in a rush of pounding blood to her face, *Caroline knows. Somehow she has figured it out.*

The matron's eyes shifted to Rafe as she added, "It's been good for us."

There was a subtle but definite emphasis on the word *us*. As if she were warning Rafe to walk the straight and narrow for the sake of the Patriarchy, or face dire consequences.

"Come along, Ward," she added, and the two of them glided off, leaving Rafe and Mystere both impressed into silence. It was a full thirty seconds before Rafe broke it.

" 'The devil is sailing on a sinking ship, and the place where he reigns is called Doomed Domains.' I heard a preacher spout that once."

"Yes," Mystere agreed softly, studying his chiseled-coin profile in the shadowy gaslight. "But which devil must I fear?"

"Our name is Legion," he assured her. "And you can't say you haven't been properly warned about us. Behave with good sense and be damned careful what you say to whom, Sheridan included. Caroline has just made it clear: we buy her silence by announcing a September wedding date. And so we shall cooperate."

"Until *you* decide not to, right?"

"Strong dogs dominate."

"And you're stronger than Caroline, is that it?"

"I—*damn* it," he muttered in annoyance as Abbot Pollard's bulk suddenly blocked their path just inside the gates. *At least he appears sober,* Mystere thought.

His annoyed face confused her until he nodded in the direction of the noisy protestors. "Angry peasants with pitchforks. And we permit them to vote, so in a sense they're right—America's troubles *are* all our fault. As generously as we bribe our elected officials, and they still betray us by kowtowing to these mudsills."

"Yes, yes, the public be damned and all that rot," Rafe snapped impatiently, brushing past Abbot and propelling Mystere with him. "Look, Abbot, hurry up and get drunk. You're more entertaining that way."

"Ahh, of course," Abbot called out behind them, loud enough for others to hear. "I've interrupted you in a 'heated moment.' You two strike me as shameless exhibitionists."

"Worthless old nancy," Rafe muttered. "I don't doubt he keeps a catamite somewhere."

The rest of the evening proved uneventful and anticlimactic to Mystere, who had arrived hoping she was on the verge of some critical revelation about her past. Instead, with Rafe refusing to give her any free leash, she ended up exchanging only brief, polite remarks with the duke and duchess, and speaking briefly to Alana Sheridan and not at all with her infamous husband Trevor. In fact, it might be easier to pet a wild bear—the Irishman had an intimidating, imposing manner and seemed little concerned with the banal exchanges of "socializing." In that respect, at least, he was like Rafe.

They left little over two hours after they had arrived. Mystere felt sore around the mouth from all her insincere smiling. However, the evening's pretending had produced an unintended—and very unwelcome—response within her. Rafe's attentions all evening in public, his little touches and compliments, the way he smiled into her eyes, his masculine solidity at her side—she was beginning to wonder if some of his acting might not be genuine affection.

When he had first intruded his way into her life, she had heard only his words. But by now his every tone of voice had taken on new meaning, every nuance of accent becoming crucial to her. That was all new, and she found herself, more and more, wondering, Was *he,* too, possibly losing the war with his own heart? She thought, sometimes, that he looked at her with something besides lust or cunning; thought, too, that he might have protected her from Caroline, and now from Sparky and Lorenzo, for kind reasons.

But *no,* she resolved anew as Rafe's carriage rolled off into the night, carrying her home, and she coldly resisted his physical advances. She must cling to cold logic, not to longing. She was vulnerable now, in her growing desperation, and had to remember that Rafe was probably the most serious danger of them all. She must pin her hopes on finding Bram and learning more about their family—and perhaps on somehow getting away from New York well before September.

You would begin with Sheridan's attorneys, not with him.

All right, then, she vowed. *They should be in their offices on Monday. So that's when I'll begin.*

Chapter 31

Monday morning dawned gloomy and sunless, a solid pewter sky threatening rain. In her nervous anticipation of Sheridan's attorneys, however, Mystere failed to plan for bad weather. She would soon bitterly regret that failure of foresight, among others even greater.

The Manhattan Phone Directory listed Trevor Sheridan's business address as a suite in the Commerce Building on Wall Street, and she could only hope that office included his attorneys. She spent much of the weekend rehearsing what she would say. Her situation was fraught with dangers, and she must carefully avoid revealing too much, which in turn would make it harder for her to elicit information.

Another problem was the danger of being recognized. She briefly considered telephoning, but decided it was too easy for them to hang up on a stranger. After considering the problem further, she found a solution that would alter her usual physical appearance without clumsy disguises. Since, in public, she almost always wore her long hair drawn back tightly in a chignon, she would let it down to cover the sides of her face before knotting it to her nape. And today she would not bind her chest. She knew from experience that if she wore the right dress, most men wouldn't waste much attention on her face anyway.

There was one brief item of business before she made her much-anticipated, much-dreaded visit to Wall Street. She wrote a brief note to Helzer, Paul's fence, requesting a meeting about "an object of unusually high quality." Then she went searching for Hush.

It was still early, not quite eight A.M., and Paul had not yet come down for his papers and coffee. Mystere found Hush out back in the carriage house, which was merely a stable with a few stalls knocked out. By arbitrary decree of Baylis, it was the lad's job to take care of the team, carriage, and tack.

"Good morning, Hush," she greeted him after angling between the open doors. "Are you too busy to do me a favor?"

He was kneeling beside a front wheel of the carriage, smearing grease on the hub. Hush gaped when he saw her, for she literally looked like a new woman. And the light garden dress of cream-color cotton—he had never seen her with her breasts unrestrained, she realized, and the sheer material only emphasized the change.

Slowly he put down the grease pail and stood up. "Mystere?"

She laughed. "Who else would I be?"

"Well, it's your voice, anyhow, that ain't changed."

His prolonged stare made her uncomfortable. "I have a face, too," she reminded him, and he flushed slightly, raising his glance.

She handed him the note, sealed in a blank envelope. "Would you please take this to Mr. Jerome Helzer at Helzer's Salvage Yard on Water Street? It must go to him personally. And then you must wait for his reply. It would be a great favor to me, Hush."

"Shoot, you can't ask *me* for favors," he scoffed, still sneaking peeks at her full bosom. "I'll go right now."

"*Thank* you. Here's some money for the omnibus. If Paul is cranky with you when you get back, just tell him . . . tell him I sent you out to drop off some shoes for repairing."

They both left the stable together, Hush banging the doors shut and securing the latch.

"Mystere?" he said before they headed their separate ways on Great Jones Street.

"Yes?"

"I won't ask where you're goin' nor nothing, but—you gonna be okay?"

"I'll be fine," she assured him even as another tickling spasm of nervous fear made her worry she might not be up to this visit. So much weighed on her mind, and she was so desperate to answer some vexing questions. And there was always the very real risk that her visit today would blow up in her face, exposing the tangled web of lies and deceptions for all to see.

Thus preoccupied, she commanded Baylis to get the carriage, hardly aware that the first great, splattering drops of rain were falling. When the downpour began in earnest she rued not grabbing an umbrella.

Her letter, at least, would remain safe inside her leather handbag.

During the ride to Wall Street she tried to make herself more presentable, but she shivered despite the morning's balmy temperature. It wasn't just the damp air that chilled her. The tightrope she had been walking for some time was becoming infinitely more dangerous. If her visit to the lawyers somehow became public, the results could be catastrophic. Paul, always unpredictable, was capable of any desperate act if he felt cornered. And Caroline, while perhaps more predictable, was just as dangerous in her own way.

The rain slacked off as the carriage turned east on Wall Street, bearing toward the river. But she could not shake the memory of Caroline's eyes, glinting like new, hard steel, as she seemed to reveal to Rafe and Mystere the chilling suspicion that *she*, too, had guessed the truth about Lady Moonlight's true identity.

How or why she had guessed was irrelevant now, although Mystere had a hunch it began with that shocking scene in Rafe's drawing room. Caroline must have put her considerable intelligence to the baffling puzzle of Mystere's chest bindings, and that clue would have led to others. Including Caroline's inevitable conclusion that Paul must be the mastermind of a great hoax.

With the wisdom born of ceaseless calculation, Caroline had so far revealed no outward sign of strain between herself and Paul. But Mystere knew that was just cosmetic to save the precious "respectability" of the Old Guard. Paul would, indeed, be "cut" socially, but probably not until after the September wedding Caroline was determined to force. This kind of scandal, since Mrs. Astor herself had championed the Rillieuxs, could stain her and the Four Hundred indelibly.

And that, Mystere told herself, was the greatest irony of all. For Rafe was planning to foment just such a scandal—planning, too, to lock horns with Caroline in a final death struggle—and it appeared that Caroline had begun to sense his true intentions.

"Commerce Building, Ma-dame," Baylis taunted, wheels sending up a little swell of water as the conveyance pulled up at the curb.

She allowed him to disembark and help her to the curb. Becoming drenched, she turned to face the four-story office building with its lancet-arched windows and Gothic-style gargoyles.

Her legs refused, at first, to take that first marble step. She felt the annoyance of those on the busy sidewalk, forced to steer around her.

"For Bram," she whispered, and moments later, soaked and scared, she found strength to hurry up the steps.

"And what concern is it to you," demanded the stern-faced man who had finally come to the counter to talk with her, "whether or not Mr. Sheridan's lawyer is available?"

This man was around thirty, better dressed than the half dozen clerks in eyeshades and sleeve garters who were busy in the big central office behind the counter. Typewriters rang and banged all around her, and she had to raise her voice to be heard.

"Are you an attorney?" she inquired politely, for he had not even had the decency to introduce himself.

"That's none of your concern," he snapped, and she noticed how his vandyke beard made him look like a devil. "Just state your business here."

Her wet clothing felt even colder now, a clammy, chilling pressure that made it difficult to control her trembling. Now it was time to actually say it, and she felt utterly foolish.

"I'm trying to find out," she replied as bravely as she could with Baylis waiting across the room, out of earshot, "if perhaps Mr. Sheridan might have some knowledge about my family."

"Why? Do you think he's a public genealogist?"

"Of course not. But my famil—"

"And just which family might that be? Oh, but don't tell me," the clerk or whatever he was mocked, "you don't really *know* your surname, is that it?"

Heat leaped into her face. The man had deliberately raised his voice so those working nearby could overhear.

"Actually, that's . . . that's right," she managed.

"Yes, and what you'd *really* like to know," he continued, ruthless mirth glinting in his unblinking gray eyes, "is whether or not you're related to either Mr. Sheridan or his sister's Granville line?"

"Perhaps not related," she qualified, "but in some way linked. You see, I have a letter. . . ."

Before she could open her purse, however, the man exclaimed loudly, "Say, fellows! This one has a *letter.* Now that's a different matter, hey?"

Howls of derisive laughter momentarily replaced the typewriter noises. Her adversary stood behind the long wooden counter that kept visitors out of the working office. He banged open a drawer, then thumped a thick stack of correspondence down on the counter in front of her.

"We have perhaps fifty or so letters of our own right here," he retorted. "And these are only those we've collected. Care to add yours to the heap?"

He riffled quickly through the stack, and she felt her heart plummet when she realized at least half the letters were written under the Granville crest.

"Your confidence game is old," the man assured her harshly. "It's not just the house of Granville—every established family of the aristocracy is deluged with greedy, lazy claimants."

Only now did she become fully aware of the way he, and others in the office, were staring at her soaked form. She had been too preoccupied and nervous, at first, to think about the physical picture she must present. A thin dress, with only a chemise and slip beneath, all soaked clear through—and those bright, unshaded electric lights suspended from the ceiling cast a cruelly clear view of her . . . *much* of her, she realized as the men's eyes seemed to touch her like probing hands.

"I make no claims whatsoever," she insisted. "But if I might have just a brief appointment with—"

"*Bother* your appointment," the man cut her off impatiently. "I assure you that Mr. Sheridan wants nothing to do with your inquiries. Just because a man is wealthy, and his sister has married well, does not mean he's related to every gold digger who ever sailed to America in steerage class."

"She thought that fine figger would open doors," jeered a clerk. "Deliberately came in here soaking wet, she did, to get us all het up. So I say let's take 'er back in the storeroom and show 'er *our* 'roots.' "

His filthy pun evoked a chorus of taunts and laughter.

"It's far easier to sponge off the rich than to earn your way; that's how so many of you comely young wenches think," the man assured her. "Now get the hell out of here before I have you arrested."

Crushed, she hadn't even had a chance to show them her letter before a uniformed doorman hustled her out onto the sidewalk again. She was gone so quickly Baylis didn't even see her leave.

The rain had stopped; but a gray pallor filled the sky, and everything seemed to be dripping. Wall Street looked ugly and cold, dirty puddles covering it like pockmarks. A trolley lumbered past, the big dray horse marked by deep girth galls and open sores. She could not only read the resigned misery in the horse's eyes, but at that moment she felt a deep affinity with the hopeless creature.

At first, so devastated and emotionally drained, she could manage no other reaction than to start dumbly walking. Her newfound freedom from Baylis should have been embraced, but she felt nothing except loneliness and despair. She headed northwest on Wall Street toward the spire of Trinity Church a few blocks ahead. With each lapsed second, however, she realized how completely her hopes had been dashed, how utterly common and foolish she had looked in that office. *Say, fellows! She has a letter.*

For far too long now she had borne so many troubles in silence, kept her heartfelt hopes and dreams to herself. But the miserable failure at Sheridan's office was the final straw, the death of her hopes. Right now she needed to share her misery with someone, anyone who might care. The one person, in fact, who knew all of it.

A cab discharged a fare just ahead of her, and Mystere called out to the driver, bidding him wait. It was only a few blocks around the corner on Broadway to her destination, but suddenly she didn't want to waste any time getting there. She hurried forward and took the driver's hand as he helped her into the passenger compartment beneath his high seat.

"Where to, ma'am?"

"The Astor House Hotel," she replied, a new tone of resolution in her voice.

She savored this new feeling of actually wanting Rafe's company for a change. Of course, she must not let desperate hope cloud her vision. But it seemed to her that he was her friend, though he wouldn't call himself that. It also appeared to her as if he was somewhat indecisive about his reckless plans, and she was secretly praying he would change his mind.

Despite her terrible setback at Sheridan's office, she had decided to remain hopeful that disaster was not imminent. Rafe could well be right about Paul—the Breaux letter may have served notice without forcing a crisis.

Ultimately, to be sure, it hardly mattered. She must flee New York before Rafe, friend or not, was forced into a dangerous marriage with her. And perhaps her disappearance, its subsequent shock to the Four Hundred, would accomplish all Rafe's plans for him—a fitting ironic end to this turbulent episode of her life.

Right now, however, as the cab turned in toward the curb in front of the hotel, Mystere found herself hoping Rafe was there, for she had neither desire nor courage to visit his corporate offices. The need to talk, to be held and kissed to the point of sweet oblivion, seemed to pulse in every cell of her being.

She paid the driver and turned toward the big revolving front door of the hotel. She was cold and wet and looked no better than a beggar from the streets, but somehow she prayed she could find him. Suddenly he seemed very much like a kind of salvation, and she desperately wanted to be saved.

She was perhaps ten paces from the door when Rafe suddenly emerged as if coughed out by the building. Their eyes locked in the next instant.

A hopeful smile pulled at her lips; a fractional second later, however, Antonia Butler spun out the door right behind him, linking her arm through Rafe's, and Mystere felt all the misery of her life suddenly pinpointed to that moment.

Chapter 32

Rafe watched the beginning of a smile part her expressive lips, watched the first gleam of joy in her eyes as Mystere recognized him. He was still looking moments later when she spotted Antonia. The smile wilted in a heartbeat, and Mystere turned abruptly away, recklessly dodging traffic as she crossed Broadway and escaped into City Hall Park.

Damnit, he thought, on the verge of chasing her. But already Antonia, who evidently hadn't seen Mystere, was trying to engage him in more of her tiresome, "clever," thinly veiled sexual banter. And why not, for he had just spent the past hour or so playing along with it himself.

He ignored it now, however, still watching Mystere's retreating figure. At first he had not been sure it was she, so wildly weather mussed was she, so frankly provocative in her damp clothing and literally unrestrained beauty. But those forget-me-not eyes had been unmistakable.

Of all the damned rotten luck, he cursed mentally. All his efforts to create a shocking impression, and look who took the brunt of it. And most irritating of all, the fact that he had found himself unexpectedly bound to Mystere's crushed feelings.

Antonia repeated something, her tone offended, and he realized she was waiting for his response.

"What?" he asked somewhat brusquely.

She stopped in her tracks, tugging him to an abrupt halt also.

" 'What?' " she mimicked his absent interrogative. "You haven't been listening to me at all, have you, Rafe Belloch?"

"Of course I have," he insisted with the rote conviction of a parrot.

"You have not, and it's as obvious as clown make-up," she accused. "Suddenly your unique sense of daring adventure seems more like a standard guilty conscience."

"That right?" he replied absently. He was so distracted that he added with unintended honesty, "You don't say anything anyway."

She frowned, and with good reason, for it was he who had initiated their insipid seduction ritual.

"I don't . . . ?" Antonia's flirtatious pique suddenly became real anger. Her pretty face had the tendency to distort itself into a vengeful mask when she was offended. *"You* called me, Rafe, remember? It was your idea to be 'boldly bohemian,' not mine."

"I'll never accuse you of ideas," Rafe promised, his tone so mild he only confused her more. He continued to ignore the woman at his side and everything else except Mystere, disappearing behind a tall hedgerow.

Sam Farrell had been right, Rafe thought, he could, indeed, wear Mrs. Astor's scorn as a badge of honor. But not, he was devastated to learn now, Mystere's.

He made up his mind and reached for his wallet, pulling a banknote out and tucking it into Antonia's hand.

"I'd loan you my carriage," he explained as he extracted his arm from hers, "but I may have need of it. You'll have no trouble finding a cab. Please excuse me, something's come up."

Antonia's jaw fell open in astonishment at his manners, but Rafe was off in the next moment, eliciting curses from drivers as he tore across Broadway with as little heed as Mystere had paid.

Rafe skidded round the hedgerow and caught up with a sodden Mystere just before she reached the Chambers Street exit.

"Mystere! Wait up a moment!"

Even swept up in the turmoil of her distraught emotions, she couldn't help realizing he had called her by her real name—something he usually did only for the benefit of others.

"You must have finished with Antonia," she flung at him as she quickened her step, "to part so suddenly now."

He was faster, sprinting in front of her to block a narrow gate in the iron fence surrounding the park.

"It's not what you think," he protested.

"I agree—it's what you *are*. Let me pass."

"No, not until you let me explain. We merely had coffee and dessert in the hotel restaurant. We did not go upstairs." He frowned and added, "Not that it's technically any of your damned business."

"I never said it was. Now let me pass, I said!"

"You little fool, I set all this up to cause a buzz of scandal, don't you see? To push Caroline, for I knew it would get back to her, which it will. Perhaps has already."

"And that makes it all acceptable?" she demanded, wide-eyed with outrage. Hot anger knotted her insides. "You know full well Lance Streeter and that blood-sucking pack of scandalmongers will make a public fuss over it. So what if our engagement is a sham; the public accepts it as real. And what you've done today will humiliate *me* more than anyone else. You swore you had no plan to destroy me."

He shook his head. "Wrong, you're all wrong. You speak of the public, but to them a provincial morality has no place in the sinful city. It's Caroline who will seethe, for it shows that her tight reins are slipping."

"Oh, you make me ill, Rafe, do you know that? The masses this, Mrs. Astor that . . . you and Abbot really are alike. It's Mrs. Astor's closed world versus the steaming dung-heap, and you seem determined to show her the dung-heap is winning. But where's the victory in being right?"

Rafe was not used to being concilliatory. But neither could he deny that for the moment at least, she had him dead to rights.

"I see your side of it," he conceded, "and you're right, to a point. I've sunk to some base tactics, granted. But look at my side of it. For the price of high tea, and a couple hours of boredom with Antonia, I can outrage my enemy. With no actual transgression, I have upped the ante in my contest of wills with Caroline."

"Fine. Then, why are you here now, blocking my path, once again trapping me? Why aren't you still with Miss Horse Grin, creating your precious 'impression of sin'?"

"Because of that look you gave me a few minutes ago, that's why. It felt like I'd been knifed. The question really is—why were you coming to my hotel?"

A sudden blush was only part of her answer, but the best part, judging from his smile.

"I . . . I went to Sheridan's office this morning," she explained, rubbing the rain from her miserable sodden face.

"I thought you might. And . . . ?"

Her chin trembled for a moment before she got control of herself and replied, "It was a disaster. I did manage to protect my identity, I think; but they laughed to my face, and who could blame them?"

His eyes traveled the length of her, from sodden hair to well-turned ankles. Her limp, soaked dress only made her tangled hair seem even wilder. The dinted fabric of the thin cotton bodice clearly marked her nipples. "Beauty Unbound," he remarked with a smile through the rain.

"I look horrid," she retorted stubbornly.

"Wrong. You look uncivilized and insatiable . . . really quite fetching." He kissed her wet nose. "Tell me, what do we do now? Sit and play a harp?"

"Don't you already have Antonia to entertain?"

"Nope. I was rude with her, now it's your turn."

"Well, I'm used to your rudeness. But I'll tell you this much," she rallied in a burst of defiant indignation, "I'm *not* going into that hotel with you now. Not after you've just been there playing kissy-face with her."

"Fine by me. How's this for a plan? The sun's due back out. I'll take you by your place so you can change into some dry things. Then we'll both play hooky and go for a little cruise up the Hudson. How 'bout it?"

Actually, she thought, it was a wonderful idea. She needed a respite from the close, crowded, frenetic world of Manhattan. And even if it was only self-delusion, only his lust masquerading as affection, she also needed attention, comforting. . . .

"Only one stipulation," he added. "When you change—don't wear those damned binding cloths."

Her eyes fled from his, but she nodded. "If you think you can control yourself."

"Hell, I won't even try. But I'm sure you'll manage to do that."

Their eyes met and held.

Together they both laughed.

While Mystere changed into dry clothing and brushed out the wild, tangled thatch of her hair, Rafe telephoned his yacht crew at their Manhattan slip and told them to ready the *Courageous Kate* for cruising.

The steam turbines were at full capacity by the time Rafe and Mystere arrived, and within minutes the yacht was already tacking around the Battery, bearing north through City Harbor into the mouth of the Hudson, while Rafe gave her a quick tour of the sleek craft.

Mystere was especially impressed by the luxury and quality of the master stateroom, with its gold velvet curtains and compact stove with nickel trimmings. An onboard generator powered by the engines provided electric lights throughout the yacht.

They both finally settled near the bow, leaning against the gunnel to watch the city gradually dwindle into rural pastures as they steamed farther north. Grassy banks teeming with timothy and clover marked the New Jersey shore, from which fishermen idly waved at them. Simply by turning her back, Mystere could pretend there was no city at all. The sun was stuck high in the sky as if pegged there, and to her it felt good burning on her neck and shoulders, comforting to feel its weight.

As the smoky, clamorous city receded farther behind them, a kind of lazy peace settled over her. Rafe was in a different mood, too, and hadn't been sniping at her as usual but actually conversing with her.

"Who's the original Courageous Kate?" she asked him. "Some beauty you squired until she broke your heart?"

"No, but in a sense she is my sweetheart. She's a brave little girl out west who saved one of our trains after a trestle washed out. Crossed a raging river in pitch-black darkness to flag down the approaching train. Just fifteen years old when it happened and she's become a heroine to railroad men everywhere."

"A heroine," Mystere repeated with thoughtful softness. "So unlike the Lady Moonlight. The difference between fame and infamy."

He studied her in silence, seemingly transfixed by her in that moment. She had brushed out her long, coffee-colored hair but left it free to cascade down over her back and shoulders. Sunlight spun a golden crown on her head.

"That difference," he suggested, "is perhaps less clearly defined than we think."

She wasn't sure if the odd contortion of his mouth was meant as a smile. She only knew that she was drawn to him, suddenly kissing his harsh lips with a burning passion even hotter than the July sun.

"I admit it," she confessed in a voice just above a whisper. "Sometimes I dread thinking of the time when you won't be with me."

Stop now, an inner voice warned her. *Do not ruin this closeness, even if it's illusory, because even a temporary illusion is better than a cold, lonely, dangerous existence without comfort, without the intimate touch of this man.*

He kissed her, beginning with her mouth and then tasting the soft skin of her throat, his lips causing an electric response that made her shudder.

"We don't need to think about that now," he whispered close to her ear. "The day's waning now. Come back with me to Staten Island—for the night, I mean."

She remained silent for some time, watching the river part before the prow of the yacht in a white curl. The silent lull became painful, then excruciating.

As if to break it, or perhaps to remind her, he moved the hand that was resting on her left hip—moved it up to caress her breast.

"Rafe," she protested at his shocking frankness, but without any effort to pull away from him.

"Shall I tell Skeels to head back to Staten Island now?"

She looked up into his teal gaze, shading her eyes from the sun.

"Yes," she surrendered, tired of the battles and the threats, tired of fighting her attraction to him.

Soon she would have to flee from everything and everyone she knew, flee from the known and familiar into an unknown future fraught with dangers. But tonight, at least, she would seize a few hours of happiness in Rafe Belloch's bed, knowing that in the morning, if she was smart, she would take her chance to be free from Rillieux and disappear forever.

Chapter 33

The sun had burned down to dying embers on the western horizon by the time the *Courageous Kate* was moored in her Staten Island berth.

"Hungry?" Rafe asked her as the two of them walked, arm in arm, toward the massive gates of his Garden Cove estate.

"Famished," she admitted, realizing she had eaten nothing since breakfast, and then only coffee and a croissant. "Well, this does feel odd," she added, smiling up at him in the grainy twilight.

"What does?"

"You asking me such innocent questions, and look—for a change you aren't tugging me along like I'm a bad child. I'm actually walking beside you of my own volition."

"You sound disappointed. Would you prefer to be forced?"

His tone was playful, but the double entendre did not escape her.

"Force," she replied, "does relieve one of responsibility. But I prefer being the ruler of my own fate."

"Choices, some sage once said, are the hinges of destiny."

"Yes," she almost whispered, for Rafe had no idea how true his words sounded in her ears. Her own destiny had reached a fork in the road, and very soon now she had to make the hard decision which turn to take. Both directions were crowded with danger, but for tonight, she vowed, she would think no more about it. Even though Rafe did not love her, and probably never could, she would settle for lies. She wanted to stop worrying about everything, to feel pleasure and closeness and warmth, to feel wanted and needed instead of always being used, hunted, and afraid.

"It's just us, Jimmy," Rafe said as they reached the gate in near darkness. "After we're in, run round to Milly's quarters, will you, and ask her to prepare a light supper for two. She needn't cook."

"Will do, boss."

"Oh, and then run down to the wine cellar, would you, and bring up a bottle of . . . burgundy, I guess."

The heavy iron gates groaned as Jimmy swung them open, then shut again. Mystere felt his eyes taking her measure, and she blushed unseen, suddenly wondering how many times the handsome Rafe Belloch had brought home a wench to bed. But she mustered her newfound resolve and chased off such thoughts. *Never mind grim reality,* she thought. *Just for tonight you live in a fairy-tale world, and you'll write your own happy ending.*

While the cook prepared their meal, Rafe and Mystere sipped wine in the front parlor.

She wandered about the room, studying framed photographs from a happier time in Rafe's life. To augment the meager candlelight, he built a small fire. It glowed blood orange behind an embroidered fire screen, and he silently studied Mystere in the flattering light. She studied him right back.

"I see where you got your good looks," she commented, nodding toward a photo on the mantel. "Your parents were a handsome couple."

"I always thought so, too," he replied, his tone more wistful than bitter. "And although not publicly demonstrative, they were very much in love. The years never seemed to diminish that."

Despite her newfound resolve, his poignant words stabbed at her heart.

"Rafe?"

"Hmm?"

"What do you plan on doing about Caroline's ultimatum? The September wedding date, I mean?"

"Don't worry about September," he dismissed her in a matter-of-fact tone. "Things will come to a head before then."

That reply only raised more questions. But just then Ruth appeared in the doorway to announce that their meal was already laid out in the dining room.

They both enjoyed a light repast of sandwiches, cheese, and fresh fruit, Mystere reveling in their peaceful, enjoyable conversation. She had never seen this side of Rafe, or realized he could be so personable and authentically charming. For a hard-hearted man of empire he certainly seemed well read in poetry and the classics, and spoke with enthusiasm about the novels of the expatriate American Henry James.

"But to hell with James," he said abruptly, watching her in a way that made her stomach flutter nervously. "Let's go upstairs. I want to show you something quite beautiful."

Carrying a three-branch candelabra to light their way, he led her up the magnificent central staircase with the turned balustrade. The master bedroom occupied a northeast-facing wing. He set the candelabra on a bureau near the door and led her by the hand across the big room to a wide expanse of full-length windows.

"This house sits on high ground," he explained as he tugged the sheer lace curtains and brocade overdrapery apart. "You can't fully appreciate the view until after dark."

Mystere very nearly gasped at the startling, magnificent beauty of Manhattan lit by gas and electricity after dark. Lights glittered like millions of stars across the dark expanse of the Upper Bay.

Rafe drew back the latches and opened the casements, and she felt the balmy night wind caressing her face like exploring fingers.

He stood close behind her, arms encircling her, chin resting on her head as they gazed for some minutes in silence, absorbed in the vista spread out before them like some grand diorama.

"There's no ugliness or suffering in this view of it," she finally remarked softly. "I wish I could always see the city from here, like this."

"Then, time stops here, tonight," he replied, kissing the side of her neck, then turning her to face him and pulling her close to kiss her mouth.

"Yes," she agreed in bittersweet surrender. "And the only world we'll have is the world we'll make."

He led her across the room to a mahogany poster bed with an arched canopy. When she modestly stepped behind a two-panel dressing screen near the bed, Rafe protested.

"No. I want to watch you disrobe just as I did that night in the drawing room."

"Is it an order this time, too?"

"No. A request."

"Then, you shall have your wish."

He kicked off his shoes and removed his shirt and vest, now bare to the waist. She already knew he was strong, but the hard, sloping pectorals and flat-as-a-board stomach took her again by pleasant surprise. In the gaslight, muscle wrapped his shoulders like taut steel cables.

He sat at the foot of the bed, watching in rapt fascination as she left her clothing in a pile at her feet. This time, however, she did not feel a burning shame, only a mounting heat that felt very different from shame.

"Turn around slowly," he told her when she stood naked, studying her figure bathed in soft light.

She did, watching desire transform his face, his own excitment fueling hers. He stood up and lifted his arms, a silent beckoning that drew her closer with magnetic power. When her bare breasts met his muscular torso, a groan escaped both of them simultaneously.

The tenderness of his kiss quickly heated to a greedy, needful hunger. The fact that they were both worlds apart and at each other's throats over everything from a robbery to a forced marriage seemed trivial to Mystere now. They had spent too much time battling.

Time stops here.

The phrase reverberated through her mind like a poem.

Rafe picked her up easily in both arms and carried her to the bed, laying her down on the silk sheets and then kneeling beside the bed to kiss and tease her nipples. Mystere gasped as he took first one, then the other into his mouth, knowing just exactly how much light pressure with his teeth would stoke her desire even hotter.

He caressed her body until she felt like she was burning up from within.

"Be with me now," she urged in a breathless whisper, tugging at him.

He stood up and pulled off his trousers, and she thrilled at the forbidden sight of his arousal. As he lay beside her she murmured in his ear, "I want you inside me."

He slid one hand high up the inside of her thighs, and she moaned at the pleasurable contact as his fingers spread her open like the petals of a dewy flower.

Only for a few brief moments, as he first entered her, was she again aware of his size. But the pleasure far outweighed any pain, and once he had slowly, carefully penetrated her to his full length, she felt herself opening to him, adjusting; and a blessed cry of pleasure rose from her when he began moving harder, faster.

He surprised her again as a lover, forceful and commanding, yes, but also tender and passionate, as eager to give pleasure as he was to receive. Again and again he took her with him to peaks of ecstasy, her insatiable need matching his own. Behind them, beyond the open windows, the lights of Manhattan winked out as the night edged toward midnight and then far beyond.

She wasn't sure precisely when the words "I love you" began to rise from her throat to her lips, but somehow she managed to stifle them. Even though she now realized it was true—not just the passion of the moment—she also realized it mustn't be. Not only because he didn't love her, but because this night must be their last.

Finally, exhausted and depleted, they dozed off together in a sleepy tangle of naked limbs. Mystere dreamt she was a great lady riding in a coach bearing the Granville coat of arms, with Rafe seated on one side of her, a smiling Bram on the other.

But then everything turned all wrong. Bram's handsome features melted, metamorphosed into Paul's fox face, laughing savagely at her, and when she turned to Rafe for help, he had become a horned, Satanic version of Mrs. Astor, who shrieked at her with demonic joy: *What about bub 'n' sis now, you filthy little thief?*

It was the sound of birds celebrating sunup that woke Mystere from her fitful rest.

The windows still stood wide open, and a cool, steady wind blew in off the bay, making her shiver a little when she peeled the covers back. Rafe still slept deeply beside her, even more handsome in repose, for his features showed no sign of his usual scorn for the world at large. The bed was a shambles from the force of their passion, which had pulled the sheets loose and even tugged the feather mattress partway off the bed.

She felt a pleasant soreness between her legs when she carefully, silently disentangled her legs from his. She kissed him once on the lips, very gently, before she got out of bed and began gathering up her clothing.

She dressed before the open windows, the breeze making goose-flesh on her skin while she watched the eastern horizon begin to glow salmon pink with the new day's sunrise. Already she could see the first ferry loading below at the public slip, and she hurried so she could catch it.

When she turned and saw Rafe lying there, however, she almost lost her courage. It would be so easy to just deny and postpone, crawl back in that warm bed with him . . . but no, *no,* she commanded herself with a merciless sense of purpose. That was the easy way now, perhaps, but by staying she would only endure the pain of watching all of it be destroyed.

Caroline Astor and Paul both expected a wedding, for different reasons, and either one of them was potentially dangerous; Paul if the wedding did happen, Caroline if it didn't. And Rafe was the most troublesome of the three.

If he did by some unlucky chance marry her, it would be a loveless match against his wishes; or he might sabotage everything in his implacable vengeance quest. No matter what, her best chance to remain free and search for Bram lay in flight. Especially now that her disastrous visit to Sheridan's office had convinced her she and Bram had no logical connection to the house of Granville. It was pointless to remain in New York any longer, pointless and dangerous.

Yesterday, when Rafe took her home to change into a dress of light French muslin, Hush had given her Helzer's reply to her note. She was to meet with him later today about the ring. With luck, she would only need to hide in her room on Centre Street for a few days at most.

She finished dressing and quickly located paper, a steel nib, and a pot of ink in the console table by the door. She left a brief note for Rafe, casting one long look back at him from the doorway.

The room suddenly seemed to melt as tears sprang from her eyes, and the constricting pain in her throat felt like a nail had lodged there. *You must leave him,* her mind admonished. *This hurt now is nothing compared to what's in store if you stay. Paul's desperation, Caroline's pride, Rafe's vengefulness—all of it will crush you unless you disappear.*

Then, vowing never to look back again, she left the man she now realized she loved and went forth to confront an uncertain destiny.

"God*damn* it," Rafe muttered, doing a slow boil as he read the short message Mystere had left on the bureau for him. She had taken no

time to blot it, and some of the letters had smeared, but it was read-
able.

> *I've gone forever and I beg you not to search for me. It's far bet-*
> *ter this way. Thank you for last night. You made it easy for me to*
> *pretend you love me.*

And in a final show of rebellious spirit that brought a bitter twist to
his lips, she had signed it, *Lady Moonlight.*

For a few minutes, as he hurriedly dressed, Rafe was almost wild
with fury at her. He was a man accustomed to calling the shots, to
being in complete control, and when it came to women, it was *he* who
did the rejecting, not they.

But as his anger began to subside, a cold, gnawing worry rushed in
to take its place. Despite his claims, he had not protected her secret
from Mrs. Astor, and scared those inept blackmailers away, simply to
retain control of events. It wasn't just a matter of control, of his bruised
male pride—the woman he had taken into his arms last night, that demure little beauty who had become such a passionate firebrand, was
the one woman in all the world to match him. He knew he *must* find
her before she could get too far away.

It's your fault she couldn't sign her name Mystere, he thought with bitter
honesty. *You hardly ever used her name. . . .*

The search for her wouldn't be easy, not with her survival knowledge of the streets. He would have to have help, but he would find the
men he needed. He was, after all, the man who moved mountains. He
would find her, even if it meant moving heaven and earth.

Chapter 34

"In summation, gentlemen, the decision to consolidate all of our Midwestern short lines is now final. This will entail a radical reorganization at the management level, and the current system with seventeen field managers will be revised into a system with three regional supervisors located in Detroit, Cincinnati, and Omaha."

Rafe's clear, steady, strong voice easily filled the big meeting room where almost thirty executives of Belloch Enterprises sat around a long, rectangular table of polished oak. It was just past ten A.M., and the meeting was nearing the end of its second hour.

Although concise and well organized, Rafe looked tired, seemed at times distracted. Sam Farrell, seated at one end of the table, saw his boss impatiently consulting his watch every few minutes.

Rafe started to speak again. But suddenly a commotion could be heard out in the anteroom, a woman's voice protesting with forceful authority.

"I don't care if Jesus Christ is in there with his disciples. I said I *will* see Rafe Belloch and I'll see him right now!"

The doors flew open to admit a glowering Caroline Astor, Ward scuttling beside her like a general's aide-de-camp. He carried a beautiful rosewood case under one arm. Two of Belloch Enterprises' private guards trailed them, shrugging their apologies at Rafe.

"She said we'd have to shoot her to stop her," one of them offered, his tone embarrassed.

"You missed your chance, boys," Rafe muttered, aware that all the men now assembled were staring in openmouthed astonishment. The few who didn't recognize this intrusive female were quickly informed it was *the* Mrs. Astor.

"Gentlemen," she called out in her most magisterial manner, "I must ask all of you to leave the room. I have some private words for Mr. Belloch, and they will not wait."

The room went as silent as a lecture hall after a call for volunteers. All eyes shifted from Mrs. Astor to their corporate chief. Never had Rafe so acutely felt the weight of leadership as he did now. But it was Sam's quick diplomacy that saved him.

"Fellows," Sam suggested, rising from his chair, "we could all use a break anyway. I, for one, have no doubt that Mrs. Astor must have urgent business, or she'd not be here now. So let's adjourn until further notice."

"Thank you, sir," she responded with formal politeness. "And would you remain behind?" she asked Sam.

He glanced at Rafe, who shrugged and nodded permission. The moment the room was empty except for the four of them, Caroline got right to the point Rafe was expecting.

"Have you *seen* the newspapers, you unprincipled scoundrel?" she demanded.

"No," he replied flatly. "I've been busy."

"Not too busy for your little performance with Antonia yesterday, though, were you?"

"Coffee and napoleons?" he protested. "Where's the scandal in that?"

"You *are* vile, Rafe. You are a Patriarch of the Four Hundred, formally engaged, and you knew perfectly well how your actions would be interpreted."

"Oh? Has there been some mention?" he asked with galling innocence.

"Mention?" she repeated, outrage deepening her already stern voice. "The gossip writers are all squealing with glee over your apparent rejection of propriety. And since I've 'championed' your engagement, they're calling it the revenge of Father Knickerbocker."

Despite her outrage, Rafe liked the dig and barely managed to keep his face sober.

"What would they be writing instead, Caroline," he asked her quietly, "if you had seduced me as you once planned to?"

Sam, who had remained standing because Mrs. Astor did, looked astounded, a rare reaction for him. Ward turned white, no doubt in fear as he anticipated Caroline's reaction.

For a moment her anger was so severe that she visibly trembled. But in seconds her iron will asserted itself again, and a cool sense of determination was clear in her voice. "Ward, bring me the case."

She looked at Rafe. "All right, you want to be blunt, do you? Then allow me to play along. You have accused me of killing your parents. If you truly believe that, then honor requires you to kill *me.*"

Caroline lifted the lid of the felt-lined case.

Rafe stared at two handsome dueling pistols with ornate ivory and silver inlays. The initials W. B. A. were inscribed on the butts.

"My husband's family heirlooms," she explained needlessly. "And no, he doesn't know I took them."

"Am I to murder you in cold blood?" Rafe inquired, keeping a straight face only with effort. "Or are you challenging me to a duel?"

"Why not a duel? I know the rules. I have my second, you have yours, so it'll be properly witnessed. We can easily take ten paces in this huge room. Isn't that how 'offended' gentlemen such as yourself settle serious matters?"

"Caroline, you're showing your age. Dueling is illegal; we let lawyers fight our battles these days."

"Illegal? Come now! So is aiding and abetting a thief, Mr. Belloch, but laws haven't stopped you from keeping Mystere's secret, have they?"

Rafe wanted to laugh, yet her intensity intimidated him. She removed one pistol and held it out to him, offering it butt first.

"Take it," she demanded. "I believe you'll find it's properly loaded and primed. I will not have my name constantly dragged through the mud because you nurture a grudge. *Take* it, Rafe. If I killed your father, then shoot me for it. Or I'll shoot you, whichever the outcome."

"Caroline, don't—"

"You can't scare me, Rafe, nor make me feel guilty for your father's cowardice. So shoot me—it's your only alternative."

Rafe took the pistol, but he also snatched the case away from Caroline. He put the gun away and handed the case to Sam.

"Ward, for heaven's sake," Caroline snapped, suddenly offering him support for he seemed on the verge of fainting.

"I'll be outside with the others," Sam excused himself, seeing that his services would not be required.

Rafe paced a little in silence, feeling Caroline's eyes on him the entire time. It was she who spoke first after she had helped Ward into a chair.

"You're going to stop this vicious little game you're playing, Rafe. And there *will* be a wedding by the end of September. One more trick like the one you played yesterday with Antonia, and I'll destroy you, Rafe Belloch, one way or another. Bullet or bankruptcy."

"That's nice, Caroline," he replied wearily, still too preoccupied with thoughts and images of Mystere to care much about anything else. But oddly, Caroline's melodrama with the pistols had somehow eliminated his desire to destroy the matron. For in the depths of her willful anger and offended dignity, he saw the same class fanaticism that had destroyed his own father.

I've not been up against any individual villain, he realized, *despite focusing all my resentment on Caroline—it's an outmoded way of life I'm up against, and it's already in its death throes.*

All these years he had lived to kill a chimera that existed only in the mind. And thanks to his myopic spite, the best thing that had ever happened to him was, even now, fleeing from his life forever.

"Actually, Caroline," he said after a minute, "you're partly right. My father did show a moment of cowardice at the end. No one murdered him, death was his choice, and to that extent I've harbored an illogical grudge. But you'll never convince me he wasn't wronged, after his death, by those who owed him better treatment. Yourself included."

Mrs. Astor softened a little at this image of him, so brilliant and virile and good-looking . . . and unattainable.

"Perhaps, after all, we did wrong you somewhat," she relented.

"Not I, my parents."

"Yes, well, the pronoun isn't important. My point is that you're a fool. You are obviously in love with Mystere or whoever she really is;

and yet you've been prepared to destroy her just to vent a childish spite."

He took her words in silence, for she had him dead to rights.

Her voice became more reasonable. "The whole secret to survival, Rafe, is to simply deflect pain and move on. You *reflect* too much. Self-absorption in one's own misery is a prerogative of the middle classes only, not we who are their social betters. I was hoping Mystere would help you see that."

Mystere . . . Rafe knew that Mrs. Astor couldn't possibly have learned yet that she had run away, gone into hiding. If it was scandal Caroline dreaded, then the lid would definitely blow off when Mystere's absence was noticed. In fact, Rafe suddenly realized, suspicion would center on him, the last person to be with her.

"Oh, don't misunderstand me," Caroline added. "Of course it knocked me sick and silly when I finally surmised who, and what, she must be. Of course the public must not find out or we'll all become laughingstocks. But I don't care if she's the Whore of Babylon; I *like* the girl."

Rafe nodded. "I know that. You've always been fond of her."

"One cannot help it; she's compelling, Rafe, and vital. I can't put a name to it, but there's something in her eyes. She's searching for something. . . ."

"Transcendent?" he supplied.

"Yes, exactly. She may not find it, of course, but bless her heart for the search. Lord knows she's no angel, but I wish I could be like her. If you ever quote me on any of this, I'll call you a liar."

"Oh, Ward will back me," he said with absentminded cynicism. He knew damn well Ward would never contradict one word Mrs. Astor claimed, fearing his tongue would be torn out for blasphemy.

"Can we strike a truce, you and I?" Caroline asked him. Her voice had softened with feeling.

Rafe met her imploring gaze and saw how Mystere had been right all along. Only Mrs. Astor still stood, wounded but victorious, on the battleground where powerful wills had clashed.

"Truce," he conceded, for all he really wanted now was to find Mystere.

His surrender moved Caroline to a rare candor.

"I shan't be a total hypocrite now that Sam's gone. I, too, was willing to foolishly risk a great deal, Rafe, to be your lover. Even my self-respect if you used me once and then rejected me. You knew that, didn't you?"

"It crossed my mind," he said diplomatically.

"But in any case you won't do it now because you're in love," she added, placing slightly jealous emphasis on the last three words. "By the way, I've been unable to reach Mystere. Her . . . 'uncle' claims she did not come home last night. I assume she's staying with you?"

"Yes," he lied.

"For God's sake be discreet. And keep her away from your hotel. And ask her to call me," Caroline requested, adding, "Come along, Ward. Rafe must get back to his work."

But Rafe had no such intention.

"You close out the meeting," he ordered Sam the moment the latter poked his head inside the room. "I'm going to see Paul Rillieux. Jesus, I've made a hell of a mess of things."

"Perhaps you have," Sam replied. "But you'll set it all to rights, boss. Remember what you told your engineers when the Rock Island Line got bogged down at Walnut Creek? The subsoil wouldn't hold deep pylons, and everybody was ready to give up."

Rafe grinned. "Sure I remember. I said if we can't raise the bridge, then we must lower the river. And damn me if we didn't lower the river."

"I'll take care of things here," Sam assured him. "You go find Mystere."

Paul Rillieux seemed amused, and somewhat disdainful, at Rafe Belloch's manner and tone. Paul had been expecting this visit ever since he realized, some time late last night, that Mystere had finally run away.

"Where is she?" Rillieux repeated his visitor's question, placing his cane across his knees and leaning back in his chair. "She's working her way west, as we used to say of women traveling alone. Although I doubt she's selling her body, for she's a stubbornly high-minded—"

"I know what she's like, Rillieux," Rafe cut him off impatiently.

The fox face grinned at him. "I'm sure you must."

"Old man, you have fewer friends than you think. And age does not keep a man from prison, once convicted."

"Sir, you enter my home and threaten me?"

"Your home?" Rafe stood up and took a few steps across the parlor, advancing on Rillieux. "I asked you where Mystere is, and I expect an answer."

"Let's not be precipitate, Mr. Belloch." He banged the floor three times with the tip of his cane. Almost immediately a side door was flung open, and the burly "butler" Rafe knew only as Evan stepped into the room, a shotgun tucked under one arm.

"You best hark to your manners, you lily-livered mange pot," he advised Rafe in a surly tone, "or you'll get a load of Blue Whistlers in your belly."

Rafe had no choice but to back off. The homicidal glint in Evan's hostile eyes was unmistakable, and it only served as a reminder that Mystere's trespass was not so great, after all, in the scheme of things. It was Rillieux's evil that had controlled her so long in this den of thieves.

"When one pleads guilty," Rillieux told his visitor, "he skips the jury. I admit to everything you've accused me of, more or less. As to your inquiry about Mystere's whereabouts—I have every intention of cooperating with you. I am quite confident that she could not have left the city yet. But at the moment I do not know her precise location. I have several people working on that as we speak."

"I shouldn't wonder, for she's the key to the mint as far as you're concerned. *You* got rid of her brother, didn't you, Rillieux? Tipped off an impress gang to nab him because if there was any wealth to be inherited, you figured Mystere would be easier to control."

"I see she told you about her precious letter."

The topic didn't seem to bother Rillieux at all. Obviously having read the letter from the law firm in New Orleans, he would know there was no need to lie, no point for pretense with Belloch.

"So what if I did arrange the boy's abduction?" Rillieux countered. "Although I mean the question rhetorically. Remember, the mere fact that those children possessed a certain letter, and I knew about it, doesn't make that letter at all significant. I made some quiet inquiries over the years, but to no avail."

"And it doesn't matter to you any longer," Rafe supplied, "since your sights are fixed on my money now."

Paul made a deprecatory gesture with one hand. "You attribute too much power to a sick old man. However, since you've touched on the topic of money—my network has been alerted, and Mystere will not get out of this city undetected."

"This is an offer, I take it?"

Rillieux shrugged. "Right now you're neither up the well nor down. If you want to find Mystere, your best chance is with me. I'm in constant contact with my people."

"Yes, and so far you've come up with nothing."

"That will change, I assure you. And when it does, you will be the first person I contact."

Rafe nodded at this, for he was too desperate not to. But he had agreed to nothing so far as payment; let the old blackguard believe what he chose.

The moment Rafe had left the house, Rillieux began to fret. Belloch, too, had extensive resources at his command. There were really only two feasible ways Mystere could leave the city: by water or by rail. That meant watching the waterfront ticket offices and Grand Central Station. And Belloch's men might spot her first—or the police if any of this went public.

Rillieux had reached a critical conclusion: Belloch had no intention whatsoever of surrendering his fortune to anyone, and Mystere was no longer the obedient little girl susceptible to suggestions. If Paul wanted to profit, he must do so now, not later, and then flee before Caroline could crush him.

"Put the word out on the street," he instructed Evan. "Three hundred dollars cash reward for whoever captures Mystere and brings her to me. Belloch is badly smitten—he'll pay a king's ransom to get her back in his arms again."

Chapter 35

Three days spent as a virtual prisoner in her room on Centre Street was sufficient to remind Mystere how spoiled and pampered she had become while posing as Rillieux's debutante niece. She also quickly realized what a blind fool she had been to think grabbing one night of pleasure and happiness could excise Rafe from her thoughts. Just the opposite: torrid memories of him became sheer torture during the long, sleepless nights in her strange and uncomfortable bed with its lumpy mattress.

There had been a few fine old furnishings in the room when it was shown to her. But when she arrived on Tuesday, after fleeing from Rafe, the nice pieces had vanished; instead, she found a rustic rope bed and a crudely fashioned washstand of the type sold through catalogs.

She now shared a drabby, windowless water closet with three other tenants, all of whom seemed to resent her presence. And she was forced to a spartan diet of items that would not spoil quickly, for the room was always hot and she had neither icebox nor cooking stove. There were some clean restaurants nearby on Broadway or Sixth Avenue, but she feared being recognized and fared forth only when necessary.

Her landlady, Mrs. Cunningham, was humorless and petty, a stout, aging widow with folds of excess flesh ruining the interesting bone structure of her face. She was barely civil and seemed always resentful of something, but at least she wasn't a snoop and did not bother to interrogate Mystere.

The other tenants, however, had not shown such discretion. She coolly rebuffed their attempts at conversation, always polite but deliberately haughty, hoping such snobbery would seem familiar enough to keep her from appearing "different." It apparently worked, for yesterday morning a brief dialogue was staged outside her door. The mocking voices were raised deliberately so she would hear their new name for her:

"Shall we invite the new tenant to lunch, girls?"

"Oh, don't you know? The marchioness does not take her meals with commoners."

"No, for the marchioness would far rather gnaw on cold penny rolls all by her superior self."

Their laughter sounded coarse, somewhat forced, for they truly resented her.

Let them vent their petty spite, she thought. Anything to keep them from wondering about her. Soon, with luck, she would be gone and this place merely a fading memory.

She had concluded her business with Jerome Helzer, and now her escape from the city was at least funded if not assured. She still shuddered at the memory of Water Street, the tenements looming nearby amid their malodorous school-sink privies and the stink of rot and decay.

Helzer had treated her with professional courtesy, but at first feigned a crafty reluctance to buy, implying that the Butler emerald was too notorious, thus too risky. But no doubt he had his emery wheel and diamond-tip saw in motion before she even got back to her room, for she had heard no man was better at transforming a gem than he—or quicker to get rid of one. She hardly cared, for he had paid her one thousand dollars cash, no questions, and that was enough to allow her to relocate and survive awhile. With luck, long enough to find some means of gainful employment.

She had decided on Boston, for she knew of respectable areas where rooms were let at reasonable rates. She also knew she mustn't delay, for too many persons were after her. At least she felt somewhat lifted by the realization that it was in almost everyone's interest to suppress word of her escape. No one benefitted by the newspapers playing it up except the newspapers themselves. Nonetheless, word would get out, for there were too many informants among the domestic staffs of the Four Hundred.

So she devised the best plan she could, knowing that Grand Central Station and the shipping offices of Trans-Atlantic and the other passenger ship lines would be under close surveillance. There would probably be less attention paid to the rivers, and Mystere had already booked passage on the Hudson River Line to the town of Croton-on-Hudson. From there she would travel to Boston by rail.

Her boat was set to disembark from its West Street berth at nine A.M. today, and she had been awake since well before dawn, confronting the fear that by now had caused a piercing headache. She did not just dread the unknown, but also the fact that she was leaving Rafe's life forever. At one time she had prayed for this; now she secretly hoped he would somehow appear and stop her.

At eight A.M. she walked to the cab stand at Fourteenth Street and quickly arranged to have a second driver pick up her trunk and deliver it to the steamboat terminal.

Face obscured by the lace veil of her widow's bonnet, Mystere pressed well back into the seat of her cab, feeling naked and exposed, vulnerable to countless eyes. She thought again, with sinking dread, of the big, drab, frame terminal building, where anyone off the street could easily lurk among the ticketed passengers.

Preoccupied, at first, by such worries, it took her some time to realize the cab was heading toward the Lower East Side, not the City Harbor.

"Sir!" she called up to the driver, vexed. "You're going the wrong way to reach West Street!"

"I know 'zacly where I am, lady," he assured her, snapping his quirt across the horse's rump to quicken the pace, assuring that his passenger could not flee.

Only now did she realize she had no idea what happened to the cab that was hauling her trunk. Dread sickened her as the speeding hackney careened into a series of unpaved alleys along the docks.

Suddenly they halted beside a deserted loading dock, so abruptly she almost slid forward off the seat.

"I think I've nabbed that sly little piece you been looking for," the driver called out to someone she couldn't see. "Come glom her face."

She fought hard to control her breathing, fear seeming to paralyze her muscles. For a few seconds she debated leaping from the cab. Before she could do anything, however, a big, mean, unshaven face thrust around the canvas fender to look at her. The breath suddenly blasting her nostrils stank of rotgut whiskey.

"Let's have a better look at you, muffin," Sparky said, reaching up to grab her veil.

"Leave your hands off me!" she protested, pushing his hand away.

"You're a feisty little bitch, ain'tcher?" he demanded with approval. "P'raps I'd better check you for guns, anh?"

He reached toward her breasts, and quick as a snake striking, Mystere bit his hand hard. Sparky loosed a bray of rage and pain.

"You like to cut up rough, eh?" he goaded, his voice suddenly hoarse with excitment. "That's *my* game, too."

She saw him double up his right fist, but before she could protect herself, Sparky struck her so hard in her left temple that the blow literally stunned her. She was helpless to interfere when he reached up and yanked her bonnet off.

A wide smile creased his big, moon face as he recognized her. The cab rocked wildly when the big man heaved himself up beside her, forced to push her out of his way.

"Good eye, Hiram, you've bagged our quail," he called up to the driver. "Now let's head toward Great Jones Street and collect the bounty."

"I'll take that," Paul told Rose, rising from his chair. He hooked his cane over one forearm so he could take the tray from her. "I told you when Mystere was first brought here that you are to stay away from her. Is that clear?"

"But, Paul, I only—"

"Rose, you have grown too sympathetic to her."

"*Some*one has to," she bristled. "I saw that bruise on her, la!"

"Now, now, she's safe here and no one's going to hurt her. I won't have you scheming with her, do you mark me? She has become my— I mean our last chance to raise a bit of capital before we all must flee. Rafe Belloch can afford to pay our needs out of his postage drawer."

The tray held a bowl of soup, bread and butter, a glass of milk and some toiletries. Walking slowly, Paul took it downstairs into the gaslit basement room used as the servants' dining hall. He removed a key from his pocket and unlocked a door at the far end of the room, hidden by the big coal furnace.

It opened onto a small, windowless storage room cluttered with garden tools and food staples. Enough light spilled in to reveal Mystere, lying on her side on a quilt pallet. Her wrists and ankles were bound with ropes.

Paul set the tray down on a nearby wooden crate. Then he removed her cloth gag.

"Must you keep that in my mouth?" she protested. "I'm not the screaming type."

"I know, but it's difficult to predict just who might pop by, and I'd rather not risk it. Here's some delicous beef-and-barley soup Rose has made," he added in a coaxing tone. "I'm sorry the boys are out right now, so I can't take the chance of untying your hands. It's come to this, that my little girl can now overpower me. You'll have to let me feed you."

"I'm not hungry," she tried to snap. But her voice sounded thick and sluggish; the words came to her slower than usual. She vaguely recalled her arrival, how Paul had forced some not-unpleasant-tasting liquid down her throat. Whatever it was, she had blacked out soon after.

"What time is it?" she asked him.

"About five P.M. You've been asleep all day."

"Asleep? Drugged, you mean."

Paul shrugged. "If it pounds nails, call it a hammer. Here, try a bite of this."

"No," she insisted, turning her head away. "If you make me taste it, I'll spit it on you."

Paul gave up with a sigh, setting the bowl aside again. He winced when he glanced at the big, grape-colored swelling over her temple. Even in the stingy light it was ugly.

"Sweet love, you were foolish to resist a pig like Sparky," he lectured her.

Mystere said nothing to this, although secretly she was glad she fought with him, for evidently it made him give up the idea of raping her. Sparky had gone no further.

"I don't want Belloch upset," Paul added. "It won't do to sell him damaged goods when the man's a hothead like you."

A sense of helpless frustration made her actually groan. "Paul, no, please reconsider what you're doing. Just let me go, please."

He shook his hoary head, lips pursed like a coldhearted accountant. "Out of the question, dear. Hush has already been sent to fetch him."

There must have been a telltale gleam of hope in her eyes at this, for he added wryly, "Don't expect the boy to rescue you like Tom Sawyer, for he doesn't know you're here. And don't look at me like that; I have no choice in the matter. I realize now that all my grand schemes are hopeless. I am a tattered old man who must save his breath to cool his porridge. I've lost control of you, and I'm losing the others, too. Most troubling of all, I suspect that Caroline is 'cooling out' toward me—that could signal real damage. But I still have one thing of value to Rafe Belloch: his fiancée."

"Paul, you've got it all wrong. Rafe has no intention of marrying me."

"No, you're the one who has it wrong. I've talked to the man, and he wants you the way they want ice water in hell. He's in love with you, and you with him. Don't deny it."

"I admit I love him, so what? He does *not* love me, and he will not marry me. How many times do I have to tell you that? He is a dangerous, unpredictable man, and you are a fool to think you can manipulate him just because you're desperate."

"I'm a fool, all right," he conceded sadly. "An old fool who played a fool's game far too long. But I have no intention of dying in prison, dear heart. Belloch will be here soon, I expect, and the bargaining will begin in earnest. Now, if you insist on not eating, I must tie this gag on you again."

"Oh, Paul," she protested, close to tears as she realized the game was finally, at long last, up. And she had come so close to freedom. So close to protecting the man she loved. The despair choked her like a noose. "I beg of you, please don't hurt him."

They were her last words before he tied the gag.

"Well then," he replied, "if we are all bound for hell, Mystere, at least *I'm* whipping the team."

Chapter 36

Darkness had begun to settle over the city by the time Hush returned with Rafe Belloch. Paul, Baylis, and Evan had all joined forces to wait in the parlor. The shotgun lay conspicuously across Evan's lap.

Hush didn't bother with the bellpull, using his own key to open the front door. Rafe stopped in the doorway of the parlor to stare at the trio for a moment.

"Ahh, Mr. Belloch," Paul greeted him smugly. "So glad you could stop by."

"So here's the cock of the dung-heap," Rafe replied. "A thief and grifter who expertly imitates Mrs. Astor's supercilious tone."

Evan scowled and patted the scattergun. "You're valiant as an Essex lion," he said scornfully. "You'll watch your mouth, you banker's pimp, or I'll let daylight into you."

Rafe ignored him, still staring at Rillieux. "All right, I'm here. Where is Mystere?"

"You'll *pay* me for that information, Mr. Belloch, and you'll pay handsomely."

"I'll see you bark in hell first. Where is she?"

Evan and Baylis exchanged sneering smiles. Evan pushed up out of his chair, leveling the shotgun on Rafe.

"Your robber-baron ways don't cut no ice here, Belloch," Evan snarled. "You're in *our* home now, and under law we can blow you away as an intruder."

"Hush," Rafe spoke quietly, for the lad stood just behind him in the hallway. "Step well aside. That's the lad. Boys, you're on."

Rafe took several steps into the room, making space for Jimmy and Skeels, who suddenly stepped in from the hallway where they had been waiting. Both men held pistols at the ready and took up positions well to either side of their boss.

Between his vest and his coat Rafe, too, wore a pistol in an armpit holster. In a moment it was out, and there was a muzzle trained on each of the three adversaries.

"You can probably kill me," Rafe told Evan in a cold, authoritative voice. "But that's a single-barrel gun with one shot. My life for all three of yours. Now either put down that shotgun or pull the trigger."

Evan, whose face had turned pale as fresh linen, did not wait for Paul's order. Not one of the three men confronting him looked in the least bit afraid. He set the gun down on the floor, and Jimmy came over to claim it.

"Now, let's take it from the top," Rafe told Rillieux. "Where are you keeping Mystere?"

"Rot in hell," Rillieux replied savagely. "I said you'll pay for that information."

Rafe stared from one to the other. "There's nothing wrong with you three that a can of blasting powder couldn't fix. Hush!"

"Sir?"

"Could Mystere be somewhere in the house?"

"I dunno, sir. I ain't seen her."

"Wasting your time," Rillieux assured Rafe. "She's nowhere near this house."

All the commotion had brought Rose from her quarters. She poked her head into the room, then gasped when she saw all the drawn weapons.

"Rose?" Hush said. "Honest Injun now. Are they keeping Mystere here in the house?"

Rafe turned to stare at the redheaded servant. She paled, but only shook her head, too intimidated to even speak.

"You've got them all afraid of you, old man," he told Rillieux. "But you've a telephone in the hallway. Perhaps Inspector Byrnes would take some interest in this matter."

Rillieux calmly called the bluff. "Perhaps he would, at that. Particularly when he learns the identity of Lady Moonlight—and the fact that *you've* been protecting her to maintain your bedroom privileges."

Paul's mocking face seemed to ask Rafe if he was so God-almighty tough *now*. But it was Rose who finally broke the impasse.

"Sir?" she said hesitantly to Rafe. "I know where Mystere is."

"Damn you, Rose, put a sock in it!" Paul exploded, his angry eyes warning her. "I've told you before that disloyalty will—"

"Oh, shut up, Paul," she snapped. "I've kept quiet far too long while you've abused that poor girl. I'm sick of you and your bullying ways. Do what you want to me, I'll not play the good dog for you any longer."

"He'll do nothing to you," Rafe assured her. "I'll see to that. Is she here in the house, Rose?"

"Yessir. Down in the basement, I'll show you."

"Rillieux," Rafe ordered tersely, "you'll come with us. Jimmy, you and Skeels stay here and keep an eye on these two. If you have to shoot them, fine by me. It'll save the citizens the cost of feeding them in prison."

Absolutely nothing, Mystere realized with a sinking sensation of despair, *focuses the mind like captivity.*

In the darkness she had no idea how much time had passed. Her hands and feet had gone numb from being tied so long, and the air in the storeroom was heavy and close. The gag hurt her mouth and made it difficult to breathe. But it was her mind that tormented her even more than her body.

With so much time to ponder her stark situation, she had given up all hope of a positive outcome. Many things could happen, depending on Paul and on events she could not predict or control. But one terrible conclusion seemed inevitable: Rillieux would see her dead.

Never, in the bleakest depths of misery, had she felt such helpless loneliness. She cried until she had no more tears left. When the door was finally flung open, and she heard Rafe's angry curse, instead of joy she felt only a terrible dread.

"Damn you, Rillieux," Rafe muttered as he hurriedly untied her ropes. Rose held a candle to augment the dim light spilling in, and it clearly revealed Mystere's badly bruised left temple. "Were you planning on delivering a corpse as my bride?"

Terrified at Rafe's sudden fury, Rillieux began loudly protesting. "See here, Rafe, I did not—"

"Shut up, you ruthless old bastard." He began gently chafing Mystere's limbs, restoring her circulation. "You've drugged her, too. I see it in her pupils."

"Merely a good dose of Miss Pinkerton's to help her slee—"

"That stuff is pure laudanum; you might have killed her. Get out of my sight before I shoot you. Give me a hand, would you, Rose?"

Rose went to help him, but they were interrupted by Rillieux's cold announcement.

"She is not yours to save, Belloch."

Rafe's head snapped up. Mystere saw the glint of the small ladies' muff pistol in Paul's hand. With utter despair, she realized her worst fears were coming true.

"No—I won't let you hurt him!" she cried out with all her strength.

"You protect him?" Paul spat. "When I am the one who took you from the streets—?"

"And kidnapped my brother!" she accused.

"If I could have ever gotten to Sheridan to see if that fortune was yours, it would have been worth it to both of us to have gotten rid of Bram," Rillieux spitefully confessed.

"What did you do to him?" Mystere was hysterical. Rafe's strong hands on her were almost not enough to keep her on the pallet.

"He went where every poor lad is doomed to go. To the sea. And by God, I hope he's rotted to fish food by now." Rillieux's face turned murderous. "He had the same traitorous spirit as you. And I'll see you die by my own hand before you'll profit from my machinations." He cocked the muff pistol and pressed it to her swollen temple.

A ferocious bellow seemed to come from the pits of hell. Before Mystere could even comprehend what was taking place, she realized Rafe was upon Rillieux, attacking him with the viciousness of a feral dog.

The old man Rillieux was no match for Rafe. If not for the gun.

A loud report sounded. Blue gunsmoke hung in the air as deadly testament.

Rafe doubled over.

Rose screamed.

In bilious rage Paul stood over Mystere, cocking and firing the now empty gun as if ignorant of its impotence. Footsteps thundered overhead as Rafe's men sounded the alarm and scuffled with Baylis and Evan.

"I'll have my vengeance on you yet, you turncoat bitch!" Rillieux screamed at Mystere. "You'll never be free of me! Every time you look across your shoulder, you'll fear it will be me at your back!" With that, he flung the useless muff pistol at Mystere's face and fled through the outside cellar stairs.

No doubt Baylis was already ahead of him with the waiting coach.

"Rafe! Rafe!" Mystere wept, nearly crawling to his doubled-over form.

"Go after him!" Rafe barked at his men when they appeared at the door. "Don't let him get away!"

"Rafe, you're hurt," Mystere cried, watching her hand that was on his side turn red.

Rafe straightened, his face tight with pain. "It would seem Ruth will have another wound to tend. But it's not too terrible. Went clean through my side."

Together they walked up the stairs to the parlor. Rose went to fetch bandages, and Rafe took a deep quaff of brandy. By the time the spirit was gone in the glass the color had returned to Rafe's face.

"Take her ladyship upstairs and draw her a bath. She looks paler than a ghost," Rafe proclaimed.

Refusing to leave his side, Mystere had to be nearly dragged upstairs with Rose's constant assurance that Rafe's wound was not lethal.

Rose quickly tended to her. Rafe waited anxiously in the upstairs hallway while Rose helped Mystere bathe and change into nightclothes.

While Rafe waited, Jimmy came upstairs. "Boss? The old man is missing. Him and his minions. Clean gone. We can't find them anywhere."

Rafe nodded, grim resignation on his face. "It's every man for himself and the devil take the hindmost. Tell Skeels to go wait for us on the yacht, all right? I want you to stay here."

Jimmy nodded and went back downstairs.

Moments later Rose emerged from Mystere's bedroom.

"She's resting now, God bless her," she reported to Rafe. "She's not very sleepy, though, and she's asked to see you. You needn't knock, she's waiting."

He nodded. As she turned to head downstairs, Rafe called after her: "Rose?"

She turned around. "Yes, sir?"

"I suppose Mystere being from Ireland was born Catholic, was she not?"

Rose looked startled. "Well, yes, sir."

"Then, I want you to send Hush for a priest." Rafe handed the startled woman some banknotes. "This should fetch one. Tell Hush to inquire at the rectory at Saint Patrick's."

"Oh, but, sir," Rose protested, "Mystere is not in any grave danger. She doesn't need Last—"

"Just go," he insisted.

Rose went downstairs, and Rafe let himself into the bedroom. He felt a sudden flood of relief when he saw Mystere resting comfortably in bed, her beautiful hair fanned out around her head on the pillows. Although her bruise was still puffy and dark, she felt good enough to greet him with a warm, if somewhat diffident, smile.

"So how are you feeling?" he asked.

"I should be asking that of you," she offered.

He ruefully grinned. "Believe it or not, I've had worse."

"I'm afraid I'm a miserable failure as a fugitive."

"You're certainly quite good at slipping out of a man's bed," he assured her, but with a smile.

"It wasn't easy. I was of a mind to crawl back in and kiss you awake."

Rafe sat down on the bed, gently pushing her hair aside to better examine the bruise. "Did Rillieux or his men do this?"

"No, it was Sparky."

Rafe nodded, saying nothing. But the man had been fairly warned, and now Rafe made a mental note to talk to Sam about it. Sparky's days of beating women would soon be over.

"Anyhow, I wish you *had* crawled back into bed," he assured her.

The covers were turned down, and Mystere's silk chemise clung flatteringly, emphasizing the fullness of her breasts. She saw his eyes lingering on her and self-consciously pulled the covers higher.

"What about Mrs. Astor?" she inquired, changing the topic. "Does she know I tried to run?"

"Caroline, I've learned over the years, generally knows much more than anyone suspects she knows. But it really doesn't matter."

"It certainly does, and you know it."

He shook his head. "For your information Caroline adores you. Do you know that she herself has started a rumor about how the Lady Moonlight has migrated to the West Coast?"

"But . . . why would she—?"

"Why, to take any suspicion off you so you can remain here in the city safely."

"Perhaps," Mystere suggested sadly, "she'll feel less charitable toward me after our wedding doesn't happen. Or when the vengeful Rafael Belloch completes his elaborate revenge scheme against her."

"As to your second point," Rafe insisted, "Caroline came to see me, even chased my top men out of our boardroom to have it out with me."

"And . . . ?"

Rafe smiled wryly at the memory. "Let's just say that she and I have settled accounts. Which is to say—she won and I accept it. As to your first point . . ."

He brought his face close to hers, gently kissing the tissue-thin skin of her eyelids. "You were right, Mrs. Belloch. Revenge is not a good enough reason for living."

Mrs. Belloch . . . his unexpected words made her heart race as new hope surged within her. But outwardly doubts clouded her eyes.

Rafe frowned, misunderstanding. "Unless," he corrected himself, pulling back from her a bit, "you are rejecting me?"

"I've tried so hard not to fall in love with you," she confessed miserably.

"Then, we have no problem. I'm making an honest woman out of you. I've sent for a priest. We'll be married right here in the house— tonight."

"Rafe. We can't."

"Can and will. You needn't worry about Rillieux, for the old goat has fled. Besides, for all I know you're pregnant. Are you?"

"It's too soon to know yet," she replied, blushing.

"Let's play it safe, then. And after all, it will quiet Caroline. She just wants a marriage, not a grand wedding. Unless it's you who—"

"I've had enough publicity for two lifetimes," she assured him. "I don't care about the grand wedding."

Her gaze fled from his.

"Then, why this strange reluctance?" he demanded. "You just said you're in love with me."

"Rafe, don't you see? That's my reason—love. It's the only reason I'd ever get married. You aren't the problem; it's your motives. Quieting Caroline, making an honest woman of me . . . if you can't—can't love me, I must find another man who will."

He bent close to her again, so close she felt the warmth radiating from him.

"That morning you left me," he told her, his voice enlivened by passion, "my first reaction was anger. But then . . . do you remember telling me how you felt when Bram was taken? As if half of your soul went with him?"

She nodded, fighting back tears of feeling.

"Well, that's how I felt when I feared you were out of my life forever. Mystere, the truth is your wounded soul matches mine in every way. The only way we can mend is to be together. I love you, my mystery girl, love you with all my heart. Please marry me?"

"I will," she whispered, her heart ripping away the bindings that had prevented her from hoping, from loving in return. Almost afraid to believe, she hesitated, but when she joyously felt his arms go around her, she began to hope again. Even when she thought the laudanum and her own mind were playing wretched tricks on her, she watched his expression fill with love for her and helplessly surrendered to his long and passionate kiss.

Only a timid knock broke them apart.

"Yes?" Mystere called out.

Hush and Rose stepped in.

"Hush brought a priest," Rose explained. The smile she couldn't quite suppress showed that she had guessed why Rafe sent for one. "A nice old gent named Father Perry. He's waiting downstairs."

"Send him up," Rafe said. "And you two come with him, for I believe two witnesses are required. By the way—would both of you be willing to come live with us at Garden Cove? There's to be no more stealing, just honest work for honest wages."

"Man alive!" Hush exclaimed, face brightening as he realized he would be with his beloved Mystere. "You bet, Mr. Belloch!"

"Now, sir, I'm warning you," Rafe added with mock solemnity, "I will *not* have you courting and sparking my wife behind my back. Gentleman's word?"

"Cross my heart," the youth promised, flushing with pride.

"Now you two men clear out of here," Rose fussed, her flurry of sudden activity meant to detract attention from her tears of joy. "There'll be no marriage in a bedroom. Go keep the priest company until Mystere is properly dressed and I bring her down. La, she shan't be married in her underclothing! What will Father Perry think of us?"

Within the hour Rafe's wound had been bandaged, and he and Mystere had exchanged nuptials. It was too late by then to bother returning to Staten Island, so the newly wed couple decided to spend their first night as man and wife at the Great Jones Street residence.

Baylis, Evan and Rillieux were long gone, but Jimmy spent the night downstairs just in case any of them were fool enough to return.

Later that evening, as Rafe unbuttoned the back of Mystere's dress, he murmured in her ear, "Well, you haven't found your brother, but at least you've found your true husband. Are you happy?"

Tears filmed her eyes, and she felt like bursting from the fullness of joy within her.

"One does not replace the other," she replied. "But yes, Mr. Belloch, I am exceedingly happy."

Both of them undressed in the glow of a small electric lamp on Mystere's chest of drawers. The moment she turned out the lamp, however, Rafe noticed shafts of bright moonlight streaming through the room's dormer windows.

"Walk over by the windows," he whispered in her ear just before they got into bed.

"But why?"

"Please, just for a moment."

Completely naked, Mystere crossed silently to the windows and slowly turned around. Silver-white moonlight bathed her in a luminous aura like stardust. In that moment, with Rafe's worshipful gaze upon her, she felt like a nocturnal goddess that had been carved from ivory and then brought to life by some divine spark.

He was silent for a long time.

"The Lady Moonlight," he finally said in a voice softened by love, deepened by desire. "So come to bed now, my lady," he added, raising his arms.

And as she crossed the room to join her husband, she did not seem to be walking at all, but rather gliding like moonbeams across a gentle sea.

Epilogue

November 1883

Trevor Sheridan leaned forward in his upholstered walnut armchair, resting both forearms on the desk to read a neatly typed note lying on his blotter. It had turned up two days earlier in his inter-office correspondence. The author was one of his best clerks, a man who had started with the firm seven years ago as a messenger boy and had an exemplary work record.

> *Sir,*
>
> *A few months ago a young woman arrived at the offices to make inquiries about a possible connection between herself and the Sheridan or Granville ancestral line. I mention it at this late date only because, just recently, I saw a photograph of Rafe Belloch's new wife in the* Times. *I'd swear it's the same woman who came to your office.*
>
> *One or two others present in the office that day have remarked the same thing. I felt it my duty to mention this, sir, because she claimed to have a letter of some kind, and I thought you might like to see it.*
>
> *Yrs. respectfully,*
> *Nathan Winkler*

Even as Sheridan finished reading and folded the note again, he heard footsteps in the hallway outside the open door of his second-story office in the Commerce Building. He looked up and saw Rafe and Mystere Belloch in the doorway.

"Come in, come in, please," he greeted them, rising to his feet as they entered. He indicated a pair of Louis XVI carved giltwood fauteuils in front of his desk. "Please have a seat. I'm glad you agreed to come."

His casual greeting struck Mystere as somewhat forced, as if civility was foreign to his nature. One side of Sheridan's mouth made what might have been the beginning of a smile. *Or just as likely,* she thought, *it's merely a growl.*

This was the first time she had actually met him, and she disliked Trevor Sheridan instantly. His grim intensity was even more noticeable at close range, and she decided the Predator was an apt name for him if first impressions could be trusted. But she reminded herself how she had also disliked her own husband at first, an aversion that had since turned to a passionate love.

"I must admit," she began somewhat nervously, "that I've been consumed with curiosity since your call, Mr. Sheridan."

"As have I, Mrs. Belloch, since only belatedly learning of your visit. Thankfully, a sharp employee brought your visit to my attention after realizing who you were."

Despite her burning curiosity, Mystere could not help an indignant frown at the memory of that rainy day. Or his implicit admission that only women with social rank deserved serious notice.

"The reception I was accorded by your office staff, Mr. Sheridan, was not deserved by even a murderer."

He raised his hands from the blotter and spread them in a helpless gesture. "Excuse us, Mrs. Belloch, if we've become a cynical fraternity around here. I am not, I confess, a good model of chivalry for my subordinates. Too, the stories we're told are all drearily similar, yours included, from what I've heard of it."

"Yes, well, all that's nothing to the matter," Rafe intervened impatiently, all business and used to taking charge. "Just look at the letter."

Hands trembling, Mystere opened the silver clasp of her bag, then the protective chamois pouch holding the letter. She removed the dog-eared sheet of stationery. Careful of the worn creases, she unfolded it.

"It's gotten wet and smeared the ink at some point long ago," she explained. "It becomes illegible toward the end, including the signature."

"Of all places," Sheridan observed, his cynical tone causing Rafe's fists to clench on the arms of his chair. But Mystere's imploring glance settled him down again, and Rafe couldn't help a little grin, probably realizing it was just the tone he might have used himself.

Sheridan accepted the letter and said nothing for perhaps the next two or three minutes, face turned downward to study the letter. He tilted the bronze Sinumbra lamp on his desk, its long-faceted prisms ringing, to throw more light on it. Mystere watched with growing anxiety, unconsciously perched on the edge of her chair.

Finally he looked up from the letter and scrutinized her face as if he had been ordered to sculpt its likeness. His hazel eyes were unusually dark, and even now wrathful.

"Of course you could always favor the female side," he remarked as if thinking outloud. "I never met Maureen or saw a likeness of her. Frankly you're a bit too classically wrought for a Sheridan. Mara proves we have our female beauties, but not of your kind."

"For a Sheridan?" she repeated uncertainly.

His tone became unexpectedly emotional. "I wrote this letter to my cousin Brendan, all right. More than twenty years ago when I first began to make my fortune."

"Then, my father was a Sheridan," she repeated, looking at Rafe, then off at the windows for a moment. "Oh, thank God, I know it at last," she added in a murmur, suddenly overcome with emotion. Shock, wonder, joy washed over her in a floodgate-opening tide. "I'm somebody. *Bram* is somebody," she wept, wishing with all her heart Bram was there by her side now, sharing in the happiness she now knew was hers.

"Brendan's mother was a Sheridan," he stipulated. "But of course her name changed with marriage. Mine did not as my father was a Sheridan. All you need do, to prove you are Brendan's girl, is tell me your surname."

"You know she cannot," Rafe interceded. "She told you that when you called her."

Sheridan nodded slowly. "I know she did. But I will assume nothing where kinship claims are concerned. You must prove to me that Cousin Brendan was, indeed, your father. If you can prove that, you will become a Sheridan with all the rights of our name."

"Now see here, Sheridan," Rafe remonstrated. "I understand such skepticism in other claims you've dealt with. But you just admitted you wrote this letter. Surely that is not part of the routine?"

"No, but so what? I have no idea whatsoever how this letter came into your wife's possession."

"Yes, you have," Rafe objected. "Her word that her mother gave it to her and her brother. But I suppose you're implying Mystere stole it, no doubt to sink her hooks into your vast fortune."

"You might sound less scornful," Sheridan reprimanded, "if you knew the actual amount of that vast fortune, Mr. Belloch."

"Look, I'm duly impressed by you. Anybody who matters in this city knows that you own bulging warehouses on Pearl Street and that your fortune can buy entire nations. But let's be candid: So can mine. My wife has no need for two fortunes—just a family."

Sheridan made that one-sided smile again. "She may well be speaking the truth—so far as she knows it, that is. But I have no way of knowing who gave her this letter or how that party came to acquire it. If she could at least tell me her surname, I'd be far more convinced."

Sheridan fell silent a moment, studying Mystere's prosperous appearance in the generous illumination of the electrified lamp. She had already explained, during his questioning when he called her the day before yesterday, the rather remarkable claim that she did not know her own surname. She had implored him, reasoning that it was possible she did not know it, however, given her young age then.

"Perhaps life has played a scurvy trick on you in the past," he remarked. "Obviously your fortunes have been reversed."

"Both of you think like men," she upbraided the two of them. "You home in on 'fortunes' as if that's all I care about. You don't understand—money has never been the issue. I rate finding my brother Bram above all else. And next comes the desire to know, absolutely and unmistakably, our surname."

"Yes, of course. In your case it's not money at all, it's only love," Sheridan summarized, his sarcasm subtle but detectable.

Rafe's jaw muscles suddenly bunched tightly. "Don't step on me, Sheridan. I won't be so easy to crush as some others you've ruined."

"Oh, stop it, both of you," Mystere pleaded, in no mood to get embroiled in a clash of proud males.

"Look, I find Mrs. Belloch quite persuasive," Sheridan conceded. "But I must have a little more knowledge of your family back in

Ireland. Come back here with some proof—your brother himself would be ideal, for he's older and must recall more—and we'll declare both of you legal Sheridans."

"I warned you he's a hard twist," Rafe declared the moment they had collected their overcoats from the porter downstairs and exited the Commerce Building. "But to hell with his scruples. You're his kin, God help you, I'd wager on it. His admitting he wrote the letter as good as warrants it."

He handed Mystere into the carriage and told Wilson to head down to the Battery.

"No, he's right," Mystere said. "I can't prove I have a right to own his letter. And I realize now that even if I could—he doesn't have any idea, either, where Bram might be. You've been right all along, I suppose."

"I? How do you mean?"

"My quest for Bram. I know you think it's a waste of time."

Tears threatened to overwhelm her. She glanced outside at the late-autumn evening, watching pedestrians with their chins tucked in against the chilly wind. Here and there she spotted trees already mulched for the coming freezes.

"You're wrong," Rafe assured her, cupping her chin with one hand and turning her face toward him. "The old veterans in my father's regiment always told me no man is truly dead until he's forgotten. You've kept your brother alive in your own way; I'll never fault you for that."

Rafe's words, meant to solace, instead sent hot tears quivering onto her long lashes. "It was Paul," she said, more convinced than ever. "It was he who was behind Bram's disappearance."

Rafe, after a moment's debate with himself, replied, "Last summer, when you were hiding, I questioned Rillieux about it. Technically, of course, he admitted nothing, the old weasel. But he as much as confessed he sold Bram to an impress gang, his motive being to have you in the line of inheritance in case a fortune turned up."

Cold, numbing despair hit her like an Arctic squall.

"All those years and all that money I spent," she lamented, "in a useless quest for Bram. Oh, Rafe, at least then I had *hope* to cling to. I'll never, ever be able to find him."

With her final word, her voice gave out in a great sob, and she collapsed against Rafe, weeping.

"Never mind now," he soothed gently in her ear. "All is not lost, Lady Moonlight."

She looked up at him from swollen, red-rimmed eyes. "I can think of nothing else."

"I turned the problem over to the best answer man I know," he assured her.

"Sam Farrell?"

He nodded.

"You don't mean—then Sam knows where—?"

"No, not Sam. But he has found the one person in this wide world who stands the best chance of finding Bram. And I have already arranged to take some time off from the office because I'm going to take you to this person myself. We're going to find your brother."

Mystere looked at him in awe and wonder. If she had ever doubted he loved her, she had no doubts now. Unable to help herself she flung her arms around him and hugged him in unspeakable joy.

"They should have warned me," Rafe murmured against her hair.

"About what?" she asked, her face beatific with happiness.

"That your talent lay in stealing hearts as well." He kissed her. "I love you, Lady Moonlight."